John and Sean walked toward the barn where they could be alone and talk. "Life is funny," Sean said and smiled. "I was just thinking of all the things that could have gone wrong. We could have missed each other on the streets of London. I would have died back there if you hadn't risked your skin to save me during the hold-up. And Christ, I still shiver me bones thinking about the close call we had in Scotland. And our luck—yours and Suzanne's—getting here to buy the plantation at the right time. Maybe life's all a matter of throwing the dice."

"No maudlin Irish sentiment tonight, Sean," Jean said in a voice of mock serenity. "We're here to celebrate a good harvest, a fine year with our friends."

They were suddenly interrupted when Suzanne burst into the barn. "There are you!" she cried, taking John's arm. "Sorry, Sean, but I haven't danced in years. John belongs to me for the rest of the night."

Sean raised his empty glass in a salute. "A toast to the most beautiful hostess in the world."

Sean stood quietly and watched his friends walk back toward the dance platform. He raised his empty glass and sipped the last drops. Belle Meade was a place of peace, tranquil skies and love—an eternal land created by the angels many eons ago. He prayed that it would always stay that way . . .

SENSATIONAL SAGAS

THE FRONTIER RAKERS   (633, $2.50)
by David Norman
With half their lives packed in their covered wagons and the other half staked on the future of the great frontier, these brave pioneers begin their arduous journey down the Oregon Trail.

THE FRONTIER RAKERS #2: THE FORTY-NINERS
by David Norman   (634, $2.50)
Lured by the promise of gold the pioneers journeyed west, coming face to face with hardship, struggling to survive. But their need for adventure, wide open spaces and new-found wealth led them to meet the challenge of taming the wild frontier.

THE FRONTIER RAKERS #3: GOLD FEVER
by David Norman   (621, $2.50)
The brave and determined forty-niners are blazing their way across the wilderness, heading toward California, the land of gold. Neither murder, thieves nor Indian attacks can deter them from staking their claims and fulfilling the great American dream.

WHITEWATER DYNASTY: HUDSON!   (607, $2.50)
by Helen Lee Poole
This is the first in a new historical-romantic-adventure epic that traces the growth of America by its magnificent and powerful waterways—and the proud, passionate people who built their lives around them.

Available wherever paperbacks are sold, or order direct from the Publisher. Send cover price plus 50¢ per copy for mailing and handling to Zebra Books, 21 East 40th Street, New York, N.Y. 10016. DO NOT SEND CASH!

THE CONRAD CHRONICLES 3

BELLE MEADE
THE DESTINED

BY
JOANNA
WARREN

ZEBRA BOOKS

KENSINGTON PUBLISHING CORP.

ZEBRA BOOKS

are published by

KENSINGTON PUBLISHING CORP.
21 East 40th Street
New York, N.Y. 10016

Printed in the United States of America

Chapter One

South of the high bluffs at Memphis, Tennessee, the Mississippi River took a great curving swing to the east. The waters were swift and deep at this point. The powerful river seemed to be testing the endurance of a long, low hillock that formed the eastern bank. This small rise in the land formed a natural levee, which protected the low-lying cotton fields from spring floods. Always dangerous, the powerful Mississippi was very treacherous at this point. The muddy waters often formed a swirling whirlpool, moving from the shallow depths to the onrushing main channel.

This particular day was bright: a warm afternoon in late spring, 1832, when all the sunlight in the universe seemed focused on Belle Meade plantation. Nonetheless, the day was pleasant. A cooling breeze blew gently from the west, crossing the river, past the bottom fields, rustling twin rows of stately trees guarding a lane leading to a great southern manor house.

The great house at Belle Meade shone like a white pearl in the sunlight. The house had just been completed. It was a loving tribute by the plantation owner, John Conrad, to his English-born wife, Suzanne. Tall and stately pillars were set in front of a low veranda that led to thick double doors. The sprawling three-story structure was built with white brick, white boards and marble. There was a profusion of airy windows and white shutters. The front doors were elaborately carved. They opened onto a spacious visitor's hall and reception area. The house had been constructed with painstaking care, built to stand for a thousand years. The great house at Belle Meade was set on a crest in the land, looking out over the Mississippi River. Steamboat captains going past the plantation often saluted with a friendly blast of their steam whistles. Everyone who traveled up and down the river, whether captain, crewmen or passengers, realized Belle Meade was a symbol of gracious living in the mid-southern states.

Beyond the great house were a large number of outbuildings. The first was a white frame carriage house. Beyond that was a horse barn containing fifty stalls — everyone knew the master of Belle Meade was a fervent breeder of fine horses. The large pasture lay south of the stable. It was cross-fenced by whitewashed wood railings. One section of the pasture contained several frisky young colts and their mothers.

Off to the other side of the great house was a working barn. This huge structure fronted a large pasture containing a small herd of blooded cattle. Beyond this pasture was a smaller acreage, also fenced with railing, that held a herd of sheep. John Conrad, the master of Belle Meade, had imported these animals from Scotland in hopes of developing a hardy local breed.

Off beyond the great house was a row of small but neat cabins. These buildings were the living quarters for the slaves on Belle Meade. Many of these cabins were rude, ugly structures put up by Otto Korrman, a German immigrant who was the original founder of the plantation. A flinty and tight-fisted individual, Korrman spent very little on his slaves.

6

The newer cabins were larger, had windows, and each was fronted with a porch. John Conrad had designed these units to shelter families. Each contained two bedrooms—one for parents, the other for children—a living room and a kitchen. Each family could draw provisions from Belle Meade's storehouses. This food could be cooked to their wishes in the cabin's kitchen. The single men, notably the field hands, were fed ample meals from a communal kitchen in the center of the slave quarters. This building also served as a community hall and meeting place during the evening. Two wells, operated with rope and pulleys, were located at each end of the row of cabins.

Now, a tall and handsome man with a slender build came strolling out of the house. He paused on the marble veranda, admiring the beauty of the balmy spring weather. Although he was not yet thirty years old, John Conrad was master of all his eyes could see. A dim dream had been transformed into reality. A tenacious and stubborn man, Conrad was unwilling to accept a low view of human potential. He held a lofty view of man's tenure on earth. Other men might be vile, grubbing for money in some terrible endeavor. John Conrad held fast to his vision.

The door of the house opened behind him. Conrad turned as a dark-haired man of his own age stepped out onto the veranda.

"Ahh! A penny for your thoughts, bucko," said Sean Porter.

"I'm wondering when my wife will be home."

"Missing your colleen?" asked Sean.

"And the twins as well."

John Conrad's wife, Suzanne, had gone back to England for the birth of their first child—which turned out to be twins. Daniel Joseph and Denise

7

Elizabeth Conrad were born without complications. Suzanne's letters said they were beautiful, healthy babies. But Denise developed a complicated respiratory infection, and Suzanne thought it best to remain in England until the condition cleared up. The twins were now almost six months old. John was anxious to see his children, welcome them to Belle Meade. He was also lonesome for the return of his wife.

Sean Porter asked, "Waiting for the mail?"

John nodded. "Noah should have been back an hour ago."

"Methinks he lingers too long in Memphis."

"Noah will be lingering when he's called to judgment day," said John.

Sean looked up into the cloudless sky. "Care to go cat fishing this evening? I'm told by the field hands that they're biting."

"My heart wouldn't be in it."

The Irishman shrugged. "Merely trying to get you out into the world, bucko. I know you're pining away to see your lass and the wee ones. That's natural when a man loves his lady, especially as you love Suzanne. But she's been gone for most of a year. A man must make the best of things."

"I'm trying," John said.

"Lad, mayhaps you should take a bed wench."

"Not likely."

"John, there's a lovely lass out back. She can't be more than sixteen years old. Delicate features and a body that will delight any man. She's not coal black like the rest of these gals. Her skin is golden brown. She would be a prize in any man's bed. Oh, I tell you, John, she's the prettiest colleen I've seen in many a moon. Just sweet and slender. An armful for a lonely husband whose wife is away."

Sean continued to laud the virtues of the young slave girl. John listened faintly, his mind on his wife and children. This conversation was unique because slave-owning southern aristocrats seldom discussed bed wenches. The subject was never brought up in mixed company, and rarely discussed among males. An aura of shamefulness hung over a man who slept with his slaves. Yet, as the number of mulatto slaves attested, the practice was widespread. Slave traders and auctioneers sold their most beautiful young females for that exact purpose. At certain plantations young girls were trained to please their masters.

Some wives deplored the practice of their husband's sleeping with a darkie. They were revolted by the thought. Every section of the South knew of one or more women who had left their husbands over a bed wench in the master's bed. Why, these wives clucked, Negroes were property. A decent man did not lay out with a heifer or sheep. A black concubine was no better than an animal.

Other wives accepted their husband's bed wenches. They ignored the nightly opening and closing of their husband's bedroom door, the creaking of mattresses and bed springs. Such things were expected, they said with a cynical expression, because men would always be men.

A few wives asked their husbands to take a bed wench. These were women who had never enjoyed sex, or grown tired of their husband's constant attention. With a black girl to dally with, they figured, their husbands would be happy. He would not ask his wife to particpate in "that nasty stuff."

Sean Porter had been chiding John about a bed wench for several weeks. The Irishman knew that John Conrad was a loyal husband. But as Suzanne's stay in England lengthened into months, Sean had watched his friend become more nervous and irritable. A practical and direct man, Sean saw no harm in John's releasing his physical tension with a bed wench.

"Most men," Sean was saying, "would give a year of their life for a tumble with this bronze-skinned gal. She's cute. She'd be a delight under the covers."

"I don't force anyone to sleep with me," John retorted.

Sean gave forth a lilting Irish laugh.

"You miss my point, boyo," he said. "This poor girl is in love."

"One of the workers?"

Sean grinned. "She's in love with Ole Massa. You've been too preoccupied to notice. She keeps her distance, but her eyes follow you whenever you come into view."

"Quit talking like that," John said in a peevish tone. "My wife will be home soon."

"You don't have to tell Suzanne." Sean laughed again. "I won't tell either. So you're safe."

"Sean," John said with exasperation. "You're getting me into a bad mood."

The Irishman shrugged. "Just trying to cheer you up."

"I wonder what you've been doing on the other house." John referred to a plantation formerly owned by Julian Burnside, a planter. Burnside had caught the pox from a slave girl. He had sold out, gone off to seek a cure. John had borrowed the purchase price from Suzanne's grandmother, Dorcas, and her new husband, Dr. Matthew Jamison. That elderly couple had managed the plantation until they accompanied Suzanne on her trip to England. Now the plantation was being managed by Sean Porter.

"I don't sleep alone too many nights," Sean said,

reddening somewhat.

John looked alarmed. "You'll catch the pox like Burnside."

"I use a sheath."

"They don't work all the time," John pointed out.

Sean chuckled. "I'll burn a candle the next time I'm in church."

John felt a sudden stirring in his loins. His resolution to remain true to his wife was still strong. Yet at the same time he wondered which of his slave girls was interested in Ole Massa.

II

To end their discussion of bed wenches, John led his friend on a tour of Belle Meade. They went out to the pasture, one foot on the railing, and watched the horses for some time. They talked about bloodlines, the spiritedness of an Arabian stallion, the merits of a gelding versus a mare. Next, they strolled leisurely out to the slave quarters. They stopped and talked with Uncle Eli, a gray-haired old black man with skin the color of dark walnut. Uncle Eli was too old to work in the fields. Upon buying the plantation from Otto Korrman, John placed the elderly Negro in charge of the storehouses. With his new found leisure time, Uncle Eli became the slaves' wise man. Whatever their woes, spiritually, physically or financially, Uncle Eli gave forth with good advice. Uncle Eli was Belle Meade's marriage counselor, psychologist, child guidance expert, labor arbitrator, negotiator with management, wise old gentleman and giver of advice to the lovelorn. His advice had stopped feuds, prevented fights, kept an aura of family among the slaves.

Uncle Eli wanted to know about Suzanne and the

twins. He asked, "Ye heered from Miz Suzanne?"

"Expecting a letter any day," John replied.

"Where she stayin' at?"

"England. Her dad lives there."

"She got no mommy?"

"Her mama died a long time ago."

"Pore chile. Y'all babies doin' good?"

"I guess so."

"When's Miz Suzanne comin' home?"

John shrugged. "I don't know, Uncle Eli."

"We's got to have a partyin' when they gets here."

"We will," said John. "Now, are you taking care of everyone's troubles?"

Uncle Eli's face became somber. "Boys runnin' the sawmill're kinda mad."

"How come?"

"Y'all expectin' them to do a lot."

"Their quota is that hard?"

"They's havin' trouble with that junk."

"The sawmill?"

"Naw suh! That ole engine ain't workin' right."

John looked surprised. "I just had a mechanic in from Memphis the other day."

"They say he do worse'n when it was before."

After leaving Uncle Eli, John and Sean walked across the field toward the hills that formed Belle Meade's back boundary. One of John's first ventures was to set up a lumbering operation. A steam-powered sawmill had been purchased and brought upriver from New Orleans. It was set up on level ground in front of the hills. Trees were axed down in the woods, limbs trimmed away, snaked down to the mill by mules. Once cut into boards, the lumber was sold in Memphis.

The sawmill put John Conrad into a separate category from other planters. Most plantation owners were concerned only with raising cotton. Some planters even refused to raise food and animals to feed themselves and their slaves. They purchased foodstuffs in town from wholesalers.

"I'm going in the other direction," John told Sean as they walked to the sawmill. "Everybody's buying all the cotton the South can raise. That's well and good, but the price might drop someday. You can't have good years forever. I figure Belle Meade has a good chance of surviving if our eggs are spread out. Cotton can go down; we still have the mill."

Sean asked, "Will Memphis continue to grow?"

"New families move in every week. Plus there's lots of new business firms setting up. They all need lumber."

"And you've also got the land company," said Sean.

"That, too," John agreed.

John owned half interest in the Belle Meade Land Company. His partner was a Memphis attorney, Roy Lanning. With a surplus of lawyers in the city, Lanning had suggested the enterprise. Land speculation was at a fever's pitch in Memphis. They would purchase raw land, hold it for a few weeks. If a profit could not be made on the property, Lanning hired carpenters to build a small single-family dwelling. Lumber was purchased from Belle Meade at the standard wholesale figure. Once the house was built, it was offered for sale for a few weeks. Then, if no buyers came forth, the house was rented out. Since Suzanne had left for England Lanning had built thirteen houses. Three had sold quickly. The remaining ten were rented out at a profitable rate.

When they arrived at the sawmill, John talked with the foreman. Bobby was a handsome young black man with thick shoulders, a flat stomach, muscular arms and strong legs.

"We sure ain't runnin' right," Bobby told John. "Been tryin' to fix it ourselves. Saw ain't been spinnin' right since that fellow come down from town."

John walked around the mill. He saw that the mechanic had failed to adjust the tension on the huge driving belt. He pointed out the problem to Bobby, waited until the spinning saw blade was stopped. Then the shaft was adjusted and some dressing applied to the belt. Bobby smiled brightly when the saw spun with its original power.

"Shoulda called you 'fore now," Bobby said, shamefaced.

"Let me know next time," John said.

"Massa John?"

"Yeah, Bobby?"

"Me 'n the fellars been talkin' 'bout somethin'."

"Got an idea?"

The Negro looked down at the ground. "We bin thinkin' 'bout how to keep the mill runnin' all year long."

John listened as the black man suggested that a mill house be built over the equipment. The structure could be heated in winter and work would not stop during the cold-weather months. This would allow the mill to double output. Bobby added, "We'uns natch'ly 'pect you to be mindful we'd be workin' instead of restin' in the winter."

"What'd you have in mind?" John wondered.

"We be makin' more money for y'all," Bobby said. "We likin' to have a bit of it."

John smiled. "The worker is worth his salt, Bobby. Let me see what I can work out. I promise to be fair with you and the others."

"We know that, Massa." Bobby grinned. "But we don't want money."

14

John looked surprised.

Bobby went on. "Niggers don't need much money. Me 'n the others been talkin' 'bout what we'd like to have best of all. We been thinkin' that would be a li'l piece of land 'a our own. Som'thin' we could have . . . just like you're ownin' this big place."

"You'd have to be a freed man for that to happen."

Bobby looked down at the ground again. "Yas suh!" He glanced up slyly. "We thinkin' maybe to speed up the bean baggin'."

"I'll see what I can do," John promised.

Upon his purchase of Belle Meade, John had instituted a way for each slave to earn his freedom. The matter had been complicated because many of the slaves were unable to comprehend the passage of time in months or years. They were additionally unable to understand mathematics. So John devised a system of giving each slave a black bean on the eve of each full moon. Depending on the slave's purchase price, he could earn his freedom in a certain interval of time.

Conrad's "beanbag niggers" were a sore point with several planters in the northwestern region of Mississippi. Most plantation owners felt Belle Meade's system was an erosion of the traditional master-slave relationship. Others were fearful their slaves would demand the same method of earning freedom. Fortunately, "bean bagging" had improved the efficiency of workers on the plantation. Everyone was happier, more concerned with their performance as workers.

On their way back to the house, Sean said: "Bucko, I'm wondering how far your beanbagging proposition will go." He sounded worried.

John smiled. "I'm going to make the sawmill crew a nice offer. They've been talking among themselves. Do you realize they've got the first tiny glimpse of free enterprise? They're starting to think, Sean, and I'll

15

wager Bobby will be a freed man in a short while."

Sean moaned. "Don't let the other planters hear about this."

"Why not?"

"The last thing they want on their place is a slave who thinks."

Chapter Two

Since Suzanne had gone to England, John had sent a coach into Memphis each day to pick up the mail. First, he wanted to quickly get any letters that Suzanne might send from England. Second, with his wife absent, John had become a voracious reader. He whiled away his idle hours reading newspapers, magazines and books.

Each day the coach left the plantation shortly after lunch. It came back near suppertime with the mail and, usually, some reading material. The driver was a genial slave, Noah Purdy, about twenty-five years old. He had a pleasant and ambitious personality. Noah relished this new position. He enjoyed seeing the sights in Memphis, something that few slaves were allowed to do.

Since slave Nat Turner led a rebellion of slaves in Virginia in 1831, killing more than fifty white people, the South had imposed rigid restrictions on travel by slaves. Few black people were allowed beyond the boundaries of their plantations. This was the law. Slaves sent on an errand to a neighboring plantation were required to carry a written pass from their masters. All socializing between slaves from neighboring plantations was forbidden. Let the darkies get together, reasoned the planters, and no telling what might happen. A man never knew what those dark devils might be stirring up! They might plot rebellion like those darkies up in Virginia, heaven forbid. They might pass along information on the underground railroad, a network of people who assisted slaves to get North to freedom. Or, God forbid, they might plot to kill Ole Massa, his wife and children some terrible night.

So a trip to Memphis was a journey of wonderment for any slave. The daily visit to town set Noah Purdy apart from the other slaves on Belle Meade. This new freedom, the ability to come and go beyond the eyes of his master, was a status symbol. He was somebody! Noah was soon raised to a new level of respect. Some slaves reckoned that Noah was higher than a house servant, and everyone knew they were pretty hot stuff. The house nigger lorded it over the common field hands and other workers. But Noah occupied a position of trust that went beyond menial work in the great house.

Noah Purdy's position allowed him to provide news of the outside world to the other slaves. He kept them informed of the day's happenings in Memphis. Each night, after the chores were done and everyone had supped, they gathered in the community building and listened to his daily reports. His listeners asked many questions, went over the daily information in detail, discussed the happenings during the next twenty-four hours.

At first Noah's information was interesting. During the first month on the job, Noah described the town, sketched out a map of Memphis, talked about the tall buildings. He mentioned the big steamboats moving up and down the Mississippi, described the finery of the captain's garments, went over the clothing worn by the passengers. This was a time of great enjoyment for Noah. The people were content with his reports. He had been able to catch the attention of several young slave girls who had been cool to his advances.

But there came a time when his listeners' enthusiasm plummeted. Martha, the big and genial black woman who ran the kitchen at Belle Meade, summed up their discontent.

"I'm gwine tell you the honest truth," she informed Noah one evening. "Me 'n the others are gettin' tired of hearin' the same ole thing 'bout them steamboats 'n big buildin's in Memphis. We can stand in our yard right here on Belle Meade, catch sight of them boats chuggin' up and down the river. And for buildin's"—Martha snapped her thick black fingers—"we got plenty of fine buildin's right here on Belle Meade. Them fellers on steamboats don't toot 'n hollar when they goes past 'cause massa's livin' in a shanty. We ain't been hearin' nothin' new for quite a while. Noah, you needs to open yore eyes and sharpen up yore ears. Otherwise, I ain't listenin' to no more of this stuff 'bout steamboats and buildin's. I'se tired of them things."

Like all men who become accustomed to newfound respect, Noah did not want to lose his exalted status. The next day in Memphis, Noah looked for something that was new and different. The town was slow and lackadaisical that afternoon. Noah was depressed on the return trip to Belle Meade. Then his mind brightened and the young slave devised a plan. The other slaves were unable to travel to Memphis. Chances were, they would never get off the plantation. There was no way anyone could check the truth of his stories. With a wide grin of satisfaction, Noah decided to use his overly active imagination.

During his visit to the post office that afternoon, Noah had cautiously sneaked a look at an attractive young white woman. She had entered the post office wearing an ankle-length white dress. She carried a blue parasol and purse. Noah thought about the woman the rest of the way home.

When his audience gathered that evening for another lackluster tale, Noah gave them an enchanting story.

"Lotsa things happenin' in town," he explained. "The big she-queen of the whole country is visitin' Memphis. Nicer woman never been born. Pretty, too. She got the color of fresh sweet milk just bein' drawn into the bucket. Wears dresses that must've cost more'n all us darkies are worth. She went right past me, she did, in a big yallar coach pulled by twenty-leven white horses. Lotsa white horses that were holdin' they heads high. And the harness had little stones that just glowed in the sunlight like Miz Suzanne's rings."

"Queen of the whole world," said Martha in wonderment.

"She was thinkin' of comin' here," Noah went on. "She say how darkies are her fav'rite people. She think Belle Meade the best place in the whole world."

"When she comin'?" asked Uncle Eli.

Noah's face took on a somber look. "They's needin' her back north. Black folks up there's got they's freedom. They been cryin' cause she left 'em and come down t'here to see us. But the next time she's comin' visitin' she gonna stop off and say hello to us darkies at Belle Meade."

Martha asked, "She say what it was like up north?"

"Nobody ever work."

Uncle Eli asked, "How long folks live up there?"

"Twenty-leven years."

"How long's that?"

"Longer'n folks ever live before now."

A young girl chimed in. "What color was she hair?"

"Yaller as the sun. My eyes were hurtin' to look at

20

that she-queen."

"Shore 'nuff?"

"You better believe it," answered Noah.

Each day after that liar's success, Noah dreamed up a fanciful tale to enchant his audience. One day he returned breathless with excitement. He swore an army of dwarves had marched through Memphis heading for the land where the sun set. They were going off to battle a tribe of giants that lived far west across the Mississippi River. Each dwarf carried a slingshot as a weapon. Each man carried a monstrously complicated machine called a knee-cracker. As the dwarves were so small, and the giants so tall, the knee-crackers were their first line of defense.

The dwarves were followed by twenty-leven witch doctors—more'n anyone could ever hope to count—convening in the city for a contest of supremacy. These wizards chanted, cast spells, threw fits and made up potions. During the next ten days, everyone talked about nothing but the wizard's convention. They learned of Hiptomaloco, the wiliest sorcerer of all times, a black man with a scarface from Africa. There was Tumulla, a rival of Hiptomaloco, who lived in a tree in a far-off land called Philadelphia. And many others who came from equally fascinating lands. When people became tired of the witch doctors, Noah declared Hiptomaloco a winner. Everyone had expected him to win all along.

Thunder and lightning—didn't you darkies know they was married?—lived in a hotel in Memphis. They were forever getting into marital spats. Ole thunder roared and grumbled while his wife jolted him with bolts of fire. After that, a strange menagerie of animals came to exist in Memphis. Purple horses, polka-dotted mules, a cow with satin skin softer than

21

a baby's behind, dancing dogs and cats were all part of the city's scenes. So were walking pumpkins, talking trees, watermelons the size of a steamboat and tobacco plants that spit juice at passers-by. The skies of Memphis were bluer, the sun hotter, the nights darker, the wind stronger, the rain heavier and the hailstones bigger than any place on earth.

A few of Noah's listeners voiced their skepticism. But there was scant opportunity to dispute his lies. Emboldened by his success, Noah invented wild and domestic animals that boggled everyone's mind. The first, and perhaps the most notable, was the turbit. This creature was half turtle, half rabbit. It hopped about with a thick shell on its back. The turbit also liked to leap through the air. It seemed that leaping turbits covered every inch of space in Memphis. But, unlike the speedier rabbits, a turbit leaped at a turtle's pace. It might take all morning for a turbit to complete a single leap. They were that slow, Noah insisted.

"Man can do half a day's work while a turbit's making one leap," Noah explained. "Slowest thing y'all will ever see."

A field hand asked, "Why didn't you ketch a turbit?"

Noah had anticipated this skepticism. "Can't be caught."

"But dey leap lazy. Just reach 'n grab one. We like to be seein' one of them turbits."

"Can't be done."

"Bet I kin ketch 'im."

"Turbits are funnier than you realize," said Noah. "They don't like bein' tied up. So they jump smack dab outta they shells if'n they's grabbed whilst they's jumpin'."

"Think 'a dat," chimed in another field hand. He

was truly filled with wonderment about the amazing creatures living in Memphis.

A few days later, Noah returned with a turbit shell he claimed to have grabbed in Memphis. It looked suspiciously like a regular turtle shell. Everyone made a close examination of the artifact. One of the field hands pointed out the little tufts of rabbit hair clinging to the inside of the shell.

"That sucker almost skinnin' hisself gettin' away," Noah rejoiced.

Now, on his return trip back to Belle Meade on this balmy spring day, Noah have the horse its lead. He leaned back in the buggy seat and thought up another imaginative creature. The sasscoon was composed of equal parts duck, raccoon, and tomcat. The duck contributed webbed feet and feathers. The raccoon provided the body and head. The cat gave the sasscoon eyes, a tail and a nasty disposition. Whenever someone approached a sasscoon, the creature reared back on its webbed feet, stuck out its tongue, quacked like a duck and made a terribly rude noise.

Noah smiled. In his mind's eye came a vision of a mother on Belle Meade admonishing her children, "Shut yore mouf'. Ah won't have a pickaninny sasscoonin' me."

The buggy came to the lane going up to Belle Meade. Noah sat up in the seat, assumed an erect position, straightened his clothing, wiped the dust from his trousers and boots. He took on the air of a man engaged in important work.

The horse and rig went through the tree-lined lane, out beyond the great house and stopped at the carriage barn. Noah got down and unhitched the animal. He got feed and water for the beast. After the horse was fed and watered, it was let out into the pasture. Meanwhile, Noah had wheeled the carriage inside the building. Massa John became upset when tools and equipment were left out in the weather. When these chores were finished, Noah picked up the leather mail pouch and went into the house.

Chapter Three

Late that same afternoon John Conrad cut through the garden on his way back to the house. He had spent an hour, after Sean left, walking across the fields of Belle Meade. This was his usual custom. He liked to visit each part of the plantation at least once each week. These walks kept him in touch with the land. The previous owner, Otto Korrman, had neglected the land. Deep gullies cut through some of the most fertile acres. Drainage was a problem at other points.

Nonetheless, John felt a certain sense of serenity on the way back to the house. Everything took time, but there was noticeable progress in fixing the land. He stopped in the garden and picked a sprig of mint. In the kitchen, he poured a small whiskey, added the mint leaves and some cold water. He carried the drink to his bedroom, where he washed and changed his shirt; then he came back downstairs to his study.

The leather mail pouch was on his desk. John took out the mail and laid aside a copy of the *New York Herald*. The newspaper was read each evening before going to bed. It provided an overview of world news that was lacking in the southern newspapers. The *Southern Review,* published in Charleston, was also put aside, as was a copy of *Nile's Register,* a monthly publication published in Baltimore.

Next, a flyer from *Ambrose and Co.*, New Orleans,

advertised a line of stone crockware that appeared to be reasonably priced. John wrote a short note to the company asking that samples of each crock be sent upriver by steamboat, that his note be taken to his New Orleans bank for payment. Another letter was from a steamship company headquartered in Cincinnati. The general manager of the firm asked John's help in securing a supply of firewood in Memphis for their boats. "We have had bad experiences with several other suppliers," the manager wrote. "We will pay a fair and reasonable price to a supplier who will keep wood there for us at all times. Our boats have had to lay over on several occasions to obtain wood. We want to avoid these delays in our schedule. We would appreciate hearing from you on this matter."

John laid the letter aside, wondering whether to expand the lumbering operation. Every worker on the plantation was busy. An expansion of work would mean purchasing more slaves. He was idly reflecting on this decision when his eyes caught sight of a pale blue envelope tucked inside the *New York Herald*. His heart quickened. How could he have missed it? He grabbed the envelope, saw the London postmark, and quickly opened it.

Suzanne's familiar handwriting read:

Dear John:

Just a brief note, husband of mine. We will be leaving here as soon as passage can be booked. The children are fine. Denise has been released by the doctor. She is a fine and healthy child, so there are no worries from that direction. We will leave on the next ship bound for New Orleans. I have no way of knowing what steamboat connections will be like there. We will get to Memphis as quickly as possible.

Your loving wife, Suzanne
and the two wee ones

John leaned back in his chair and reread the letter. He held up the notepaper, let the perfumed scent fill his nostrils. Then, with a wild whoop of joy, he leaped up and did a foolish little jig around the study. It was a joyous dance of celebration. He was still jigging around the room when Martha, the cook, opened the door.

She asked, "Massa, you awright?" Her expression indicated that the master had plainly gone crazy.

John calmed down. He waved the letter at the black woman.

"My wife's coming home," he said.

"Glory be!" Martha beamed. "Now yore frettin' days are over. Won't be no more long faces from Massa John. How 'bout yore chillun?"

"They're fine."

"Praise the Lord! We fin'ly gettin' a fam'ly 'round this place. Nothin' like a baby or two to liven up a house."

"God, Martha. I'm so happy."

She beamed. "I know you been missin' her."

"This calls for a celebration. We ought to barbecue a hog for everyone."

Martha looked dubious. "Save that for when they gets here. Right now, I'se goin' out and fix you 'nother whiskey. Nice big glass. You sit out on the porch and be happy whilst I finish yore supper."

Drink and letter in hand, John went out onto the back porch a few minutes later. He settled back into a comfortably cushioned rocker and gazed into the evening. It was not quite sundown, but the sun was fading. Dark shadows stretched like blue fingers across the buildings. He sipped his drink, feeling the

27

glow of good whiskey inside him, and wondered if he could wait until his family got home. At that moment, John Conrad was a truly happy man.

II

At that same time in Memphis, a short, round man with a cherubic expression left the steamboat wharves and walked up the bluff to the center of town. He came out of the fading sunlight and stood silently in the doorway of a livery stable. Raymond Fisher, the owner of the establishment, was resting his head on his arms atop his battered oak desk. Fisher got the feeling that someone was looking at him. He raised his head, eyes blinking, and saw the stranger silhouetted against the light.

The man stood motionless as if awaiting some personal doomsday. One hand was hooked inside his worn leather belt. The other held a dusty leather satchel. He was not more than five feet, six inches in height. His boots were caked with mud and his battered black hat was dusty. His thick neck was hidden behind a red bandana. His round face was pale, the expression uncertain, and his liquid brown eyes looked innocent.

Raymond Fisher suppressed an urge to laugh. No telling what comes walking into town these days, he thought. This one took the cake. Not more than twenty, maybe twenty-two years old. Why didn't he crawl back under his rock and stay there? Raymond wiped his nose, sucked his teeth and waited for the stranger to speak. He decided the stranger was another of those blamed book agents. They were everywhere these days, running up and down the river via steamboat, popping in and out of every frontier settlement. They sold the works of various authors, or peddled anthologies on a variety of subjects. They implied that purchasers of their books would receive a heavy dose of culture. This jasper, reckoned Raymond, was probably touting a fancy bound volume of Shakespeare's works. Regardless of what the stranger was selling, Raymond Fisher had no plans to buy. His wife, a mousy woman with cultural aspirations, had bought enough books to start a library. When she should be doing housework, Anna Fisher sat and read. She was reading all the time, but she was still as dumb as ever. Worse, she moved her lips when she read. Raymond couldn't read, didn't want to learn. But if he ever figured it out, bedamned if he'd move his lips. So Raymond didn't plan on adding to Anna's shelves of foolishness.

The two men continued to stare at each other. Raymond recalled his childhood days when he got into a staring contest. Bedamned, he wouldn't be the first to blink or speak.

At last, the young man opened his mouth.

"Aaaaaugh . . ." he said in a shrill, almost girlish, voice.

One of those kind, Raymond reflected.

He asked, "Hep ye?"

"Aaah . . . that is . . . maybe you . . I . . ."

Raymond shook his head with puzzlement. This gent was the queerest duck he'd come across in thirty-two years on this earth. He couldn't be a book agent. The most cold-hearted and order-hungry publisher wouldn't send a tonguetied fool out on the road. This jasper would scare bejusus out of the kids, make the cows go dry.

Raymond smiled his best horse-trader's look of sincerity.

"Son," he said, "Ah can't hep ye less'n ye open yore mouf 'n say what ye want. Ye sure yore awright?"

"I'm looking for . . ." The stranger halted again.

"Take yore time, son. We don' close 'til ten o'clock."

"I'm looking for Major Winchester." The man expelled his breath, seemingly relieved.

"Yeah, the major lives heah. That's a fact."

"Do you know where he's staying?"

"At his house, ah reckon."

"Oooh!" There was that high pitched wail again. "I hadn't thought about the major being married."

Raymond snickered. "Married? Ole major went . . ." He hesitated. "Ye kin to major?"

"No sir."

"Reckon ye don' know 'bout Major Winchester?"

"I was told to look him up."

"Well suh, Major Winchester is a strange ole bird. That's a fact."

Raymond launched into a discussion of the man who served as the first mayor of Memphis. Major Marcus Winchester was also justice of the peace, postmaster and representative of Judge John Overton, the Nashville land speculator who founded Memphis. Winchester laid out streets, established roads, set up a mail route to Jackson, Tennessee, and became a friend to poor people, black and white. An expert on investments, Major Winchester had done private banking for poor people and slaves for many years. Orphans and widows placed their funds in his care. That trust was never abused.

What happened to Major Winchester was love, Raymond reckoned. Thomas Hart Benton, after serving with General Andrew Jackson in New Orleans, met a lovely "woman of color" and brought her back to Tennessee. Her name was Lucy Lenoa. She was a wonderment, the prettiest female in Memphis according to most folks. Benton worried about his political fortunes. The future senator of Missouri decided voters would look with disfavor on a politician with a colored wife or mistress.

Thomas Hart Benton gave money and property to Lucy Lenoa and let Major Marcus Winchester handle these investments. "Right from the git go," said Raymond Fisher, "old Winchester fell in love with that gal. But he warn't willin' to just sleep with her, like ole Isaac Rawlings does with his nigger housekeeper. Nosiree! The major married Lucy Lenoa 'n ever'body in a hunnerd miles was scandalized outta their socks. A bunch of them gamblin' folks 'n a few crooks tried to run 'im outta town. Figger they was wantin' to get their hands on money from them widows 'n orphans. But old major held fast. True, he lost the 'lection in twenty-nine to ole Isaac Rawlings. But Major's still postmaster, justice of the Peace, and banker. See, I figger it must be awright to sleep with nigger ladies. You jus' can't *marry* 'em."

"I didn't know that," admitted the stranger. "What sort of man is the major?"

"Heerd a lady tellin' some folks 'bout 'im," Raymond answered. "Said he was"—and here he stopped for a moment to refresh his memory—"the most el-lee-gant, courtly and graceful gent that ever walked on Main Street. Yessiree, that's what she said."

"Is he a wealthy man?" the stranger wondered.

"Tol'able. Major shoulda made money runnin' with Overton, McLemore 'n that packa land boomers."

The short, round man looked out the door, saw the dusk thickening to darkness. He said, "Maybe I'd better see the major tomorrow."

Raymond agreed. "Sounds sensible t'me."

"Any place to stay in town?"

Raymond got up and came around the desk. He walked to the front of the office, where a large grime-smeared window looked out onto the street. He pointed directly across the way.

"Go crost the street," he said. "That's the City Hotel thar. Nice place 'n the vittles are good. Ye can't miss 'er. Sign says in great big letters: City Hotel. Ye git a good clean room thar for cheaper'n most places. Ye brung the missus with ye?"

"I'm not married."

"Reckon ye be luckier'n ye figger," said Raymond, thinking of his addled wife, her books and passel of in-laws. "Man don't know 'is blessin's till it is way too late. 'Spect yore not the marryin' kind."

The stranger grinned bashfully. "I . . . well . . . my work . . ."

"What'll ye do for a livin'?"

"Nothing lately. I been busy with my studies."

"Afore that?"

"I did some clerking."

"'Magine that," said Raymond. The poor soul looked prissy enough to be a clerk. "Well, suh, yore sleep'll be restful at t'hotel."

"I hope so." The short, round man looked as if he wanted to stay and chat. But he suddenly croaked out a "thank you," turned and walked out into the evening. He stood motionless on the sidewalk for a long time, blinking into the deepening night. Then he walked across the street toward the City Hotel.

Raymond Fisher stood in the door of the livery stable, watching the stranger. Strange bird, he reflected. Sure was a lot of loonies running loose these days. Made a body wonder what the world was coming to. He sighed loudly, went back to his desk, cradled his head and was soon sleeping again.

III

The stranger stood for several minutes in front of

the City Hotel. He hesitated going inside, debating whether to spend so much money for a room. Money was getting low again. He would soon have to stop traveling and go to work for a while. His senses picked up the sounds and smells of Memphis. Maybe this would be the place, he hoped. It was tiresome moving from place to place, man to man, town to town, searching for that right person. He was weary of searching for a single man with vision. And the money to back it up. Someday he would find that man, in that place that could be called home. There had to be people who thought as he did. Surely he was not an alien plunked down on earth—the only member of his species. It was so lonely being without friends and acquaintances. He never stayed too long anywhere because he didn't fit in.

With a heavy sigh, he went into the hotel and registered for a room. He signed the card with an uncharacteristic flourish: *Ruskin W. Ward, Philadelphia, Pennsylvania.*

IV

Sean Porter was bored. Which was one reson he welcomed a visit from two neighboring planters that same evening. Albert Spearman and James Courtland owned plantations in the neighborhood. Their spreads were not as large as Belle Meade, but both men owned sizable acreages. Sean walked out in the yard to greet them, then led the two men into the library. He ordered whiskies for everyone. Next, Sean inquired about their families.

James Courtland said his wife and daughters—both of marriage age—missed Sean's visits. The Irishman promised to call and pay his respects within the week.

"I've been busy with planting," he lied. "The

darkies here don't work without supervision. John's got most of his people working without an overseer."

"Don't know how he does it," marveled Albert Spearman.

"The man's a genius," said James Courtland. "Of course, it probably helps to have a rich wife. My womenfolk are a drain on my purse."

Sean felt no compulsion to inform his visitors of John's financial condition. But the Irishman knew the money to purchase Belle Meade had come from robbing the Dover mail coach in England. Sean and John had done the job as a favor for Israel Goldman, an investment banker and English patriot. Goldman learned of a conspiracy to overthrow the English government. There was no time to inform the authorities and, even if there had been time, Goldman preferred to remain in the background.

The robbery turned messy. An English nobleman refused to give up a packet containing a list of names of his fellow conspirators. Instead of the documents, the fellow whipped out a pistol. Sean was shot. He owed his life and freedom to John's refusal to abandon him on the Dover road. Israel Goldman had made certain Sean received the best of medical care. Meanwhile, John and Suzanne were being pursued by the police during a widespread manhunt. As a result of Israel Goldman's efforts, they escaped from England and came to the United States to build a new life. Yes indeed, gentlemen, Sean thought, he earned every single dollar and, perhaps, saved the English government.

While his guests talked, Sean reflected on people. We knew so little about each other's lives. We rise each morning, knuckle the sleep from our eyes, reach over and put on a mask. We hide our true selves from others, not wanting someone else to know who we

34

really are. We pretend. We pose. We lie. We hide the past. Our humanness is suppressed and a totally false image is presented to the world. Everyone keeps forgetting that humans bleed, hurt, are sad and sorry at certain times. But a forcedChuile comes on the face, a mask is drawn across our emotions and we deceive each other. All because humans, the highest form of life, are fearful of opening up to another person.

Sitting across the way was Albert Spearman, playing the role of an unconcerned planter. The slaves on the former Burnside plantation had hinted, then finally told, Sean about the wild parties at the mansion. Julian Burnside and Albert Spearman held weekly orgies with slave girls in an upstairs bedroom. Burnside had caught the pox. He was forced to sell his plantation and go searching for a cure. Sean was forced to kill a large Negro slave on the Spearman plantation. The hulking fellow was found in the barn holding Caroline Spearman as his prisoner. The black man was armed, ready to kill. He had fired at Sean and missed. The real truth had never been brought to light. Sean felt Caroline had secretly been meeting with the slave. One thing was certain: the facade of southern aristocratic respectability hid many secrets.

". . . so this should be a good time to buy," James Courtland was saying. "Do you agree, Sean?"

The Irishman gave his attention to his visitors. He lied, "Sorry, buckos, I've been daydreaming. Thinking about buying a place of my own around here."

"We were discussing this week's slave auction in Memphis," Courtland said. "Supposed to be the largest sale of the year. If you're thinking of buying your own place, you should attend. There may be bargains."

"I doubt that," said Albert Spearman. "Price of blacks keeps going higher each year."

Sean chuckled. "Almost like the cotton market. I suppose I'll attend the auction with John."

"So you're looking for a place," said Courtland.

"Aye, the thought has crossed my mind."

"Land's getting higher each year, too," Spearman pointed out. "Looks as if there's nothing but good times ahead for the next century."

"You looked at any places?" This came from Courtland.

Sean shook his head. "Nothing yet. I'm just running the idea over in my mind." He got up and walked to the liquor cabinet, came back and refilled their glasses with ice and bourbon.

Courtland said, "You need a good butler to do those things for you."

Sean laughed. "He'd just drink up the whiskey."

"True," said Spearman with a hearty chuckle. "But a good planter puts on airs, even if the whiskey bill is atrocious."

Courtland took a sip of his fresh drink. "You heard what happened to Delano Street over in Holly Springs?"

"Nope." Sean added a sprig of mint to his glass, an addition he enjoyed with whiskey.

"Seems there's a band of slave stealers operating in this area," said the planter. "Part of that new thing called an underground railroad. You know, that's the people who help runaways get north to freedom. Call themselves abolitionists. I hear they've even set up a newspaper in Boston. Some fellow named Garrison runs it. Called the *Liberator*. Anyway, a half-dozen slaves ran away from Street's plantation last weekend. The whole bunch just vanished. Not a sign of them. Trackers and dogs couldn't get a scent. Delano's madder than a hornet. Lost one whole family. Father, mother and a nice kid growing up to be a strong buck. The other runaways were field hands. Makes a man wonder what this world is coming to, seeing folks out stealing his property. We've been out most of the day looking for those runaways. Figured they'd head for Memphis and try to sneak aboard a steamboat heading north to Cincinnati."

Sean asked, "Any sign of them?"

"Nothing at all," Courtland answered.

Spearman drained his glass. "Seen any strangers around the neighborhood the past few days?"

Sean was thoughtful for some time. He replied at last, "Nobody has been through that I've seen. Unless you count Doc Fletcher and his medicine show."

"Naw, that rascal works out of Memphis. He's safe. Biggest nigger-hater in the country." Spearman rose from his chair.

"Doc's all right," agreed Courtland.

"We better get going," Spearman said, pulling a gold watch from his waist pocket and examing the instrument. "My wife worries if I'm out much after dark."

Courtland laughed richly. "I'd worry like the dickens if I was married to an old goat like you."

Spearman opened his hands in a gesture of innocence. "Gentlemen, I do not deserve such notoriety."

Laughing with the two men, Sean walked them to the door. He stood on the porch as they mounted up and rode away.

Chapter Four

The gaudy medicine-show wagon moved through the dark streets of Memphis. Red-and-gilt scrollwork glowed brightly when the rig passed a torch or shaft of light. The wagon was custom designed for the purpose of giving shows. The interior was enclosed, but any or all of the four sides could be opened. The top of the wagon was rimmed with bright polished brass fringed with gold and silver tassels. Emblazoned across the side in gilt letters were these words: DOC FLETCHER'S WORLD FAMOUS MEDICINE SHOW. A small placard contained a sketch of what was purported to be *Attila—The Caveman of the North Pole*. This savage prehistoric creature was said to have been found in the frozen Arctic, thawed out and brought to life. He was depicted wearing a furry loincloth. One arm was raised above Attila's head. It held a bonelike club of enormous size.

No one paid any attention as the wagon passed by. It was just good old Doc Fletcher heading out into the boondocks. Fletcher was known as a man with a golden tongue, a gent who could charm the fangs off a rattlesnake. His periodic trips through the mid-south were eagerly awaited by the folks in small towns and villages. They enjoyed listening to Doc lecture on the evils of drink, tobacco and gluttonous eating. Some folks claimed Doc was better than most preachers, especially since he didn't get too all-fired worked up about living the golden rule. After delivering his lectures, Doc went into a spellbinding spiel about the merits of his medicine. The concoction was not bad. It contained essential vitamins and minerals and a few medicinal herbs. As people in the rural areas were often malnourished from lack of one or more nutrients, the medicine did some good.

Now Doc Fletcher sat on the front seat of the wagon. He held the reins as the wagon moved north out of Memphis. His real name was Randolph Fletcher. He was thirty-three years old. After the death of his wife during childbirth, Fletcher had given up a promising career on the stage. He became a full-time drunk mourning the loss of his wife and child.

Fletcher's father-in-law was a fiery abolitionist, a Boston clergyman who lived a moral and temperate life. Fletcher was in a Boston tavern, drowning his grief, when his father-in-law bodily forced Fletcher to come to his home. There, Fletcher was nursed back to a sober condition. Next, the minister got in touch with other abolitionists in New England. They financed Fletcher's first venture into the slave-holding states.

Now, after several years in the south, Fletcher had put together a network of abolitionists. Several hundred slaves had been helped to run away from their masters. They had been sent along this embryonic underground railroad to freedom in the North. Fletcher's latest project was the escape of seven slaves from a plantation owned by Delano Smith in the Holly Springs, Mississippi, region.

As the wagon moved out of Memphis, Fletcher rapped on the door behind his back. Instantly, the door opened and Jesse Hawkins' craggy face came into view.

Fletcher asked, "Everything okeh back there?"

"Goin' fine," answered the big man. Hawkins had given up a job as foreman on the wharfs in Cincinnati to accompany Doc Fletcher on a trip south. Big Jesse was general handyman, bodyguard and companion. Clad in a furry loincloth, waving the thighbone of a cow, Big Jesse played the role of *Attila—The Caveman from the North Pole*.

Doc Fletcher whispered, "Keep everyone quiet. It'll be another half hour before we get to the pick-up spot."

"Same place?" Jesse wondered.

"Yeah. But we got to find another," Fletcher replied. "I don't like setting up a pattern. Too easy for someone to watch and catch us."

They rode along for another half hour, the road becoming little more than a wilderness trail. The people hidden inside the wagon remained silent. Big Jesse hated the dark stuffiness of the wagon's interior. He suffered from a mild case of claustrophobia, hated to be in a small enclosed space for any length of time. In addition, the seven blacks had hidden out in a small building that served as Doc Fletcher's warehouse. They had been there for several days awaiting an escape-route north, and their body odor was sour.

At last the wagon halted. Doc Fletcher stepped down and pretended to inspect the hub of a wheel. He waved his lantern in a wide arc. After a moment, an answering wave of light came from far off in a field. Moving quickly, fearful of a traveler's coming along the road, Doc Fletcher opened the rear of the wagon. Seven black men and women, their eyes wide with fright, scrambled out of the vehicle. They gethered behind the wagon, standing in the middle of the road, uncertain about what to do.

"Quick!" hissed Doc Fletcher. "Follow me!" He extinguished the lantern and started across the field toward the river bank. The only light now was a pale moon that moved in and out of a scudding mass of clouds.

Midway across the field, one of the slaves fell to the ground.

"Oooh, Lawd!" he cried out. "Ah can't go no more. I'se busted my ankle . . ."

"Jesus!" said Fletcher. He called to a passing black man. "Help me get him to the river bank."

They raised the injured Negro, put his arm around their necks and moved slowly across the field. At one point all three men went sprawling into the grass. Finally, panting from the exertion, they caught up with the other slaves. They were standing by the edge of the river on a sandy beach.

A white man came out of the darkness and greeted Doc Fletcher.

"Looks like a real bunch this time," he said.

Fletcher asked, "Can you get them all in the boat?"

"Sure. It'll be crowded but we'll make it. That is, if they sit quiet and don't move around."

"The steamboat'll be here in another half hour."

"Captain Johnson?"

"One and the same."

"We using the same method?"

"Johnson will pull up in the river for about five minutes," said Fletcher. "He'll pretend to have engine trouble. Row to the back of the boat. He'll be there to help everyone on board."

"What about his passengers seeing us?" asked the white man.

Doc Fletcher smiled. "The captain's buying a round of drinks for everyone in the salon. That should keep the passengers occupied."

After a few minutes, they saw the lights of a steamboat moving toward them from Memphis. The slaves got into the boat. Fletcher cautioned them to remain silent, to follow Captain Johnson's instructions when they got on board the vessel. "He's a good man," he told the black men and women. "He'll keep you below deck in the cargo area. Don't leave there under any circumstances. Johnson will see that you've got food and water. Be quiet and you'll soon be in Cincinnati. If anything goes wrong, don't talk about what's happened the past few days. Don't mention my name under any circumstances. If you get caught before you reach Ohio, I'll do my best to get you out of trouble."

A tall man walked out of the group of slaves. He extended his hand to the medicine-show operator. "All I can say is thank you, suh!"

Fletcher smiled. "My pleasure. God be with you."

As the boat pulled away from the beach, Doc Fletcher took one last look at the runaways. Then he turned and hurried back to the wagon. Big Jesse Hawkins was nervously pacing up and down in the road. Wordlessly, they crawled up on the wagon seat, slapped the reins and set out. When they came to the nearest crossroad, they cut eastward and then doubled back to Memphis. The first faint gray streaks of dawn could be seen in the eastern sky when they arrived home.

"A good week's work," said Fletcher.

"You're takin' lotsa chances, Doc," Big Jesse replied.

"Have to in this work."

"I worry about us bein' caught." Big Jesse leaped down from the wagon seat, opened the doors to the warehouse. Fletcher drove the wagon inside the musty building. The horses were unhitched and led to their stalls. After that, the two men walked to a small cottage in back of the large building. This was their living quarters. Doc Fletcher cooked breakfast and, after eating, they went to sleep.

II

Doc Fletcher prided himself on his ability to play a real-life role to perfection. His life depended on suppressing his true beliefs to fool the southerners. Long tours with the medicine show had sharpened Fletcher's wits. In Kentucky he was the grandest of Kentuckians, a neutralist on the slavery question. But when his gaudy wagon rolled into the Carolinas or Virginia, Fletcher favored state's rights—God bless 'em! That infernal government in Washington, D.C., should suppress those rabid abolitionists. In Georgia he talked about the inferiority of the Negro race, the depth of the white man's burden. He was a fervent pro-slaver in Alabama, Louisiana and Tennessee. In Mississippi Fletcher could sit on the veranda of a plantation, sip a mint julep, admire the ladies and condemn those rabble-rousers in the north.

Doc Fletcher was welcome wherever he went. Well educated, up-to-date on the latest news, he was a born conversationalist. Like a true actor, he could drop his New England accent and drawl with the best of southerners. Traveling across the land, selling his medicine, delivering his lectures, Fletcher gained a deep knowledge of southern character.

Southerners of every class were hospitable people. Strangers were welcomed into their homes. They were genial company. But there was also a darker side to their character. They wore honor and chivalry like a badge. Cross a southerner, whether he was a mountaineer from east Teneessee or a planter from the rich Delta of Mississippi, and you had a fight on your hands. A southern male never forgot a slight to his honor. They were quick tempered, fast to fight, slow to forgive.

Aristocrats defended their honor with dueling pistols. The rest of the men fought like demons with pistols, knives, swords, clubs, teeth and toenails. Fletcher had seen dozens of men with an ear missing, bitten off during a wild brawl. Yet they could laugh about such incidents, displaying that curious humor so vital to their existence.

Fletcher knew the South. He had hunted foxes in Virginia, gone on trips into the Great Smoky Mountains, strolled the streets of Charleston. He marveled at the street scenes, sights and smells of New Orleans — the most cosmopolitan of American cities. Fletcher and Big Jesse planned to linger in New Orleans, but an outbreak of Asiatic cholera hastened their departure. They had driven hard and fast over obscure back roads to outrun the epidemic.

Although Big Jesse was the larger and stronger of the two men, Fletcher had a will of iron. He was seldom fatigued. With the heart of a true thespian, Fletcher could go without sleep for long intervals. He was barely bothered by bad weather or hot sun. There was always a healthy glow on his face. There was always a humorous sparkle in his eyes.

Both Fletcher and Big Jesse loved the South.

"These are the grandest people in the world," Fletcher said frequently. "We must remember to keep the land and people separate from our hatred of slavery."

Big Jesse did not fully share Fletcher's hatred of slavery. He was not thick-witted, but seldom cared to think about the subject. Big Jesse received an equal share of the profits from the medicine show. He enjoyed dressing up in the fur loincloth, baring his teeth and howling at the wide-eyes natives in some town or village. His sense of showmanship was superb. Flexing his mighty muscles, waving the bone club above his head, Big Jesse would blast forth with a ferocious yell. The howl would curdle milk for a half mile in every direction.

Doc Fletcher always tantalized the crowd with a fanciful tale of how Big Jesse was found in a glacier. "Ladies and gentlemen," he would spiel, "Attila was frozen stiff when they chipped away that dreadful ice. Stiff as an ironin' board. When he thawed out, he began to talk in the language of the North Pole cavemen. But he was addled, folks, truly addled and unable to speak more than a few words. They concluded his brain was frozen solid. They tried everything to thaw his head. As a last and certainly pathetic effort, they carried the poor creature to New Orleans via steamboat. They felt the warm southern sunshine might do the trick. It didn't work. Then an elderly lady who knew of their efforts succeeded in giving Attila a tablespoonful of my golden-nectar medicine. Within a few hours, Attila was revived. He became a normal, healthy man. But he kept trying to escape from his cage. On those occasions Attila always yelled 'Atkachnmipa! Atkachnmipa!' And he would rattle the bars of his cage like a truly wild man. Of course, the scientists at that time could not speak true North Pole-ese. They could not understand this simple-minded savage. But on their way back to the university back east, Attila saw a group of young maidens get on the steamboat. He pointed at these pretty women and smilingly said, 'Atkachnmipa! Atkachnmipa!' Everyone knew what that meant."

Doc Fletcher would pause to allow the crowd to laugh. Upon proceeding, he said: "The North Pole caveman has one characteristic common only to his race. He has a seventh sense. Now, some of you may find this hard to believe. But Attila is able to use his seventh sense to find women who have been neglected in matters of"—And here Fletcher paused, looked bashful—"shall we say, loving? He knows intuitively when a woman has been neglected. Science does not understand how this wonderous seventh sense works. But work it does. And now, ladies and gentlemen, I shall demonstrate his perceptive abilities."

Saying this, Fletcher would open the door of the cage. Big Jesse would come waddling out. His bone club would be slung over his bare shoulder. He always paused in the doorway to hitch up his fur loincloth. Walking through the crowd, Big Jesse's face would suddenly take on a moonstruck expression. The object of his adoration was always pointed out beforehand by a local townsman. She was always a spinster or long-time-widowed woman. The crowd roared with delight if the lady took flight from the ardent caveman. They were equally pleased if Big Jesse planted a loud, wet kiss on the woman's cheek. The next gambit brought an even louder roar from the crowd. On his way back to the cage, Big Jesse would once again assume a moonstruck expression. Rolling his eyes, Big Jesse would advance on the wife of a leading businessman or farmer. While the crowd went wild, Doc Fletcher always awarded a bottle of medicine to the wife.

"A teaspoon a day for the next three weeks in his coffee," Fletcher would say, "and you can cure your condition, madam. He will be back in his prime again."

The customers knew that Big Jesse Hawkins was Attila, the North Pole caveman. But they enjoyed a good show and the act was good theater. Everyone liked the genial giant. He was a welcome visitor to their communities. Big Jesse was always willing to work on a local project. Both Hawkins and Fletcher donated liberally to local charities. Big Jesse always made an appearance at local hospitals, jails, schools. Big Jesse enjoyed his celebrity status. The fringe benefits were appealing. Spinsters and widows were attracted to the amorous caveman. Doc Fletcher might sleep in the wagon or rent a hotel room. Big Jesse always had free bed, board and other benefits.

III

Morning came. Doc Fletcher and Big Jesse ate a late breakfast. The big man had cooked eggs, ham, fried potatoes and picked some fresh tomatoes from a small garden plot in back of the warehouse. When he finished eating, Big Jesse looked gloomily down at his plate.

"Worried?" Doc Fletcher asked.

"Just thinkin'."

"I'm sure everyone is safe. They'll be in Cincinnati before long."

"I wasn't thinking of them darkies," said Big Jesse. "Reckon I'm thinkin' about money. Doc, we got a real good business here. It could be a gold mine if we paid attention. What'd we do in Holly Springs? Sold maybe forth bottles of medicine. We got people cryin' for a bottle of this stuff. You ain't been payin' attention to things. Look here!" Big Jesse went to a desk in the living room, pulled out a stack of letters and postcards. "These folks are wantin' us to send them medicine. Most've sent along a couple dollars to cover the cost and postage for mailin' it. So whatta we doin'? Spendin' our time messin' with a bunch of darkies. If we hadn't messed with them people last week, we coulda made three of four hundred dollars. Doc, we could be rich."

"Rich?" The idea seemed foreign to Doc Fletcher.

"The whole idea of the medicine wagon is to provide us with cover."

"Why help those folks? They seem awful shiftless and lazy to me."

"Would you work without being paid?"

"Not for long."

"That explains why they're lazy," Fletcher pointed out.

"Well, maybe so," admitted Big Jesse. "But they smell like they've been raised back of a barn."

"Most just own the clothes they're wearing."

"Soap 'n water don't cost much."

Fletcher disagreed. "It does if you don't have a cent of money."

"We could make lotsa money," Big Jesse said grudgingly.

"We've been over this once a week for the past year."

"Facts are facts," contended the big man. "We could make a fortune."

"Maybe someday."

"We could own our own plantation."

Fletcher rolled his eyes. "God forbid!"

"I didn't say we had to work niggers."

"We'll talk about it later," Doc Fletcher said, getting up from the table. "Right now I have to get downtown."

"Shucks, Doc. You say that ever time I mention makin' money. Ain't nothin' wrong with layin' a little back for bad times. Now you're runnin' off. I'll have to fill these orders, mix up a new batch of medicine. What's so all-fired important?"

"There's a big slave sale coming up."

"Sure, I saw the posters all over town. Can't miss 'em."

"I'm trying to plan a surprise for everyone."

Big Jesse looked suspicious. "Like what?"

Fletcher grinned. "Not sure yet. But there must be some kind of devilment we can dream up for the planters. They'll be coming in from all over the South. This is a good time to create a little trouble."

"Dang it! Lotsa money out there and you're thinkin' of devilin' folks."

Fletcher reached up and took his coat off a wall peg. "Got to keep things stirred up, Jesse. Otherwise these smug planters will forget there's an abolitionist movement."

He went out the door. Big Jesse sat glumly and stared out the window. He was tired of saving darkies. He wanted to make some big money and enjoy his new-found celebrity status.

Chapter Five

Although he appeared awkward and incompetent, Ruskin W. Ward possessed a deep streak of practicality. For the form, the balance and the method of his mind prevented Rusty Ward from idle conversation. It was not a trait that commended him to other people. They felt the young man was conceited. Neither was Rusty Ward able to easily hold a conversation with strangers. He seemed tonguetied on those occasions. But when he talked about the things of his dreams, an instant change came over the young man. His eyes glowed with a visionary glint, his tongue became facile, his mind mashed into a direct and sensible drive.

He had gotten up early at the City Hotel that morning, breakfasted in the dining room and gone directly to the Memphis post office. He found Major Marcus Winchester to be a genial, engaging man with a calm disposition. He was flawlessly dressed in a black waistcoat, pearl gray trousers, polished boots and a white shirt and gray tie. Rusty Ward introduced himself, asked permission to lunch with Major Winchester. Although he had never met the young man, the major was agreeable to the meeting.

Promptly at noon, Rusty Ward returned to the post office. Major Winchester was just starting to close up.

"Thunderation! You're punctual," said the major. "Delighted to meet a man who keeps his word in matters of time. Times have changed since I was a lad. Nowadays, people have things too easy. Don't have to gnab and grub for a living. Lost all sense of time. Hot ain't it? Believe this must be the hottest summer in Memphis that I can recollect. And I came here right after Judge Overton, General Jackson and those other scalaways swiped these western lands from the Indians. Sometimes I get to wondering if this is truly healthy country. Maybe we're too close to the river. You've heard of river fever, of course, and how certain locations seem to be poorly situated for people. Damnation! Here comes ole Dan Spaulding. He runs the tavern here in town. Got too many of those infernal saloons here. But grog shops are hard to close down. You wait a couple minutes. I'll have to wait on ole Spaulding, or he'll pour some lye soap in my drink the next time I visit his den of vice and curruption. Soap lubricates your insides, you know, and you go like Billy Wizard the next day."

After serving his customer, Major Winchester locked the post office. He suggested they eat in the dining room of the Union Hotel. The major was well known at that eatery. They were greeted by an amiable man, who was evidently the proprietor, and led to a back booth.

The major slid into the booth. "Food's just as good over at the City Hotel," he said. "But you'll notice these folks have the comfort of their customers in mind. See those Negroes sitting on the stools when we came in?"

Rusty Ward looked around before he sat down. He saw a man in each corner of the room. They sat on high stools, held palm leaf fans in their hands. They moved the fans up and down in a slow, steady motion.

"Keeps the air circulating," said Major Winchester.

"When they serve out food, another Negro will come out of the back with another stool and fan. He'll sit right beside us while we eat, shooing away the flies and keeping us cool."

Rusty Ward was appalled by the system. He said so.

"You have a better idea?" wondered the major.

"You only need one man."

A humorous glint came into Major Winchester's eyes. "You'll have to explain that to an old gentlemen like me."

Rusty was thoughtful for some time. "Attach fans at all four corners of the room," he said at last. "Run a rope around the ceiling. Hook the rope to each of the four fans. One man could move the rope up and down, activating each fan. With that system, one man does the work of four."

Major Winchester pondered that thought for some time. "Son, that sounds right sensible. About the most sensible thing I've heard all day. 'Course, I've been talking to an inspector from the post office department. Down here to see if my office is operating efficiently. Can't understand why I don't return letters after they've been here for a month. Hell, I kept telling him that some people don't get into town but once a month. But, please"—Major Winchester drew a pencil and sheet of paper from his waistcoat—" make me a sketch of your plan. While you're doing that I'll put in our order. This is Thursday so we'll be having liver and onions? Or they got some excellent catfish if organ meats aren't your favorite dish."

Rusty Ward was already sketching. "Liver and onions suits me fine."

Major Winchester beckoned to a white-smocked black waiter. He gave their order, then watched

Ward make his drawings. He said, "You got a mighty fine hand drawing things, son. Makes me wonder why the good Lord neglected to give me the gift of artistry with pen and pencil. Expect he was figuring I would just get all blowed up and conceited with that power."

Rusty sketched a few more details of his system. He explained the diagram to the older man. He summed up, "All you'd need would be a few pulleys, a few ropes and four fans."

"Amazing," said Major Winchester. "I do believe that would work."

"I know it will." There was no smugness in the young man's statement. He spoke with an inventor's assurance.

II

As they ate their lunch, Rusty Ward began to feel at ease. He had not known what to expect from a man of Winchester's caliber. Especially after hearing the former mayor had married a colored woman, fathered several mulatto children and was ostracized from polite society in Memphis. He found the major to be a sharpminded man with liberal tendencies. There was a aura of culture about his luncheon companion. The major was well read, knowledgeable about many subjects. For the tenth time during their meal, Rusty Ward cast a covert sidelong glance across the table. The major seemed to be the perfect symbol of southern aristocratic upbringing. That such a man had flourished in a frontier town like Memphis was astonishing.

The major finished his meal, pushed back his plate. "I've been yammering away at you most of the time," he said, smiling. "That is one of the dangers of aging. We try to give younger folks the benefits of our experience, knowing full well that each man must make his personal mistakes in life. Now, sir, who told you to call on me?"

"Leland Shearer, the cotton broker in Natchez."

"That old rascal? I haven't seen Leland Shearer since he helped Mr. and Mrs. John Conrad buy the old Korrman plantation. Thought Leland might have been shearing the sheep a bit, if you know my meaning. But the Conrads have prospered on that place, turned it into something of an institution in a short time. So I owe an apology to that sharp old scalawag. No, I won't apologize because he still has a copy of my works of Homer. Borrowed the book a few years ago and, like all who do so, has never returned it. There must be something about the nature of books that causes people to neglect their return to the rightful owner. Now, are you in the cotton factoring business like Mr. Shearer?"

"No, sir. Mr. Shearer said I should call on you."

"A salesman?" An expression of curiosity came onto the major's face.

"I'm not sure I'll ever amount to anything, major," Rusty confessed.

"Never downgrade yourself, son. Plenty of others to do that for you. Just why are you calling on me?"

Rusty Ward's mind meshed into a fine gear. It was time to make his presentation. He plunged ahead.

"Well . . . aaah! . . . I've never been very good at anything. My mother used to say I was the dreamy one. She swore I could sit for hours and watch ants carrying food to their hill. I never did too well in school. Seems like I was always daydreaming. Got boxed on the ears by my teachers. One lady held me back a year and that embarrassed me. I also took a lot of kidding from the other children. My best ability isn't playing games. I'm not coordinated good enough to win a footrace. Can't catch a ball. Or do much of anything for that matter. I can't sit around like most folks and chitchat. I get all nervous and tensed up. Want to scream out that we're wasting time, that we should get busy doing something rather than chew the fat."

Rusty paused and Major Winchester said, "Son, this isn't the way you start a sales talk."

Afraid that the major might start rattling off again, Rusty went on:

"About the only thing I'm good at doing is fixing machines. Ain't nothing been made that I can't fix. That ain't bragging. I figure the lord made me extra strong in that department because I'm weak in everything else. I was doing this even when I was a child. Maw's favorite spinning wheel got contrary and wouldn't work right. Took me most of two weeks, but I fixed it when Paw couldn't. Even back then, I could look at something and start figuring out how to improve it. Or, I'd watch maw do something and put together a gadget to do the job better. My baby brother was a colicky baby. Always cried at night and poor Maw had to get up and rock him. I invented a little cradle with a rope and pulley. When Elmer cried, Maw could just reach up and move the rope up and down. She didn't have to get out of bed. That's where I learned about ropes and pulleys. Used them to build all kinds of things around the house. Maw was always churning milk, bouncing little Elmer on her knee. I devised a gadget that moved the churn handle up and down when she raised and lowered her foot. Worked perfect! Maw liked to read and Paw was always complaining about the cost of candles. So I worked out a way to rig up a lantern using pine wood. Gave a better light, too.

"But Paw wasn't real pleased with my inventing. He figured a son of his should be hoeing corn, doing chores. I wasn't much good for that because, like Maw said, I'm kind of dreamy. Addled, Paw said. My mind would get to thinking about a way of hoeing corn without actually doing it. I would forget to hoe and draw sketches in the dust. Used to drive Paw straight up a fencepost. He said people were put on earth to work, dagnabit! — that was his favorite word — and thinking never got a single ear of corn from the field to the barn. I — "

Major Winchester interrupted. "Mister Ward, I checked with the hotel this morning after you called at the post office. You registered as being from Philadelphia, Pennsylvania."

Rusty grinned. "You're thinking I'm a bunco artist? I always say me home is Philadelphia. Our farm was located north of the city limits about fifteen miles. I got my papers and everything at the hotel and — "

"Proceed," said the major. "I just wanted to clear up that point."

"It got so bad, what with Paw and my brothers, that I had to leave the farm. Paw said I was headed straight for perdition. My brothers just laughed and said I'd starve to death out on my own. Sir, I admit to getting fired from quite a few jobs. Got dreamy again. These were mostly clerking positions. I would be staring off in space when I should have been waiting on customers. Now, I went down to New Orleans. Spent some time there, working when I had to. But I live frugal. When I got fired from the first store I spent a month trying to find someone to back one of my inventions. You see, my satchel is full of drawings about my ideas. No one in New Orleans cared to back me. Most thought I was balmy. So I worked some more, saved my money and came upriver to Natchez. I thought a wealthy planter might be interested. Nobody was. The last man I called on was Leland Shearer. He listened courteously but said his funds were tied up in factoring for the planters. I was so depressed I neglected to ask him what factoring was."

Major Winchester cleared his throat. "A factor loans money to planters for seed, equipment and expenses to raise their crops. When the cotton is harvested, the planter often sells his crop to the factor at a price agreed upon when the loan is made. Or for a few cents under the market price when the cotton is delivered to the factor's warehouses. Some planters sell their cotton for a few cents more in New Orleans, paying off the loan in cash money."

Rusty Ward looked puzzled. "But I thought planters were rich."

"Land rich, son."

"But what about those big houses?"

The major chuckled. "Those houses are why they have to use a factor. Their money is tied up in land, houses, slaves, animals and a high standard of living. So Leland Shearer sent you to me. That right?"

"He knew I was coming to Memphis. I asked for the name of a leading citizen."

The major leaned across the table. "Son, I wish I could help. Unfortunately, my fortunes are not as large as they should be."

Rusty Ward's expression sagged.

"Nothing to do with the value of your ideas, son. Let me explain something to you about Memphis. It probably holds true for the entire South. Cotton is king right now, riding in the catbird seat. Every man with two coins to rub together wants to buy land to grow cotton. If they have ten dollars and an old mule, they're thinking of a great plantation. I've been here in Memphis from the start. This is cotton country. It isn't manufacturing country. People eat, drink and sleep cotton. The thing to do is go back north to Pennsylvania, or up in the New England states, where people understand factories and making things. Those folks could see the value in your ideas."

"Aaaahh . . ." said Rusty in a strangled murmur. "I was up there last year. All they think about is looms making cotton into cloth. They said my best promise was in the South, where labor is cheap."

Winchester dabbed his mouth with his napkin. "I must admit—with a certain reluctance—that has a partiality of truth. However, the cheapness of labor in the south is based on slavery. It is a curse that will be a burden on this country for the next two hundred years. Free men and slaves cannot exist in the same society. We must—"

Rusty interrupted. "Could you tell me of another person who might be interested? I would appreciate your help."

Major Winchester was thoughtful. "I'm sorry, son. I can't think of anyone."

"A businessman, perhaps?"

"Everyone I know is expanding. Their finances are extended to the breaking point."

"A banker?"

"They're cold blooded and never loan money on ideas."

"A plantation owner?"

Winchester mused on this for a moment. "The rishest would be John Conrad, the gentleman who was associated with Leland Shearer. However, I must caution you that I don't know anything about his finances. Conrad does not discuss his affairs in public. He's a very private man."

"Do you think he might give me an interview?"

"His man comes to the post office each day to pick up the mail," Winchester replied. "The only way to find out is to ride out to Belle Meade and present yourself."

After a few moments of general conversation on the weather, they rose from the booth. Major Winchester insisted on paying for the meal. They walked back to the post office. The man from Belle Meade had not yet arrived to pick up the mail. Ward thanked the major for his time and interest, then went outside to sit under a shade tree and await Noah's arrival.

Rusty Ward was totally depressed. He felt doomed to wander the world searching for a nonexistent financial backer. How could he continue to prolong this agony when even his own family was unconvinced of his achievements? How many more times could he present his ideas, find a cold, hostile stare — worse yet, indifference — in another man's eyes? Would his life be squandered in his pursuit? But he realized there was really no choice. He could not exist as a clerk. He did not fit into the mold demanded by society. Like the homeless wanderer he was, Rusty decided his journey would continue until the right man was found.

Chapter Six

The next morning a steamboat, the *Natchez Rocket,* pulled up to the wharf in Memphis. Two drummers, a book agent, a land speculator and his wife and Caroline Spearman walked down the gangplank. Miss Spearman was a thin girl, now twenty years old, with a frail look to her pale face. The daughter of Albert and Margaret Spearman, Caroline was returning from a stay of several months in Boston. There, she had attended Miss Markson's Finishing School for Girls.

Life at Miss Markson's school had been unpleasant. The lady and her staff kept close watch on the students. The girls were in bed each evening by nine o'clock. Beds were checked every two hours. They rose early each morning and spend the day in regimented training. In addition of liberal arts classes, the students were taught how to be young ladies. They were shown the proper way to walk, talk, dance, address a servant, write a thank you note, host a party, set a table. Caroline found the whole routine very boring. She loathed Miss Markson, who brooked no nonsense from her students.

Two weeks after her arrival, Caroline tried to sneak out of the dormitory one night. She was caught by an alert dorm attendent. Miss Markson put the girl on probation. Caroline was also forced to write a thousand-word essay on ethics, honor and integrity. She had to rewrite the essay four times. Even then Miss Markson criticized her sentence structure and spelling.

Caroline's mother, Margaret, was a religious woman who lived a gentle and blameless life. Her father, Albert Spearman, was a devil-may-care rake who slipped away from home for women, bourbon and whatever else was available. As a result of these conflicting examples, Caroline grew into a confused child. In her late teens, she was bashful and tonguetied in company. She worried about becoming s spinster. She wondered about sex, what it was all about, how it was done.

Albert Spearman's weekly "hunting trips" with Julian Burnside aroused his wife's suspicions. She sent Caroline out into the night to spy on the Burnside plantation. Caroline was shocked, then excited at Julian and her father pleasuring themselves with several Negro slave girls. She never informed her mother of these orgies. But each week she waited until her mother retired, then slipped off to watch the show. Alone in the darkness, watching the bodies twist and heave inside the Burnside mansion, created a change in Caroline Spearman.

She became obsessed with sex.

She began to blackmail her father, demanding that he become her lover. He resisted. One night coming home from Burnside's place, she was raped, somewhat willingly, by a large black slave named Sam. They became lovers, meeting in the dark nights to vent their lust. Even Sam's sexual prowess was not enough. Caroline continued to pursue her father. He was flesh, weak flesh and eventually succumbed to her advances. Caroline enjoyed these incestuous trysts, but her father drank himself into a stupor each night.

Problems resulted when Caroline tried to end her affair with Sam, the black man. Sam turned ugly—which had surprised her. Did some smelly black men believe everything they were told? Nobody was that stupid. Luckily, that handsome Sean Porter came to her rescue. Sam got off a shot at the Irishman, but the big black man was killed by Sean's return shot.

Caroline did not mourn the slave's death. That would have caused everyone to wonder about their relationship. Sam had been someone to dally with, nothing more. Caroline planned on becoming daddy's little girl. She figured on slipping from her room most every night, sneaking down the hall and tumbling with daddy.

She was surprised when her father turned surly. Maybe he knew more than she realized about her trysts with Sam. One day when Margaret was visiting a sick friend, Caroline flirted outrageously with her father. He became angry and said she was going to Boston to attend finishing school.

"I'll tell Mama," she threatened.

Albert sighed. "I hope to Heaven she'll understand about Julian and me just having some fun."

"I mean about you and me," Caroline told him.

"Jesus H. Christ!" thundered her father. "That would kill your mother. She's a religious woman, kind and considerate to everyone. For the love of God, what kind of person are you?"

"I'm not going North."

"You leave tomorrow morning."

"I won't go."

"I've already purchased the tickets."

"Mama's going to be awful unhappy," said Caroline. She walked to a liquor cabinet. "Want me to fix a little drinkie for you? You sound on edge."

Albert shook his head. "You'd better start packing."

"I'll play sick. Mama won't let you send her sick baby away."

He laughed without mirth. "You'll be on that steamboat if I have to drag you aboard."

The following morning Caroline left for Boston. She did not want to leave Daddy. Neither did she wish to destroy her family by telling the truth.

Her departure from school was a result of Miss Markson's snoopy disposition. The old crab came sneaking into the dormitory one night, found Caroline and one of the new girls in bed together. Miss Markson threw a fit, when all they'd been doing was playing around.

She marched both girls to her apartment and launched into a bitter tirade. Most of Miss Markson's hate spewed in Caroline's direction. Hands trembling, she said, "This . . . this incident can't be tolerated. You will both be leaving school in the morning."

Caroline smiled sweetly. "But, Miss Markson, all the girls do it."

"You're unfit for our school. I'll write your folks tomorrow and give them the details."

Caroline looked at the new girl. She was trembling. No help could be expected from that direction. But she launched a surprise attack. "You tell my folks," she said evenly, "and both of us will swear you taught us to sleep with another woman. We'll claim that you brought us here and—"

"Caroline!" This came from the new girl.

"Shut up!" Caroline snarled. "We're not letting this creepy spinster ruin our lives. Miss Markson is a greedy old bitch scared to death of scandal. The authorities will close down this place when we spill our story to the newspapers and the police."

"Oh lord!" Miss Markson knew she was whipped.

"You'll write my folks that I've finished up here," Caroline went on. "And her folks—" Caroline's head jerked in the direction of the new girl— "will be told that she's sick and has to go home. Do you agree to that?"

Miss Markson sighed heavily. "I'll go along with you to protect the school. The reputation of our students must be maintained. As for you . . . the time will come when your true nature will become known. You'll be exposed for what you really are, young lady."

"Just write the letters," Caroline demanded. She took the new girl's hand and started to walk in the direction of the bedroom.

Miss Markson was stunned. "What're you doing?"

Caroline smiled sweetly. "You're going to be writing letters. We'll be using your bedroom until morning."

Grimly, Miss Markson went to her desk and pulled out a sheet of paper. She ignored the giggles coming from her bedroom, began to write in a shaky script. Still later, she chose to ignore the thrashing sounds coming from her bedroom.

II

Now, standing at the top of the bluffs at Memphis, Caroline embraced her parents. She held her mother at arm's length, said, "I'm so happy to be home."

"Things haven't been the same without you around," Margaret Spearman told her daughter.

Caroline turned to Albert Spearman with a sly smile. She purred, "Miss me, Daddy?"

"Sure."

"You don't sound enthusiastic."

Margaret Spearman ventured, "You know your father, dear. He gets all involved during growing season. I know it is a trial, trying to get the darkies to work. They're always so slow and dull-witted."

Caroline looked boldly into her father's eyes. "I'll help cheer you up, Daddy. Things are going to be just great." She winked. "Lots of good family fun."

Albert Spearman looked away from her stare.

"Nothing's ever the same," he declared.

"But was can try to keep things as they were, Daddy." Caroline went over and embraced the stiff body of her father. He did not respond, letting his arms hang limp.

"Well, I never—" Margaret blurted out. "Albert, give your daughter a nice hug."

Albert's arms came up and encircled Caroline's upper body. His mind was confused, his soul in torment. His face crimsoned as his daughter pressed against him. Everything had been going smoothly with Caroline away. Now his daughter was perversely flaunting herself before him, her pride wounded by the fact that she had been sent north for schooling. He recalled the Biblical verse about the sins of the fathers, knowing Caroline understood his weaknesses and needs. She knew his longing for sexual release, knew that Margaret held little regard for that problem. He recognized that Caroline was a shrewd and stubborn young woman who, through intuition or feminine power, would get to the core of him. He would be bent to her will. She seemed obsessed with this notion, and he was unable to halt it. He wished the past could be erased, the clock turned back to eliminate those parties at Julian Burnside's house. Caroline had spied upon them, the wild scenes unsettling her mind, scrambling her morals. He wished to die. That might solve the problem.

Albert moved away from Caroline's embrace with a contorted smile.

His voice was strangled when he said, "We'd better get started home."

"Anything you say, Daddy," Caroline replied sweetly.

III

That same morning John Conrad was in Memphis checking into schools. Although his children were infants, John was displaying a typical father's instincts. His first stop was a private school ran by Miss Lillian Trainman, a kind and gentle woman devoted to her students. Miss Trainman was one of those obscure unmarried females found in every community. Their lives were spent pounding knowledge and manners into other people's children. She worked tirelessly to endow perfectly horrible children with perfect behavior. She was a thin, gray-haired woman with birdlike hands and a nervous habit of twisting her hands when she talked.

John waited until the morning recess, then went inside the small schoolhouse. After introductions, he found Miss Trainman to be an honest and sincere woman. She was mildly amused by his concern about schooling.

"After all, Mr. Conrad, I may be dead before your children are ready to be taught," she said.

"True, but I hoped to get an idea of what's available locally."

"Not much in the way of proper schooling, I'm afraid." Miss Trainman moved her hands, as if washing them.

"What is your philosophy of teaching?"

"I try to teach the children the rudimentary

writing, reading and arithmetic," she answered. "I also try to give them a heavy dose of Christian character."

"Could you explain that?"

"I try to raise the child to live according to the words of Jesus."

John asked, "Is that wise?"

"We should all try to emulate his life. Are you a Christian, Mr. Conrad?"

"I believe in God."

"But have you been baptized?"

"No, Ma'am."

"What about your children?"

"My wife takes care of those things."

"Indeed, and where is she?"

"In England. The kids were born there."

Miss Trainman raised her eyebrows. "Land sakes! Your children may be baptized in the Church of England."

"Is that bad?" wondered John.

"Nothing but lukewarm Christians," Miss Trainman declared. "The Lord will spit them out at judgment day. Such people are an abomination to the Lord. The day of judgment approaches and the pits of hell await those who play at serving the Lord. They have no purity and little piety. They—"

John listened to the woman with growing amazement. She was clearly obsessed with religion. His children would be raised with a proper respect for the diety, but they would never be taught by this fanatic. He cut the interview short, promised to keep in touch with Miss Trainman.

At noon he spent an hour with Clarence Barlow, headmaster of a small academy established over a store on Main Street. Barlow was a thin, scrawny man in a dark suit, white shirt with soiled collar and a perpetual look of hunger. John inquired about the Barlow Academy's educational philosophy.

"Main thing's keepin' 'em in line," replied Barlow. "Spare the rod 'n you spile the chile. Yoh kid'll do fine heah, Mistuh Conrad. Me 'n the teachers don't take any sass. Ever' kid toes the mark or gets switched. We kin take the biggest brat in town. Amazin' what a little switchin' will do. We jus' talk 'n they hop to like soldiers. Not sayin' yore kids'll need it, suh, bein's they's high born. Sure yoh kids'll have good manners 'n be models of deportment. But if they need a bit of switchin', suh, yoh kin be sure we ain't sparin' the rod at Barlow Academy."

John inquired about the academy's educational philosophy.

"We ain't cottonin' to anything new fangled," answered Clarence Barlow. "No suh. Ain't likely a chile's gonna need Latin or them other fancy languages. No, suh, we don't teach it. Plain speakin' folks speak good ole U.S. of A. when they's talkin'. Yoh kin rest assured knowin' yore kid'll learn the multiplication tables right up to twelves. Spellin' is strong heah, suh, b'cause even a clerk needs that. Hold a spellin' bee ever' spring. 'Course, kids who miss a word on their daily spellin' lists gits ole Dan Switch." He chuckled. "Oughta see them kids studyin' they lessons."

Clarence Barlow insisted on taking John on a tour of the grounds. As the two men approached the playground, which was nothing more than a vacant lot in back of the building, the kids warily watched their approach. They fell silent, subdued. Their game of running tag stopped. They were suddenly transformed into nervous little adults.

"What ah tell yoh?" chorkled Mr. Barlow. "Switchin' turns 'em all into ladies and gents. We don't mess with 'em. Nosiree." He went over and tossled the hair of a boy, who was about seven. "How're yoh doin', Timmy?"

"Fine, sir."

John asked, "You teach them to call everyone *sir*?"

"Sure do."

"I might not want my children to do that."

Barlow looked surprised. "Deportment is important, suh."

"A person should address everyone on an equal basis."

Barlow looked dumbfounded. "Suh, kids ain't equals to adults."

"Depends on the adult, Mister Barlow."

"Nevah had anyone dispute kids havin' manners."

"My children won't say *sir* to a man who doesn't earn it."

"Heavens, Mr. Conrad. Don' yoh realize kids ain't people?"

"No offense, Mr. Barlow, but my opinion differs."

"That makes hoss races, suh," A servile tone came into the schoolmaster's voice. "Yore kid'll find goin' heah a pleasant experience."

John did not wish to pursue the matter. He replied tactfully. "They're babies now. We can discuss things again, perhaps, when the children are approaching school age."

"Ah hope so," said Barlow.

They shook hands. John walked away with a frown of displeasure.

Chapter Seven

John was uncomfortable during the hot, dusty ride back to Belle Meade. He slumped in the saddle and sweated under the blistering sun. His mind dwelled on the morning's experience. He was troubled by a sense of guilt, a feeling he could not shrug off. The words of the two schoolteachers haunted him. The woman was clearly a religious fanatic. Why, she would twist young minds into blindly accepting any "ism" disguised as religion.

And terrible Clarence Barlow was no better—an uneducated sadist who loved to whip young bottoms with a willow switch. Forget it, his mind counseled, and hire a tutor for your children. But then another idea came leaping into his consciousness: Start your own school! Oh, yes, that's what you've been thinking about for the past couple of hours. A half-dozen children lived within walking distance of Belle Meade. Something's got to be done about educating them. The law says the children of slaves can't be educated. That was the law, but Roy Manning was a good attorney. Maybe he could find a way to circumvent it. His thoughts went racing happily into the future. He envisioned a picturesque schoolhouse with bright and dutiful children listening to an intelligent teacher. A feeling of excitement surged through his body. He felt positive, energetic and enthusiastic. He grinned and reached up to take off his hat. He held it with one hand, slapped his horse on the rump with the other. The animal's head came up. John slapped the horse again, yelling at the top of his lungs. The creature reared up, his hooves bit into the dirt and they went off in a wild gallop. This was more like it, John decided. Why, he hadn't felt this good since before Suzanne went off to England.

He still felt good when he rode up to the stable at Belle Meade. He jumped down from the horse with a high heart, handing the reins to the stable boy. Walking briskly toward the house, John was honest in his thoughts. Like all people who achieved their goals, he was profoundly touched by sentiment. He had been born in the backwoods, in a log cabin, with little opportunity for education. His entry into the world had been traumatic. There were other kids like he'd been: poor, uneducated, backward, endowed with the aura of a country bumpkin. The whole thing went back to his childhood, a feeling that he must be honest with the world and pay his debts.

John was smiling when he crossed the back porch and entered the kitchen.

"Hello, Martha, isn't this a marvelous day?" He grinned at the black cook.

"Still smilin' cause yore wife's comin' home?" she asked.

"That and a few other things."

"Uh . . . Mister John . . ." Martha paused for a moment, as if to recollect her thoughts. "A gentleman come ridin' back with Noah. Funny sort. Didn't know what to do with him, so's I put him in the parlor."

"A visitor, eh?" John wondered who it might be. "He give a name?"

"Randall something," the woman replied. "Or maybe it was Rust or something like that."

"I'll go in and see him," John said. "You did the right thing."

John found Rusty Ward pacing the floor of the parlor. The short, round man's eyes widened when John came into the room.

"Aaauuggh . . ." said Rusty Ward, attempting to move forward. His short, thick arm jerked up and his hand was extended.

"I'm John Conrad," John introduced himself. He took the man's moist hand. It was cold and sticky.

Rusty's eyes swung away from John's direct gaze.

"Ayeh! Aaaahhhh" said the visitor.

John thought the young man might be choking.

"Can I help you?" he inquired.

"Hate to . . . Don't like . . . Hesitated to intrude."

John realized his visitor was embarassed.

"Sit down, sir," he said, trying to ease the man's tension. "I'll fix a couple of whiskeys. I hope you like bourbon and branch water. The whiskey is smooth. Brought down from Kentucky."

Rusty Ward stood quietly as John opened the liquor cabinet and prepared their drinks.

"I . . . ah . . ." Ward began when John handed a tumbler to the young man.

"Sit down," John said, somewhat forcefully. "Relax. We can enjoy our drinks and, hopefully, you can join me for dinner. My wife is away, sir, and I hate eating alone." John raised his glass. "Cheers, sir!"

Rusty took a tentative sip.

"F-f-fine whiskey," he stuttered.

"The best money can buy," replied John.

"I always wondered how they make it."

"A very exacting process, I'm told."

Rusty took another sip. "Best I've ever tasted."

"Thank you, sir. Now, what can I do for you?"

Rusty moved to a chair directly across from John and recited his story. His speech was at first halting and imprecise. He went over the inventive nature of his personality. John was interested by the narration, appreciating men whose ideas changed the world. Rusty explained that he had gone over the country, from town to town, hamlet to hamlet, seeking capital; his visit to Major Winchester in Memphis.

"An interesting man," John remarked.

Rusty's face reddened. He asked, "Did the major marry a woman of color?"

"One of the most beautiful women in these parts. An attractive woman and well educated. She has the high regard of anyone who knows her. But her black blood means the Winchesters are unwelcome at any social function in Memphis. That's one of the problems with slavery. A race of people are condemned because of their skin coloration." John was thoughtful for a moment, then raised is tumbler and finished his whiskey. He turned back to his guest. "Are you asking for my help, Mr. Ward?"

"I'm hoping you'll back my patents."

"An interesting thought."

"I need money to think and tinker," explained Rusty.

"Do you think your ideas will work?"

"Most of them will." Ward said this with forceful passion. "Oh, sometimes my mind goes racing off on come fanciful notion. I'm uncertain as to why that happens. Maybe my mind needs to play for a while. But that is a harmless pasttime, an indulgence I allow myself once in a while."

"Do you know anything about systems?"

Rusty Ward's eyes blinked furiously. His short, round body seemed to sink down in his chair.

"Perhaps you'd better explain that, sir," he said.

"Call me *John*."

"All right . . . John. What do you mean by 'systems'?"

"Be back in a moment." John got up and went into his study. He came back with the letter from the steamship company. "This shipping line operates steamboats up and down the Mississippi River," he explained. "They're asking for a steady and reliable source of firewood. They need the wood to operate their engines. This is an opportunity that exists right now. What would you do with the problem?"

John handed the letter to his guest. Rusty Ward held the sheet between his thumb and forefinger, staring solemnly at the flowery script.

Rusty asked, "Are there other boats needing wood?"

"I don't know."

"How much wood will they need?"

"That's unknown, as well."

"How often?"

John grinned. "An other unknown factor."

Rusty replied tersely, "It helps to have a few facts."

John laughed. "I agree. Let's create a situation where we can sell eight cords of wood each day. The steamboat captains have a devil's time finding wood up and down the river. They depend on people living along the river for their supply. I haven't researched this aspect of the project. But I presume most of their suppliers are fairly reliable. But a few are probably forgetful, maybe a bit lazy. In that event, wood might not be available to the steamboat captain. Perhaps the boat has to wait for wood, which throws them off schedule. Or they may be forced to carry extra wood in the event it isn't available when the supply runs low. If Memphis is going to be a large, growing city—as I believe it will be—the town has to have firewood when a steamboat pulls into shore."

Rusty asked, "The wood has to be hauled to Memphis?"

"That's mentioned in the letter."

"Why?"

"Because the boats stop there."

"That's not a reason," Rusty ventured.

"Well, they want the wood delivered there," John said, somewhat impatiently.

Rusty Ward's face took on a cherubic expression.

"Will the wood come from your land here?" the young man asked.

"Of course."

"Why not build a landing right here on the river?"

"I never thought of that," John admitted.

"Does your land run to the river?"

"Yes."

"A wharf," Rusty cried, jumping up and pacing to and fro. "A wharf that's manned day and night. A reliable supply of wood whenever a captain goes past. This letter—" He waved the paper at John—"says there is difficulty in finding wood in Memphis. They'll have to purchase from us. We'll provide a good reliable source—" He stopped and seemed afraid to continue talking. "Ayeh! . . . well . . . you see . . . I didn't mean we'd be partners. Ahhh . . . you see . . . I meant that we are solving . . . not quite . . ."

"Forget it." John's eyes glittered with excitement. He walked over to the liquor cabinet, brought back a decanter and a bottle of tepid water. He was thoughtful as he made their drinks. "A wharf right here would save a lot of work."

"You have plenty of trees on your land?"

"All over the place." John handed a tumbler to his guest.

"Clear the level ground first," Rusty suggested.

"Each acre cleared can be planted the following spring. You're clearing land and making a profit at the same time."

"Good thinking. How would you handle the details?"

Rusty Ward took a sip of his drink. "The steamboats I've ridden on have stopped for wood in some pretty risky spots. I know those captains enjoy showing off in front of their passengers. A needless danger in some instances. Now, I would run a wharf put in the river a good ways. Not so far that it would interfere with navigation. A wharf that would float, but which could also be permanently attached to something for security. I think we should have one large enough to handle three or four boats simultaneously."

John looked doubtful. "Why so large?"

"Do you agree that the number of boats will increase?"

"Yes. That's going to be the transportation system for the Mississippi River towns."

"We build to meet future needs," Rusty said. "Now, do you have quill and paper?"

"In my office." John rose, picked up his drink and headed toward his study. Rusty followed.

Moments later, Rusty sat at John's desk. The quill began to move across a blank sheet of paper. "Here's the wharf. Fairly wide. Now, these are large wooden boxes built to the exact dimensions of a cord of wood. You attach the boxes to a wagon frame. The rig goes off to the sawmill, the woodlands, or wherever you get the wood. You get an exact measurement of wood in each box. Bring the wagon back to the wharf, loosen the device holding the box on the wagon frame. Bolts will do for now. We'll add hooks on top of the box. Attach a chain to the hooks and use a winch to unload the wagon. We can even put the winch on a rail so the wood can be stacked in long rows. Now here"—the quill moved at a rapid pace—"we'll build a swinging iron arm. The arm will pick up the box of wood, swing over and deliver it on the deck of the steamboat. Once the wood is placed in a box, we don't have to handle it ever again. Machinery does the rest. The winch and swinging arm can be powered by mules. But what I'd really like to do is use a steam engine and a series of gears."

John asked, "What would it cost to build that?"

"We'd need gears," Rusty said, talking rapidly. His eyes were fixed on the sketches. "Some blacksmith could jack-leh up the rest of it. Hey! Wait a minute! Look here . . . we could attach the swinging arm to an invented rail that runs the length of the wharf. That way, we could swing the arm to either side of the wharf for loading." Rusty grabbed another sheet of paper and silently sketched the device.

John picked up the sheet of initial sketches.

He settled down into a chair beside the desk and studied the drawings.

"Those are just for getting the idea down," Rusty said, apologetically. "I'll do better drawings tomorrow."

John chuckled. "Rusty, you're a wonderment."

The young man stopped sketching. His round face was solemn. "You mean that? You're not just saying it to make me feel good?"

"I mean it."

"Thank you," Rusty said, somewhat shyly. "You're the first person to say that about my ideas."

"No one's listened before now?"

"Sometimes they humor me like an adult pretending to understand a baby's first efforts at speech."

"I thought our nation was open for new ideas."

"Not if it involves money," Rusty explained.

"Speaking of that, what arrangement do you want to build me this modern wharf?"

Rusty Ward's mouth went agape. His pudgy fingers slawed at his hair. He tugged his left ear with his other hand. "I . . . well . . . never figured that far . . . you see . . . I don't . . . Shucks, You pay the materials and I'll build it for free."

"You must have considered some arrangement," John said gently. "You've been going from town to town to raise money."

"I haven't thought much about that part," Rusty replied.

"Not at all?"

"Been too busy looking for a backer."

"Let me make you an offer," said John. "We'll use workers from Belle Meade. I'll put up the money, supply the wood and either of us can manage the operation. I —"

"You manage," said Rusty. "I don't have any talent for actual business."

"Looks like you have a fine brain."

"But only for thinking," Rusty explained. "I get bored with details. Once I learn how to do something, understand it, I sort of lose interest in it."

"All right. I'll manage or get someone," John went on. "You draw a reasonable salary while you're putting the wharf together. When we get operating we'll draw up papers giving you twenty five percent of the profits. That is making an assumption there will be some profits to divide. Does that sound fair?"

Rusty Ward nodded happily.

"Next, you can move out here. My wife will be coming home so we'll want some privacy. There's another plantation down the road managed by my friend, Sean Porter. We call it Belle Meade Two.

There's plenty of room over at the old Burnside place and Sean would appreciate having some company."

"I don't know . . ." Rusty hesitated.

"You don't like the deal?"

"Oh, I love that. Most folks don't think much of my company, to be honest about it."

"Do you have bad habits?"

"I snore a little."

"Then what's the problem?"

"I'm not much of a talker. But I like to listen to other folks talk."

"God, man!" John slapped Rusty on the shoulder. "You'll get along with us. Sean and me can out talk a patent medicine salesman. Besides, I'll tell Sean you're a genius. He'll make allowances for your moods."

"What if I just want to think by myself?"

"Sean will understand. He's the finest man I know."

"In that case," Rusty said, extending his hand, "I am delighted to be a part of your plantation."

They shook hands.

"Welcome to Belle Meade, Rusty," John said with a grin.

Tears glistened in the young inventor's eyes.

His voice cracked with emotion when he spoke.

"This is the place I've been searching for all this time."

Rusty felt like crying.

"Come on," John said, to spare his new friend embarassment, "let's go see what Martha has cooked for supper."

Chapter Eight

There was a section of Memphis that was notorious rather than respectable, dirty rather than clean, poor instead of rich. There was an absence of green lawns, prosperous businesses and neat buildings in this area. Most of the proper citizens deplored the existence of such an area in an up-and-coming town. The ladies of Memphis were particularly offended, yet they were eager to hear gossip about what took place there. Knowing the way of hypocrites, many people thought those who loudly objected to the slum area were those who kept it prosperous. The section was known as Pinchgut, so named because those who lived there were poor. The section consisted of a ramshackle collection of shanties and log cabins, houseboats, cheap hotels, brothels, restaurants serving greasy fried food, saloons pouring cheap home-brewed whiskey. Here lived the prostitutes, gamblers, river rats, shanty boatmen, shysters, bunco artists, and cripples who existed on the hungry side of the dollar.

Pinchgut was as quiet as a corpse during the daylight hours. The summer heat was thick and humid along the river; the broiling heat kept everyone indoors or in the shade. Shimmering heat waves bothered the eyes causing a witchery effect wherever a person looked. Everyone waited for darkness; night would bring relief from the heat and sun. Most folks in Pinchgut seldom stirred until the noon hour. They hated the harsh brightness of daylight, felt at home only after the sun was gone from the sky.

They were night people destined to live in darkness. That was to their liking. Most felt day people were stubborn, abrasive and always in a hurry. Day folks liked to get things done, work hard and gather up treasures on this earth. The night people liked treasure — maybe more than the daylighters — but hard work didn't sit too well. Easier ways could be found to earn a dollar. Who needed early-to-bed, early-to-rise when the world was filled with lonely people waiting to be entertained?

Pinchgut became a relaxed place when the sun went down. Tension went out of their voice; the people relaxed. There was a magical quality about the night, a time when all things seemed possible. Hustlers could dream of a big score, feel like the money was in their hands. Prostitutes could dream of handsome gentlemen begging for their hand, whisking them off in a fancy carriage to a storybook plantation with servants and elegant furniture. Cripples thought about a new leg, or maybe two in some cases. And best of all the night hid the seediness of Pinchgut, the street lights transforming it into a golden place.

Nighttime was when Pinchgut did business. Suddenly, the first group of dandies from Memphis came swaggering into the quarter, money in their pockets to be spent. Little Negro boys rushed up to watch the fancy rigs, hoping for a sizable tip. The pretty young prostitutes in their finest dresses giggled and laughed as they waited on the corners for a gentleman to entertain. They bantered with the bashful young men off the farm for a spree in town.

Older men, more experienced in the ways of Pinchgut, headed for Madame Rose's brothel. The house was an asset for Memphis, many reflected, because Rose ran the finest brothel between New Orleans and Cincinnati. Madame Rose, an attractive woman in her forties, was whispered to be the wife of a judge from Nashville. She had run away with a young lawyer, who abandoned the woman in Memphis. The town loved stories about fallen women and Madame Rose encouraged the rumor. She had learned a few legal terms and hinted at her knowledge of jurispuridence. Rose was actually a former crib girl from New Orleans. She robbed a wealthy customer one night and hurried upriver on the first steamboat.

A man needed credentials to enjoy the carnal pleasures at Madame Rose's place. Looking and acting like a gentleman was important. Wearing a hat, shirt, coat and cravat helped get one through the front door. Once inside, a willingness to spend money was essential. Those who wanted the best girls always ordered a bottle of champagne for Madame Rose and the girls. At twenty dollars a bottle, this endeared the customer to Madame Rose. Hereafter, he would be called a sporting gentleman.

Occasionally one or another of the gentlemen might become boisterous. Or a group of river men, fresh off a steamboat with their pay in their pockets, might try to enter the elegant brothel. Whatever scandal threatened to mar the reputation of the house was quickly squelched by a huge Negro bouncer. His hulking appearance and stony face stopped the rowdiness. His name was Jumbo. Simply Jumbo. Some folks claimed Marie and Jumbo were lovers, although that fact had never been actually established.

On this night Doc Fletcher came walking out of Hancher's Saloon in Pinchgut. He stopped and consulted his watch under a street lamp. It was ten minutes after ten. Behind him from the saloon came the tinkle of a piano. Several businessmen and a few planters were celebrating the end of the day. The market price for cotton was up, the weather was fine and all was right in the world. A couple of prostitutes came walking past. They eyed Doc Fletcher speculatively, decided he was a drinker rather than a lover. Across the street two men weaved drunkenly toward a carriage. They stopped under a street lamp and began to sing boisterously. The two streetwalkers headed in their direction.

Doc Fletcher had spent the afternoon and evening in Hancher's Saloon. He stood in the dirty sawdust and sipped cheap whiskey, talking with Clarence Hancher and passing the time with customers who drifted in. Finding someone to help sabotage the upcoming slave auction was his goal. Hancher's saloon had been a poor choice; everyone there was a pro-slaver who would kill an abolitionist on principle.

Fletcher walked down the street, glad to be in the dark. There was comfort in the night. A man could let down his guard for a moment, knowing no eyes could penetrate the blackness. He was tired of his solitary life wandering the South. Yet the mission had become his burden until slavery was abolished. He thought about his dead wife, reflected on what the ravages of the grave had done to her body. He shuddered.

The destination that Doc Fletcher had in mind was Madame Rose's brothel. It was a large, nondescript building on a corner. The entrance was protected by a wrought iron structure with an awning on top. Two large windows covered with velvet drapes flanked the doorway. A young Negro man with a cheerful smile guarded the entrance. He gave Doc Fletcher a cheerful smile.

"Th' gennulman lookin' for entertainment?" inquired the doorman.

"Considering it," said Fletcher. The building was larger than he anticipated, four floors high with a vacant lot serving as a parking spot for carriages and horses. Another Negro was moving through the lot, feeding and watering the customer's horses.

"Madame Rose had the fines' house on the whole Mississippi River," said the doorman. "We's got white gals, black girls, and a few high yallers. Each gal's bin specially trained to pleasure her visitors." He grinned widely. "They can do anythin' yuh want — and some things yuh ain't ever heard of."

"Expensive?"

The doorman smiled again. "Yuh gets what yuh pays for. Yuh can get a streetwalkin' gal a whole lot cheapner'n our gals. Thass a fack. Mayhap yuh heered Madame Rose don' 'low no white trash in her house."

"White trash?" Fletcher gave the Negro an intimidating look.

"Yuh knows what I means, suh," said the man, quickly.

"Is Jumbo around?"

"Who askin' for Jumbo?"

"Doc Fletcher."

"He know yuh?"

"Not likely."

"Yuh come back tomorry. Jumbo don' like bein' bothered durin' workin' hours. Thass a fack!"

"Jumbo can be the judge of that," said Fletcher. He gave the doorman another hard look.

The man wilted. "Deed he can, suh!" He bowed low, opened the door. As Fletcher went past, the doorman whispered. "Bes' ways t'buy the gals a bottle'a champagny. Sportin' men're always treated right. Yes suh! A sportin' man don' have t'worry at our place."

Fletcher stopped in the entryway. "How'll I know Jumbo?"

"Yuh'll know when yuh sees him. Bigges' man yuh'll ever see, suh."

Flectcher fished a coin from his pocket, handed it to the doorman.

The man's eyes brightened. "Yuh're sportin' awright."

Doc Fletcher walked into the brothel. The carpeting was vivid red, gaudier than he expected from rumors about the brothel. The windows were covered with bright red drapes. The bottom floor was apparently used as a bar and get-acquainted area. Several women lounged around the room, sitting on sofas or leaning against a small bar. Most wore abbreviated clothing or negligees. Their garments looked as if they belonged in a brothel. A tall woman in a low-cut, black gown came up. Her bearing was regal, almost haughty. Fletcher noticed that her shoulders, face and the exposed flesh of her breasts were rouged and heavily powdered. Doc Fletcher had expected a much older woman, but Madame Rose was about thirty-five. That seemed young to be the owner of a brothel. The conversation at Hancher's Saloon suggested she was a much older woman.

Madame Rose extended her hand.

"Welcome!" she smiled. "I'm Madame Rose."

Fletcher was tonguetied. The woman's attractive face was framed by long black hair. She was a tall woman, at least five feet, ten inches. He had always been attracted to tall, slender women and Madame Rose was certainly that.

"I . . . ahhh . . ." Doc Fletcher reddened.

"Don't be bashful!"

"This is my first—"

Madame Rose beamed. "I know, darling! You're embarassed! This must be your first visit to a palace of pleasure. We're not ogres! Really, darling, we are not! We are not evil women! Not at all! We're here to transform your fantasies into reality, to take those fantasies out of your imagination and transform them into something sweet and sensual. We do not lure married men from the embraces of their wives. Nosiree! We don't know if you're married or not and it doesn't make a smidgen of difference! Ha! Madame Rose and her darling girls never tell tales. We merely do what every wife should do—which is please their husbands in the boudoir. But we only entertain gentlemen and, darling, I can trust my eyes that you're one of the gentry. Nothing wrong with some feminine companionship after a hard day of work. My girls? Misty is sitting on the coach. Wonderful girl! Blonde and sleek as a cat. But, darling, she's like a snake in bed. Nice, yes? See that beautiful dark-haired girl sitting beside Misty? She's Marcella. Beautiful! She just finished two years of schooling at a lady's academy in Charleston. South Carolina, that is! Marcella comes from an aristocratic family in Virginia. The poor girl was abandoned by her lover. A cad! A double-dealing cad who left the poor girl penniless after she'd given up her inheritance to become his lover. Her mission in life is to make every man feel the most intense carnal pleasure. My next girl"—Madame Rose looked at Fletcher with an expression of rapture—"is Stormy. She's the strawberry blonde standing by the bar drinking her cocktail. Champagne! Real French champagne! Stormy and the girls love to drink champagne. Most gentlemen order a bottle or two while they're getting acquainted with the girls. Girls! Such delightful companions for a lonely man on a nice evening. Heavens! I don't know what I'd do without these beautiful girls to keep me company."

Fletcher was amazed at how Madame Rose could fill a room with words. He grinned, "You've got the wrong calling."

"Indeed?" Madame Rose gave him a critical look.

"You should have been a medicine show barker," he told her.

"My! Don't you recover quick from being bashful!"

"You've got a great line," he said quietly.

"Land's sake! How you do go on," said Madame Rose, cocking her head and giving him a coquettish look.

"You're wasting your talent here."

"I'll be the judge of that, mister!" Madame Rose looked solemn. "Maybe I'm wasting my talent on white trash that just galloped in to look around. I could tell you what you are, sir, but my delicate nature forbids it. We serve only those gentlemen with sporting blood. Real sports! You look like a man with a thin purse in the wrong pew, buster!"

"Don't get your dander up," said Fletcher. "How much is a bottle of champagne?"

"Twenty-five dollars!"

"I'm not buying the winery," he complained.

Madame Rose looked aghast. She cast a scornful expression in Fletcher's direction.

"Leave, sir!" She cried. "Begone! My girls and I do not entertain cheapskates."

"Don't you serve cheaper champagne?"

She pretended to be bewildered. "Cheap champagne? Oh my God! Did you hear the man, girls? He wants to ruin our gullets with cheap champagne. Lordy sir, we're too delicate for rotgut. We drink only the finest wines, sir! You would save a few dollars and blemish our insides. Ha!"

Fletcher was impressed with the woman's act. Money could be made selling tickets to such a show. Madame Rose was haughty enough to frighten the average customer into buying the champagne. She displayed just the right amount of counterfeit culture. Her attractive face could suggest rapturous agreement or scornful discontent.

Fletcher cocked his head. He looked at Madame Rose with profound respect.

"Dear Lady," he said, lightly. "I thought there was a hint of nobility in your speech. But I do believe that's an affectation. During my travels around the south I've studied local accents and dialects. I—"

"A poor scholar," said Rose, scathingly.

Fletcher noticed that the other women were listening. He wondered if they believed Rose'e lies about her origins. No matter. He spoke frankly, "As a student of speech patterns I think you're from Catfish Row south of New Orleans. Are you?"

Marcella and Stormy sucked in their breath. Misty giggled, then covered her mouth and looked innocent. Madame Rose was plainly astonished, her eyes bugging, mouth dropping open. Then the woman recovered her senses and drew up stiff as a ramrod. Her face colored.

"I've always lived in Tennessee," she lied. She was amazed that Fletcher knew that she'd been born in the swamplands around New Orleans.

"Then you moved to the swamps of Louisiana," said Fletcher. "I'm seldom wrong about these things."

Her face reddened to a deeper hue. "Of all the silly men, you're the worst!"

Marcella rose from the couch. "What about me, mister? Can you tell where I'm from just by listening to me?"

"Don't be foolish, Marcella," Madame Rose objected. "The man's clearly a fake."

Fletcher ignored Madame Rose. "Do you think I can do it?" he asked Marcella.

"I don't know," she admitted. "But it'd be fun to see if you could."

Fletcher was thoughtful. He steepled his hands beneath his chin and asked the girl to speak several words. He listened intently to the subtle accent in her speech.

"Can't you do it?" asked Marcella.

"You were born near Knoxville, Tennessee," Fletcher said, at last. "Not in the city but on a nearby farm or in a small town. You lived there until you were about ten or twelve years old, then your family moved to Georgia. Probably close to Atlanta. You've been in Memphis about a year."

"Well, I swear," sighed Marcella. "That's absolutely right. I was eleven when we moved to this itty-bitty place right outside of Atlanta. Land's sake! A gift like yours can tell a lot about people. How'd you do it?"

Fletcher shrugged. "Just listen to how people talk."

Marcella winked. "Course you're just batting fifty percent because you missed Rose's background."

"She still sounds like a swamprat to me," Fletcher answered.

"Jumbo!" Madame Rose's shrill voice made everyone jump.

A curtain parted behind the bar and a tall man, his skin the color of black walnut, came into view. He was at least six feet, six inches in height, his muscular body weighing almost three hundred pounds.

"You call me, Miz Rose?" Jumbo's gaze fastened on Fletcher's face.

"This man is bothering us," his mistress replied in a whiny voice.

"Want me to whump his tail?" Jumbo moved from

89

behind the bar with remarkable swiftness. He came foreward on the balls of his feet, his huge black hands balled into fists.

"Just see that he leaves," Madame Rose replied.

Fletcher was already backing toward the door. "I just decided to go by myself," he grinned.

Jumbo walked behind Fletcher until they were past the doorman and out into the street. Madame Rose pulled aside a drape, looked out into the darkness. The two men were talking quietly. After a few moments, they walked to the other side of the street and talked there for several minutes. She was surprised to see Fletcher shake hands with Jumbo before walking away.

When Jumbo came back into the house, Madame Rose asked about his discussion with the man.

"Wasn't nothing," Jumbo lied. "Like all whities. He was just making chin music."

Chapter Nine

The night was hot and humid. Big Jesse Hawkins had trouble falling asleep because of the heat. During the night he awoke in the sultry bedroom of the house shared with Doc Fletcher. The air was oppressively hot, almost stifling. The sheets on his bed were damp with sweat and so was the cover of Jesse's feather mattress. Grumbling aloud, Big Jesse got up, pulled on his trousers and picked up a blanket. He went out to the kitchen, drank a dipperful of the tepid water. It did not slake his thirst. Still grumbling, Jesse went out on the front porch and spread the blanket on the hard wood floor. He thought about going back in for the mattress, but decided it would fold around his body and be wet for a week. Finally he drifted off into a restless sleep.

Big Jesse came to his senses about eleven o'clock in the morning. A buzzing horse fly was feasting on his arm. He slapped the pesky insect, sat up and knuckled his eyes. He became alert at the sight of a skinny boy sitting in the porch swing. The boy was about ten years old, freckled lightly over his face. His hair was sun-bleached, cut short. The child was silently staring at Big Jesse; he was chewing slowly on a blade of grass.

"Dangnation!" Jesse said, taken aback. "What're you doing here?"

"You don't look like no wild man," replied the boy.

"I ain't no wild man."

"Maw said you were."

"Well," said Big Jesse, "maybe your maw don't know everything about other folks."

"My maw's smart," responded the boy, still chewing his blade of grass.

"I don't doubt that. She had you, didn't she?" Big Jesse's voice was sarcastic. "Now, son, you run along and let me get started on my day."

"Maw wants you to hep her."

"Boy, I'm tired of making chin music. Skedaddle!"

"Maw said you'd be like this. It ain't gonna take long."

"What's wrong with you maw? Why's she need help?" wondered Big Jesse.

"We need somebody to fix the porch."

"Go find a carpenter."

"Maw said you'd be growling."

Big Jesse looked at the boy as if the child was a village idiot. When he spoke again, his words came slow and each syllable was pronounced carefully.

"Boy, I don't know your maw. That's a fact!" said Big Jesse. "Never laid my eyes on you till just now. Being's I don't know your maw, don't have any intention of getting acquainted with her, don't even know her name or yours either, why, you just run on home. I got business to attend to. That's a fact!"

"Maw said it won't take more'n a half hour."

Big Jesse slapped a sweat bee on his wrist. "Damnation! Insects'll take over the world someday."

The boy nodded solemnly. "Our porch needs fixing real bad. Maw's afraid one of us young'uns will hurt ourselves. She needs a strong man to help her."

"So you come here to get me to do your paw's work."

"No sir! Paw's gone."

"Run away from your maw, I expect."

The boy shook his head. "No sir, he's dead."

"Damnation! I'm sorry."

"Maw says the Lord giveth and the Lord taketh away. We ain't to wonder about the Lord's ways."

Big Jesse looked dismayed. "How'd it happen?"

"He worked on a steamboat. It blew up." The boy threw away his well-chewed blade of grass. "'Spect we'll have to make do with our old porch. It wouldn't take long for someone who's strong to fix it. If someone wanted to help a widow lady and four fatherless children. Maw says Memphis folks can't be expected to hep. They're all talk about hospitality and no doing the work. Maw told us children you'd be muley about it."

"Muley?" croaked Big Jesse.

"Mules won't do nothing lessen they get whacked on the head."

Big Jesse looked astonished. "Don't try whacking me, son."

"No sir," said the boy. "Maw does the whacking around the house. She whacked one of my sisters last week. Got Angel all ready to go to church. She was wearing her best white dress. Maw turned her back and Angel went outside and played in the dirt. Maw whacked her hard. Angel crossed her heart and said she saw stars."

"Your maw carries a good whack, huh?"

"Yep."

"She'd better not try and whack me," said Big Jesse, defiantly.

"Maw whacks whoever don't do what she wants."

Big Jesse frowned. "Are you warning me 'bout your maw?"

"No sir. Nothing 'cepting maw needs hep fixing the porch."

Big Jesse looked mystified. "But why me? I don't know your maw."

"She explained that, too. We kids can't be too choosy."

"About what?"

"Our new daddy."

"New *daddy*!" Big Jesse's voice was a strangled wail.

"Maw says she ain't getting any younger and she ain't a spring chicken."

"None of us are," said Big Jesse, trying to reason the thing through. He felt depressed. Somewhere out in Memphis was a widow woman with four children who had maybe earmarked him as her new husband. The thought was frightening. The huge man swallowed hard, then asked: "Son, how old is your maw?"

"She's thirty-five."

"Hmmm! She pretty?"

"Said she used to be the prettiest girl on Big Ugly Creek."

"Big what?" Jesse was taken back again.

"Big Ugly Creek. Back in the hills of western Virginia."

Jesse pondered that for a moment. "I bet they raise some doozies on Big Ugly Creek. How'd anybody ever name a creek that?"

"Must've been an ugly creek," said the boy. "But Maw says it isn't ugly at all. Supposed to be real pretty. Now"—and here the boy jumped down out of the porch swing—"we'd better get along. Maw's going to be worried about me. She'll have to get the porch fixed and look you over."

"Look me *over*!"

"Kids need to get acquainted with you, too. You know," said the boy, "we got some rights in saying who's gonna be our daddy. You might measure up—and then again, maybe you won't. I think us kid'll be fussier than Maw."

Big Jesse ran his hand through his hair. "What I

94

oughta do—and probably will—is drown you in the river. Coming around here this morning disturbing my sleep and—"

"I waited an hour for you to wake up," said the child in a defiant voice. "Sides, you snore awful loud. 'Spect that'll have to stop."

"*Snore?* Who snores?" demanded Jesse.

"That's what I would call it."

"I don't snore."

The boy grinned sheepishly. "Maybe you was snoring 'cause of laying out here on the porch."

"Damnation!"

"Maw don't like cussing. She'll whack anybody who does it."

"Your maw must be the whackingest woman in Tennessee."

"She's a Christian woman."

"What's wrong with this porch?" wondered Jesse.

"Needs fixing."

"Dammit, you twerp! I figured that out. How does the blamed thing need fixing?"

"Couple boards need to be nailed down."

"That's all?"

"Right now."

"Boy, your maw can do that."

"She'd rather have a man do it."

"I'd rather have a good whore to—" Jesse halted. "Well, you know how things go. Life's not set up to give us what we want."

"Maw says that ain't true."

"I suppose she's a philosopher, too."

"Maw makes do."

"I'll bet she does," Jesse agreed. "Throw her in the briar patch and she'll have rabbit stew for supper. Along with blackbery cobbler and whatever else she can devil out of people."

"We do have good vittles. Maw's a good cook."

"What's her best?"

"I like fried chicken. She fries it real golden."

"What's your name, son?"

"Billy."

"What else?"

"Billy Wells. But my maw used to be a Payne."

"What's her name?"

"Pat. That's short for Patricia."

"A good ole girl from Big Ugly, eh?" said Jesse.

"I wouldn't let Maw hear you joking about her home place."

"That a fact?"

"She might whack you for it!"

"Dammit!" Big Jesse stood up. "I reckon you'll keep pestering me until I go over and fix that porch. Tell me where you live and I'll drop over there this afternoon."

"Maw said I had to bring you with me." Billy Wells grinned. "I don't figure she trusts you off by yourself."

"I don't trust myself half the time," said Jesse. "But I got a rumble in my stomach. Got to go downtown and get something to eat."

Billy Wells considered that. "Maybe Maw will fix some grub."

"Not sure I'd want to stay there that long. Got business to attend to."

"Maw's an awful good cook,"

"Well, hell," said Jesse, running his hand over his face. "I'll shave and go over and help your maw."

"She'll be grateful for any hep she gets," said Billy.

II

The Wells home was about a block and a half away

96

from the home occupied by Big Jesse and Doc Fletcher. The house was a large two-story log home with a large front yard and a backyard consisting of five acres of fruit trees. The town had built up around the acreage. The yard contained rose bushes, violets, hollyhocks. The flowers were planted in careful rows. Off to the left side was a large garden carefully weeded and planted with an abundant variety of vegetables. Big Jesse had been raised on a farm. He was impressed with the work that had gone into Patricia Wells' place. She might be widowed but she wasn't sitting around grieving.

Billy led Big Jesse up the walk. He stopped on the steps of the front porch, pointed to the floor. "There's the boards," he said. His voice was low and the tone was grave.

Jesse bent down to inspect the wood. He studied the spot where the nails had been, noted the impressions left by a claw hammer or crow bar. He stood up, asking, "How long did it take your mama to loosen those boards?"

The boy backed away. "They need fixing."

"Dangnation! You little twerp! Someone took a hammer and loosened those boards!"

Billy looked sullen. "You can't say that for sure."

"I sure as hell do say it!"

"Maybe a big bear was under the porch and pushed 'em out with his paws." Billy blinked at him with an innocent expression.

"Dumbbell! Bears don't carry hammers!" Jesse roared, pointing to the impressions left by a tool pulling out the nails. "At least not the bears I've been acquainted with. Maybe bears are getting a little advanced these days! Maybe they ain't bears at all but widow ladies dressed in fur looking for husbands! Damnation, son, your maw's gonna ruin your house pulling these stunts!"

A woman spoke from the doorway. "Mister, watch your language! That's a small boy you're talking to."

Big Jesse spun around to see a tall slender woman in her mid-thirties step out onto the porch. Her hair was black, long, and tied in a bun on her head. She wore a white cotton blouse and a black floor-length skirt. Her face was attractive, scrubbed clean and free of makeup, and her eyes flashed angrily at Big Jesse.

Billy spoke up quickly. "He come to help me fix the porch."

"Are you this boy's maw?"

"Yes, I'm Billy's mother."

"You ought to quit tearing up your porch," said Jesse, speaking frankly. He pointed to the nailless boards lying on the cross beams of the porch structure.

The woman inspected the planking. Then she raised her face and cast a smouldering look at her son.

"Did you do that?" she asked.

The boy hung his head. He dug his bare foot into the edge of a flower bed.

"Answer me, young man."

"Yep. I did it," Billy replied, lowly.

There was an audible exhalation of the woman's breath. She sighed.

"I'll attend to you later, young man," Mrs. Wells threatened. She gave her attention to Big Jesse. "I apologize, sir. Billy has been grieving over the loss of his father. You're the fourth or fifth man he's brought home under one pretext or another. I hope he hasn't put you out."

Big Jesse felt embarassed. His big face reddened.

"Naw, I just wanted to help the little feller," he said. "Don't be too hard on the little twerp."

Billy spoke up. "He didn't either want to hep,

maw. I had to promise you'd fix lunch."

Mrs. Wells looked exasperated. "What am I going to do with you?"

"He ain't married, maw," Billy said. "You said that you weren't getting any younger."

The woman's face turned crimson.

"Bill, I—" she began.

"You said it last week, coming back from church," he stated.

She ignored her son. "I'm sorry, sir, for my son's actions."

Big Jesse shifted uncomfortably. "I'd better mosey on back."

"Thanks for showing your concern," she said.

"Don't whack the shaver too hard." Big Jesse tipped his hat.

"You ain't leaving?" This came from Billy.

"Son," Jesse said solemnly, "I got business to attend to."

"Maw's gonna fix some lunch."

"Shut up!" shouted Mrs. Wells. "Billy, you're embarassing us."

Billy ignored his mother's cries. He ran over and grabbed Big Jesse by the hand.

"He's a good man, Maw," the boy insisted. "He's got a good job and he wouldn't whack us around like some would. You said there wasn't much pickings on the tree."

Big Jesse was confused. One part of him wanted to stay and comfort the boy. Another part of his mind suggested retreat as rapidly as he could do so. His huge hand came out and he tousled Billy's sun-bleached hair. "Son, you feel free to come and see me anytime. Drop in for coffee anytime you're passing through."

The boy's expression was hopeful. "You mean it?"

"Sure," Jesse answered gruffly.

"I might do that," said Billy, with a manly swagger.

Jesse removed his hand from the boy's grip. "I'll mosey on back." He bowed toward the woman with a stiff, clumsy motion.

"Good bye, sir," she replied as Big Jesse walked away.

Patricia Wells stood on the porch, her hands resting on the railing, and watched Big Jesse walk out into the street. He was a big man, much larger than her husband. What she'd said was true, only Billy didn't have to repeat it to every man he met. She wasn't getting any younger, her best years had gone past. But she was responsible for raising four children; under those circumstances it didn't pay to take chances. She had seen a number of widows marry right after their mourning period ended. They had taken the first thing in pants that came along. The results were seldom favorable.

Rose Smith married a drunk who stayed long enough to drink away her farm and livestock. Martha O'Brien's second husband abused the poor woman and her children. They tried to hide their bruises by staying at home. Near the end, before the oldest boy killed the man, the family had become reclusive. When the grand jury saw the boy's battered body, they returned a bill of no indictment against the young man.

Losing a husband was tragic, she reflected.

Marriage to the wrong man multiplied the disaster.

Chapter Ten

After eating a light lunch, Doc Fletcher went down to Pinchgut. He cut through an alley that ran behind Madame Rose's brothel, to a small one-room shack with a single window set behind the main building. Dock Fletcher found Jumbo, the huge Negro, sitting in a cane-bottomed chair in front of the shanty.

"Hello, Doc," said Jumbo. He looked up at the sun. "Real punctual. My kinda man."

"I try."

"Still lookin' for hep?"

"Sure. Got any ideas?"

"I been thinkin'," Jumbo drawled. "Why're you wantin' to disrupt the auction?"

"I might be workin' for black people."

"Whities don't do that," said Jumbo, leaning his chair back against the shack.

"Some do."

"Never heard of it."

"You know about the North?"

Jumbo nodded gravely. "Black folk're free there."

"I promise to help you get there."

Jumbo looked suspicious. "If'n I hep you tear up the selling."

"Do Schoolcraft good to lose some sleep."

"Folks gonna get hurt?"

"They might. Depends on what we pull off."

"Tell me 'bout the North."

Doc Fletcher spent the next ten minutes explaining about states where blacks were free. At several points Jumbo interrupted to clarify something. Doc finally summarized his explanation by asking, "You want to go up there?"

"Miz Rose treats me awright."

"But you'd be free in the North."

"Have to think 'bout it."

Fletcher protested. "I need help right now."

"Sorta like Madame Rose, eh? Man pays in advance. Who'd feed me up North?"

"My father-in-law will help you get a job."

"Shoot, I got better here with Miz Rose. I just hang 'round and keep order."

"She also tells you what to do."

"Folks with jobs get tole that."

Fletcher could not dispute the black man's logic. "Well, I'll find someone else to help me."

"Don't run off. I'm plannin' to hep you."

Fletcher grinned. "You got something in mind?"

"Just an itty-bitty thing."

"I just want to keep everyone thinking," Fletcher explained.

"This might be tryin' something bad."

"Lead on, friend," Fletcher said.

"You're willing?" Jumbo seemed surprised.

"Sure, pickings are slim this season."

Jumbo rose from his chair. "I'll check with Miz Rose. She won't mind my going, but I like to keep her happy by playing scared nigger."

Fletcher laughed as the big man walked into the back entrance of the brothel.

Fifteen minutes later they walked along a back alley in Pinchgut. They were headed for Catfish Row, a conglomeration of shantyboats, riverside cabins and weather-beaten shacks on the banks of the Mississippi

River. This area was the home of poor families, alcoholics, busted gamblers, freed Negroes and a group of people known as river rats. Jumbo explained that the river rats could afford to live elsewhere, but their love for the river kept them on Catfish Row. "They're strange people," he explained. "Some of those rats could live in the nicest section of town. But they're attracted by the river. They enjoy sitting and watching water flow past. Wonderful people! But I've noticed that most have a drink in their hands when they're fishing, watching the sun go down or just sitting around talking. Maybe the booze keeps away the skeeters."

Doc Fletcher seldom pried into another man's background. But Jumbo's sudden lack of a southern accent was curious. Fletcher asked, "Jumbo, why aren't you talking like a southerner?"

The big man was thoughtful. "My first master was Major Hinston down in Louisiana. He was a fine and noble gentleman. Never did figure out why the major sort of adopted me. But he did. Brought me into that fine mansion, dressed me in fine clothes, and let me get schooling alongside his sons and daughters. Major Hinston was a good man."

"Why'd you leave?"

"Major Hinston died. The plantation went to his oldest son. He was an itty-bitty runt. Always yapping like those small dogs that women favor. His daddy kept Leroy shoved down, but when Major Hinston died the little squirt went wild. Always bullying his sisters and brothers, treating the slaves like trash. The man had no respect for anyone. Thursday morning was whipping time. Leroy lined up men and beasts for punishment that day. He gloried in using that blacksnake whip."

"I've known some men like him," Fletcher said.

103

"They usually get their just reward."

"Leroy did. He whipped a couple field hands one morning, then turned that snake on a stallion to break the animal's spirit. That big horse broke his halter that was tied to a fence post. Brought the post right out of the ground. Then the stallion swung around and liked to kick Leroy's leg right out of the socket. It was a pleasure to see Leroy laying there whimpering like a baby. I ran away that night, but not like most runaways. Leroy's brothers and sisters signed papers making me a freed man. After that, I starved in New Orleans until I met Miz Rose. She was headed for Memphis to set up her house. Figured she'd need a big man to keep order. I get two dollars a week, room and board."

Fletcher asked, "You like working for her?"

"Finest job there is," Jumbo grinned. "I get to meet the best men in town. They're usually drinking and fooling around, so they don't mind talking to me. A couple loan me books. On the sly, of course, because most whites don't cotton to a black man getting an education. I know a little bit about the law, medicine, running a business, tending a bar, handling folks who're drunk and spoiling for a fight. They're the worst. I don't want to hurt those suckers, but they can get rambunctious."

"Talking with a drawl is just playing dumb?" Fletcher asked.

Jumbo nodded. "Nigger has to pertect hisself, boss," he said in a perfect imitation of an uneducated slave. "Jumbo hasta be dumb t'keep folks off'n his black ole back."

They approached the river bank. Insects swarmed around them. They had to slap away horse flies, mostquitoes, and sweat bees.

"Know what I think 'bout skeeters?" asked Jumbo.

"Nawsah," replied Fletcher, grinning.

"Most folks'd claim these skeeters ain't big. They'd talk about skeeters bigger'n turkey gobblers."

"Big gobblers?"

"Yassuh! 'Ceptin' I ain't seen any skeeter bigger'n a chicken hawk!" Jumbo shuffled his feet, rolled his eyes. "I kin bow 'n scrape real good, too, massal!"

They walked past a number of cabins. These dilapidated structures held watermarks from the spring flood. The shantyboats were waterlogged, unpainted cabins sitting on log rafts. They rode low in the water, and occasionally a raft had been pulled ashore to avoid sinking.

The two men came to a battered shantyboat on the south edge of Catfish Row. Fletcher decided the wobbly raft and hut was the most rotten craft he'd ever encountered.

"This is it," Jumbo said, stepping onto a water-soaked gangplank. "Watch your step. Everything's slippery. So's the man living here, but he might help stir up things at the auction. Play along with him, no matter what his mood."

Jumbo stood on the deck, slammed his fist against the side of the hut.

"He's hard to rouse," the big man explained.

"What's 'at?" cried a voice.

Jumbo pounded again, slapping his palm against the wood.

"Go way!" yelled the man.

Jumbo's fist made a thundering tattoo against the hut.

"Lord! Lord," shrieked Jumbo. "I knows yuh're in thea!"

"Go way, you black devil!"

"You're afraid to step out and face Satan!"

"Ah'll throw yore sharp-tail into the pits!"

Jumbo pushed against a battered door. He roared, "Yuh're skeert to come out and face Satan and his minions! Hide yore sorry face, yuh yellow-doggin' coward! Call yoreself a man of God? Hah! Yuh're nothin' but a skarty-cat hidin' from the great tempter! You're afraid to meet the darkest of the dark, the meanest of the mean, evilest of the evil! Yuh're powerless 'gainst my legion o' demons 'n red-eyed devils. Quit readin' that fool's book 'n come forth to meet yore master!"

A strangled scream came from the hut. "Aaaah! Yuh must be the infernal prince of darkness. Knew yuh'd be comin' this way beggin' forgiveness for yore transgressions. Sneakin' like a snake to harm folks, yuh wily devil! I'll drive yore legions into a herd of pigs! Rend you senseless with a flashin' bolt o' lightnin'. Throw yore slimy soul into the fiery pits of hell! I'm a'girdin' my loins with the sword of rightousness 'cause I'm fightin' mad, yuh sorry piece of trash. Satan! Hear me! Yuh is hell-bound!"

Jumbo grinned at Doc Fletcher, rolled his eyes.

"Ain't he something?" asked the big man.

Fletcher did not join in the laughter. He wondered how a preacher could create a riot at the slave auction. The voice inside the hut sounded threatening. Fletcher figured the man was a typical southern preacher, a self-appointed soul-saver for Christiandom. Fletcher had met many preachers during his travels. At their best, they were shining examples of Christians devoting their lives to the betterment of humanity. They preached in their isolated churches in the mountain hollows and remote communities. They preached to crowds at all-day meetings with dinner on the ground, camp meetings that brought the Gospel to the backwoods. These gentle men baptized babies, saved sinners, brought kind words and message of everlasting life to the sick and ailing. They performed marriage ceremonies, presided at funerals. These men were respected by Doc Fletcher.

The dark side of the ministry was hell-and-brimstone preachers who frightened everyone with a gospel of fear. They cried an eye for an eye, a tooth for a tooth. Angry men without mercy or forgiveness, these self-appointed zealots were troublemakers who moved from hamlet to town, like dark birds of prey. A large number were schizophrenics, confusing psychotic inner voices for the word of God. They leaped from sanity to insanity like a small child jumping rope.

The door of the hut was flung open. A wraith-like figure stood in the doorway. The man was tall, middle-aged and thin with a skull-like face. The boniness of his features was dreadful to behold and, instinctively, Doc Fletcher stepped back to the edge of the raft. A deathly yellow pallor colored the man's skin. It seemed that the juices of life had been drained from his body. His dirty hair was thin and stringy without a spark of vitality, and he stared angrily at his visitors from dark eyes sunk deep into his fleshless face. A fearful brightness burned in his eyes, as if his soul was being consumed by madness.

"Satan! Yuh evil tempter!" he cried, raising his clawlike hands toward the sky. "Yuh come a-hidin' in the guise of a son of Ham. Yore minions, yore devils, yore demons are powerless 'gainst the word of God! Y'all can't stand 'gainst the glory of the Lawd! Not in a minute, a day, a month or til' eternity! Cry for mercy, yuh rotten, stinkin' sharp-tailed prince of darkness. The Lawd won't heah yore cries! My truth will prevail! Lawdy! Lawdy, tremble a-fore yore betters!"

Jumbo grinned. "How you doin' this afternoon?"

The man gave Jumbo a furious look.

" 'Member me?" Jumbo inquired.

The preacher looked confused. "Satan!" he cried.

Doc Fletcher was apprehensive. He decided the man was a religious fanatic. Fletcher was also repelled by the filthiness of the crazy man's clothing. He wore black trousers and a frock coat, although the afternoon was oppressively hot. No sign of perspiration could be seen on the man's thin face.

Suddenly the glittering eyes focused on Jumbo.

"Hello, Jumbo," he said. "How're yuh this afternoon?"

"Just fine, suh!"

"Glad to see yuh. Bring me anythin' to eat?"

Jumbo pulled a sandwich from his pocket. It was wrapped in a piece of newspaper. he handed the sandwich to the man. "Yuh eatin' regular?"

"Salvation!" cried the man, stuffing the sandwich in his mouth and chewing furiously. "No time for food! Satan's prowlin' the earth temptin' innocent people." Suddenly, the man stopped chewing. His face went blank and the skull-like head was cocked at a childish angle.

Jumbo whispered lowly. "He's listening to a voice in his head."

Crazy, absolutely nutty as a fruitcake, thought Flecher.

"Who's talkin' t'yuh?" Jumbo asked.

"Gabriel," said the man.

"What's he sayin'?"

"Fool!" shrieked the demented man. "Gabe doesn't talk! He's a-blowin' his horn to bring forth the hounds of hell." Sayin this, the wraithlike figure resumed chewing.

"Catchin' any fish?" asked Jumbo.

"Catfish yesterday. But Satan was a-foolin' around. The cat git away."

"Yuh willin' to preach the word?"

"Ah'm wound up—ready to go if'n yuh want me."

"Big meetin' comin' up," said Jumbo.

"Sinners?"

"A city plumb full of the most sinful jaspers in history."

"Yuh want me at Sodom or Gomorrah?"

"Both need preachin'," Jumbo said solemnly.

"Ah need lightnin' bolts 'n angels?"

"Might be nice to bring a few."

A slight smile crept over the skullish face. "Ah love shootin' those bolts outta the sky! Fry their sinnin' souls to a crisp!"

"Praise the Lord," Jumbo said. "Praise His holy name!"

"That's better, boah!"

"Yuh willin' to chastise the sinners?"

"Damn 'em all to the pits," croaked the man. "Lead the way, yuh black bastid!"

"I gotta gather the sinners!"

The man's eyes flashed with impatience. "Yuh don't need preachin' now?"

"Takes time to gather sinners."

"Mayhaps." The man swallowed the last of his ham-and-biscuit sandwich.

"Yuh stayin' close to yore shanty?"

"Yuh know 'bout my work. Got to stay close to keep in touch with t'angels. Never know if'n Michael needs help! He's a good boah, but the forces of evil are messin' up ever'thin'. Sin! Corruption! The stinkholes of wicked women are temptin' men with their flesh! Jehovah has seen more'n enough to damn all sinners to everlastin' fire! A lake of fire burnin' their hides forever, suh!" The preacher's face underwent a sudden transformation. He seemed to come back to reality. "Yuh got 'nother sandwich?"

"Sure have," said Jumbo, pulling another ham-and-biscuit from his pocket. The man grabbed the sandwich from Jumbo's hand. He began to eat, newspaper, sandwich and all.

"Oughta take off the paper," Jumbo suggested.

"Butterflies comin' tonight," said the man, unmindful that Jumbo was pulling the newspaper wrapping off. "Big 'uns flyin' in with wings as wide as this stinkin' river. Carryin' bags of brown liver dust. Boxes of anointed 'taters t'feed the multitudes. Plus, they bringin' flapdoodle juice for an offerin'. Flapdoodle juice! Rub it on a door 'n the first born lives! Give it t' a snake and turn it to a sieve! Mock God! Flapdoodle sneezes! Draws sinners to their knee-zes!"

Jumbo asked, "Yuh run outta juice?"

A long silence was the preacher's answer. He seemed to be listening to an inner conversation.

"Yuh need some juice?" Jumbo asked.

"What say he?" shrieked the man.

"Yuh need a bottle?"

"The God of Israel is a mean 'un," cried the man, raising his talonlike hands above his head. "Flapdoodle juice is an offerin' to please me!"

"I'll bring somethin' tonight!"

"Yore sins are forgiven."

"Yuh met my friend?" Jumbo asked.

The man directed his attention to Doc Fletcher. "Yuh forty gallon, suh, or sprinkle wrinkle?"

Fletcher glanced at Jumbo for instructions.

"He be forty gallon."

The thin bloodless lips drew back into a parody of a smile. "Yuh kin enter m'kingdom, brother! My name is God. Yore God! No tremblin' now 'cause Satan says you're forty gallon. None of that damnin' sprinkle wrinkle stuff sashays through m'pearly gates."

Jumbo gently patted the man's shoulders. "We gotta get yore flapdoodle juice, God."

The man licked his lips. "Early sacrificin' cuts a lotta mustard with me, yuh know."

"I'll be back soon."

"Nice meetin' yuh," the man said to Fletcher.

They stood silently and watched the man turn and enter the hut. A thin arm came out and bony fingers pulled the door shut. Jumbo and Doc Fletcher stepped down the gangplank to the muddy river bank. Fletcher released an audible sigh of relief.

Jumbo said, "Ain't he something?"

"WHo is he, for God's sake?"

"Crazy man."

"I assumed that," said Fletcher, giggling to relieve his nervousness. "How'd he get in that shape?"

"Yuh know"—Jumbo began, then chuckled. "I'm still talking like an old wooly-headed darkie. "My tongue gets tangled sometimes after I've been playing that role for a while. He was once a pretty fair preacher. Fell off his horse, broke a leg and started sipping patent medicine to kill the pain. That stuff is pure dynamite, Doc. 'Cepting I hear your concoction is pretty good. But most have enough dope to kill a mule dead in his tracks. The fellow back there is an addict; he's hooked on whatever patent medicine he can beg, borrow or steal. Miz Rose and the girls feel sorry for him. I bring food to him every day. We sort of give him a bottle or two of his medicine each week. Just enough to keep him from going off the deep end."

Fletcher looked astonished. "Deep end? He looked to me as if he's sitting at the bottom of the ocean."

"Naw, Doc. You ain't seen him get real squirrelly."

"I'll pass." Fletcher shuddered inwardly. "What did he mean by 'sprinkle wrinkle' and 'forty gallon'?"

"Concerns baptizing," Jumbo explained. "Some folks—the sprinkle wrinkles—claim squirting a little water on the head is all that's needed to be a Christian. Forty-gallon folks claim you got to be dunked under the water in a big creek or river."

"A doctrinal dispute?"

Jumbo nodded. "If that means rules. Folks argue about it all the time."

Fletcher asked, "How can the preacher disrupt the auction?"

"He held you spell bound back there," Jumbo chuckled. "We should be able to figure out something. When's the auction, Doc?"

"Starts tomorrow."

"Start thinking real hard." Jumbo was silent until they left Catfish Row and climbed up the bluffs.

They were shaking hands before departing. Jumbo asked, "I promised the preacher a sacrifice."

"How much does it cost?" asked Fletcher.

"A couple bucks will wind him up like a wildcat!"

Fletcher dug the money out of his purse, gave the coins to Jumbo.

"I feel bad trying to take advantage of a crazy man," he said.

"Don't," advised Jumbo. "A man has to use whatever he can find."

They parted. Doc Fletcher held a worried expression all the way home.

Chapter Eleven

A cool breeze came up around suppertime. John
Conrad ate alone that evening. Afterward, he decided to forego his usual inspection of the fields of
Belle Meade. The slave auction would start the next
day in Memphis. It was a large sale, and good
workers would be offered in such a large consignment. Rusty Ward could use a carpenter, maybe two,
and a skilled blacksmith to build the wharf. Belle
Meade II, managed by Sean Porter, needed more
hands. John decided to ride over and confer with his
friends.

John ordered up a horse. The stable boy brought a
magnificent gray gelding out of the pasture. John
stood leaning against the rail fence beside the stable,
watching a frisky colt and its mother in a holding corral. Jimmy, the stable boy, saddled the gelding and
led the animal to where John stood.

"Yuh goin' to the big sale, suh?" Jimmy asked.

"I'm planning on it."

"Spectin' Noah to drive yuh?"

"I hadn't thought about it."

"Noah's sick."

John looked concerned. "What's wrong?"

"He got the runs."

"When did this happen?"

"Come down sick 'bout an hour ago," Jimmy
related.

"Someone should have called me."

"No need, massa. Martha's doctorin' Noah. She be real good 'bout that kinda thing."

"Hold the horse for a few minutes," John told the stable boy. "I'll go see Noah."

He walked to the slave quarters and, after knocking, entered Noah's cabin. The slave was lying on a pallet, sweating profusely, while Martha, the cook, mixed a potion at a small table.

"How's Noah?" John inquired.

"He gone be awright," Martha answered. "He got some runnin' 'n his stomach is upset. First he get chillin', then feverish."

"I be awright," Noah said, looking up from his pallet. "I be ready to drive tomorry."

"You'd better rest for a couple of days."

"Naw suh! I be fine."

John looked at Martha. "You need medicine or anything?"

"This potion stops them up real fast," she answered. "I just gotta mix everything into a little ball."

"I wanna drive my massa tomorry," Noah insisted. He prayed for relief from his sickness. A fearful thought intruded into his feverish mind. If another slave drove Massa John to Memphis, that darkie might find the town was not filled with wonders. Noah would be branded a liar, a man who had deceived people. Sweat rolled down his face when Noah tried to rise from his pallet. "I be well tomorry."

"We'll see," John said. "Let me know if you feel worse."

"I'll watch Noah," Martha promised.

John left the cabin. Noah groaned aloud and wished he were dead.

II

John found Sean and Rusty in the dining room of the mansion on Belle Meade II. They were sipping an after-dinner drink. Sean was in a droll mood, proclaiming the virtues of Negro women in bed. In truth, the Irishman was rigidly proper with female slaves. But now, to tease Rusty, Sean claimed to be an expert on bed wenches.

Sean enjoyed Rusty's company. He had been teasing the young man about sex since Rusty moved into the mansion. Each night Sean made an offer to bring in a slave girl for Rusty's nocturnal amusement. Rusty blushed, stammered and acted like a tongue-tied fool. His embarrassment goaded the Irishman into more teasing. Rusty erred in telling Sean of his virginity. Sean delighted in mock attempts to alleviate Rusty's celibacy.

Sean glanced up when John entered the dining room.

He smiled wickedly.

"Come in, bucko!" Sean said, cheerfully. "Sit down! Sit down! I don't have time to talk with you at the moment. I'm giving Rusty the benefit of my considerable experience on a very important matter. The poor lad, bless his soul, is a virgin. He's never tumbled with a wench, so I'm advising the lad to learn the art with a black girl. They're the best there is in bed, as you well know. Uninhibited, wildly erotic, those girls can overpower a man with their sensuality. Ah! Lord, but I have memories of laying with wog girls that are positively delightful. I'll remember those girls when I'm stuck off in a poor-folks' home in my doddering old age."

"Still spreading the blarney, I see," John remarked.

"Blarney?" Sean gave his friend a look of mock

confusion. "I don't believe I'm familiar with that term."

"Blarney," John repeated. "You're the finest of those artists."

"Oh," Sean replied. "You mean the blarney stone on the auld sod."

"That's the one."

"And a fine art it is, my lad," Sean agreed. "But let's not discuss my character. I'm concerned about Rusty, who seems doomed to a womanless existence."

"I'm saving myself for my wife," Rusty explained.

"Hah! One might consider that a noble virtue."

"I beliive it is."

"But what about your wife?" Sean wondered. "Is she saving herself for you?"

John poured himself a drink and waited for Sean to run down. After another five minutes of gentle chiding, Sean gave up. "The lad is hopeless," he said, raising his face to the ceiling. "I pray the Good Lord will lead Rusty in the right path."

John chuckled. 'He has a better chance with the Lord than you, Sean."

"Thank you," said Rusty.

Sean refilled his glass. He looked in John's direction. "What brings you over this evening, squire?"

"The slave auction starts tomorrow in Memphis."

"That it does."

"How's your work situation here?"

"We could use three or four more field hands."

"Want to go into Memphis and pick them out?"

Sean pondered. "I can judge horse flesh, female flesh and I've been known to pick a winner once or twice at a dog fight. Picking workers is another matter. I'll leave that to you."

"What about building the wharf and running the wood crew?" John directed his attention to Rusty.

"Any idea how many hands we'll need?"

Rusty shook his head. "I've given it no thought."

"You want me to figure it?"

Rusty nodded. They discussed the matter, deciding that a couple of carpenters, a blacksmith and several laborers would be needed for the project. After completion, these same men could build the wagon boxes and operate the firewood service. When they had finished, John drained his glass and prepared to leave.

"Just a minute, boyo," Sean said. "I have a surprise for you."

"You've bought me a present," John said, smiling.

"Nope. Something better than that. You remember that black lad who's been driving my carriage?"

"You mean Donald?"

"Righto! He's a fine wog, good worker and an honest boy. But Donald looked a bit shabby sitting on the front of my rig in his homespun overalls. It wasn't befitting a fine plantation like Belle Meade. So I've been into Memphis—using my own money, mind you!—and sought out a fine seamstress. She made a nice liveryman's uniform for Donald. The boy would like to model it for you."

John left the house and went down to the slave quarters. He came back with a fifteen-year-old slave. The boy was dressed in a flashy uniform made from bright red velvet cloth trimmed with gold piping. A high stiff collar, white sash and black boots completed the costume. The crowning touch was a gold-trimmed hat with a wide brim.

Both John and Rusty were thunderstruck by the gaudiness of the outfit.

"Ain't he a pip?" laughed Sean. His dark Irish eyes flashed with humor. "Turn around, Donald. Show them how you look from the rear."

117

The slave turned slowly, his face beaming with pleasure.

"Sean, that's a winner," John admitted.

"Aye, that it is."

"You ever see anything like it?" John asked Rusty. The young inventor shook his head, negatively. "once, in a circus. The ringmaster wore something almost as bright."

"Like it?" Sean asked.

"I'll pass," Rusty shrugged.

Sean dismissed the young slave. Still smiling, the boy left the room. "There goes a proud wog," the Irishman commented.

"You know," John confided, now that the boy was out of earshot, "that uniform is the epitome of bad taste."

"Isn't that marvelous," Sean chuckled. "Israel Goldman—he's our banker in London, Rusty—claims I have a knack for *schlock*."

"What's that?" Rusty wanted to know.

"Anything that is low grade and in bad taste."

"You're proud of that?" Rusty looked incredulous.

"Aye, lad."

"You could read a few books and improve yourself."

"That was Israel's whole point. I like *schlock*." Sean looked at his friends with a wide smile.

"Can Donald drive us tomorrow?" John thought of Noah's illness.

He'd like nothing better. The lad is dying to show off his finery in Memphis."

John siad, "I'm not certain that Memphis is ready for that outfit."

"Aye, no place is."

"Agreed," Rusty chimed in.

"But wait and see, lads," Sean predicted. "When

118

the planters see Donald's outfit, they'll start dressing their wogs in the same ugly way."

"You think so?" Rusty wondered.

"Bad taste always drives out the good."

"*Schlock* rules," John told the inventor.

They agreed to meet the next morning at Belle Meade at nine o'clock. Rusty would accompany them to the auction. Donald would drive the most impressive carriage on Belle Meade, an open rig with leather cushions and upholstery.

II

"Your move, dear."

"I thought I moved last time."

"No, don't you remember? I moved this black checker from back there." Albert Spearman tapped a square on the checker board.

"You're right," Margaret sighed.

Caroline Spearman sat in a heavy upholstered chair a few feet from her parents. She was embroidering a flower pattern onto a pillow case. She hated every minute of it, sitting quietly and listening to her parents' conversation. Coming home had been a mistake, she reflected. Her parents were a couple of dull fools, content to work on the plantation during the day, play a few games of checkers after dinner. Shortly after dark her parents would finish their third of fourth game of the evening. Caroline's father would sigh, rise from his chair, and stretch. He would mention being tired, that bedtime was upon them. Within minutes her parents would be in the process of retiring for the night.

So boring!

Caroline wanted to resume her incestuous relationship with her father. Albert Spearman had become

119

elusive. Caroline conspired to catch him alone. She had succeeded on several occasions. Albert was cold and aloof, pushing her away with a stiff, awkward motion.

So boring!

This evening Caroline Spearman fidgeted in her chair and did her needlework. Her face wore an expression of total boredom. The interval since she had arrived home had worked a remarkable change in the young woman. She looked indifferent, her face passive and lifeless. But Caroline's mind was churning with ideas. She had to work out a suitable plan; and her face held tiny lines of frustration.

She worked the thread through the cloth. It was the fourth pillow case she'd embroidered. The future stretched before her as embroidery: pillow cases, sheets, doilies, curtains and, as she passed into spinsterhood, Caroline saw herself embroidering everything in the house. Given time, she would probably be embroidering fences around the fields.

Her mind quickened with memories of sexual liaisons in the past. The first had been Sam, the powerful black slave from Burnside's plantation. That had been a close call. A southern belle could be ruined if people knew about her tumbling with a slave. Daddy hadn't been bad, except he was consummed with guilt over *their* relationship.

Her mind went down a list of possible bed partners. Daddy? He was out of her bed, probably for good. There was John Conrad, whose wife was off in England. Conrad was probably satisfying himself with slave girls. Sean Porter was living on Belle Meade II, the old Burnside place. The handsome Irishman had cute black hair and charming manners. Sean was said to be spending most of his time with the Courtland girls, Patricia and Elizabeth. They were certain to be trying to get Sean to the altar. Caroline doubted either of the girls was sleeping with Sean or anyone else. They were too proper, too bloodless to admit their sensuality.

Caroline had heard of Rusty Ward, the newcomer now living at Belle Meade II. She'd made a point to appraise the young man. He seemed naive, a creature from another world. Rusty had stammered during their introduction, bashfully looked down at the floor. She mentally listed Rusty in the virgin category.

Altogether it had been a boring homecoming. But Caroline had accepted it as passively as she accepted all things now. The incident at school in Boston convinced her that every affair—whether with a man or a woman—dawned, bloomed and died.

Caroline's attention was drawn back to the present time. Her mother and father were arguing about a point in the checker game. Margaret Spearman insisted her finger had not left the checker; Albert swore she was trying to cheat.

God, Caroline thought, suffer me no fools. Dear Lord, suffer me no fools!

Chapter Twelve

The slave auction in Memphis that spring was advertised as the largest in history. Four hundred black men, women and children were going on the block for the highest bid. Whole families were being sold off. Auctioneers and slave owners preferred to keep the families together. The slaves were happier that way. But if families could not be sold together, they were broken up and sold to the highest bidder. Sentiment was not allowed to stand before profit. Whenever families were broken up, sold to different owners, contact was frequently lost forever. Wives and husbands were separated, their children often sold to a planter in another state or region.

The auction was advertised in newspapers. Handbills had been put up throughout the mid-south. Planters had been talking about the auction for weeks. It was a big one, all right. Everyone agreed. With four hundred slaves on the block a man might pick up a bargain or two. The pessimists said every man jack in four states would attend. Prices were sure to be high. Even the dourest viewer nonetheless checked the stagecoach or riverboat schedules and made plans to attend.

Buyers flocked to Memphis. They filled up hotels and boarding houses, rented spare rooms in private homes. Latecomers had to make do. They rented cots set up in the back rooms of saloons, grumbling about the high prices. Madame Rose put in a few bedrolls and cots in a vacant room in her brothel, charging twenty dollars a night and getting it.

The buyers were a mixed lot. Large cotton planters were expanding operations in response to a rising cotton market. They came to buy sturdy field hands with strong backs and a docile nature. Tobacco farmers came in from eastern Tennessee and southern Kentucky, looking for slaves to tend their fields. Many buyers were looking for bed wenches.

Others were looking for educated blacks. Although the law strictly forbade teaching slaves, a black person able to read, write and cipher went high. White workers had to be paid each month. Buy an educated slave for $750—even $1,000—and your costs were fixed. Get 20 years' work out of the man and your costs were $100 a year. A harness maker from Nashville was getting rich training slaves to work in his leather shops, a Murfreesboro planter said.

A new type of buyer was coming to auctions that year. Entrepreneurs were setting up breeding farms. They bucked the social stigma against such operations to secure future profits: Take ten females and a good buck, put them in five cabins, and a man could get eight or ten babies a year. Buy big, raw-boned women with wide hips and a broad pelvis. Babies came easy for such females.

And, the money angle looked really good. Ten women cost $300 each; a good buck was maybe $500. That represented an investment of $3,500. In ten years your first crop could be sold, returning your initial investment. Meanwhile you had a harvest of slaves to sell every year.

A far-sighted man could do well in nigger breeding. Half of those babies would be female. So a man constantly increased his supply of breeders. Cost? Very little, the enthusiasts pointed out. Each slave received seed and a hoe to raise their own food. They tended the milk cows, slopped the hogs and, under the right set-up, were self-sufficient.

"Like ownin' a bunch of money makin' machines," declared Fred Lily, a breeding enthusiast from northern Alabama. He planned on establishing a large breeding operation on a two hundred acre farm. "Darkies are the best crop goin'. Cipher it for yourselves, boys! Yuh can't miss! Raise 'n train those suckers, sell them as house niggers—they bring a fancy price that way. Yes, the cotton boom is here to stay and I 'spect the price of Nigras to keep risin' ever year. Bound to! I'll be breedin' those suckers till Gabe floats down from Heaven a-tootin' his horn. Yessirree, next fifty years will be a boomin' market for Nigras. I'm gettin' in this year, lookin' for my first harvest in 'bout ten years. You know and I know some folks're looking down on breedin' farms. Damnation! Took me a spell to figger that out, 'cause they's no difference 'tween breedin' and ownin' slaves, not an itty-bitty dab. Figured out the big planters got a conspiracy goin'. Take a man ownin' a hunnerd slaves: He's gettin' a bumper crop of babies every year. Bound to! Yuh know how Nigras like fornicatin'. So mayhap that owner gets hisself a nice annual crop of about twenty tads. That yellow dog's got a good thing goin'. Five years 'n the size of his herd is doubled. *Doubled*, mind yuh. Them yellow dogs are operatin' just like a breedin' man. 'Cepting they ain't tellin' us jack-leg boys 'bout the money they're makin'. Nosiree, they're a-tryin' to save the gravy, pretending breedin' Nigras is a mortal sin, not done by polite gentlemen. But meanwhile back on the ole plantation they's fixin' it so's them black wenches has a new one in the oven ever' year.

"Get in!

"Get rich!"

Fred Lily was correct, and mathematics proved it: Owning slaves was a profitable business!

No one in Memphis would dispute those facts.

II

The auction was scheduled to begin at noon. A half hour before that time, the carriage from Belle Meade rolled through the streets of Memphis. The rig was pulled by four white mares. The horses were neatly groomed, and on ordinary morning they would have drawn stares from onlookers. But everyone's attention on this day was fixed on Donald's dazzling red-and-gold uniform. John, Sean and Rusty sat in the back of the rig, smoking cheroots, enjoying the stares.

"Amazing, boyo!" exclaimed Sean. "Truly astonishing how a little *schlock* can draw attention. There has to be a lesson here."

John laughed. He asked, "What do you think, Rusty?"

Rusty Ward was sitting beside Sean in the rear seat of the open carriage. He was happy to be riding beside his new friends. "Maybe we'd better trade seats," he told John, who was in the front seat looking back. "Donald's uniform is starting to blind me."

"Stick around, Rusty," Sean told him with mock solemnity. "Another year and every planter hereabouts will have a man dressed like Donald."

"Heaven forbid," Rusty replied.

"Don't let this Irish lunatic fool you," added John. "Everyone except Sean has more sense."

Sean puffed his cheroot, exhaled with an expansive

grin. "True, true! But remember that I have a lot of fun."

Rusty wondered, "What's your encore for next month?"

"Whatever it is," Sean replied, "you can rely on it being *schlock*."

They were discussing Sean's bad taste when Donald parked the carriage two blocks from the auction site. Donald stayed with the rig. They started walking toward the slave block. The streets were crowded with visitors and town folk. Everyone, it seemed, had turned out for the big event. John recognized several well-dressed planters, nodding cordially to each man as they passed through the crowd.

Col. Amos J. Schoolcraft, the auctioneer, had correctly assessed the drawing power of his sale. Having foreseen that the bidding area might be overrun by onlookers, he had spent several days in thought before coming up with a solution. A large area in front of the slave auction block had been roped off. People entering the section had to obtain a yellow ribbon from a clerk who guarded the entrance. This enabled Schoolcraft and his ring men to sell to buyers, keeping the sightseers back away from the bidding area.

Col. Amos J. Schoolcraft was dressed in his finest white suit; his beard was trimmed, long white hair neatly cut. He stood on a high platform looking over the crowd, which, he decided, was the largest ever assembled for an auction. It looked as if everyone south of the Ohio was in attendance. Damnation! He made a mental note to charge ten dollars to get into the bidding arena next year. Nigger-hungry buyers would willingly pay the price.

The bidders came in all sizes, shapes and ages. Excitment raced through the colonel's mind. He figured to sell every slave for a handsome profit; even the old darkies and the cripples would bring a fair price.

The ring men, assistants who moved through the crowd spotting bidders, were strategically located in the crowd. Schoolcraft drew his large gold watch from his pocket and consulted the instrument. Both hands were pointed straight up: time to begin. The auctioneer cleared his throat and addressed the crowd.

"Gentleman," cried the auctioneer.

He paused to allow the hum of conversation to die out. Schoolcraft had spent some time on his initial statement to the crowd, knowing that might set the theme of the sale. Deliberating, he had decided to use the term "workers" rather than "slaves." No need reminding the buyers they were supporting slavery.

The crowd looked up at Schoolcraft with silent anticipation.

"Gentlemen," he said in a loud voice that carried to the back of the bidding area, "we're offering the finest selection of workers ever assembled in the South. Each worker has been carefully selected because, as you know, I do not deal in cripples, crazy people or workers with a chip on their shoulder. These are docile workers. They'll put in a good day's work, be grateful for the attention you give them. The workers offered in this sale have been culled. The bad ones were sent down river to work in the cane fields.

"I must emphasize that cotton is king in this area. Prices are up on every market, from Natchez to New Orleans. There is no better time than the present for expanding your work force. And you'll see many trained servants go over the block, any of which would be a pleasing addition to your household staff. We have cooks, blacksmiths, liverymen, carpenters, barrel makers, leather workers and saddle makers, gardeners and other occupations represented here. Many of our younger women are virgins, gentleman, who will make excellent servants for your wives and daughters. Men who appreciate beauty will recognize the value of these young women."

Schoolcraft outlined the rules of the sale. Bidders must pay in cash before receiving their property. All sales were as represented. All sales were final.

As Schoolcraft continued to talk, a voice shouted from the crowd: "Quit talking, Amos, and start selling!"

That shout was followed by, "Start sellin' Nigras!"

"Bring in the bed wenches," roared another voice.

Schoolcraft signaled to an assistant. "Bring in the first batch," he ordered.

The assistant walked to a shed and came out leading six black men whose ankles were chained together. They were sturdy, muscular young men with stolid expressions.

"Here they are, gentlemen," said Schoolcraft. "The finest field hands from Colonel Albert Ashley's fine plantation over in South Carolina. Look at these superb specimens! None of these workers is a day over eighteen. Figure on getting thirty or forty years of work for your money."

Several men stepped out of the crowd. Aided by the auctioneer's assistants, they began to examine the slaves.

"No need for having them drop their pants," said Schoolcraft. "We guarantee against hernias or disease. These are prime field hands able to work all day in the hottest sun. Best in the country! You can't find finer workers anywhere."

Once the inspections were completed, the buyers withdrew back into the crowd. Colonel Schoolcraft started his spiel. The bidding was swift. A banker from middle Tennessee, who operated a plantation as a hobby, bought the lot for $400 each. Then came more field hands in lots of six. The bidding dropped off. One group sold for $275 each.

Colonel Schoolcraft began to exhort the crowd.

"Boys, you know the price of cotton will go up for the next fifty years," he roared, "and so will the price of workers. Men with foresight are going to buy now and save money. I've talked to traders down in New Orleans. They expect the price of a good field hand, especially the young ones able to work for a long while, to go up at least two hundred dollars this year. That is the truth! You're paying more next year. Why not do yourself a favor and buy now?" He motioned to an assistant. "Bring out that next batch."

While they waited for the new group, Sean Porter turned to John Conrad.

"You planning on bidding today?" asked the Irishman.

"Prices are too high."

"They may go higher."

"Nah."

"What're you looking for?"

"Someone to help Rusty build the wharf."

"That means carpentry."

John nodded. "That's why I'm waiting for the skilled ones."

Another group of slaves were placed on the block. Bidding was slow. Schoolcraft wheedled, whined and pleaded. The six slaves went for $1,550.

"Boys, let's break the monotony," cried the colonel.

The next offering was brought out of the shed. She was a light-skinned young girl.

"This high yellow gal will be a wonderful servant for your wives or daughters," cried the auctioneer.

"Hell with my wife," yelled someone in the crowd. "That gal's ripe for a cold winter night!"

"Strip her!" shouted another man.

"Now, gentlemen," said Schoolcraft.

"We got to see what we're buying," another man insisted.

The auctioneer's assistant removed the girl's dress. She was well formed. Her breasts were full and erect, hips gently curved.

John noticed that Rusty Ward's eyes were fastened on the girl.

"Like a Greek goddess," he commented.

"She's beautiful," Rusty agreed.

"Want her?" asked Sean.

"Aaah . . ."

"Think of that chile warming your bed at night," the Irishman teased.

Rusty cleared his throat, keeping his eyes on the girl.

"We'll start the bidding," Schoolcraft announced. "Who'll give two thousand dollars?"

"How's her teeth?" demanded a man in the front of the crowd.

Everyone laughed.

"Teeth are guaranteed good," Schoolcraft retorted. He tried to obtain a bid for $2,000. None was forthcoming. Schoolcraft stopped for a moment, shook his head slowly with a sour expression. "Boys, look at this beauty. She's going to make someone mighty happy. Your wives and daughters will be pleased to have her. She's well trained, docile and doesn't have that darkie smell. Imagine this young lady dressed in silk and satin, tending to your every need."

Rusty Ward's gaze was fixed on the girl. She stood nude before the crowd. He suppressed a desire to step forward, demand the girl be allowed to put on her dress. Instead, he stood meekly and admired her beauty. He had never seen a nude female body, so he feasted on the girl's features.

Schoolcraft tried to start the bidding at $1,800. No one took the bait.

"All right, gentlemen," cried the auctioneer. "Someone start the bidding!"

"Two hundred," yelled a man from a small farm in Kentucky.

"Three," cried another bidder, a planter from northern Alabama.

The price quickly rose to $1,300, then $1,350 and seemed stalled at that point.

"Well, here goes," said Sean. He nodded to the ring man.

"We have fourteen," cried the man.

"Ayuhhh," Rusty said. "Don't buy her for me."

Sean bid fourteen-fifty. "I'm not thinking of you, bucko!"

The bidding became spirited now. When the price reached $1,600, several bidders dropped out. Sean and a planter from around Natchez were left.

"Better stop," John advised Sean.

"I want that girl," the Irishman insisted.

"Well, do what you think is best."

The bidding ended at $1,650.

Schoolcraft pointed at Sean.

"Mister, you just bought yourself a beautiful nigger. You pay in cash?"

John spoke up. "Belle Meade guarantees the purchase."

"Good enough, Mr. Conrad," said the auctioneer. "Your word is good anywhere."

The girl was taken back to the shed.

"Beautiful girl," John remarked.

"Too good to be sold to some scoundrel."

"That why you bought her?"

"Reason enough."

"Aaaaugh . . ." Rusty moaned. "What're you going to do with her?"

"A man can always find a use for a virgin."

Rusty glowered at the Irishman. "Th-that isn't nice."

Sean slapped Rusty on the shoulder. "We'll discuss her future later."

Another coffle of chained field hands was placed on the block.

"Let's get something to eat," Sean suggested.

They moved through the crowd toward a lunch wagon outside the bidding arena.

Chapter thirteen

"I'm crazy to try this."

"There's nothing else to be done."

"We're using this poor soul."

"Crazy men didn't count for much," insisted Jumbo.

Doc Fletcher and the huge Negro were walking from Catfish Row to the slave auction. They were accompanied by the preacher, the man who thought he was God. He walked with an awkward, shuffling gait, mumbling to himself in an agitated voice.

Fletcher asked, "What's his real name?"

"Don't know. He calls himself God."

"He's sick."

Jumbo nodded. "Tell me something new."

"Getting him up there to start preaching doesn't seem like much," said Fletcher. "That's all I could think of."

"Don't worry."

"What do you figure will happen?" Fletcher inquired.

"You never know about God," replied the black man. "He may push that auctioneer off the stump, start preaching. Maybe those folks will pull him down, maybe not. These folks take their religion pretty serious! They don't know God is crazy. We've cleaned him up, shaved him, got him looking like a respectable man. Why, I ain't seen the old goat looking this good since I've known him."

Fletcher asked, "How'd you meet him?"

"Miz Rose found him one morning back of the house. God was prowling through the garbage looking for something to eat."

"I'm still worried."

"God works in mysterious ways," said Jumbo.

"I don't want anyone to get hurt."

"They won't, boss."

They went through back alleys until they came to a vacant lot in back of the auction. The preacher stood there, hands trembling, muttering gibberish. He was barely able to control his emotions. His grip on reality was tenuous. One moment he seemed normal; the next instant his mind flipped out. Drooling like an idiot, eyes rolled back into their sockets, he seemed on the verge of fainting. Jumbo kept cleaning up the slobber, combing the preacher's lifeless hair into a semblance of orderliness. Fletcher left them and went to check on the auction. He came back several minutes later and told the preacher to get ready. The preacher's back stiffened, his face took on a pleasing calmness.

"Am I to preach?" he asked. "Ah'll need muh Bible."

Jumbo handed a worn book to him. "Good luck."

"Ah gwine chastise the sinners," God promised.

"Do that," Jumbo said, patting the man on the shoulder. "Just remember to defend your throne against Satan. He's somewhere in that crowd looking to take over every inch of Heaven."

God's face grew angry. "That pervert! Yuh knows ah'll whip his tail."

"Just walk right up on that place where the auctioneer is spouting away."

The man looked confused. "What's that sinner sayin'?"

"He's praying to the great god Baal." Jumbo winked at Doc Fletcher.

"Ah'll blast him to the pits with a lightnin' bolt!"

"Attaboy. Go get them sinners!" He gave the preacher a gentle push toward the platform occupied by Colonel Schoolcraft.

The preacher marched rather than walked to the platform, then squared his shoulders and started up the steps.

Meanwhile, Jumbo hurried off to mingle with the crowd gathered outside the bidding area. Doc Fletcher walked behind the platform and crossed over to the shed holding the slaves. Before he could turn around, he sensed that something was amiss. He directed his gaze to the platform where the preacher was shoving Colonel Schoolcraft, who had a startled expression on his face. A ring man started to run up the steps to assist the colonel. Suddenly the preacher moved to the edge of the platform and held the Bible above his head. The expression on his face was that of a wrathful man.

"Sinners! Listen to me, yuh sons of Baal!" He roared these words like a cannonade.

"Yuh stand in the sight of yore Lawd. Sodom 'n Gomorrah was the last to feel the Lawd's wrath. But woe Ah say to yuh—before nightfall the plague of Egypt will visit ever home in this town. The wrath of a vengeful Lawd is upon yuh. Hear me, sinners. Repent!" The man's eyes blazed and he held the Bible before him like a shield.

Colonel Schoolcraft stood beside the platform. He was bewildered by the preacher's sudden appearance.

"Get that coot off there," cried a man.

"Leave him be," yelled another.

"Kick 'is tail! We come t'buy niggers," shouted another onlooker.

A scattering of cries, shouts and yells burst from the crowd.

"This ain't the Sabbath," roared a planter from Mississippi.

"Hah! Give these fools some hellfire and brimstone!"

"Get his ass offen thar!"

The preacher glowered down at the crowd. Fletcher watched the skull-like face take on an expression of pure hate. He started to preach, but a ring man came up from behind and grabbed his arm just as Colonel Schoolcraft approached from the other side.

"Sir, you seem to be misguided," said Schoolcraft. "This is a slave auction, not a church service."

The crowd roared appreciatively.

The preacher wheeled about when the ring man's hand touched his wrist. He held the Bible up. "The Lawd must speak," he cried.

The ring man's grip faltered. He looked at Schoolcraft with a quizzical expression. "What yuh want to do?"

"Don't manhandle the ole fool," Schoolcraft hissed.

The ring man shrugged and left the platform. He was a practical man and realized that nothing but brute force would dislodge the preacher from the platform.

"Sir, you must leave," Schoolcraft told the preacher.

"Repent!" cried the preacher. There was a crazed edge in his voice. "Fall on yore knees, yuh sinner, and bow to the Lawd."

"Yeah, Amos!" cried a planter from Mississippi. "Confess your sins! You can start with that lazy nigger you sold me last year—the one you said would outwork ten men."

"Tell him 'bout bein' at Madame Rose's last week,"

roared a young man from the back of the crowd.

Two of the men moving slaves to and from the block were standing near Doc Fletcher.

"What's going on?" Fletcher asked, pretending to be mystified. "Is this part of the auction?"

A burly man chuckled. "The colonel will get rid of this nut."

Fletcher pointed to a terrified slave standing on the block. "Maybe you'd better get him off there. That crowd sounds ugly."

"Good idea," the man agreed. He left Fletcher's side and headed for the auction block.

On the platform, Colonel Schoolcraft was negotiating with the preacher.

"Five minutes," the auctioneer insisted. "You got five minutes and then we're resuming the auction."

"Repent!"

"Three minutes," said Schoolcraft.

"Yuh whorin' hell-bound sinner!"

While the auctioneer and the preacher argued, and the crowd grew restless, Doc Fletcher disappeared around the corner of the shed. The building was actually a holding room for slaves to be sold. It was attached to a larger building that housed slaves until auction day. This larger building was divided into two compartments—a large open room for the men, another for the women. Neither building contained windows, although the larger structure had a skylight. Off to the side, opposite the shed, was a large unpainted shack that served as a kitchen.

Fletcher noted that the area surrounding these buildings led down to the river. Once out of sight of everyone he inspected the premises, discovering that the back doors were locked on the outside with loose bolts slipped into U-bolts. Without considering the consequences, he opened the side door to the holding shed. A hundred black faces blinked against the sunlight.

"Start running," Fletcher hissed.

The slaves looked blankly in his direction. A middle-aged man with skin the color of ebony stood up. He was one of six men chained together. "Git movin'," he told the other men.

"Be quiet!" Fletcher told them.

They picked up the chain and headed out the door.

Fletcher moved to the large building. He found a side door, removed the bolt from the hasp, threw open the doors. Three hundred men and women were imprisoned there. They leaped up from the floor, came toward him.

"Take off!" Fletcher said.

It took a moment for the slaves to get his message. Then they silently filed out of the building. A muscular black man rushed off to the women's quarters, pulled the bolt and opened the door.

Fletcher moved around the building into a thick crowd of onlookers. On stage, Colonel Schoolcraft was still arguing with the preacher. Each time a ring man moved toward the thin figure, the crowd called out for fair play. During all this maneuvering, the preacher continued to exhort the sinners to come forth and accept God. Fletcher watched this with catlike intensity, all the time wondering if the slaves were running away.

By now the crowd sensed trouble was coming. Two deputies started up the steps of the platform. At that point the first rock sailed through the air. It arced high above the crowd and struck the platform with a loud, sharp sound. More rocks were thrown from the back of the crowd. Some came down on the platform, causing everyone to hide under it.

The only man who remained on the stage was the preacher, who shook his Bible at the onslaught of stones. His gestures were the choppy movements of an enraged man. Some stones fell short of their destination and landed among planters in the bidding area. A sharp-edged rock knocked the hat off a planter from Alabama, then a stone struck his forehead. Blood gushing from the wound, the man howled with pain; from back of the roped-off area there came another anguished scream. Fletcher looked beyond the crowd, saw a rough-looking gang of young men throwing the rocks as they cackled with laughter.

When a stone struck its side a horse neighed shrilly and reared up in wild-eyed fury. The animal was part of a four-horse team, all of which reared in their traces. Terrorized, the animals bolted and took off. The owner of the coach tried to reach the reins, but the horses knocked him to the ground and the team and empty coach shot forward into the crowd.

After that it was difficult to know what was taking place. People ran in all directions, causing other horses and wagons to run away. Animals ran in a pell-mell manner, striking each other and knocking down people. Women and children from the crowd of onlookers were crying out; a hysterical man kept roaring "runaway!"

The first team to bolt had smashed through the crowd leaving a trail of people lying on the ground. The straining team ran directly toward the shed housing the cooking facilities. At the last minute the frightened team veered away from the structure, slamming the coach against the building. The force of the impact smashed the wooden structure. The horses were pulled back by the coach. Then the traces broke and the animals went free. The coach careened into the building, upsetting stoves and destroying everything. A shower of sparks and burning wood was knocked against the side of the main building. Hot embers were flung up onto the roof of that structure and dry shingles burst into flames.

"Fire! Fire!" cried a man.

On stage, the preacher yelled with a crazed intensity.

"The wrath of God!" he yelled. "Sinners repent or yore God will destroy yuh!"

It was time to start moving out, Doc Fletcher reckoned. He looked around and saw everything in shambles. People were lying on the ground, crippled or hurt, moaning in pain. The slave buildings were ablaze. The crowd milled in turmoil. Chaos existed in every direction.

Fletcher moved through the crowd. No one paid any heed when he came up on the platform, took the preacher by the arm.

"Come on, God," Fletcher said. "Time to go home."

The man blinked. "Ooh! Is my time up?"

"We'll go get some flapdoodle juice."

The preacher smiled and allowed himself to be led away.

Chapter Fourteen

Col. Amos J. Schoolcraft was hiding under the auction platform. The front of the structure was draped in red, white and blue bunting. This prevented the auctioneer from seeing the crowd in front of the auction block; it also hid the colonel and his companions from view. Schoolcraft had been joined by a ring man and two deputy sheriffs. Their faces were white with fear.

The colonel's breath came in hard, quick gasps. He was numbed by the violent behavior of the crowd. Hands and legs trembling wildly, the colonel tried to remain calm. His reeling mind flashed with kaleidoscopic images of that damned preacher. The man's skull-like face flashed into the colonel's mind and, for one crazy instant, Schoolcraft wished he'd killed the fanatical idiot.

A sudden high-pitched howl came from the left side of the platform. Schoolcraft wheeled and saw a fat man running under the platform. The man's bloodied face was twisted with terror, his eyes wide and bulging. The man sobbed as he came under the platform. His coat and shirt were half torn from his back.

"Save me!" pleaded the newcomer.

Schoolcraft's mouth dropped open. He recognized the voice of Elmer Hathaway, a well-known planter from northwestern Tennessee. Hathaway had been buying slaves from Schoolcraft's auctions for years.

"Elmer! What hap—"

A half dozen young toughs came up to the side of the platform.

"C'mon, Fatty," one hoodlum yelled. "Come take your punishment like a good feller."

The faces of the young men held bestial expressions.

Elmer Hathaway kicked out at their clawing hands, all the while howling in a high-pitched wail.

"Go 'way," Schoolcraft commanded.

The answer was cackling laughter.

A deputy came up. "You boys get outta here," he commanded.

The gang of toughs appraised the deputy. One man started to move under the platform. The deputy pulled his revolver. He said, "I mean business. Another step and you're a dead man!"

The burly hoodlum studied the deputy for a moment, shrugged and turned away. "We can find other pickings, boys," he said, looking for another victim.

Elmer Hathaway whimpered like a small child. Schoolcraft looked at the planter, then quickly moved away. He didn't want to be a part of Hathaway's humiliation.

The ring man grabbed Schoolcraft's arm.

"Boss! Boss! The slave building is on fire!" he cried.

Schoolcraft rushed to the other side of the platform. The holding shed and the main building were in flames. The roof of the larger building was blazing.

"The nigras!" cried Schoolcraft. "Save the Nigras!"

"Open the doors!" yelled the ring man. He ran toward the holding shed.

Schoolcraft raced along behind the ring man, veering over to the large building. Flames were shooting up one side of the structure. Heat seared the auctioneer's face as he pulled the bolt. The metal was hot, as Schoolcraft found out when his fingers blistered. As he tried to open the door a shooting flame burned his hand.

"Let me help!" said a voice. Schoolcraft looked frantically as John Conrad came up. Conrad kicked the door. The blow knocked the door off its hinges.

Schoolcraft yelled into the building, "You Nigras get outta there!"

His mouth dropped open when he saw that the building was empty.

The ring man came running up.

"Boss," he cried, "the shed's empty!"

Schoolcraft looked around with a confused expression. He saw men fighting in a free-for-all in front of the platform, and everywhere people were going crazy: a hysterical woman wandered around screaming for her baby; a wild-eyed man climbed atop the wrecked coach and swung a piece of wood at a gang of young toughs. The whole scene was like a hideous nightmare.

"Do something," Schoolcraft yelled to a deputy.

The man gave the auctioneer a bewildered look.

"Give me your gun," ordered John Conrad.

The deputy unholstered his pistol. Conrad pointed the weapon to the sky and pulled the trigger. The explosion boomed above the noise of the crowd. Everyone stopped fighting, looked to see who was shooting.

"Stop it!" John roared.

The crowd wheeled, to see John standing before the flaming buildings. They stared with wonderment at the flames.

John pulled Schoolcraft in the direction of the platform.

"Get up there. Calm them down," John told the auctioneer. "Be quick about it, Amos."

Schoolcraft hurried up the steps. He stumbled to his knees, then rose and scrambled up onto the platform. He walked to the front of the platform, holding his hands high in a conciliatory gesture.

"Folks! Folks!" Schoolcraft yelled in a croaking shout. "Things are all right! The Nigras are out of the buildings; no one's inside. Enjoy a nice fire—she's too far gone to stop. Let's be good neighbors and help the folks who've been injured. We can start by"—Schoolcraft stopped. He turned back to John. "How can we get started?"

John came up on the platform.

"This is Mr. Conrad of Belle Meade," said Schoolcraft in a relieved tone. "He'll tell you what to do."

John looked out over the crowd.

"We'll start by asking people with wagons and carriages to drive the injured to the doctor's office and hospital," John told them. "The rest of you can bandage up people who're bleeding. Folks who've just been cut lightly or bruised wait while the folks who've been seriously injured get fixed up. If anyone's found a lost child, bring him over to the lunch wagon. All kids are to be taken there." John pointed to a small frame building across the street. "Women who've been separated from their husbands are to go there. This will stop everyone from milling around looking for their kin."

Already the gangs of young toughs were in flight. They moved to the perimeter of the crowd and headed for the nearest saloon to discuss their exploits. The remainder of the crowd looked sheepish. They watched the fire, or stayed to help the injured. Wagons were pulled in and the injured crawled into them to be taken for medical treatment. John sent a man ahead to alert the doctors.

There was still noise on the fringes of the crowd: running feet, the sound of crying men and women, and the rattle of carriages pulling out. But it was a sound of exhaustion. From his vantage point on the platform, John saw a semblance of order take shape.

He gave his attention to Amos Schoolcraft.

"You all right?"

Schoolcraft looked exhausted. His hands continued to shake. "I . . . I . . . who was that crazy preacher?"

"Sit down, Amos," John advised the auctioneer. He led the stunned man to the steps of the platform. Schoolcraft slumped down to the top step, body sagging, legs jerking with a staccato trembling. A crashing sound thundered behind them and both men turned to see the roof of the large slave building fall into roaring flames. Schoolcraft blinked, then tears rolled down his face.

"You can always rebuild," John told the auctioneer.

Schoolcraft did not answer, but sat quietly and watched his building burn.

"I've got to find my friends," John told Schoolcraft. He patted the man's shoulder and went off to find Rusty and Sean. He was depressed; the riot had been a dreadful experience.

The air was filled with smoke and the smell of burning wood. Men stood at a respectful distance from the fire, talking quietly, staring at the flames.

II

The sheriff in Memphis was Walter "Bull" Frazer, a stockily built man of medium height. The nickname came from Frazer's practice of bulling into a situation to restore law and order. Hoodlums on a spree often mistook Bull's big belly, which hung over his gunbelt, for weakness, but the error was never repeated. Miscreants came away with new respect for law and order after tangling with the sheriff.

Bull Frazer was a likable man, a cynic about the human race. He figured 70 percent of the world's inhabitants were crazy: their behavior made that a solid conclusion. The next 25 percent schemed to gull the crazies, and the remaining 5 percent were honest, forthright citizens who minded their own business.

Ten years before, Bull Frazer and his brother had come downriver on a flatboat seeking their destiny. Both men fell in love with the high bluffs. It was the nicest stretch of river they'd seen since leaving their father's farm in Ohio. They decided a town had to grow there. His faith in the future of Memphis kept Bull Frazer a happy man.

One or two men had tried to take Bull's job, but Bull seldom worried about an election. He sat back, smiled, provided impartial law enforcement, and gave his opponents rope to hang themselves at the polls. Take the last election when Bull faced Urban J. Wallace as his opponent: Urban J. Wallace looked and acted like an intelligent man but Bull was cynical enough to know Wallace would ruin the sheriff's office.

Urban went around claiming Bull Frazer was doomed. Look at him, Urban told everyone, he's a total mess. He doesn't look like a sheriff, but like something thrown together by a forgetful God. His belly was big enough to qualify as the world's largest tumor; he had a problem with indigestion and was always passing gas. He wasn't very handsome, his nose having been battered in by miscreants, lawbreakers and general hell-raisers. Furthermore, everyone knew about Bull's escapade with Bob Valentine's wife. If they hadn't heard, Urban J. Wallace was willing to spread it at every chance he got.

"Old Bob Valentine runs that saddle shop down on Main Street," Urban confided. "He came home one night to find his wife playing cards with our sheriff. Nothing wrong with that pastime, I suppose, 'cepting Bull and Mrs. Valentine were sitting on Bob's best bed. A man might overlook that 'cepting Bull and Adele were playing strip poker. The sheriff was down to his boots an' socks. Adele lost everything 'cepting her drawers. Course, seeing something like that was bound to upset ole Bob. Reckon most husbands would be a little peeved seeing someone as ugly as Bull sitting jaybird naked on their bed. Which explains why Bob grabbed his rifle and took a shot at Bull. They swear old Bull went out the Valentine's bedroom window stark naked. And"—at this point Urban J. Wallace always leaned close to his listener and spoke in a confidential tone—"they say it took Adele a month to get the brown stains outta her bedspread."

Nonetheless, the voters of Shelby county went to the polls and reelected Bull Frazer by a large majority.

Now as he rode up to the auction Sheriff Bull Frazer was in a dark mood. Damn fools! Schoolcraft should have known better than to gather several hundred people in one spot. All it took was one fool to wheedle everyone into killing their neighbors. As he rode through the fringe of the crowd, Bull Frazer shook his head from side to side. He halted his horse, sat quietly and ignored the shouts of men asking for his attention. He spied Amos Schoolcraft sitting on the steps of the auction platform. Bull nudged his horse with a light kick, rode over and dismounted.

"What happened, Amos?" Bull Frazer inquired.

The auctioneer's eyes were red from crying.

"A riot."

"Christ!" Bull roared. "I got eyes. I can see there was a riot. How did it get started?"

"Preacher," sobbed Schoolcraft.

Bull looked incredulous. "A preacher started a riot?"

Schoolcraft nodded.

"What kind of preacher?"

"Funny-looking buzzard."

"Can you spot him in the crowd."

"He's gone."

"What was his name?"

"I don't know."

"What did he look like?"

"He carried a black Bible."

Bull grimaced, then snorted. "Any damned fool knows a preacher carries a Bible. I know that most Bibles have black covers. Ever seen this jasper before?"

"No," sniffed Schoolcraft.

"Who set your building on fire?"

Schoolcraft shrugged. "I don't know."

"How many slaves did you lose?"

"They got out in time," replied the auctioneer.

"You sure all of them got out?"

" 'Spect so."

"You made a head count?

"No. Haven't had time for that, sheriff."

"Where've you got them?"

Schoolcraft looked bewildered. "I don't know."

Bull Frazer's voice rose to a thundering roar. "You telling me you got four hundred slaves and don't know where they're at?"

"They're around someplace."

"I don't believe it," said Bull Frazer, shaking his head in disbelief. "You damned fool! You ever thought they might have run away?"

"Sheriff, you got to understand," implored Schoolcraft. "Everything happened too fast."

"Fast? Maybe some jasper took off with a few hundred of your slaves."

"They're probably around someplace."

Bull snorted again. "Amos, you don't have a building over there. All you've got is a smoldering mess that's burnt down. Now, I am looking around. Four hundred darkies should be easy to find if they're here. Wouldn't you say that was a fact?"

"Yes, sheriff."

"Amos, I don't see a single darkie."

Schoolcraft stirred his lips, but there was only the flash of his teeth. He remained silent.

"Where are your darkies?" demanded Bull Frazer. "I'm responsible for the safety of people in this county. I got to know if there's four hundred runaway darkies spreading over the countryside."

"Aaah," murmured Schoolcraft. "They're around someplace." He shook his head sadly.

Bull spoke loudly, "I ought to arrest you."

A scowl appeared on the auctioneer's face. "Why arrest me? I've lost everything. I'm the victim, not the criminal."

"You were running the auction."

"That's not against the law," Schoolcraft replied, heatedly.

"I'll decide that," Bull replied. "Now quit crying your heart out, stand up and tell me what happened to those four hundred darkies."

For a whole minute the auctioneer did not stir. Bull Frazer waited for the man to compose himself.

A convulsive shudder went through Schoolcraft's

body. It was the first indication that he might be breaking down. Bull saw a vague blankness appear in the auctioneer's eyes. The strain was also telling in his face. A cheek trembled. His lips quivered.

"You all right, Amos?"

Schoolcraft stammered, "I gotta bid f-fi-fi-fifive."

Bull Frazer studied the other man's face for another thirty seconds. Then he turned away and went off and found a deputy.

"Take care of Amos," he informed the man. "I think he's having a nervous breakdown."

The deputy looked dumbfounded.

"Get moving," Bull roared.

The man blurted out, "Thought you might want a report on what happened."

"You fool! I can see what happened." Bull was already moving away. "Get over there and find someone to take care of Amos. Then get your tail over here! I want you to help me find the darkies."

The deputy said, "They ain't hurt. They got out before the fire got bad."

"I know that. Where are they?"

"They're—" The deputy looked around in bewilderment.

"Hurry up!" Bull roared. He hitched up his gunbelt and walked toward the smoking remains of the slave buildings.

Chapter Fifteen

The preacher babbled as Doc Fletcher led him through the back alleys to his shantyboat in Pinchgut. The crazed man begged for flapdoodle juice, threatened to destroy the world, and condemned all of humanity to the fiery pits of hell. Nearing Catfish Row, the preacher seemed to come back to reality for a moment or two. He balked at going down the slopes to home, muttering that he needed a sacrifice of flapdoodle juice. Doc Fletcher begged him to come along, but the man's jaw set and the last vestige of sanity left his eyes.

"Come on," Doc pleaded. "I'll get you home and come back for some juice."

The preacher stared vacantly into space.

"C'mon, God," Doc told the man. "We're not far from your shantyboat. I promise to get you a bottle."

The preacher remained silent. His face held a wrathful expression.

"Just a little ways more," Doc said. "I promise."

It required five minutes to get the thin man to proceed. Going down the slope, the preacher lost his footing and almost tumbled down the bluffs. Doc grabbed the man's skinny wrist, held tight until he regained his balance.

By the time they reached the upper end of Catfish Row, the preacher was howling like a lunatic. Doc tried to quiet his cries, but nothing worked. He figured the preacher was undergoing withdrawal symptoms. The howling attracted the attention of people in the shantyboats and cabins, and a be-whiskered man with a paunch rose from his chair on a shantyboat, came ashore and slipped the preacher's arm over his shoulder.

Above the preacher's cries, the river rat said, "He needs his medicine."

Fletcher nodded. "Will you take him home?"

"Sure," replied the man. "He's nothing but skin and bones, he won't cause trouble. You going for his medicine?"

"Yeah."

"Better hurry. He tries to kill hisself when he gets in this condition."

Doc Fletcher turned and started back up the bluffs.

Twenty minutes later he came up to the preacher's shantyboat. The man was still howling, but not so loud. A pitiful whining quality came from the cabin.

The river rat poked his head out the door. "Got it?"

Doc Fletcher handed over a bottle of a powerful patent medicine. The river rat opened the bottle and poured the dark liquid into a tin cup. "Be right back," he said. "Hey, preacher, I got some juice for you."

Fletcher stood awkwardly on the log-raft portion of the shantyboat, thinking of the horror of being ad-dicted to a patent medicine, wondering what could be done to help the preacher. His mind went back to the auction, wondering if the slaves had gotten away. If they spread out over the countryside, all of Shelby County would be in a turmoil. Whatever happened, Fletcher knew it would be days, possibly weeks before the slaves were rounded up and the auction resumed.

The shantyboat rocked from the waves churned up

by a passing steamboat. The preacher howled inside the cabin, Fletcher closed his eyes and took a deep breath. Suddenly he did not see the boat, bluffs and river but a pastoral scene in Maine. A gravel road ran through the pine forest, a lake on one side and a field of shocked corn on the other. It was fall and he was vacationing with his wife. They were visiting his grandfather, Mark Fletcher, who lived in a big white frame house.

It was odd that he should remember now, he thought. How vividly he could see his bride. Grandpaw Fletcher enjoyed teaching his wife to fish in the lake. His grandpaw loved telling the neighborhood gossip in a rasping voice. He recalled the old man going on about people: Remember, son, it doesn't matter what people call themselves or what the color of their skin may be. You put people together and you'll find some good folks, some bad ones and a handful of sons-of-bitches. Those high-society folks down in Boston put on airs, but most make their money blackbirding slaves from Africa to the southern states.

And his mind went back to when he was nine or ten years old, spending the summer with his grandpaw. That was the year his grandmaw died and the old man needed company. Grandmaw Gladys had passed away that spring: just went to sleep one night and never woke up. His grandpaw rose early each morning, started breakfast with biscuits or johnny-cakes and then came in to wake his grandson. After a man-sized country breakfast, they gathered duck feathers and spent the morning making fish lures. While they worked, his grandpaw talked about the Revolutionary War and fighting the British. Doc remembered a faraway look coming into his grandpaw's eyes when he talked about George Washington

153

and the cold winter at Valley Forge, starving and freezing, and the dying soldiers—all the while wondering what was going on back home, where Grandmaw Gladys was doing her best to plant and harvest the crops.

He recalled nostalgically how his grandpaw never had much use for religion. The old man liked to tell a story about a preacher at the crossroads church. A model of propriety, the old man said with amusement, until the day Emma Nelson, a widow, found the preacher in bed with her sister, Carla. Emma had been putting out to the preacher, grandpaw chuckled, and she was mad to know the preacher was sharing his goodies. That afternoon the preacher stole two hundred dollars of the church money and ran off with Sam Deprue's teenaged daughter.

Doc grinned about the old man's fiesty nature. His grandmaw and mother used to get mad for the old man's habits of swearing, of refusing to go to church, of sitting around and telling stories about the war. The women claimed those weren't fitting things for a small boy's ears. But the old man would pull his grandson up on his knee and claim he knew what Heaven was all about: It was not a place with golden streets and pearly gates; that was a fool's Heaven. A man's Heaven was where you went hunting or fishing every day, getting a clean shot at a big buck, or feeling the pull of a huge bass on your line. "Son," he'd say, "if you want to get a man's measure, take him out hunting or fishing. The hypocrites and the sons-of-bitches get found out real quick in the outdoors."

Doc's wife had loved his grandpaw. The old man liked showing her off like a young swain. He found her beauty and youth a tonic, starting the juices flowing in his aging body. Doc and his wife held each other and cried when news came of the old man's death. His boat overturned in the lake, and he drowned trying to swim to shore. Yet Doc held the belief that his grandpaw was not really dead. A spirited man never truly died—his body might be buried in the ground, but his spirit was still out on a supernatural lake sharing a boat with a few cronies, swapping war stories, sipping a rum toddy in the evening.

Doc wondered why he should be remembering his grandpaw now. He was so engrossed in his memories that he did not hear the river rat come out of the preacher's cabin.

"Preacher's asleep now," the man said.

"Thanks for helping me," Fletcher said.

"I'm Charlie Flynt." the man said, extending his hand. "The preacher's a friend of mine. I know he's all messed up with that medicine. But he wasn't a bad person when he came here. The juice didn't have him too bad in those days."

"How long has he been living here?" Doc asked.

"Couple years."

"He got a name?"

"Just preacher." Charlie Flynt nudged his head toward his boat. "Wanna come over for a sip of whiskey?"

Fletcher declined, asking for another time. They walked together back to Flynt's cabin.

"Don't worry," Flynt said when they parted. "Jumbo or me will look out for the preacher."

"He needs it," Doc said.

Halfway up the bluff it began to rain. Doc took a deep breath of the cool air. He paused at the top, the rain stinging his face, and looked toward the oppostie shore, where a rainbow had formed. Back at his house, Fletcher found Big Jesse was mixing a large vat of tonic. Doc told his partner what had happened at the auction. Jesse listened with a sober expression and when the story ended, he was worried.

"We'd better get out of town," he said.

Doc shrugged. "There's nothing to tie me with the riot."

"It don't seem right to use a crazy man like that."

"I know."

"Then why'd you do it?"

"He was the only weapon I had."

"What about the Negro . . . what's his name?"

"Jumbo."

"Is he liable to talk?"

"He's trustworthy." Doc sighed, went to the water bucket and drank a dipper of water. Exhausted, he removed his shirt and went off to take a nap. Jesse remained and finished mixing the tonic.

II

Bull Frazer had deputized a half-hundred men and sent them hunting the missing slaves. They fanned out and went down into the thickets along the river. By evening 127 slaves had been recaptured. Most had been hiding in the weeds along the river bank, and they meekly submitted to being marched back to the auction site. One bully cuffed the ears of his captives, driving them like oxen. When Sheriff Bull Frazer saw the man strike an aging Negro he walked over and slapped the bully across the temple. The man yelled out in pain, went away muttering to himself.

The slave quarters were a smoldering ruin, with no accommodations for the recaptured slaves. Bull Frazer was wondering how to solve the problem when Sean Porter came up. The Irishman suggested an open-air compound be set up in a couple of vacant lots. Frazer appreciated the advice and set up a round-the-clock guard detail.

"Wait a minute," Sean said. "You given any thought to feeding them?"

The sheriff's face sagged. "Jesus! I forgot the kitchen was destroyed."

"Does Schoolcraft have any extra equipment?"

"I don't know."

"I'll go ask him."

"Amos had a nervous breakdown. All he does is babble in an auctioneer's chant."

"Bucko, we can't let them starve."

Bull Frazer was at the end of his patience. "Damnation! I know that. You don't have to tell me they have to be fed. I don't aim to mistreat any darkies." The sheriff's face took on a cunning expression. "Maybe I'll deputize you to take charge of feeding."

Sean shook his head. "I have my own people to attend to."

The sheriff smiled. "Next time you point out a problem I'm going to pin a star on your chest."

Sean turned and walked away quickly. He went over to the lunch wagon. Rusty was babysitting a group of children. During the turmoil, thirty or so had become separated from their parents, and eleven were still waiting to be picked up.

"Any idea where the parents are?" Sean inquired.

"Figure they're in the hospital," Rusty said. "Get me a replacement. I'm ready to go home."

Sean went off and came back with a matronly lady of indeterminate age who agreed to watch the children. He told her to stay there until the sheriff gave orders on what to do with the children. They would need beds and shelter before nightfall.

Sean and Rusty found John Conrad helping a deputy get Amos Schoolcraft into a carriage. The auctioneer trembled and babbled a meaningless chant. Life was drained from Schoolcraft's face and he seemed unaware of his surroundings.

The driver of the rig looked concerned. "You sure he won't jump out?"

John said the deputy would ride inside the rig with Schoolcraft.

"Sheriff ain't said nothing about it," said the deputy.

"He'll understand."

"Naw, you don't know Bull Frazer."

"Then find somebody to ride along," John suggested.

"How do I do that?" the deputy looked tired, mouth drooping, eyes glazed.

"I'll ride with Amos," Sean said.

"We'll follow in our carriage," said John, "pick you up and head home."

"Where're we taking him?" the driver asked.

"You know where he lives?"

The man said, "Sure, everyone knows the colonel's mansion."

"Take him home," said Sean, crawling in beside the auctioneer. The driver clucked at the horses, shook the reins and the rig went rolling away.

A few minutes later John and Rusty climbed into their carriage. Donald swung the rig around, set out after the carriage containing Sean and Amos Schoolcraft. The two vehicles proceeded along Main Street and out to a residential area. Schoolcraft was helped from the rig and led into his home, where his wife, who looked like everyone's favorite aunt, accepted the news calmly.

"I always told Amos that sellin' niggers meant trouble," she said matter-of-factly.

"I hope he comes around real soon," Rusty stammered.

"Happened before," the woman replied. "Amos has a delicate nervous system. It goes to pieces when he gets frustrated. Was there trouble today?"

John nodded. "As much as a man can take in a lifetime."

John gave the woman a brief account of the day's events while Sean and Rusty helped the auctioneer up the stairs to his bedroom. They came downstairs just as his narration ended.

"Better watch him, ma'am," said Sean.

"He'll be fine," Mrs. Schoolcraft said. "Amos goes to pieces, lays in bed till his nerves mend. We tried doctorin' when this happened the first time, but he seems to mend about as fast layin' in bed. 'Nother week and he'll be back to normal."

She then expressed her grateful thanks.

After leaving the Schoolcraft residence, they got in their carriage and headed back to Belle Meade. Each man sat quietly, staring out into the countryside, mulling over the day's events.

A mile out of town they saw a coffle of six chained slaves walking down the road.

"Be damned!" said Sean. "What're those poor devils doing out here?"

"Probably lost," said John.

He ordered Donald to stop. The six slaves looked fearfully at them as the carriage came to a halt.

"Where're you going?" John asked.

The black men looked down at their feet.

"Anyone speak English?" John wondered.

"Yassuh!" This came from a muscular young man wearing a ragged red shirt and homespun trousers.

"What are you doing out here?"

"Massa, folks is killin' theyselves back thar!" He pointed in the direction of Memphis. "We ain't runnin'. We jes' wanna stay outta trouble."

"Hungry?"

"Gettin' that way."

"I got a place down the road," John said. "I'll send a wagon back for you. Just keep walking in this direction. We'll feed you and put you up."

"Yassuh." The black man smiled. "'Preciate it, suh."

"Don't go back to Memphis," John warned. "There's no place to sleep and nothing to eat."

"Ah understand, suh."

"We'll get back for you as soon as we can."

"We's gettin' a gut rumblin' for food, suh. Me an' the others are thirsty."

"I'll send back water," John replied.

Altogether, they came upon thirty-two slaves walking along the road. There were another two coffles of men chained together, a large group of women and young girls, and several men walking alone, solitary figures moving through the dusk. John told everyone to head for Belle Meade.

When they got to the plantation, wagons and drivers were sent out to bring in the slaves. The last wagon returned with six chained slaves just at sundown. The slaves looked scared as they silently watched the activities going on around them.

Two slaves cleared out the stable to provide shelter for the newcomers. Martha had started cooking as soon as she heard the slaves were coming. She set two girls frying eggs and ham in the kitchen of the main house. A young boy was helping Martha mix up cornbread and biscuit dough. Two Belle Meade slaves set up a table in the backyard to hold the food. The newcomers lined up and, as they passed the table, were given two eggs, a large slab of ham and a tin cup of milk.

By the time the meal was over, a bonfire was blazing in the outdoor cooking area between the slave quarters and the main house. Uncle Eli, an elderly slave, brought a barrel of chestnuts from the storehouse. The newcomers were made welcome as they gathered around the fire.

John, Rusty and Sean watched the festivities from the back porch of the great house.

John raised his drink and toasted his two friends.

"To an exciting day," he said.

Their drinks were raised in a salute.

Sean asked, "Not a bad day, bucko. You've picked up an extra thirty-two hands."

"Don't be ridiculous," John said.

"You're turning them back to Schoolcraft?" The Irishman seemed incredulous.

"I'll ride into Memphis and notify the sheriff."

"Hah! A man finds a windfall and doesn't know when he's lucky."

"Honesty is the best policy," John told his friend.

"Except when you get a windfall like this," Sean replied. "Look at those poor wogs out there. Scared to death till they found Belle Meade. Their bellies are full, their minds at ease, and now you're going to spoil their lives by sending them back to the auction block."

John started to reply when the slaves raised their voices in song. The men fell silent and listened to a spiritual. Sean got up and left the porch to walk out into the back yard. He stood there for some time listening to the singing.

Suddenly Sean's face broke into a wide grin.

"Come here," he said in a low voice.

"Anything wrong?" John asked, walking out into the yard. Rusty followed.

"Back there in the lane," said Sean. "Take a look."

A large group of black men and women were

161

standing in the darkness. They looked apprehensively toward the fire where the slaves were gathered around.

"Bedamned!" said John. "More visitors."

Rusty stammered, "th-th-the front row."

"What about it?"

"The girl you bought is standing on the end."

"Let's go and invite them to stay," John said, walking off to meet the frightened black men and women.

Chapter Sixteen

The riot at the slave auction occupied conversations in Memphis that evening and the following morning. Some folks felt Schoolcraft's auctions were becoming too large, too prone to violence: It was foolish to allow such activities. A number of businessmen pointed out that auctions were good for business, although others said Madam Rose's brothel, saloons and hotels got most of the money. A number of groups gathered in the business section to solemnly discuss the riot. Respectable people would take their business someplace else if Mephis became a lawless, rowdy town, a few men ventured.

The town fathers met after breakfast to hear Sheriff Bull Frazer's report. He had spent most of the night chasing and caring for slaves. By noon everyone calmed down, except for folks who'd been injured or wounded. They muttered darkly about Amos Schoolcraft's responsibility to keep law and order at the auction. Lawyers spent the morning and afternoon signing up clients for lawsuits.

Fortunately, injuries were not serious: One man's leg had been broken by a runaway wagon. A woman broke her wrist when she fell during the melee. A number of people had been hit by rocks, and a large number were bruised when the fighting, gouging and kicking took place. Privately, the injured admitted luck had been with them. Runaway horses, careening carriages, rock throwing and a fire could have killed or seriously injured numerous bystanders, but these same people publicly deplored the riot and conferred with lawyers.

Sheriff Bull Frazer was ready to explode. The aftermath of the slave riot occupied all of his time, interfering with his routine duties — the town fathers had thrown the whole mess in his lap. Wishing the whole bunch had murdered each other, Bull did the best he could. Carpenters were rounded up and set to hammering up a kitchen for the slaves, who slept that night on the ground of the vacant lots.

Twenty or thirty slaves kept trying to escape, so Bull made a quick review of the prisoners in his jail. They were a sorry lot, mostly small-time crooks, drunks and ne'er-do-wells. Bull went back to the cells and bellowed a warning that prisoners given their freedom had better make tracks out of Memphis, then he brought the slaves who tried to escape into the jail.

Bull's tally showed 225 slaves had been caught. They needed shelter because even darkies couldn't sleep on the ground without getting sick. Hotels and boarding houses were full of planters waiting to see if the auction would be resumed. The saloons were full. Warehouses were crammed with merchandise.

To complicate the sheriff's task, a number of angry slave traders besieged his office. Most of the slaves had been consigned to Schoolcraft's auction and many of the traders had every cent tied up in darkies. Schoolcraft had touted his auction as a place to make a fortune and now the traders were unhappy. God, were they unhappy! They kept telling the sheriff that he had to do something — that he was responsible for the whole mess. They bellowed at the sheriff, threatening to bring the wrath of lawyers down on his head, demanding that he deputize a posse to round up their slaves.

Bull angrily dismissed these threats. He countered the traders' arguments by threatening to jail them for contempt.

One trader asked, "Contempt of what?"

"Whatever I say," roared Bull.

The fellow had gone off quickly, recognizing the sheriff was in no mood to be threatened.

But one man, a slick trader in fancy clothes with a pencil-thin mustache, stood his ground. He let the sheriff bellow until he ran down, then asked where his slaves were being held.

"I don't know which darkies belong to you," roared Bull. "We've been rounding up slaves all night. Isn't that right, boys?" Two sleepy deputies slumped in chairs against the wall nodded. "Hell, mister, I don't know your darkies from anyone else's. They're likely running as fast as their legs will take them in all directions! Give us time—we're doing the best we can. The riot wasn't my fault. I could charge every damned trader with creating a public nuisance, and if you fool with me I'll do just that! Stick you back there with those big darkies, let you work out your own damned destiny."

The sheriff glared darkly at the slave trader and remembered he hadn't slept the whole night, that he'd forgotten to eat breakfast.

The slave trader lit a cheroot and blew smoke in the sheriff's direction.

"My dear sir," he said suavely. "I don't intend being treated like a common thief. I've lost twenty-two slaves because your men could not keep law and order. I planned to work with you in recovering my slaves, but with your attitude I may look elsewhere for justice. I am an innocent man who has been seriously injured by a lack of law enforcement in this town."

Sheriff Frazer's face took on a cunning expression. "So you're a reasonable man looking for justice, eh?"

The trader grunted.

"Let me introduce myself," said the trader. "I am Beauregard Franklin of Natchez, sir. Of the Mississippi Franklins. My daddy is a judge on the court down there."

Bull Frazer looked grim. "I don't care if your daddy is president of the loyal order of idiots, lunatics and scalawags."

"Part of daddy's money is tied up in those slaves," said Beauregard Franklin. "Daddy will be upset if I come home without our slaves or a pretty penny of profit."

A plan was forming in Bull's mind. He smiled genially at Beau Franklin.

"Go ahead, bring on the dogs!" roared Bull. Lord, what a burden being sheriff was, he thought inwardly. "I wished to God I didn't have to do this, but you fellows are just pressing me too hard. Now, you own those slaves. Is that right?"

"Yes. I have a bill of sale."

Bull felt elated. Salvation was near at hand.

"Mr. Franklin, I suggest you start hunting for your property. They're endangering the life and limb of every citizen in Memphis and the surrounding town. You better get in touch with your daddy and ask for more money. This county is not about to foot the bill for housing and feeding darkies that belong to someone else. Every cent—every last red cent—is going to be charged to the traders for the care we're giving your darkies. Every cent, you damned fool. I'm having the county attorney attach a lien on your slaves and you don't get them back until you've paid the price of keeping, finding and feeding that horde of darkies." Bull crossed his arms in front of his massive chest and gave the trader a pugnacious look.

"Now, sheriff—" Franklin tried to mollify the lawman.

"Bed and board is going for up to $25 a night in this town," the sheriff bellowed. "Watch your step, you simpering idiot, or Shelby County will have a bill that'll rip the eyes outta your daddy's head!"

"Just a mom-"

"Get your tail outta my office!" Bull Frazer's expression indicated his limit had been passed. "Give me any more sappy talk and I'll throw you in jail."

"On what charge?" demanded the trader.

Bull Frazer grinned slyly. "Interfering with official acts. You're getting in my way, you little piss ant!"

Beauregard Franklin started to argue with the sheriff. Then he caught sight of the determined glint in the lawman's eyes.

He said, "I'll see you when I find a lawyer."

Bull chuckled. "Do that, boy. You do that!"

Franklin left the office, head jutting forward like a man walking into a wind of gale force.

Bull laughed. "Boys, I'm glad that peckerhead doesn't belong to me."

The deputies chuckled appreciatively.

II

Belle Meade was in an uproar. Forty-three extra slaves had sought shelter and food on the plantation. Another dozen or so had come wandering onto Belle Meade II, shuffling up the path with a bewildered expression, hungry and thirsty. Others had been given bed and board on the plantation owned by Albert Spearman. A number of blacks had sought refuge at James Courtland's plantation, but the planter had chased them off his property. It was Courtland's belief that helping the slaves would be harboring a runaway, even though his wife, Sarah, pointedly remarked that feeding people did not violate the law.

"Those poor people are hungry and tired," she told her husband.

James Courtland was a stubborn man, and his mind was set. He posted an armed guard at the end of the lane with instructions to keep black people moving along the road.

John Conrad realized that morning that an overseer was needed for Belle Meade. He had postponed doing so because he liked to have contact with his slaves, and the system worked fine during normal times. But this morning, during an emergency, John knew an overseer was sorely needed, a competent man to lead the slaves.

After breakfast, John called a meeting of the slaves in the community center in the slave quarters.

"Listen, everybody," he said, holding a clipboard in his hands. "This is a list of what we've got to accomplish today. How many new people do we have this morning?"

The forty-three slaves raised their hands.

"The people who work on Belle Meade will explain the rules," John said. "I think we have one of the nicer plantations in this area. We don't believe in whipping and try not to mistreat anyone."

"Massa's speakin' truth," Martha the cook chimed in.

"He be awright," Uncle Eli added.

John looked at Uncle Eli, who ran the plantation's storehouse. "What's our food supply, uncle?"

The old man answered, "We be fine."

"We won't run short?"

"Plenty stuff there. We be fine."

John nodded and turned to Martha. "Do you need extra help with the cooking?"

Martha sighed. "Reckon Ah could do it, but more hep would be nice."

"Pick out the women you'll need."

Martha smiled. "I could use a couple boys to peel 'taters."

"Pick them out."

"How's everyone doing in the stable?" John asked. "Any complaints?"

The new slaves looked down at their feet and no one spoke.

"Come on," John said in a cheerful voice. "We can't fix things unless we know the problem."

This brought a response from a muscular young black. "They's fleas in thar, massa."

"Ah gots spray for that," Uncle Eli spoke up.

"Do what you can," John said. "We'll need about three men to help uncle. You new people want to volunteer?"

Several hands rose. John pointed to three men. "You're now the official crew for getting rid of the fleas."

John jerked his thumb toward an outdoor barbecue pit. "Noah, you have Uncle Eli pick out a nice hog. Kill it and we'll have barbecue tonight for supper. Martha, you get that big black kettle out of the barn, clean it and start cooking up pinto beans for this crew. Be sure to throw in a lot of pork and fatback for seasoning. Now, is there anything else?"

Uncle Eli raised his hand. "We could use a couple more outhouses for these new folks, massa."

"Get a few men to dig holes," John replied. He pointed to the plantation's carpenter, a light tan-skinned man with an impassive expression. "Roy, you take a couple of new people for your assistants and build outhouses."

The carpenter nodded. "Yuh got any idear whar yuh want them?"

"A long ways from the house and living quarters," John replied. "Now, we have work to do around here. If you new people haven't been given anything to do, go out with the field hands and help pull weeds. Any other problems?"

There was a long silence. Hesitantly, a buxom woman of about twenty-five raised her hand. She was dressed in a thin cotton dress that fell down to her bare feet.

"Yes?"

She swallowed hard before speaking. "Massa, do we's b'long to yuh?"

"No. You're just staying here until things get straightened out."

"Who's we b'long to?"

John shrugged lightly. "I don't know. I imagine most of you were to be sold at the auction."

The woman shook her head in agreement. "We'uns wanna stay heah. Kin yuh keep us heah?"

"I don't know."

"We'uns likes livin' heah," the woman continued.

"What's your name?"

"Beulah."

"I'll do the best I can, Beulah."

"Thank yuh, massa."

After the meeting broke up, John spent several minutes discussing the future with the new slaves. They were troubled to be in a state of limbo, did not fully comprehend what was happening. John sent a messenger to Belle Meade II to get Rusty, who was needed to oversee activities. When he came back with the errand boy, John put him in charge and then saddled up a horse and rode into Memphis.

A diverse group of men were gathered in front of the sheriff's office. John had never looked upon such a collection of different types. His instincts said these were the slave traders, who had consigned slaves to Schoolcraft's auction. One group was dressed in expensive silk coats and trousers, embroidered vests, ruffled shirts and colorful cravats with diamond stickpins. They stood in the center of the crowd projecting confidence and wealth. Their authoritative voices offered opinions on every subject.

They had florid faces that were thick and jowly, flushed with whiskey. Sideburns and hair were elegantly barbered, beards and mustaches trimmed neatly. Their fat pink hands held enameled canes capped with expensive gold or silver heads. Boots were of the finest leather, polished to a gleaming richness, and gold rings, some with large diamond or ruby sets, glistened on their thick fingers. These were the wealthy traders who bought or sold slaves, using hired hands to tend their property. They never soiled themselves by actually having direct contact with their slaves.

Around this inner crowd milled a collection of smaller traders, hard-faced men who traveled with their coffles. They roamed the countryside trying to purchase slaves from plantations at low prices, hoping to profit by selling at auction in the cities. They were dressed in cheaper clothes, often homespun shirts and trousers with patches. Their clothing was stained with food, sweat and dirt. Facial features were sharp, often pockmarked and pinched into an expression of bitter money-lust. Their boots were old, heels run down, splattered with dirt and mud. They envied the wealthier traders in the inner circle, but also were contemptuous of their dandified ways.

The traders were talking with each other, joking and taking an occasional drink from a small pint bottle of whiskey.

John excused himself and started to enter the sheriff's office.

"No need going inside," said a plump middle-aged man with a pink face. "The sheriff's home sleeping."

"What about deputies?" John asked.

The trader's glittering hard eyes gave John an appraising look.

"They're on duty," he said in a thick, whiskey voice. "But you'll get nothing out of those yahoos. They don't dare do anything without Bull Frazer's permission."

"I'll go inside and make a report to them," John said.

The man's features quickened. He placed his hand on John's arm, although the touch was gentle and not offensive. "Are you a planter, sir?"

"John Conrad of Belle Meade."

"I see." The man's thick lips pursed into a thin line. "I take it that your plantation is nearby?"

"About twelve miles from here."

The man beamed. "May I have a private word with you, Mr. Conrad?"

"Sure."

John followed the trader around the corner, out of earshot of the others.

"May I speak frankly?" The trader's voice was rich.

"Of course."

"As you may have discerned, Mr. Conrad, I am one of the traders who consigned slaves to that scoundrel, Amos Schoolcraft, to auction off."

"I know Amos. He's no scoundrel."

The trader's eyes glowed with money lust. "No offense, sir! A manner of speaking after the unfortunate incident yesterday. It occurred to me that your plantation is close by. Niggers might be passing by such a place and be picked up by an intelligent man. I'm talking of money, sir! Big money!"

"How many slaves did you bring?"

"That's of no matter," replied the planter. His eyes narrowed. "A smart planter like yourself could keep a sharp eye for the runaways. I would be willing"—and here John could also see the man's mind meshing into gear—"to pay fifty dollars for every slave you find."

"Is this a reward?"

The trader chuckled indulgently. "Let's say I'm paying a finder's fee."

"You'd pay a fee for slaves belonging to the other folks over there?" John asked, pretending to be a bumpkin.

"No need to worry yourself with those yahoos, sir! They're all a bunch of unprincipled cads. Not an honest man in the pack."

"I'll keep watching for a runaway. Where can I find you?"

"I'm staying at Madam Rose's place," answered the trader. "My name is Colonel Elijah Danworth."

"I'll get in touch if any show up."

Colonel Danworth could not hide his pleasure. He rubbed his fat hands together, smiling richly. "Any time, sir! Call me day or night and I will pay in cash. *Cash*, sir. Remember that I'm an honorable man, but these other traders will not pay a reward."

John thanked the man for his interest, then went into the sheriff's office. There was a sleepy-eyed deputy dozing in the sheriff's chair, his boots resting on the surface of the desk. His name was Roger Regenmeyer, and he had been one of the two lawmen who hid under the platform with Amos Schoolcraft.

"How're things going?" John said, greeting the deputy with a friendly wave.

"Terrible," moaned Regenmeyer.

"Where's the sheriff?"

"Dead to the world by now."

"Bad night?"

"It was hell," the deputy answered. "They're sleeping now—the sheriff and the other deputies—and I'm fighting to stay awake. I can hardly wait to get home and stretch out on a bed."

"That's quite a pack of men outside."

"Traders, waiting for news. They'd do better if they were out looking for their slaves."

John mentioned the offer from Colonel Danworth.

"They'll be stealing each other's slaves by tomorrow," said the deputy.

"I've got a bunch of runaways out at my place," said John. "Any idea what Bull wants to do with them?"

"We sure don't need any more niggers," the deputy moaned. "We can't feed and house the ones we've got."

"Want me to keep them?"

The deputy hesitated. "Well, hell, I reckon you might as well. Bull ain't here. But we can't take care of the ones we got."

"Any idea when you'll be able to take them off my hands?"

Deputy Regenmeyer sighed. "Damned if I know."

"It might be wise not to mention anything about this," John advised.

"Good advice. Those traders will be claiming anything that's black and looks human."

"I'll ride in tomorrow and talk with Bull."

"We 'preciate what you're doing," said the deputy. He hesitated. "I plumb forgot in all the excitement.

Captain Strawman of the *Dixie Belle* went upriver this morning. He sent a man over with this note. It was addressed to you, but we were too short-handed to run it to your plantation."

"Much obliged." John took the note and left the office.

Deputy Regenmeyer settled back in the sheriff's chair and closed his eyes.

Chapter Seventeen

It was almost noon when John left the sheriff's office, and the traders were milling around on the sidewalk. Colonel Danworth came running up to him.

"Any news?" the trader asked.

"Nothing about your slaves," John replied.

"Damnation!" A fat man in a brown waistcoat came up. "This two-bit sheriff's gone to sleep. He should be looking for our slaves."

"The man needs rest," John answered.

"Hell, Bull's always sleepin'," said a trader with a hectoring voice. He wore dirty homespun clothes. "Never mind. Gents in business ain't worth nothin' to his highness Bull Frazer, nosiree. Taxpayers be damned! Gov'mint's gettin' too big fer its britches — folks like Bull need a little somethin' to whip 'em into shape."

John asked," You a taxpayer in Shelby County?"

"I pays taxes in Knoxville," whined the pinch-faced trader.

By now a number of men had gathered around, quiet men with deadly eyes. They talked in a subdued manner on the fringes of the group, wearing expensive fluted shirts and richly tailored suits. These were truly wealthy men, bankers and financiers who fueled the slave trade with money. Their interest rates were exorbitant, but traders paid their terms. Ten percent a week was high rental for money, but $3,000 spent on bargain slaves in Alabama could be turned into $6,000 in Memphis or Natchez. These ruthless men also loaned money to planters, taking a mortgage on their plantations for collateral.

Planters who borrowed from them often experienced an amazing amount of distress. Slaves were stolen from the mortgaged plantations, horses and mules were lost, fires broke out in their woods and fields. These lenders never loaned to small farmers, going exclusively after bigger game. Many of them owned a dozen or more plantations. There was an excellent profit in lending money — particularly if a man made certain the borrower didn't meet his obligations.

John spent a few minutes in idle conversation with the traders. Then he drifted away across the street and read the note the deputy had given him.

It was from Suzanne!

It read:

Dear John:

We are booking passage on the *Natchez Queen*. I am sending this ahead with the *Dixie Belle*'s captain. He has promised to deliver it to the sheriff's office in Memphis. I'm sure Mr. Frazer will get the news to you. We are doing some last minute shopping in New Orleans and will be arriving in Memphis on Friday. We will be there around noon.

Love,
Suzanne

He could smell the perfumed fragrance from the paper. An urge to yell out with a joyous whoop was suppressed, although his heart pounded in his throat.

Grinning, he moved with rapid steps toward the steamboat landing, unaware of the passage of time. The sun, heat and humidity did not matter as he thought of his wife and the babies he'd never seen. Gone were his worries about caring for the newcomers at Belle Meade, chores needing attention, his plans for the future; his only concern was to meet the *Natchez Queen* upon arrival.

John was panting when he got to the steamboat landing, where he saw only a couple of flatboats. A solitary Negro was moving a stack of boxes from the wharf to a warehouse. The black man said the steamboat had not arrived, that the *Natchez Queen* was often late. John sought the shade beside the warehouse, sat down on a bale of cotton and watched the coppery river.

Time passed.

After a while it began to cloud up and thunder roared in the west. Dark stormclouds came drifting lowly over the river and huge rain drops splattered the wharf. The Negro stevedore covered the boxes with a tarp, then came running toward the warehouse. He threw open the door and invited John inside.

The Negro was a huge man, muscular with broad shoulders and a body tapering down to cordlike legs. He gave John an appraising look.

"Suh, yuh from 'round heah?" the Negro asked.

"I own a plantation south of town." John extended his hand. "I'm John Conrad."

"Glad to meetcha," the Negro smiled. "Muh name's Jumbo, suh." He hesitated, then took John's hand.

"Glad to meet you," John said. "You work here on the docks?"

"Naw suh! Jes' today. Feller got sick. Miz Rose

loaned me out t'hep a friend of hers. Feller wanted them boxes under cover. Pickin' m'self up some extry money. What kinda crop're yuh raisin?"

"Cotton, mostly."

"That all?"

"Corn and barley. Some other things."

"Why ain't yuh raisin' nothin' but cotton?"

"Don't want to be tied to one crop. A bad year for cotton and most planters lose everything."

The Negro rolled his eyes, laughed gently. "That a fact, suh?"

"I also like to raise everything we eat on the place."

"Shucks, mos' planters buy their vittles in town. I heah them talkin' lak that at Miz Rose's place."

"You like working in a cathouse?"

"Sure."

"Ever have any trouble?"

Jumbo played the black fool. "Naw suh. White folk're gentlemen."

John laughed. "You ain't connin' me, are you? I get the feeling you're an intelligent person."

"Naw suh, massa. Jumbo jes' does a job."

"Miss Rose own you?"

" 'Spect so."

"Don't you know?"

"Actually, Ah'm a freed man," Jumbo confided.

"You seem like a good worker." John had been impressed that the man worked steadily without supervision.

"Ah try t'be, suh."

"Ever think of leaving the brothel?"

"Naw suh! I got's a good job. Jes' right fer a lazy nigger like me."

"I was just wondering."

"Why's yuh askin' me 'bout leavin'?"

"I'm looking for an overseer."

"On yore plantation?"

"A black overseer might get along better with my people. Seen too many white overseers get mean with the blacks."

"That's a fact, ah knows."

"You interested in a job?"

Jumbo's brows shot up. "Yuh serious?"

"Jumbo, I tell you I was never more serious in my life. I've got to find an overseer."

Jumbo looked out into the rain. His face was impassive. "Miz Rose treats me awright. Jumbo got no worries to speak of. That's a fact, suh!"

"I'd need to know a lot more about you before making a decision."

"I knows. Understandable."

John caught the lack of accent in the black man's reply. "Yuh does, huh?" he said, mimicking Jumbo's accent.

Jumbo laughed. "Ah does."

"Why not stop and see me some day? My place is called Belle Meade. Across the line in Mississippi."

The rain was coming down hard. Jumbo gazed up into the mass of dark thunderclouds.

He said, "Ah be thinkin' 'bout it."

They discussed farming. John explained his theories of agriculture, claiming that a good plantation was a self-sufficient unit. Jumbo listened. He did not know what to make of this white man. First Doc Fletcher had come into his life preaching freedom and equality, and this planter talked about how slaves on Belle Meade could earn their freedom. Jumbo smiled and rolled his eyes, still pretending to be an uneducated man.

The thunderclouds passed to the east. When the rain stopped and the sun came out, Jumbo went back to work. John stayed inside the warehouse, hot and stifling now, and regretted sharing his aspirations with the black man. The excitement of the day had kept his tongue wagging, and he had gone on like a chatterbox. Intuitively he felt that Jumbo was holding something back, that there was more to the man than his surface image.

John thought of his children, coming upriver, and vowed to raise them as passionate people with a gift of laughter. The enchantment of childhood flashed into his reveries. It had been a time of great wonderment: rainbows, the delight of a glorious sunny day, the belief that anything was possible. Those magic moments would never be known again to him, but he would do his best to give his children similar ones.

They could savor their youth, treasure moments when the spirit soared above the mundane chores of the world. They would become children of compassion, giving love instead of hate. His was the power to develop wonderment, to apply sorcery to the imagination of their minds. He could give the knowledge of the world to them, emphasizing the need for sympathy directed toward other people. Their vision would be based on the power of wisdom, the knowledge that good men lived beside evil, detestable people. The boundless evil of humans was as unlimited as their capacity to fool themselves, to dream without acting, to cherish unrealistic goals that would never come to fruition. His children would know beforehand that sadness, pity, grief and the loss of innocence were all part of the human condition. Each person's life was touched by disappointments, but these dark shadows must be overcome.

The blast of a steamboat whistle sounded downriver.

John's heart quickened. He raised his eyes and scanned the horizon until he saw a tiny black dot moving north on the Mississippi River.

Jumbo yelled, "That might be the Queen, suh!"

John walked over to where the Negro stood, but neither spoke. The minutes passed slowly, smoke rising from the stacks as the boat moved closer, blowing its whistle incessantly to alert the town. From his vantage point John watched the paddlewheel churn the muddy water. He squinted to read the name of the vessel.

Jumbo's big hand came up to shield his eyes.

"That's the Queen!"

John was thunderstruck. The big man could read.

"How'd you know that?" he inquired.

"Says so on th' fron—" Jumbo went dumb. "Boss, Ah recollect what it looks lak."

"You can't read?"

"Nah suh! Ah's just a dumb nigger."

"Jumbo, I'd like to know your secret some day."

"Nothin' 'bout me worth knowin', boss."

They stood together and watched the boat come upriver. The blasts from the whistle had brought people hurrying down to the wharf. Major Winchester was waiting to pick up whatever mail the *Natchez Queen* carried. Two drummers, bearded and neatly dressed, came down the bluffs. They were followed by black hotel porters carrying their heavy trunks of samples. A tearful woman was saying goodby to her husband and children.

"Christ, Maude, you're only goin' to Cincinnati to visit your sister!"

The crying woman ignored her husband's remarks and turned to her children. "You all be good. Mind your daddy!"

The *Natchez Queen* wheeled in midriver, paddlewheel churning the water to a froth. The big boat was painted a bright white that glistened in the sunlight. Elaborate scrollwork railings ran around the boat's four decks, and a long, wide gangplank was attached to the side and front of the craft. John saw the captain standing beside the wheelhouse, a stocky, gray-haired man dressed in a blue uniform with bright brass buttons.

People were gathering on the decks, and John scanned the crowd for some sign of his wife but could not find her. Heart thumping in anticipation, he fidgeted as the boat came closer.

A Negro standing on the front of the boat threw out a thick rope. Jumbo caught the line as a group of stevedores came running up. Another line came snaking off the boat, and the Negroes pulled the ship snugly against the wharf. The gangplank was lowered and passengers began to disembark.

John inhaled sharply when Suzanne appeared on deck, his chest swelling with joy. She looked as lovely as ever. Her long blond hair fell over her shoulders and the bright sun turned her tresses to a bright golden color. Her fine and sensitive face shone with healthy vitality. Although she was blonde, her dark eyes added an exotic touch. She was wearing a brown velvet ankle-length dress decorated with white lace and ribbons, two ruby earrings cast a pink glow on her small ears. She stood by the railing and looked at the crowd on the wharf.

John waved.

Suzanne's face brightened, and even from that distance John could see the loving gleam in her eyes. She lifted her fingers to her mouth and blew a kiss. Then her lips formed the words: "I love you!"

John saw the captain of the *Natchez Queen* approach her, diverting her attention. Then the captain stepped aside as a large woman came up carrying two tiny blanketed packages.

The twins!

Preening like a peacock, the captain walked Suzanne along the deck and down the gangplank. John's mind and heart were filled with love as he moved forward.

The captain smiled richly.

"Mr. Conrad?"

"Yes sir," John replied.

"You have a lovely wife."

Indeed, I do, John thought. Suzanne stood with a joyful smile on her face.

"Hello, Papa!" she said. Then she came into his arms. She felt soft and warm as they clung together. She raised her face and they kissed.

Their lips parted.

"Welcome home," he said.

"Miss me?"

"More than anyone in the world."

"God, I'm glad to be back!"

"Where are the kids?"

"Coming down the plank, sir," replied the captain.

The large black-haired woman came up. She carried a child in each arm, a light blanket covering their faces. Suzanne raised one blanket to let John see an infant's face and curly blond hair, eyes closed tight in sleep.

"Daddy, may I introduce your daughter Denise?"

He smiled. "Hello, Denise! How are you?"

"Tired," said Suzanne.

She covered the infant's face again, then drew the covering from the other baby.

"Daniel, say hello to your father."

John looked down into the fat, healthy pink face. The baby's eyes opened for an instant, then closed against the brightness of the sun.

"A real sleeper," Suzanne laughed. "He's the lazy one."

"A laze-about," said the large woman.

Suzanne introduced the woman. "This is Thelma. I had trouble keeping my milk. She's a wet nurse. Guards the kids like they were gold."

The captain tapped John on the shoulder. "What do you want to do with Mrs. Conrad's luggage?"

Suzanne laughed. "There's quite a lot."

"At least two wagons," said the captain.

"Two wagons?" John was astonished.

"At least that," the captain replied.

Suzanne grinned. "I did a bit of shopping in London."

John remembered he'd ridden a horse into town. He asked the captain, "When will you be sailing?"

"Not for another two hours."

"I'll take my wife and children into town, rent a couple wagons and come back," John said.

"We'll be waiting for more passengers. No hurry."

John took Suzanne's hand. They walked up the bluff toward the town, the nurse following with the children. The hotels were filled, so John led them to his attorney's office. Roy Lanning greeted Suzanne warmly, slapped John on the shoulder and volunteered to help with the luggage. Then he and John left the office, walked to the livery stable and rented two wagons and teams.

Jumbo and some other Negroes were hired to carry the luggage up the bluffs. At one point, John wondered if another wagon might be needed. But by rearranging the crates, boxes and bags they got everything aboard. Lanning offered to drive one wagon to Belle Meade, and Jumbo agreed to handle the other rig. John went back to the livery stable and hired a carriage for his wife, nurse and twins.

He was still excited when they rolled up the lane to Belle Meade.

Chapter Eighteen

"Miss me?" Suzanne asked teasingly.

"Mmmm."

"I'll bet you had a bed wench."

John sighed happily. "Two of them."

"Were they good?"

"Absolute animals." He shifted in the bed.

Suzanne lay her head on his chest. "Want me to go back to London?"

"Leave the babies here."

"Aren't they darling?"

"You're prejudiced."

"So are you."

"I'll be impartial about it! They're the cutest babies I've ever seen."

"Daniel isn't anything like his father. He sleeps all the time."

"That's all right. He'll be a go-getter when he gets older."

"How's your dad?"

"Great! He's investing in railroads—thinks they're the future of transportation."

"Dorcas?" She was Suzanne's grandmother.

"Dr. Jamison is a good husband."

"I figured he might be."

"He keeps a tight rein of Dorcas. Every time she starts venting her bile against something or someone, Matt chides her into calming down."

John wondered, "I'll never understand what Matt saw in your grandmother."

"Simple. She's good in bed."

"Old people do it?"

"Remember when they were visiting here on their honeymoon? You were marveling at the way the bed was creaking."

"I'd forgotten."

He gently kissed her forehead. "What's in all those boxes you brought back?"

"A little of everything."

"Do I have any money left?"

"Scads."

"Seriously, did you spend a lot of money?"

"About ten thousand pounds!"

"Good grief! We're broke."

"No, silly. Daddy gave it to me."

"Nice father."

"He really is. He's quit drinking."

"I never really knew him."

"He remembers you," giggled Suzanne. "We sat around laughing about how you stole the bride. Right up to the altar battling with Rodney and taking his bride."

"Hear anything about Rodney?" John questioned.

"His humiliation was too great to stay in London."

"Poor thing."

"He's supposed to have come over here."

"The U.S.?"

"That's what father said. Wherever Rodney went, someone brought up the fact that you stole his bride."

"I should have killed him."

"He might have preferred that to public ridicule."

"Did you see Israel Goldman?"

Suzanne nibbled on his shoulder. "Israel and Daddy are partners in a half-dozen ventures."

"I'll be damned!"

"Daddy's gained an appreciation for Jews. Claims Israel is the smartest man he's ever met."

"That's probably true. Is Israel involved with railroads?"

"A couple of them."

"What other investments do they have?"

"A horse farm—Arabians. A slaughterhouse that's very profitable. A coal mine in Wales, a foundry and lots of other things. Israel sent a letter to you. Want to read it now?"

"Not tonight."

"Anything else you have in mind?"

John pulled her on top of him. He loved the faint scent of her body, the smooth satin of her nightgown.

"Stick around," he said. "I'll think of something."

Her arms went around his neck. "I'll wait until you do. Just let me stay here, husband of mine."

Suzanne felt his hardness pressing against her.

"Looks as if you've already been thinking."

"It has a mind of its own."

"I'll bet the bed wenches loved your style."

"Only if I fed them pork chops beforehand."

She moved her hips, felt his manhood throbbing beneath her.

She asked, "Do you remember how it's done?"

"I put my finger in your ear, right?"

"Lord, I've stayed away too long."

A warm desire stirred within her. Suzanne felt a quickening as John's warm and hungry mouth touched her lips. His tongue caressed her lips, gently with a loving lightness.

"Wait!" Suzanne leaped from the bed, undid her gown and came under the covers nude.

John lay on his side and pulled her close. The musky scent of his body heightened her desire. Her flesh tightened over his erectness. His hand came down, cupping her hip, his hardened shaft moved to and fro between her legs. Undulating feverishly, they clung to each other. Then with a pleasurable growl deep in his throat, John rose above Suzanne and they made love.

Afterward they lay with arms entwined.

"Tell me about love," Suzanne said.

"I don't understand."

"You remember our first time?"

"I'll never forget it."

"After we finished you talked about love. That was precious."

He chided. "Sure that wasn't someone else?"

"Nope."

"Hussy! Go to sleep."

"Shameless hussy," she corrected.

"That's right," he chuckled. "Hussies are always shameless."

"That's part of being a hussy."

"I see."

She kissed his cheek. "Tell me again."

He whispered a story to her:

Eons ago, a male star streaked across the sky making a dazzling journey through the firmament of space. The earth did not exist in that day so the star was lonely. He moved through the great void with a desperate sense of unfulfillment. The star continued shooting across the heavens on an eternal quest, not knowing what would bring him happiness.

Then a dazzling light appeared on earth. A new planet was born. The dazzling beauty of the new world bejeweled the heavens. The star came closer and saw the seas, the continents with their great mountains, flat and fertile plains, great rivers flowing to the sea, the emerald beauty of mountain lakes, the foamy descent of a mountain brook. The star was awed by the Lord's creation. Like a moth approaching a flame, the star encircled the earth and, during one pass around the globe, dipped close to the surface. The lonely star smashed into a mountain.

The Lord wanted to share his creativity with someone. So the star was transformed into man. He was named Adam. And the Lord was happy to share Adam's delight in an earth with abundant beauty. Through Adam, the Lord caught the fragrant scent of wild flowers, felt the cool wind on a summer's night, studied the shimmer of hummingbird wings, the grace of a wild animal prowling through the forest.

The Lord came down to earth and walked with Adam. They strolled through the Garden of Eden exchanging views on many subjects. But the Lord was busy and Adam spent long intervals alone in paradise. He was lonely. Again the dark despair of unfulfillment descended on his brow like morning dew bending a blade of grass.

Recognizing Adam's loneliness, the Lord touched his forehead. Adam went to sleep and the Lord removed a rib from under his heart. This piece of flesh and bone, closest to his heart, was the starter for Eve. Eve became Adam's companion and loneliness went away. She was Eternal Woman, a helpmate, friend, wife, lover and sharer of his destiny.

With Eve by his side, loneliness was banished. They were soul mates, flesh of flesh, bone of bone. Since those days back in the dim mists of time, each man has hunted for his true love. Each woman must seek the man who makes her become alive.

"The peak of human existence," John related, "is two people coming together on three levels: body, mind, spirit. When this happens they are blessed beyond all humanity. Their happiness multiplies geometrically because of their union. They do not hoard love, do not ration it, but find happiness in giving and receiving the greatest of gifts.

"With a soul mate, each partner receives more than they are given. That is the first law of romance. An abundance of love conquers nature. Love transcends all laws except God's. Chop down a pine and the forest has lost one tree. Sink a ship and you've diminished the fleet by a single vessel. A man or woman dies and humanity has lost a single person. But if a soul mate dies their spouse is an unwhole person. Because without love, and being loved in return, a person loses the vital spark of life."

John told of his despair before meeting Suzanne. "I pity the man or woman who never finds their soul mate," he related. "Loneliness can be a cancer growing inside your breast. There is a throbbing ache to love, to hold, to cherish. Somewhere in the world, in another state, in another country, that flesh of flesh exists. The search can be endless, a bitter journey without end. When that bitterness festers into a psychic wound, a disease of the soul, these loveless creatures promote wars, create revolutions against the people, kill everyone they can."

He described another pitiful scenario, finding the flesh of flesh and failing to bond together. The bonding is essential to holding a steadfast love, because time and familiarity erode romance: The flame goes out and the dazzling blaze of love turns to a cold ember. Once the warmth is gone it can seldom be ignited again. Cold ashes, he explained, make poor kindling.

Body.

Mind.

Spirit.

That is all we have to give each other. Earthly treasures eventually crumble into dust. To receive fulfillment, there must be soul mates and romantic love. True love has to be fanned to a blaze, fueled by honesty, integrity, romance. Love is a vaporous substance that could never be dissected in a laboratory. Romance escapes philosophers, professors and scientists. A thousand volumes written by learned men could never capture the thrill of true love, nor explain the spiritual essence of their bonding. Only the poets know.

"Since you've been gone," John went on, "I've decided love is the essence of life. I've missed you."

"I was lonely, too," she whispered.

"There's a polarity between men and women," John said. "Energy flows between us, a positive/ negative charge that changes according to our moods. If my psyche has a negative charge, I gain strength by lying next to you. Energy flows through your skin and revitalizes me. When the polarity changes, you gain from me. Touching, feeling and caring will heal a person with a negative charge. It's an unseen and unrecognized phenomenon, but it exists as surely as that oak tree in the front yard. In another two or three hundred years we'll come to recognize the importance of skin-to-skin contact. We'll have places where people can go to recharge their psyche."

Suzanne kissed his lips. She whispered, "I believe they exist now. They're called brothels."

"A brothel serves the flesh," he protested. "What I'm thinking of is a place where people are somehow matched to meet the needs of their partners, either temporarily or permanently."

"A do-it-yourself healing house?"

"Something like that."

Suzanne moved closer. "Mmmm! Skin-to-skin contact does have its points."

"Don't get greedy," he chided.

"It *has* been several months."

He felt his desire stirring. "Perhaps I can raise some enthusiasm for the damsel."

"Thanks a lot!"

"I know! You're only interested in my body."

She encircled his shaft with her fingers. "The spirit seems willing, m'lord."

"So it does."

"What about the mind?"

"Fuzzy."

She giggled. "I believe I've hit the jackpot."

They made love again.

Chapter Nineteen

Sheriff Bull Frazer visited Belle Meade early the next morning. He apologized for disturbing John and Suzanne's breakfast, accepted with a smile when asked to join them. Martha served up bacon and eggs, fried potatoes, grits and fresh biscuits. The sheriff devoured his food like a starving man. He did not say a word during the meal but kept shoveling food into his mouth until at last, after a second helping of eggs and two additional strips of home-cured bacon, he shoved his plate away and patted his huge stomach with his hands, a smile of contentment brightening his face. His appetite was sated, he got to the point of his visit.

"My deputy said you rounded up a few slaves."

"Quite a few," John agreed.

"Here's what I want you to do." Bull rested his elbows on the table, cupped his chin with his thick hands. "The county's going broke chasing slaves. Once they're caught we've got to feed and keep them. Right now, we have tents set up all over town. Costly."

"Why not give them back to their owners?"

"That's the problem," Bull explained. "The traders are claiming everything with a black skin. I brought one coffle of field hands down to the office and asked if they belonged to anyone. Fourteen men swore the slaves were their property. See my problem? I could go back to Memphis with a black-and-tan hound dog and twenty traders would swear it was their slave. We have no way of knowing who belongs to which trader."

"What about Schoolcraft?"

"Still in his bedroom auctioning off imaginary items. His wife said Amos sold the British Empire yesterday morning, China in the afternoon. She figures he'll come out of it, but I'm uncertain. Amos doesn't look too good."

"Did he have a list?"

"His assistants figure it burned up in the fire."

"What're you planning on?"

Bull spread his big hands in a gesture of desperation. "Town fathers dumped in my lap. It's my problem now. 'Cepting they emphasize—hell, they practically stomped it into my head—that the county and city don't plan on spending a cent. The traders ain't likely to be very generous. That group would steal the clothes off a nun. Never saw such a greedy bunch. Distressing, Conrad, very distressing!"

"I'm sorry to hear that."

"How many slaves you holding out here?"

A couple more stragglers had drifted in even the previous day. "With those over on Belle Meade II we've got more than fifty."

"I'd be in your debt if you'd keep them out here. Secret-like."

John asked, "For how long?"

"God knows. Till this mess in town gets straightened out."

John was dubious about keeping the slaves a secret. "My neighbors know they're here. What do I tell a trader if he comes snooping around?"

Bull smiled. "I got a court order that says no one can take a slave off your place."

The sheriff withdrew a legal document from his hip pocket. He unfolded the paper, smoothed out the creases.

"They're costing a fortune to feed," John responded.

"Keep track of your costs. Be reasonable and I'll not quibble."

"What are you planning?"

A cunning glint sparkled in Bull's eyes. "We keep these darkies here. I'll divide the rest among the traders. I reckon Amos won't be auctioning off anything for quite a spell. The sale of the darkies you keep will cover the county's expenses and pay off the bills."

"How much have you spent to date?"

"Almost two thousand dollars."

John whistled in disbelief. "That's a lot of money."

"Carpenters to set up a kitchen; stoves, pots and pans; salary for cooks," Bull said, ticking these items off on his fingers. "Tents—bought up every tent in town. God bless merchants! They didn't charge more than double, knowing we had to have them. Food, doctor bills. Think of it, Conrad. I've had to hire a man and a wagon, team of horses, to carry water for those darkies. Lord, man, you don't know my tribulation tending to those people. Guards day and night to make sure they don't run, extra pay for my deputies. Money goes faster than spit on a hot stove, and that's the truth. So I'm asking you to help me keep a few off to the side here at Belle Meade, where we got a chance to pay these bills."

John looked at the court order. Signed by a judge and notarized, it authorized John Conrad of Belle Meade to retain any and all runaway slaves on his property until further notice.

"Looks legal," he remarked.

"Judge Ralson covered everything," Bull replied.

John was thoughtful. "Do I get a chance to bid on the slaves?"

"Sure. We might even let you make an offer for the whole bunch. If it's fair it might get them."

"You got a deal," John said, extending his hand over the table.

Bull Frazer smiled.

II

Doc Fletcher rose early that morning. He dressed in pearl gray trousers, expensive black boots, fluted shirt, silk cravat and a black waistcoat. Before leaving the house, he splashed a liberal amount of bay rum on his face, rubbed the liquid over his face and neck.

Big Jesse whistled when Fletcher strolled out of his bedroom.

"Getting married?" Jesse grinned.

"Going prowling. Traders are hanging around town waiting to take over their slaves."

Jesse raised his eyebrows. "So?"

"Thought I might mosey around and listen in."

"Don't start another riot, for God's sake!"

"You never know," said Fletcher, chuckling. "Slave traders are the wickedest, greediest men in Christendom. They'd sell their grandmother for a couple of dollars."

"I'll stay here and bottle up our tonic," Jesse told him. "We're liable to have to make a fast getaway."

"I'll be careful," Doc promised.

Jesse slumped back in his chair and scratched his head. "Doc, we're going to get caught some day. Bound to happen. What then?"

"Head north."

"What if we don't make it?"

"Don't worry. Everything's under control."

Jesse shook his shaggy head. "I wish I believed that."

Doc's first stop was in front of the jailhouse. Although it was still early, traders were gathering there. The entire group, wealthy traders and men barely skinning by, were in a sour mood.

A ruddy-faced man, expensively dressed, expressed his displeasure.

"Gentlemen, we must band together and force the sheriff to relinquish our slaves," said Beauregard Franklin. "Every cent I have is tied up in slaves. The sheriff captured my slaves, but they're sitting out there on that vacant lot. We should demand that our property be returned to us."

A portly man chuckled richly. "Of course you'll demand first pick?"

"So will everyone else."

"I'm a man of honor, sir!"

"You wouldn't think of fudging for a minute, huh?"

"I brought forty slaves to this auction," Beau lied. "I expect to have the same number when I leave Memphis."

The other man laughed. "Four hundred slaves were to be auctioned," he said. "I've been doing a little tallying. The boys are quoting some pretty wild claims. Colonel Danworth says he brought sixty darkies to the auction—except I saw the colonel pass through town with ten darkies. Somehow the colonel has mastered the art of instant birth. I'd love to have his gift. Turning ten slaves into sixty overnight is a real fine thing to know."

Beau had to grin. "Danworth wouldn't like hearing that."

The trader shrugged. "He's nothing but an

alcoholic piss ant."

"I've noticed you were knocking back a few last night."

"Hell, nothing like good booze to ease a man's mind."

"Too much will kill you."

The man growled, "You getting religion?"

"No."

"You're sounding like that hell-and-brimstone preacher."

Doc Fletcher joined the conversation. "That preacher was really a hellraiser."

Beau gave Fletcher an appraisal. "Don't believe we've met, stranger."

"Doc Fletcher." He extended his hand. They shook.

"You a trader?"

"Not really. I just dabble."

"What's your line?" asked the other trader. He introduced himself as Flannagan of New Orleans.

"Medicine show. I sell tonic."

"You from Memphis?" Beau asked.

"I headquarter here."

"Seems like a nothing town."

"Kinda sleepy," Doc admitted.

"Sleepy, hell!" Flannagan announced. "We bring four hundred slaves into town, the auction gets disrupted and we're stuck. The sheriff won't return our property."

Doc Fletcher's mind flashed with an idea. He suggested, "Maybe you're barking at the wrong man."

Beau Franklin was suddenly alert. "The sheriff's in charge of things."

"Your quarrel isn't with him."

"Then who do we bone for our slaves?"

Doc smiled. "If it was me, which it isn't because I

didn't consign any darkies, I'd be talking with Amos Schoolcraft."

Flannagan looked doubtful. "Stranger, I don't get your drift. But let's go off by ourselves and talk."

They walked out of earshot of the other traders.

"What's your idea?" Beau asked.

"Schoolcraft accepted your slaves on consignment, right?"

"He sure as hell did."

"Then your legal bet is to take the matter up with Amos Schoolcraft. He was supposed to keep your niggers secure, sell them and give you the money minus his commission. Any jack-leg lawyer will tell you that."

Pat Flannagan's eyes narrowed into suspicious slits.

"How come a medicine man knows so much about law?"

Fletcher shrugged. "Started out to be a lawyer. Read some in a lawyer's office in Pennsylvania."

"Sheee-it! That don't count for nothin'," said Beau Franklin.

"Plus, I left some medicine with a storekeeper up in Kentucky once," Fletcher went on, ignoring Franklin's comments. "He was supposed to sell the stuff, deduct a twenty-five percent commission and pay me the remainder. That's what you call consigning merchandise."

"Just like bringing niggers to Schoolcraft's auction," mused Flannagan.

"This jasper in Kentucky claimed a burglar broke into his store. Stole every bottle of my tonic. He was sorry, hoped I'd give him another batch to sell. Now, I had given the man a hundred bottles of tonic. He signed a paper stating he was going to exercise due caution in watching over my goods. So I went to a justice of the peace, swore out a civil suit for seventy-five dollars plus court costs. Nothing to it! I got a judgment in my favor, filed a lien against the man's property, and had my seventy-five dollars a couple days later."

"Bedamned!" swore Beau.

Flannagan looked doubtful. "Schoolcraft didn't sign any papers. All we had was an agreement betwixt ourselves."

"Doesn't matter," Doc went on. "The law recognizes a verbal agreement in lieu of a written contract. All you need is one witness to back up your word."

Beau Franklin and Pat Flannagan exchanged meaningful glances.

"Pat could be my witness?" asked Beau.

"Sure."

"And I could be his."

Fletcher nodded. "Incidentally, Schoolcraft owns a big house. One of the finest in town."

Flannagan chorkled. "God almighty, we been fooling around here when paydirt is just around the corner."

"I brought fifty slaves," said Beau.

"I had a hunnerd," claimed Flannagan.

Fletcher remained silent, watching greed seize both men as their minds meshed into gear, catching fleeting images of leaving Memphis with a trunkload of money.

Flannagan was the first to break the spell. He inhaled deeply and smiled at Fletcher.

"That's good advice, Mr. Fletcher." Flannagan brought forth a dazzling smile. "Both Mr. Franklin and I are obliged. Don't worry. We'll give you a ten percent finder's fee when we've settled with Schoolcraft. That scoundrel Amos has hornswaggled everyone. But"—and Flannagan lowered his voice to a conspiratorial whisper—"it wouldn't do right for every trader in town to go after the old man. No one would get anything, right? So you get quiet about this. We'll see a lawyer, get our claims filed first and be in the catbird seat. Understand?"

"I'd rather have twenty-five percent as my share." Beau started to protest. "After all—"

"Never mind," Flannagan said hastily. "We'll gladly pay."

"Maybe we ought to draw up an agreement," said Fletcher.

"Later, Fletcher," said Beau. "We'd better hightail it to a lawyer's office."

Fletcher nodded. "Maybe you'd better go see Schoolcraft first. He might be willing to pay straight out. That way you wouldn't have to split with a lawyer, and they charge high fees."

"Splendid!" Beau looked as if salvation was at hand.

"Folks say he's crazy," Flannagan said, looking unhappy.

"Maybe that's just a pretense," suggested Doc.

Flannagan's eyebrows shot up. "Damnation! He gets in all this trouble, and what's the man do? Run home and play crazy to fool honest folks like us."

"Remember," said Beau, fidgeting. "Don't tell another trader."

"Promise." Doc crossed his heart.

"Thanks again," said Flannagan. Both men turned and started off at a rapid walk.

After the two left, Doc Fletcher wandered down to Pinchgut to check on Jumbo, rousing the big man from sleep by his knock on the door of his shack. Jumbo explained that he'd left the auction early, not wanting to be around when the trouble started. He said folks had a way of going after black people first in a free-for-all. He mentioned meeting John Conrad down on the wharf, said he seemed like a fair man. Doc gave Jumbo a five-dollar gold piece to buy flapdoodle juice for the preacher, then headed back to the traders crowded in front of the sheriff's office.

They proved to be dumber than he had expected. Their intelligence was overwhelmed, Doc decided later, by an all-consuming greed. As the day progressed, he pulled first this trader, then another over to the side and suggested they file suite against Amos Schoolcraft. Occasionally it took some time for the idea to penetrate their brains. But once it was implanted there, it stuck like molasses in January. To a man, they wanted to have Schoolcraft pay for their forty, fifty, seventy or one hundred slaves. By Doc's unofficial tabulation, the traders claimed to have brought more than twelve hundred Negroes to Memphis for the auction. Like many liars, most of the traders sincerely believed they had brought that many blacks into the city. He saw the greedy expressions cross their faces, money lust consuming their souls. Once the idea had sunk into their consciousness, each trader promised a share to Fletcher and hurried off to raise hell with Schoolcraft. If they couldn't get satisfaction from the auctioneer, they planned on suing till hell froze over.

Things were looking up, Doc decided.

It was going to be a very interesting day.

Chapter Nineteen

Rusty Ward agreed to oversee the operation of Belle Meade for a few days, so John Conrad could spend the time with his wife and babies. John was filled with joy as Suzanne spread a blanket on the carpeted floor of the parlor and he lay there with the babies. Danny was a chubby infant, pink cheeked, his small blue eyes watching everyone in a marvelously curious gaze. Denise was thinner, healthy and active. She pulled herself to a sitting position, but immediately lost her balance due to a round, diapered bottom. John became alarmed when she fell over and cried.

"Nothing wrong, sir," said the nurse, Abigail Mc-Crae, picking up and cuddling the child. "A dry diaper will cure her bawling."

"What about Daniel?" John asked, looking up at the woman.

"Better control, sir! His bladder must be made of iron!"

John laid down beside the infant. "What do you think of all this, Danny?"

The baby looked at John, eyes wide and watchful.

"We'll start you out with a pony. That interest you?"

Danny's tiny hand came up. He touched John's face.

"I'm your dad."

The child's face clouded. He cried.

"As bad as all that, eh?" John rose to a sitting position, cradled the child in his arms. He crooned a soft lullaby and Danny's eyes closed. He was asleep.

Martha came in from the kitchen. "Massa, yuh got a winner!"

"He's a fat one."

"They lose weight growin' up."

"I hope so."

"Folks're waitin' to see them."

"In a couple days," John said. He had seen several slaves come to the back door of the house during breakfast. "The babies are tired from traveling."

"Crost the big sea." Martha was impressed. "Fancy that!"

Suzanne came back into the room. She had gone upstairs with an armload of new dresses, and her face brightened when she saw Martha. She said, "I'm going to need help unpacking. Can you find Elsie Mae?"

"Yuh don't need that chile," Martha said. "Worthless."

"She's able to carry things."

Martha looked doubtful. "She'll talk yore leg off. Once she sees the babies she'll be addled. But"—Martha sighed—"I'll get her. Want me to bring Hazel 'long too? She's a good worker."

"That'll be fine."

Martha left. John asked Suzanne, "Want me to help you?"

"No. This is woman's work."

"What did you buy?"

"I didn't forget your present," Suzanne teased.

"Give me a hint?"

"You'll like it."

"Is it bigger than a watermelon?"

"Depends on the melon."

"The size of a horse?"

"You'll have to wait. I shipped a lot of things by freight. Furniture, some new carpeting, a couple of beautiful paintings. A supply of sheets and coverlets for the beds."

"My god!" John said with mock horror. "You must have bought out every store in London."

"Down to the bare shelves," she laughed. "I want Belle Meade to be a fine home. We're in need of everything, so I took time to shop."

"Books?"

"A whole library."

"You serious?"

"We'll need a carpenter to build shelves."

"Maybe I'd better add another wing to the house."

"Not yet," Suzanne laughed. "I can use that empty room where we've stored our old furniture."

"Where does that go?"

"We can pitch it."

"Too good for that."

"Use it to furnish one of your rental houses in Memphis."

"Not a bad idea." John made a mental note to discuss the matter with his attorney, Roy Lanning. He needed to go over the books with Lanning, anyway; several weeks had passed since he had conferred with him.

Suzanne left the room. When she came back, she handed a letter to John. "From Israel Goldman," she said.

"What's he say?"

"I didn't read it."

"Why not?"

"It's addressed to you."

Martha came back with an air of importance. She was accompanied by Hazel, a strong and healthy black woman in her early twenties. Behind them came Elsie Mae, a teen-aged slave girl.

"Lawsy mercy!" cried Elsie Mae, catching sight of the baby. "Is this 'un the new baby? Fat, ain' it? Must eat like a pig! Bet it cuts through po'chops faster'n a saw through butter. Can I touch it? Love that fuzzy li'l hair. Lawdy, Massa John, it look just like you. Tell that right away, I did. Lawdy, baby sure be purty."

"Hush now, Elsie," admonished Martha. "Yuh're here to hep Miz Suzanne with her things."

"Spittin' image of his pappy."

"You think so?" John was pleased.

"Any fool see that, massa," said Elsie Mae, giving the baby's hair a light touch. "A pretty li'l sucker. It be older 'n Elsie Mae'll get Uncle Eli to teach this sucker to make a mojo."

"Scat!" Martha said. "This chile ain't makin' no voodoo charms."

"It is pretty," Hazel said, beaming down at the baby. "What's its name?"

John told them.

"Fine name!" exclaimed Elsie Mae. "Pretty name for a beautiful baby!"

"Lawdy, yuh do run on," Martha said. "Talk, talk, talk!"

"I does my work. Ain't no law 'gainst talking," Elsie Mae said sullenly.

The nurse came downstairs and announced Danny's feeding time. She took the infant and went upstairs to the nursery.

The black women went off to help Suzanne unpack.

John walked out to the kitchen, poured a cup of coffee, and sat down at the dining room table. A letter from Israel Goldman was a rarity, since he usually communicated through the manager of his bank in

New Orleans. Even those letters were infrequent, warning John of things that might endanger his finances.

Israel was a private investment banker in London. Sean Porter had been a highwayman, banking his loot with Israel. Goldman had doubled, quadrupled Sean's money until the Irishman was independently wealthy. Sean need not worry about money for the rest of his life. Israel was called King of the Jews as a result of his financial wizardry. The banker could call a turn of the market with uncanny precision. Some bankers swore Israel was endowed with psychic gifts, others swore his success was a result of his Jewish heritage, while still others muttered darkly that he was allied with a coven of witches, the Druids or other cultish groups.

Sean explained Israel's secret to John one day.

"Bucko, they're all wrong," said the Irishman. "Israel knows that information is worth money — particularly if you know something before anyone else. Take cotton. A nice fibrous plant that feeds the mills of England. Suppose a drought creates a shortage of cotton. Knowing that, a wise man might sell his cotton mill before anyone else knew of the shortage. He could buy up cotton, knowing the price will go up in the future. See, lad, there's all sorts of investment opportunities if you know the cotton supply is down. That's why Israel operates the best spy service in the world, bucko. Not spies on his payroll, but blokes working for other people. A butler hears his master talking about the drought on his cotton plantation in America, and he receives a dandy reward for letting Israel know. A pattern takes shape if reports come in from other sources. Israel's clerks read, assemble and record this information — call it gossip if you like, lad — and bring it to Israel's attention. A sculpin can start with a thousand dollars and double it ten times. You're a millionaire, lad, a regular dandy. A blooming swell. You just have to know something before anyone else gets an earful. Most men are lazy: They get wealthy and sit back, take it easy. Israel loves business, outfoxing other people, making deals. Mind you, not just doubling or tripling his money. That's fine, but he also loves to find new inventions, new systems and build a new business around them. He's one of the few men who can foresee future trends. Not like a fortune-teller, although I expect Israel has some second sight. His greatest skill is in taking something and applying it to benefit the people. Israel invested heavily when automatic looms came along. He wanted to make a profit, but more, he knew women would be freed from the spinning wheel. We should think like him, lad."

John read the letter from the banker:

Dear John:

I take this opportunity to send this with your lovely wife. You are indeed a fortunate man to have such an intelligent woman as your helpmate.

It occurred to me that the United States is a vast nation with growth potential beyond anyone's imagination. Suzanne's father, Henry Winston, and I have invested in railroads—the mechanical horse, as most people call them. My friends think I'm crazy to back such an enterprise. They say nothing that belches smoke and makes noise will replace the horse and carriage. They do not realize that railroads are like your babies—infants! Improvements are coming. We'll have larger locomotives, quieter methods of operating them. Steam power will change the way we travel, the method in which we move from one place to another.

The world is entering a new age. For want of a better phrase I call it the machine age. Until now, people have lived on farms. That was necessary to grow food. The machine age will see a vast migration of people to the cities. Machines will transport them to and from work in mills and shops. Machines will liberate humanity from hard labor. They will be the greatest boon in history.

My investment advice:

1. Get into railroads when their time comes in your country.

2. Study the cities that will grow. Buy land to capitalize on their increased population.

3. Watch for new trends and inventions.

4. Do not buy stock. There are mountebanks about. Set up your own company and *sell stock!* But retain control of your company and give your investors a fair return on their money.

Give my best regards to Sean. I have forwarded a statement of his account to my bank in New Orleans. Inform Sean that his account has increased by 80% in the last six months.

Sincerely,
ISRAEL GOLDMAN, ESQ.

John reread the letter several times. He ordered a horse to be saddled, informed Suzanne that he was riding over to Belle Meade II to share the news with Sean.

Nothing surprised Amy Schoolcraft. She had been married to Amos for twenty-seven years, years that had provided ample time for her to develop a shockproof shell. Not that Amos was crazy. He had his spells when he went wandering off into a mental fog, but he recovered quickly from such bouts. The first withdrawal came after the bullfrog fiasco. Amos figured every restaurant in the country was willing to serve bullfrog legs for breakfast, lunch and dinner. Amos bought a swamp, set up a fence to keep the leapers inside, hired people to scour the riverbanks for frogs. Someone forgot to close a gate. The whole crop hopped off with a joyful croak. Amos was in bed for six days after losing the frogs.

So Amy Schoolcraft was not surprised when Beau Franklin and Pat Flanagan came knocking on the front door of her home. They were polite, removed their hats and asked to see her husband. She explained that Amos was indisposed. When they insisted, she invited them inside her home.

"Nice place," said Pat Flanagan.

"Your furniture looks new," added Beau Franklin.

"Expensive, too," said Flanagan.

"Amos is not himself," Amy Schoolcraft said. "Is there anything I can do for you?"

"We've come about our slaves," Beau blurted out.

"Your mister has to pay," said Flanagan.

"I suggest you gentlemen contact the sheriff. He's in charge of rounding up runaways." Mrs. Schoolcraft's voice was icy.

Beau cleared his throat. "Lawyer says Amos was in charge of our darkies. He has to pay unless we get them back."

"We're not threatening you," said Flanagan, smiling without mirth. "But . . . well, we got a business to run."

"Good day, gentlemen," said Amy, her voice pleasant.

Beau pulled up a chair. He sat down. "We're not leaving till we get our money."

Pat Flanagan agreed. "We got rights."

Amy looked grim. "Gentlemen, I've asked you to leave my home. You're trespassing on my property."

"Your property?" Both men spoke in unison.

"My property," Amy declared. "Title to this house and land belongs to me. I'm not fool enough to let Amos keep titlement in his name. He might get sued for losing someone's darkies. The house could be sold to satisfy some trader's lien. With that in mind, gentlemen, I'm asking you to leave. You are trespassers."

Flanagan set his jaw in a determined stance. "I ain't going till I got my money."

"Me neither," Beau chimed in.

"Pardon me," Amy said. "I've got a pie in the oven."

As she disappeared into the kitchen, Beau looked at his companion.

"She telling the truth?"

"Naw!"

"Looks like a flint-nosed old biddy."

"Can't be too smart," Flanagan insisted. "She's married to Amos."

Amy Schoolcraft came back with a shotgun cradled in her arms. The weapon was pointed toward the ceiling.

"Gentlemen, I asked you to leave," she said in a quiet voice.

Flanagan's face paled. "N-nn-now, Mrs. . . ."

Beau was more courageous. "Don't you try and . . ."

Amy cocked the shotgun.

"I'm counting to three," she said matter-of-factly. "Any trespassers in my house after that get a bullet in the guts."

"Damnation!" Pat Flanagan leaped from his chair. He headed for the door.

"My money . . ." Beau stood his ground.

"One."

"I got rights!"

"Two."

"I got . . ." Beau saw Mrs. Schoolcraft lower the shotgun in his direction. He cried, "I'm going! I'm going!"

Amy watched Beau tear out the door. She walked out onto the porch. The two men were standing in the yard.

"Public property starts outside my gate," she declared.

Both men bolted for the street. Amy lowered the shotgun and sat down in a porch swing.

Beau yelled, "Your husband is a crook!"

Flanagan shook his fist. "I'll tell folks how you gyp people!"

Amy stood up. "Gentlemen, you're disturbing the peace."

"We'll sue!" said Flanagan.

"Just keep off my property," Amy smiled.

Suddenly, an unlikely figure came walking out on the porch. Amos Schoolcraft wore a nightshirt. His spindly legs were exposed beneath the short garment.

"Go back to bed, Amos," Amy told him.

"Gotta hold the auction," her husband had a blank look in his eyes. "Folks are wanting to buy niggers."

Pat Flanagan called from the sidewalk, "Amos, I

want my money."

A curious expression clouded Amos Schoolcraft's face. He started off the porch.

"Amos, come back here!" Amy called.

In his mind, Amos was standing above a crowd of slave buyers. It was time to sell. He moved to the front gate, reached out and took each man's hand. The two men were spellbound by the glazed look in the auctioneer's eyes.

Amos raised their hands. "Fi—fi—fi—" he chanted. "Who'll give me five hundred for these two niggers!"

Beau snatched his hand away. "I ain't a nigger, you old fool!"

"Humor him," whispered Flanagan. "Maybe we'll get our money."

"Fi—fi—fi—fi," chanted Amos. "Now, folks, these are prime field hands who'll do a good job. They've been fed good and they're real docile. Not a contrary bone in either one of these boys!"

Amy came up. She took Amos by the arm.

"We better stop selling," she said, gently. "These folks don't want to buy."

"Gotta sell niggers," mumbled Amos, as Amy led him across the yard and up on the porch. "Gotta sell 'em."

"Damned old fool!" muttered Beau.

Pat Flanagan laughed. "Hell, Beau, we can raise some money yet."

Beau asked, "With that crazy galoot?"

"No," Pat grinned. "We just grab the rest of the traders and have Amos sell them off to the highest bidder."

Still laughing, Flanagan turned and walked away. Beau followed.

By evening Mrs. Schoolcraft had sent a number of

traders hurrying from her yard. When one pinch-faced man stood his ground, Amy shot a blast of lead over his head. The man ran until he was three blocks from the Schoolcraft residence. Hearing this story, the traders stopped boning her for money.

Chapter Twenty

Sheriff Bull Frazer was exasperated. He sat behind his desk, chin cupped in his hands, a dark and ugly expression on his face. Bull knew the slave traders had annoyed Mrs. Schoolcraft, and he didn't like a nice lady like Amy being bothered by a gang of un-principled men. Honesty was something traders left in their cradles: They were scheming to take the Schoolcrafts, the town of Memphis or any trusting soul with two dollars in their purse or pocket. Clearly, something needed to be done—and quick.

The deputies tiptoed around the office when Bull went into a black mood. Anything could trigger a bellow of disapproval; a simple greeting caused Bull to roar like a wounded panther. Deputy sheriffs were not the highest paid men in Memphis. Working conditions weren't great. A man could get peeved ar-resting the riffraff washed off the fringes of society, but one fact was plain: Working for Bull was never dull!

Bull rested his hands on his desk. He looked at deputy Roger Regenmeyer. The deputy started to shuffle out the office door.

Bull roared, "Think of something, dangit!"

Regenmeyer looked dismayed. "Ah, 'bout what?"

"How to get those traders out of town."

"Reckon they'll be here until they get their slaves back."

"Shoot 'em," growled Bull.

Roger looked startled. "What'd you say, sir?"

"Shoot 'em! Blow their brains out!"

"Now, Bull," Roger said in a quiet voice. "You don't mean that!"

"This dang country has too many laws protecting rotten people," Bull growled. He liked to talk like this when facing a problem. "Shooting is quick. You don't worry about a rascal coming back from a firing squad. Shooting's permanent. A piece of lead, a dab of powder and society is shed of another shiftless crook."

"Now, sheriff," said Regenmeyer. "You don't mean that!"

"Blow their brains out! That's how to handle crooks."

"The judge wouldn't like it," protested Roger. He feared the sheriff might be serious.

"That's another thing that's wrong with this country," Bull bellowed. "We got judges crazier than a fruitcake. Look at ole man Girard. How many times have we arrested him for showing his ding-dong to little children?"

Roger shrugged. "Probably a dozen times."

"More like twenty."

"Well sir, maybe you're right."

"Of course I am. Old Man Girard ain't nothing but a prevert."

"Pervert."

"That's what I said," growled Bull. "An addle brained old prevert who scares the bejesus out of kids. Damnation! Shoot the old bastard, throw him in the river and let the catfish have a feast."

"The Girard family wouldn't like that at all."

"Then they'd keep the old man at home if we threatened to shoot him. Same way with those thieving traders. Blow the brains out of a couple of them and the rest will shape up or get shot out. I wish Amy Schoolcraft had blowed their heads off. I'd give her the citizen of the week award for cleaning up the town."

Roger ventured a question. "You heard what they're doing?"

"Talking with lawyers." Bull looked pained.

"They're saying you got their property."

"They're right."

"Can't we give them their slaves? Then they'd head out."

Bull cupped his chin again. His eyes took on a distant stare. Roger started to tiptoe from the room. "Stay here," Bull growled. "I'm thinking."

Roger slumped down in a chair. He fidgeted.

"Quit fiddling around," Bull ordered.

"What if I've got to scratch?"

Bull said, "Wait till I'm finished thinking."

The minutes ticked by. Roger Regenmeyer was the most uncomfortable man in Memphis. First, his nose itched; then his leg and the need to scratch became unbearable. He tried to rub his leg against the side of his chair, but couldn't reach the spot without changing his position. His back itched. Roger moved lightly, scratching in an almost imperceptible movement against the back of his chair.

"You're breaking my concentration," Bull said.

"Bull, I got to scratch."

"Dang it! Didn't you ever hear of meditating for an answer?"

"Is that like thinking?"

"Real deep thinking."

"Don't believe I've done that," Roger reported.

"Itchers probably couldn't," Bull agreed. "Whatinhell do you do in church on Sundays?"

"Sit in back and scratch."

"You ever take a bath?"

"Once a week in summer whether I need it or not."

"What time of day is it?" Bull wondered.

"Almost noon."

"How many darkies we got?"

"Counting those out on Belle Meade?"

"Not counting those, because they belong to the county."

"We got all of them except maybe a dozen. They must've run north."

Bull smiled. "Maybe they made it across the Ohio. Hope they did. Teach these shiftless traders a lesson."

Roger grinned in response to Bull's new attitude. "Reckon it would. Yes indeed, it probably would."

"Yessiree, I've got the answer," said Bull. "I'll ask each trader for the bill of sale for his slaves. Then I'll pick out that number minus the fifty out at Conrad's place. They'll get a few good ones, a few bad—"

"Sheriff, I hate to tell you this—"

"Roger, I shoot people who bring me bad news. Sounds unreal, doesn't it? But if you shoot the bearer of bad news, pretty soon all you get is nice pleasant news. Now, you go ahead and tell me what you're fixing to."

"The traders gave their bills of sale to Amos Schoolcraft. That's so Amos could sign over the darkies when the buyers picked them up. The bills burnt up."

Bull dropped his head in a hangdog fashion.

"The plagues of Job are being visited upon my weary brow," he moaned.

"Sheriff, mayhaps I could tell you how to fix things?"

"Roger, that would be a blessing."

"Sell the darkies to the traders."

"Roger, the traders already own those people."

"Th-th-that's true," Roger stammered on, mindful of Bull's glaring expression. "But when the bidding is over you distribute the money between them on a fair and even basis. A man could bid high for a good darky, knowing some of his money was coming back. It ain't the fairest thing but I reakon we got no choice."

"What about those jack-leg traders without much money?" wondered Bull.

"They'd get a share in the end like everyone else," said Roger. "And those planters who come to town to buy slaves? Let them bid, too."

"Schoolcraft's sick. You know an auctioneer?"

Roger smirked. "You could do it, Bull."

"Me?" Bull Frazer looked incredulous.

"Just stand up there and run things. The ringmen will watch out for bidders."

Bull cocked his head at an angle. He smiled in a childlike manner. "You think it would work?"

"Sure."

"I'll blow your brains out if it doesn't."

"Aw, Bull. Don't be like that."

Bull slapped his palm down on the desk. "By gosh, Roger. We're going to have us an auction tomorrow morning. Get out there and spread the word. If anyone objects, say that I'll shoot them!"

"Yes sir," said Roger, leaving the office as fast as he could.

II

The morning had been dull. There was nothing to do and Billy Wells was bored. He lay back on the steps of the front porch and let time drag by. He considered going over to see Fatty Johnson, except his friend was still mad about the marble game. Fatty lost two of his biggest agates to Billy during a shoot-out between several neighborhood boys. Fatty lost most of his marbles during the tournament; and he had been sulking like a baby.

"Billy! Billy Wells! You come here this instant!"

The sound of his mother's voice brought Billy to his feet. Mama wanted him to clean out the chicken house. That was a bad job under any conditions, but a devil of a chore when the weather was hot and humid like today.

Billy's mother called again, so the boy raced across the front yard and down the street. Mama might whack him a couple times for running off, but that punishment was easier than cleaning up the chicken house. Besides, he would worry about getting whacked on the way home.

The dusty street was hot under his bare feet. He stopped at Old Man Oake's place, picking a handful of blackberries. He walked along popping juicy berries into his mouth. Billy considered going to the jailhouse and watching the traders, but they talked dirty and Mama didn't like him to be around cussers. If she found out, he'd stay home for a week.

Mama had thrown a fit when she learned Billy watched the riot. She swore he might have been killed. Billy tried to explain he and Fatty Johnson were perched high in a big tree overlooking the crowd. It was like a grandstand seat when the riot took place. True, Fatty got excited and nearly fell from a high limb, but Fatty always did something like that.

Billy stopped in Mr. Foster's barbershop. They talked about the slaves being rounded up. Billy was warned not to go near the vacant lots. The slaves were getting restless. Mr. Foster said some people reckoned they would run again, maybe killing everyone in town, like crazy Nat Turner up in Virginia. Mr. Foster compared the slaves to old dogs. Most are pretty docile until they're mistreated. The nicest darky can turn ugly as a mud turtle when he gets the short end. Same way with dogs and other animals, he reckoned.

Leaving the barbershop, Billy went down the street and peeked in the windows of the warehouse belonging to Doc Fletcher and Big Jesse. Big Jesse was in the back bottling tonic. Billy watched as the dipper went into a barrel of tonic, came out and was emptied into a bottle. It seemed like a slow way of doing things. The front door of the warehouse was locked. Billy walked around back and went inside. Big Jesse emptied tonic into a funnel. He capped the bottle. He gave the boy a humorous smile.

"Looking for trouble again today?" asked Big Jesse.

"What do you put in that stuff?" Billy inquired.

"We sure as hell don't fill our medicine with opium and dope."

"What's in it?"

"That's a trade secret."

Billy went over and sniffed at the open barrel of tonic. "What's a trade secret?"

"For me to know," said Jesse, "and you to find out."

"Like Fatty Johnson claiming he knows how to hypnotize chickens?"

"Yep."

"He won't let us watch him do it."

"Fatty's smart—'cepting mesmerizing chickens ain't no big deal."

"Fatty thinks it is. What's that opee-yum?"

"A drug."

"What's a drug?"

"Stuff you start taking and can't stop."

"Like when the preacher comes to eat?"

Jesse looked puzzled. "What's he got to do with getting hooked?"

"Preacher can't stop eating Mama's fried chicken," said Billy. "He always gets first pick. Takes the legs every time."

"I take it you don't like preachers."

"I don't feel right when they're around."

"Me, too."

"I keep thinking they're watching everything I do."

Jesse nodded. "They probably are."

"You believe in God?"

"Sure. But not the God preachers yell about."

Billy wondered, "You mean there's more than one?"

"Might be."

"Preacher says there's only one true God. He's supposed to watch little boys and punish them for their sins."

Jesse spat. "Reckon God does watch little boys. But he's probably got a little more to do than zap you for being mischievious."

"Mama says I'm supposed to be good."

"Don't talk to me about your mama, boy."

"I'm sorry 'bout the other day." Billy pushed his big toe into the dirt floor of the warehouse.

Big Jesse filled another tonic bottle. "Here, start screwing on the caps. By the way, how is your mama?"

"She's gonna whack me when I go home," Billy said in a desolate tone.

"You probably deserve it."

"I didn't do anything bad."

"What was it?"

"Snuck off when Mama wanted me to clean the chicken house."

"That's pretty low-lifed."

"I know it. But I'd like being here with you 'stead of cleaning up after chickens."

"I'm flattered," Jesse said, "that you picked my company over shoveling chickenshit." He picked up another bottle, inserted the funnel and poured tonic out of the tin dipper.

Billy asked, "Did you see the riot?"

"Nope. I stay away from fools."

"Me and Fatty Johnson was up in a tree."

" 'Bout where I'd figure to find you."

"We saw everything. I know how it got started."

Alarm bells went off in Big Jesse's mind. "Tell me about it."

"Your buddy led that crazy preacher over there."

"I ain't got no buddies."

"Doc Fletcher's who I mean."

"What's he got to do with it?"

"Doc sicked that preacher on everybody."

"Maybe you mistook Doc for somebody else." Goosebumps crawled over Jesse's skin.

"Nope. Him and that nigger from Madame Rose's did it."

"This preacher," said Jesse. "Is he the one who gobbles up the fried chicken at your house?"

"No sir. That's Reverend Purdy. The preacher at the auction was that crazy man who lives on Catfish Row."

Big Jesse stopped working. "I suppose you been blabbing this all over town."

"Haven't tole anyone," Billy said, defiantly.

"Why not?"

"Nobody asked."

"Would you tell if they asked?"

"Reckon it would depend on who was asking."

"What about the sheriff?"

"Bull Frazer spanked me one time."

"Why'd he do a fool thing like that?" Jesse wondered.

"Me and Fatty stole a watermelon outta Widow Henson's patch."

"Smart boys, huh? I mean, letting the sheriff know you did it."

Billy scratched his head. "We didn't know the widow was watching from her back porch."

"So Bull tanned your hide."

"Yep. Said it would do us some good."

"Did it?"

"I learned to make sure nobody's looking when I steal watermelon."

Jesse grinned. "Maybe you shouldn't steal melons from a poor widow's patch. So, you ain't mentioned this preacher thing to nobody?"

"Nope."

"What about Fatty Johnson?"

"Things went fast after the preacher got there. Lordk he really stirred everybody up."

"I heard about it. So you didn't tell Fatty?"

"We ain't speaking, anyways."

"A falling out?"

"He lost his two biggest agates to me."

"That'll do it every time, Billy," Big Jesse said, solemnly. "Win a man's marbles and he'll stop being your friend. Same way with money. Never play cards with a friend 'cause, if you win, you ain't friends no more. Now, about this thing with Doc Fletcher and that darky from Rose's place. Maybe you saw what you thought—maybe you didn't. Sometimes what we think we see ain't exactly what we did see."

"You ain't talking so's I can follow you."

Jesse tried again. "I'll put it this way. Folks would get real upset if they thought Doc Fletcher had something to do with that preacher. You figure that for a fact?"

"Bull Frazer would be foaming at the mouth."

Jesse went on, "And if Doc got in trouble folks might think I was doing it with him."

"No," protested Billy. "I didn't see you there."

"But, folks might think I was. So, maybe we better not mention it to anyone."

"Okay." Billy grinned.

Big Jesse decided to spread a little frosting on the deal. "Now, you help me fill these bottles. I'll give you a quarter, walk you home and explain to your mama that I come by and talked you into coming to work for me."

"I'd have to split with the other kids."

Jesse wondered if he was being blackmailed. He thought for a moment, then said, "All right. A quarter for you and a dime for each of the kids. You won't have to tell your mama about the quarter. Might as well start learning now how to keep a secret."

The boy nodded sagely. "Will you come for dinner sometime?"

"That, too, except I wouldn't expect any miracles. Your mama and me don't see eye to eye on most things."

"Mama said that, too," Billy told him.

"She did, eh?" Jesse walked to the door and spit. "Reckon your mama knows a lot."

"She's a woman, but she's still pretty smart," Billy agreed.

"Well, let's get to work."

Big Jesse picked up a bottle and lowered the dipper into the barrel.

Chapter Twenty-One

Rusty Ward rejoined Sean Porter at Belle Meade II, grateful to be relieved of his responsibilities as overseer. John Conrad resumed management of the plantation. Rusty was too dreamy and involved with his inner thoughts to oversee Belle Meade. He was probably an authentic American genius, one of those rare creative individuals unable to handle people. The young man was overly concerned about the feelings of slaves. He kept thinking of ways to cut down on labor, while the slaves rested in the sun awaiting orders to go to work.

Rusty went off to design the wharf. John went to the slave quarters and appointed an intelligent-looking man as foreman of a timbering crew. Ten men would go out in the woods, chop down the largest trees, trim away the limbs. Muleskinners would drag the logs to the sawmill to be cut into foundation timbers for the wharf. More newcomers went out to cut firewood. That left ten men, their skills untested, to help weed out the cotton fields.

The new women were another matter. John didn't want them sitting around. The servant staff at the house was full, so a half dozen were appointed to a cooking crew helping Martha prepare meals. Sixteen women were left needing something to do.

John turned the problem over to Uncle Eli.

The aging slave's face wrinkled up with concentration.

"Need hep in the house?" Uncle Eli wondered.

"Nope. The place is swarming with people."

"Use a couple to run noon meals to the crews," the old man suggested.

"Good idea!"

Uncle Eli beamed. Gray haired, somewhat arthritic, walking with the aid of a cane, the old Negro enjoyed flattery. Although he did not work on the plantation, Uncle Eli desperately needed to be part of Belle Meade's daily operation. He carried the key to the smokehouses.

"How many's that leave?" Uncle Eli asked.

"Fourteen."

"That a heap?"

"It sure is," John answered. "We might have four strong ones curry the horses."

"Animals could use it."

"How's the berries?" John asked.

"Thicker'n grass. Blackberries real good this year."

"You got plenty of buckets?"

"We send them picking in the patches," said Uncle Eli, his features brightening.

"Berries and cool sweet milk are good eating."

Uncle Eli smacked his lips. "Blackberry wine good for stomach aches. Mayhaps we make some wine."

"You know about that?"

Uncle Eli grinned. "Massa Korrman usta be here. He a tight man. Always complainin' 'bout what folks eat. Never give any presents to folks. We made good blackberry wine one year, but Massa Korrman taken it for hisself. Not even give folks a drap when they got a stomach ache."

John grinned. "I'll bet your stomach was aching every morning."

"Yassuh!" Uncle Eli returned the smile. "Ceptin' it wasn't my stomach. I just wanted to taste that wine. Makin' it is somethin' I love to do."

"You're in charge of the berry crew," John told the old man. "Give those gals buckets and point them to the thickets."

John spent the late morning riding across the plantation. He found the muleskinners and the timber crew arguing over who should attach chains to haul the logs to the sawmill. Both crews insisted the job belonged to the opposite group. John informed the workers that he didn't care who put on the chains, but a quota of twenty logs was set for the day. Failure to meet that number would mean a loss of privileges and short rations. The crews worked hard for the rest of the day.

Down in the cotton fields, a newcomer got into a fight with one of the regular slaves. John heard the ruckus, rode in and separated the men. He sent the new man to another crew of weeders, admonishing the man to watch his temper. The black man went walking away, muttering to himself. Another new man came up. He said the slave who had fought was a troublemaker.

"He don't take to orders," explained the slave, a young man about twenty. He was tall, handsome and muscular.

"Any reason?" John asked.

"His fam'ly got sold down to where they raise cane."

"Louisiana?"

"That's hit, massa. He git squirrelly 'bout losin' his woman and chillun. He say he gonna slice my throat last night. I didn't do nothin' 'cept ask him to move over at t'supper table."

"I'll talk to him," John promised.

He left the weeders and after dismounting, walked over to the other crew. He called the argumentative slave from the group. They walked over to the edge of the field.

John said, "I hear you got problems."

The slave looked suspicious. "Who tell you that?"

"Care to talk about it?"

"Nuthin' yuh can do to hep it."

"What's your name?"

"Cottontop."

"Just that?"

"Name muh owner gives me. It awright."

"Where you from, Cottontop?"

"Nawth Caroliny."

"How'd you end up in Memphis at auction?"

Cottontop's eyes grew hard as black rock. "Yuh askin' a lotta questions, massa."

"I'm trying to help you."

"Don't need yuh hep."

John appraised the black man. He looked to be about thirty-three years old, muscular but not thick, wearing a chip on his shoulder like an emblem.

"You want to stay at Belle Meade?"

"Make no mind t'me."

"We try to work as a team here," John explained. "Belle Meade is—"

"I done been tole 'bout bean baggin' to get freed."

"People can work off their freedom," John went on. "It isn't the best system, but every slave on this plantation has an account. When the moon changes they get a bean showing they've got money on the books. When their price is paid off, they're freed men and women."

"No use Cottontop bein' free."

"Why not?"

"They taken muh woman and pickaninnies. Sole

231

'em t'pick cane. They gone."

"What did you do at your last place?"

"Hep the blacksmith."

"We could use an extra hand at that."

The man refused to look at John. "I gwine run if'n I gets the chance."

"Well, you want to work with the blacksmith till you run?"

"No matter, boss, to me."

"Work with him tomorrow." John started off, then turned and looked directly into the slave's face. "Cottontop, we don't have guards here. You don't belong to me. You're welcome to run right now if you want to."

"Yuh'd send the hounds."

"The dogs on Belle Meade are used for hunting animals—not men."

"Yuh sure 'bout that?"

"I don't lie about anything like that." John got on his horse and rode over and looked down at Cottontop. "You stay on at Belle Meade and you work with the others as a team. You want to run"—John pointed his riding crop north—"that's the direction to go. Just stay out of sight during the daylight hours and you might make it to the North."

He rode off leaving the perplexed slave standing with a confused expression on his face.

That evening, the twins were placed in cradles on a table in the back yard. The slaves were invited from their quarters to see the children. Suzanne distributed new dresses for the women, new pants and shirts for the men. Clothes were also distributed for the children. An apology was given to the newcomers, along with a promise to purchase new clothing if they stayed on Belle Meade.

Before the slaves returned to their quarters,

Suzanne distributed a bag of rock candy to each person. She had brought a small keg of candy from London, more than an ample supply for everyone. Needles were also given to the women. Each man received a plug of chewing tobacco and a long dark cigar. John did not see Cottontop in the group. Glancing toward the slave quarters, he saw the man sitting by himself and staring off into the dusk.

II

The peddler wiped the sweat from his brow, then went back to spreading his wares on a table near the auction block. A short, squat, dark-bearded man in his mid-twenties, he lined up the notions on the rickety table. He could scarcely wait on his customers, who were buying everything in sight. Dandified slave traders quickly bought out his supply of cravats and imitation-diamond stickpins. Fancy inlaid belt buckles sold out quickly. The women bought needles, thread and tiny earrings with stones that looked like rubies and sapphires.

The peddler had never tried selling his wares at a slave auction, although he was sure to do so in the future. Everyone seemed in a buying mood, inspecting the merchandise quickly. This kind of selling was much better than carrying a backpack from plantation to plantation, manor house to shanty, selling a penny's worth here, a nickel there. At the rate his merchandise was selling, everything would be gone at a good profit that day.

Making change for his customers, feeling his purse grow heavier, Jacob Stein gave thanks for his friendship with Bull Frazer. The sheriff was a *goy* with class. For three years now, Jake Stein left New Orleans each spring with four heavy backpacks filled with merchandise. He rode a steamboat to Natchez and left the boat carrying one pack. The other three packs were shipped to Memphis and locked away in Bull Frazer's jail.

Jacob was wary of Natchez-Under-the-Hill, a byword for hell-raising in America and across the ocean in Europe. Natchez-Under-the-Hill was a gathering place for the dregs of the frontier: prostitutes, riverboat gamblers, crooks, thieves, land and river pirates, highwaymen and outlaws of every description. But the bluffs looming over the "Hill" contained the town of Natchez, a pleasant community of law-abiding citizens. It was here that Jake Stein started his trips.

The old town of Natchez looked out over the Mississippi River, which flowed below in a wide curve. Jake was always touched by the yellow current and the timeless flow of water to the Gulf. It was the high elevation on the bluff that brought fortune to the town. Natchez was a striking contrast to the swamps, forest and rich river bottom land that spread for miles around the town and across the river westerly.

A student of history, Jake Stein knew that the Natchez tribe had once settled there, Indians who came up from Mexico back in prehistory. No one knew when the tribe settled there. They were there when De Soto's Spanish soldiers came exploring in 1543. Most folks claimed De Soto was buried in Lake St. John. Next, the French came, followed by the British. The Spaniards held the territory again for another nineteen years until it became a U.S. possession in 1798. The original crops were indigo and tobacco, giving way to cotton when England needed the fibrous white plant for their mills.

Although he had no money to purchase land, Jake Stein learned that the planters were becoming wealthy. They built many fine houses in Natchez. This was a result of the richness of the soil and the good climate. He was told by one planter that the purchase price of his vast plantation was paid back in two years.

After peddling house-to-house in Natchez, Jake Stein headed out along the Natchez Trace. This was a centuries-old Indian trail that ran north to Nashville. It was worn deep below the banks on either side, in some spots dropping ten or twelve feet below the surrounding terrain. A high wall of green trees rose above the Natchez Trace, almost obscuring the sun. A gentle green light guided the peddler through the historic lane.

Jake Stein found many customers along the Natchez Trace. Settlers from the older colonies were heading west to seek their destinies. Naturally, the dregs of society ventured there, often one or two steps beyond the law. They lingered for a day, a week, a month and settled down or passed on. The customers Jake liked were those who wished to own land, build a home, set up towns where their families might live and prosper.

On his first trip along the Natchez Trace, Jake had been held up and robbed of his money and merchandise. After that humiliating experience, he'd worked his way back to New Orleans on a flatboat. He labored all summer and winter scraping barnacles off ships to save money for his next pack. When he left New Orleans the following spring, Jacob carried a small pistol in his coat pocket, but he was never troubled again by hold-up men.

Soon Jake developed a regular route. He followed the Natchez Trace, then cut off onto a small dirt road through Mississippi to Memphis. With luck, his original backpack was empty when he arrived there. Next, he shouldered a pack and headed east, doubling back northward toward Memphis when his pack was half gone. In the autumn, when the trees were beginning to color, the nights were cooler, Jacob walked back to Natchez and boarded a boat downriver to New Orleans. He peddled through Louisiana during the winter months, then came north at the first sign of spring.

Jake called on everyone along his route. Certain big plantations were a windfall. The planters purchased presents for their slaves, distributing the notions and paying cash when Jake totaled the bill. Others would not allow Jake on their property, citing his Jewish heritage as proof of demonic character. The small landowners were excellent customers who welcomed Jake into their homes. These families were eager for news of the outside world. Jake always gave each child a piece of rock candy, and frequently was given a bed in their cabins. When beds were not available, he slept in the barn. Shiftless settlers were the worst. They existed on poor land, and were often too lazy to plant crops. Their families were malnourished. Nonetheless, while they lacked money to buy, Jake gave a piece of candy to each member of the family. A needle was given to each of the suffering women stuck in the wilderness with their poor husbands.

Jake maintained a rigid diet during his first year on the road. He refused to eat pork. This led to many conversations with the families he stayed with along the way. A big farmer would be chewing away on a piece of succulent ham, willing to share a slab with Jake, and the peddler sat and ate vegetables. Beef was almost nonexistent in the southern states. Breakfast meant ham, bacon or sausage. Lunch was some form of pork. Dinner meant a tasty roast, head cheese or pinto beans cooked with salt pork. Jake was gaunt and thin after his first summer on the road. The next year, he ate pork, squirrel, rabbit, whatever was placed before him. He rationalized that a man needed substantial fare to lug an eighty-pound backpack from farm to farm. Survival was put before his religious dietary laws.

Jake had come trudging up to the Memphis jail the night before the auction. Sheriff Frazer suggested Jake set up a table and display his wares for the crowd. Jake had been hesitant. But now, selling merchandise so rapidly, Jake decided that Bull Frazer knew a lot about human nature. A man could get rich selling in crowds like this.

There came a booming voice from the platform. Jake turned and saw Bull standing above the crowd.

"All right, you sonsofbitches!" roared Bull. "We're going to start selling niggers!"

Chapter Twenty-Two

The auction went smoothly, surprising even Bull Frazer. Bidding was brisk. Out-of-town buyers were ready to buy darkies and head home. On the few occasions when the bidding dropped low, traders moved in quickly to buy a cheap slave. Colonel Danworth had been appointed by the traders to keep track of the bids. He was surprised to see $200 field hands go for $275, $300 and occasionally $350.

Everyone sighed when the last slave was sold. It was as if a vast epidemic of cholera had left town.

Bull Frazer looked out over the crowd.

"Well, boys, how did I do?" he said with pleasure.

"Pretty good, Bull," yelled Colonel Danworth. "But there's still a couple of men in the crowd you forgot to insult!"

Everyone laughed. The traders rushed forward to watch the money count. Their greedy eyes glistened with excitement. Off to the side, Colonel Danworth was ciphering out the shares. Although a trader might have brought ten slaves to auction, and another only five, Bull planned to distribute the money in even shares. Surprisingly high bidding meant everyone would make money—despite the loss of the slaves being held on Belle Meade.

The money was counted by a clerk from the bank. "Almost seventy-five thousand dollars," he announced.

"Seventy-four thousand nine hundred dollars and eighteen cents," said Danworth, precisely.

Bull Frazer stood up and addressed the traders assembled around the bank clerk.

"Boys, the county and city have run a lot of expenses in caring for your slaves," he explained. "I reckon, first of all, we ought to charge a fee for auctioning. Amos charges ten percent. So if we deduct that sum it will cover our money spent out."

"Not a chance!" cried Pat Flanagan. "We had to stay here to get our money."

"Yeah!" roared Beau Franklin. "My hotel bill must be two hundred dollars!"

Bull yelled back, "Quit staying at Madame Rose's place."

The traders laughed and Bull Frazer gave in. It was dangerous for the traders to be in town. They might hear about the slaves hidden on Conrad's place.

"Boys, line up! The clerk will give out your money," Bull bellowed. "There's just one tiny matter to be settled."

An angry growl came from the traders.

"You sign off with your signature or mark on a piece of paper."

"Meaning what?" Pat Flanagan demanded.

"You're giving up claims for suing anyone over this mess," said the sheriff.

Colonel Danworth came up. "Fair enough, sheriff! This looks like a nice end to an unpleasant affair. Sir, I admit thinking you'd hold out for an auctioneer's fee, or demand we pay for feeding and sheltering the darkies. You've compromised and bent backward for us, sheriff. We'll do the same for you."

"Good enough," Frazer said.

Late that afternoon Jake Stein trudged back to the jail. His backpack was almost empty. He went into the sheriff's office, found Bull Frazer with his boots up on his desk. The sheriff had a slight smile on his lips. A jug was on the desk and the sheriff's hand held a glass of whiskey.

"Gift from the traders," Bull said lightly. "They figure I saved them from a deep hole."

Jake had heard the story from other lips. He said, "Looks like you did."

"Saved my own hide, too," Bull replied. "How'd you do?"

"Never sold so much stuff in one day," said Jake.

"You ought to think about settling down."

The peddler loosened the straps of his pack, let it drop from his shoulders. He laid the pack on one chair, sat in another. He was grateful to be rid of the weight. Even a light pack cut at a man's shoulders and chest.

Jake shrugged. "I got maybe four more years on the road before I'll have enough to start a store."

"Wanna drink?" Bull pushed the jug across the desk.

"I don't drink."

"Damnation! I make you a fortune today and you won't have a sip with me."

Jake hesitated. He did not want to offend the sheriff. "Maybe a drop or two," he said.

"Glass in the desk drawer." Bull jerked his thumb to a cabinet.

Jake opened the drawer, pulled out a dirty glass. He rinsed it and poured a half-inch of whiskey from the jug.

"Feeling might proud of myself tonight," the sheriff said, a look of satisfaction on his face. "Got to admit my deputy came up with the idea. Give him a couple days off for his troubles for thinking it up. Damnation! Traders are already heading out of town by stagecoach and boat. The whole passel ought to be gone by dinnertime tomorrow."

Jake took a small sip of whiskey. The liquid scalded his mouth and warmed his throat. Once the initial shock was gone he felt a glowing warmth inside.

"Make a gentile outta you yet," smiled Bull. "You're eating pork like a man. Hell, I'll bet you eat anything that ain't moving."

Jake nodded. "Even had some turtle meat a few nights back."

"I been thinking," Bull continued. "Would you quit carrying that backpack if you had the chance?"

Jake nodded.

"Then I got a plan," Bull said. "Open a store right here in Memphis. Nothing spectacular and you'd have a couple silent partners."

"You got investors?"

"Nope."

"I'll need quite a bit of money. It takes a lot of merchandise to open a store."

Bull drained his glass. He picked up the jug, poured a refill. "Money's not a problem. Get all that we want. Reckon you'd have a figure in mind?"

"At least five thousand dollars for a good place."

"That much?" Bull's eyebrows shot up.

"That would be a store with a wide line of goods."

"Could you do it for less?"

"Sure, but it'd be a struggle to make ends meet."

Bull averted his gaze from Jake's face. He looked across the room at the wall.

"Jake, old buddy, how old are you?"

"Twenty-four."

"That's getting up there. But you ain't nothing like me. You've got a good future ahead of you. Only prospect I got is being voted out of a job some day. Every piss-ant in town would like to be sheriff, swagger around with a pistol and act like they're cock-of-the walk. I figure I'm bound to lose an election someday. Then"—Bull spread his hands in a gesture of helplessness—"what does a broken down sheriff do when he's out on his ear?"

"You'll think of something," Jake said, quietly and confidently.

"Shee-it! I already thought of it," Bull grinned. "I'll have me a little nest-egg building up for the day when I'm defeated. You get off the road. How's that sound?"

"Real-good, sheriff."

"What I'm telling you ain't strictly kosher. You got to keep the secret."

"I will."

Bull nodded. "Here's what I've got in mind."

Bull rented a carriage and rode out to Belle Meade with Jake Stein, the next morning. He informed John Conrad that he was ready to settle up for the slaves. Moreover, Bull said, it also involved an interesting business proposition that would make money for everyone. John didn't take kindly to that last remark, wondering if the sheriff might be wanting a bribe. John suggested they ride over to the other plantation. His associates were there to help make business decisions. The sheriff would save time and energy by explaining the deal to everyone. Bull was agreeable.

A half hour later they were seated in the library at Belle Meade II. Sean was bleary-eyed, hung over from too much brandy during the night. He'd sat down in the library and read, sipping from a bottle of cognac. The Irishman had drunk half a quart of France's finest before he realized it. In contrast, Rusty Ward was bright and alert, eager to get his mind spinning on something new.

John said, "The sheriff wants to explain an idea he's got. The two of you listen in and help me make a decision."

Sean wanted to be back in bed. Nonetheless, he smiled genially and said, "Fire away, sheriff."

Bull Frazer stood up. He paced the room. "How many slaves do we have out here?"

John replied, "We've had a couple runaways. About fifty."

"That many?" Bull looked surprised.

"They came in from all over," Sean said.

"Well, the county run up expenses of around twenty-two hundred dollars after the riot. Jot that figure down, Jake. We got to pay it off. That would be fifty dollars a head for the slaves. If we were to add another one hundred dollars to the slaves, you'd be getting a good deal, Mr. Conrad."

"A steal at that price!" Sean bolted up in his chair.

"True, a real bargain," John agreed. He wondered what the sheriff was getting at.

"The county doesn't know how many slaves are here," Bull continued. "The powers-that-exist told me to handle everything. I'm going into court tomorrow and getting a bill of sale giving John Conrad titlement to all slaves for the sum of twenty-five hundred dollars. That way the county makes a small profit."

Sean's eyes narrowed. "What about the other hundred?"

"One hundred and twenty-five dollars to be exact," Bull said flatly in a tone that ruled out any argument.

"That's why we're here. At one hundred twenty-five dollars additional per head, Belle Meade would be paying one hundred seventy-five dollars each for every slave. I figure that's still a bargain. We didn't sell a single slave yesterday for less than two hundred fifty dollars."

"A bargain," said Sean. "Would you agree, John?"

"Fair. Who gets the extra money?"

Bull Frazer cleared his throat. "You're figuring ole Bull is asking for a bribe. I'm more creative than that, although the thought crossed my mind. But that's out of my line. Jake here is a peddler. Comes from New Orleans and he's packing merchandise all over hell's backbone making a few cents' profit. I've known Jake a few years, find he's a smart man, honest and intelligent. A good sort to have for a partner in business. Jake figures he can start a nice store in Memphis for about five thousand dollars. That would cover rent, whatever he needs to sell to folks, and a little capital to work on. I know how a man can figure too sharp. Jake can start a whale of a place for six thousand two hundred and fifty dollars. Jake gets half for his share. You and I split the other half between ourselves, Mr. Conrad."

Bull stopped pacing, went quiet and sat down.

They remained silent. Each man was digesting the information in their mind.

John broke the quietness. "What do you say to this, Mr. Stein?"

"Call me Jake. It sounds fine to me."

"Can you run a store?"

"I think so. What I don't know, I'll learn."

"Sean?" John looked at the Irishman.

Sean asked, "How much would the store make a year?"

Jake Stein was quick to answer. "We'll have three thousand dollars in goods. I figure on turning the inventory twice a year at thirty percent mark-up. That means our gross sales would be six thousand dollars and gross profit about two thousand dollars. After the cost of doing business, we would have about nine hundred dollars left at the end of the year. The return is fair for a store of that size."

Sean frowned. "Doesn't hardly seem worth the effort."

"Damnation!" Bull Frazer leaped from his chair. "A man can live good on two hundred dollars a year."

"Sean's used to doing business in England," John said to soothe the sheriff's feelings. "We're not saying no. I'll have to ask Rusty for his opinion."

The young inventor's round face clouded with concentration. He interrogated Jake Stein for a long time. Where did he peddle? Were his supplies purchased solely in New Orleans? Why buy in that city, so far from his peddling routes? What was the profit margin on peddler's goods? How many peddlers traveled the southern states? Did the peddler pay cash for his goods? Did the wholesale finance any portion of the merchandise? What sort of store did Jake Stein propose to set up in Memphis?

At one point Bull Frazer roared, "Damnation! We're not here to be treated like murderers. I ever need someone to ask questions I'll call for you, Mr. Ward. You could question the legs off a wooden Indian."

John intervened. "Calm down, sheriff. My friends and I will take your deal. The three of us will hold half of the store. Titlement will be in Sean's name." He looked at the Irishman. "Is that okay with you?"

245

"Sure," Sean said, without emotion.

"When do you want to start?" John looked at Jake Stein.

"Right away."

"Have you got a building to rent?"

"I . . . well, we have not looked." The young peddler smiled. "This came up rather sudden. Bull brought up the idea last night."

"And a good one it is," Bull said expansively.

The sheriff picked up his hat. "Jake and I'll get back to town — you know how things are when a man's gone — and get things started. The judge will draw up whatever papers I tell him to. Worrying about losing an election's about over for me, which makes me feel better already. If it isn't one thing being sheriff, it's another that's worse. A year or two and I might even retire, give it up without a fight at the polls, and sleep late mornings. Sit in the sun and smile a lot. Yesiree, that sounds good."

"I'll have a check waiting when you get the papers," John said, escorting the sheriff and peddler to the door. Sean and Rusty stayed in the house while John walked the two men to their carriage.

John came back inside. Sean gave him a dubious and searching glance.

"Bucko, that deal could spell trouble."

"My thoughts, too," Rusty said.

"That's why you're holding titlement," John explained. "The sheriff's enemies might get wind of the deal. It wouldn't take a mathematical wizard to figure out what's happening."

"Dangerous business," said Sean.

John shrugged. "What do you say when the sheriff drops in with an illegal offer? He's the law, Sean, and you know our stand on that score."

"Aye, boyo, that I do."

Rusty felt a heaviness in the room, but kept his silence. Only a fool would question his friends about their past.

John looked at the young inventor. "What did you think of the plan, Rusty?"

"Too short-sighted. I didn't point that out because the sheriff was here."

"How would you handle it?" Sean wondered.

Rusty's face brightened. "First off, the idea of a store in Memphis has merit, but the sheriff's going off half-cocked. Looking for a comfortable income is his main concern, rather than studying the situation and determining what type of store would be successful. A man should study what's being offered, the prices charged by existing merchants, and whether there are gaps in their line of goods. No use setting up if the market's filled up. But I'd go a lot deeper. The Memphis store would be headquarters. The thing is, this part of the country is growing and people need goods. I'd consider opening another store in Natchez, maybe one in Nashville, a few in the good-sized towns in Kentucky. To start with, I'd open the stores in river towns because transportation costs are cheaper that way. Then, if they prove successful, go to the towns along the stagecoach routes. The stores would all be under the same name, so a person looking for an axe in Memphis can buy the same axe if he happens to be in Nashville."

"God, lad, you'd need a huge warehouse," said Sean Porter.

"There's ways around that," Rusty went on. "With several stores you'd get a better price from the manufacturers. But they could break down the merchandise and ship direct to each store."

"That's saving time and money," Sean admitted.

"Each store would serve another purpose." Now, Rusty's eyes took on an inner glow. "That Jewish fellow seems like a hard worker. Most peddlers do work hard. What I'd do is have our stores become headquarters for peddlers. We'd put up backpacks and fill them with merchandise. Give a pack to any man looking for work—Jewish or gentile. Once he's proven his mettle with a pack, we could set him up into a nice peddler's wagon with a couple of mules. They could sharpen scissors, knives, sell axes, whetstones, hammers and hardware for a farm or plantation. See, a peddler could start out from Natchez, getting stocked up from our store there, and ride through to Nashville. He wouldn't have to backtrack like this Stein has to. They could draw stock in Nashville and sell their way back to Natchez."

Sean Porter's mind was flashing. He said, "We could build the wagons right here on Belle Meade. Paint them some godawful color, slap on a company name."

"That would require a lot of money to start," John cautioned.

Suddenly, Rusty leaped up and began to dance around the room.

"The wharf!" Rusty cried. "The wharf!"

"Calm down, lad," Sean smiled. "You'll just get to stuttering again and it'll be dark before we get the gist of your idea."

"Steamboats will be stopping to pick up wood, right?" Rusty looked to John for confirmation.

"We hope so."

"Steamboats have passengers, right?"

"Get to the nitty-gritty, lad," Sean said.

"The boats stop for wood. It'll take at least half an hour, maybe more, to load them up. Fact is, we don't want to load them too fast because . . . I . . . you . . . we'll set up a store over by the wharf. The biggest dang store in the whole South. Like a big tobacco shed, 'cepting we carry everything. Not just a store for harness, another for shoes and maybe a third for dry goods. We have everything under one roof. Maybe two or three floors of anything a person could ever want. Mrs. Conrad likes to read books. We could even have a section filled with books."

Sean was lost. "But people from Memphis won't come out here to do their trading."

"The passengers!" cried Rusty. "The boat stops for wood. The passengers come off and spend their time shopping. Steamboats carry a hundred or so people."

"A winner!" Sean slapped his knee. "Some of those new boats carry up to three hundred people."

John was considering the problems. "What about the spring floods?"

Rusty's spirits sagged. "I forgot about that."

"Build a store on stilts," Sean suggested.

"They would need to be high."

"Well, your fields don't flood," Sean reminded John.

"Those low hills keep the flood water away."

Sean smiled. "Build behind the hills."

"That'd mean the store would be a quarter mile or more from the river bank."

"I got it!" yelled Rusty. "We can carry the passengers over in carriages."

"Son, I hate to top you," John said, smiling. "Everyone's ridden in a rig of some kind. Not much fun in that. But what if we wrote Israel Goldman, had him act as our agent, and send us a small locomotive? We could load up the passengers and pull them to the store with steam power."

"Hot damn!" Rusty jumped around the room, unable to contain his excitement. The thought of working with a steam-powered locomotive was the most exciting thing he'd ever considered.

"It would work," Sean said.

"True," John replied. "Who do we get to help oversee it?"

"A horseless carriage!" murmured Rusty. His face beamed with a wide smile.

Chapter Twenty-Three

Bull Frazer went before a county judge and, declaring the slave problem solved, asked that a bill of sale for $2,500 be made to John Conrad for "any and all slaves captured and held at his plantation." The bill also stated that Conrad had saved the "county from the possible rebellion of runaway slaves." When the document was ready, word was sent to John. He rode into town with a check on his New Orleans bank. These documents were transferred and titlement to the slaves passed to Belle Meade. Before John returned home, he met Sheriff Bull Frazer in the lawman's office and handed over a check for $6,250. This check was drawn on John's New Orleans account in a bank owned by Israel Goldman. Leaving the sheriff, John rode down to Madame Rose's brothel in Pinchgut. He talked at length with Jumbo, but failed to persuade the black man to become an overseer at Belle Meade.

Next he went to Roy Lanning's office and asked about the availability of carpenters. The attorney agreed to round up workmen to build houses for the new slaves at Belle Meade.

Lanning offered to go over the books on their rental properties. "Things've been slow this summer," said the attorney. "Not many folks moving into town."

"How many places are empty?"

"Two since February."

"What happened to the tenants?"

"Headed west. St. Louis, I reckon."

"How's the cash flow?" John wondered.

"A couple of families are behind, but I'm working with them. The men are out of work."

"What's their line?"

"That's the problem. They don't have one."

"I need overseers out at my place. They any good at handling blacks?"

"Never thought about it," said Lanning. "Just been hoping they'd find something and, with a little time, you know, bring their rent up to date. That's if they get a job. Not much around for some ole jack-leg who's just got a strong back to sell. Never could figure out why damn fool hillbillies don't send their kids to school. I know, I know, they need help on the farm. Exploiting your own kin never did seem right to me. That's yellow-dogging your kids. They never think ahead that mayhap the kids are going to live in town where reading, writing and ciphering counts for something like three squares a day and a bed over your head at night."

John snapped his fingers. "That reminds me. I want to build a school."

Roy Lanning laughed. "Your kids can't crawl yet. Give it a couple years and start up."

"No, I want you to write an advertisement and send it to the *New York Herald* and the *Philadelphia Gazette*. I want to hire a schoolmarm. Ask them to write me a list of their qualifications."

"You're serious? Whoinhell will a schoolmarm teach out there?"

"Squatters live all the way along the river."

"You still got that trouble? I can get the sheriff to run that bunch of trash out of there."

"They don't bother me."

"Dangerous business," said Lanning. "Squatters stay too long and they get squirrely. Think they own the land instead of the rightful title-holder. How many families are squatting out there?"

"About four along the river. One family's living up in the hills."

"They making it?"

"Just barely, I'd say."

"Fish, hunt and steal a little corn from Mr. Conrad. I reckon they'll do tolable well," said Lanning with a grin.

"Except for the stealing. I give them cornmeal every fall."

"Whyinhell encourage them?"

John shrugged. "They'd steal it if I didn't."

"So you're interested in their souls." Lanning chuckled. "They ever do much in return?"

"A mess of nice catfish now and then. Folks in the hills will bring in a coon or squirrel for the pot once in a blue moon."

"One of those good ole boys might make an overseer for you."

It was John's turn to grin. Most squatters were uninterested in steady work. So long as there was corn pone and molasses on the table, and game meat to be trapped or shot, the river and hillfolk were content. These uneducated southerners settled where their fancy struck, undeterred by deeds, titles and other legal encumbrances. They hoed out a patch of corn every year, swapped extra grain to the gristmill to process it, and finagled a supply of molasses to carry them through the winter. Wives worked the spinning wheel, if the family could afford one. About all you could say for them was that they existed.

John said to Lanning, "You know those boys don't want work."

"Hell, bossing niggers ain't work."

"You know what I'm saying."

"I get worrying about you sometimes," said Lanning. "You're prospering real well out there. Making a living, I'd judge. But you're awful sympathetic to people's needs. I 'spect you're setting up a school for these squatters' children."

"The thought did cross my mind."

Lanning smiled. "Well, that schoolmarm will remember the experience. That would be teaching to a room of wild animals."

"They'd come to school."

"For a while, anyway," drawled Lanning. "I'll send out the advertisement. Won't even charge you for my legal services in writing it up. Furthermore, I reckon I can even find a couple coins to pay for it. Times are troubling right now, what with circuit court over, but maybe I can dig up a couple coppers."

John laughed. "You're getting rich off our partnership in those houses."

Lanning gave John a look of mock surprise. "You know about that, huh?"

"What're you going to do with the piles you're making?"

"Sit on it."

"No marriageable women in sight?"

"Well, I get invited out to dinner a lot. Sit there in

my suit and stiff collar and cravat, wondering why God allowed someone to invent anything that chokes the throat. I look over at the pretty girl, who averts her eyes and gets coy. Yep, I got an active social life, if that's what you're asking about, but nobody special's come wandering into my life, if you take my meaning. I was out your way a couple nights ago having dinner with your neighbors, the Spearmans. Ole man Spearman's hitting the wine jug a little hard these days. Maybe I would, too, if my wife, my future wife that is, was a religious nut like his is."

"I heard Caroline was home."

"Blossomed out some, too, up in Boston. Not as skinny as she used to be. But there's something funny about that girl."

"Maybe she's in love with this handsome young attorney who's getting rich off the poor plantation owners."

Roy didn't go along with the kidding. "I'm serious about her, which is unusual, because I can't put my finger on it. That girl has a problem."

"You heard how that slave almost raped her?"

"Just before she went to Boston, wasn't it? Well, sir, I would have to rethink that in light of what I've been trying to put my finger on about her. She's maybe the one that sort of egged that darky on."

"Come on," John was shocked.

"Wonder she hasn't tried to get her claws in you. I'm serious."

"Nothing like that's been happening."

"What about Sean?"

"Nope. Nothing to my knowledge. Of course, Sean doesn't tell me all of his bedroom adventures."

"Got time for a drink?" asked Lanning in a slow,

drawling voice.

John consulted his watch. "Another time. I want to see that patent medicine fellow, Doc Fletcher."

"I hear his juice is pretty good." Lanning was a member of the Memphis courthouse crowd. He loved to talk about the events in town, which was a polite way of saying he liked gossip.

John turned and started for the door. He asked. "How'd you do with that bunch of traders?"

"A lot of gabbing," drawled Lanning. "Dang little action when I asked for a few dollars upfront to sue the sheriff or whoever they were mad at. But like most folks, I turned a pretty good profit."

"Come out for dinner some night."

Lanning smiled with approval. "I will. I haven't seen your bride since she got back."

"We'll be having an open house, but don't wait for that."

"Oh, about those yahoos behind in their rent," Lanning remembered. "There's one fellow who might work out. Not too bright, uneducated, but most Tennesseeans would be dead if we held that against folks."

"Send him out."

"Tomorrow morning good enough?"

"Whenever he can get out."

John left the lawyer's office.

II

Doc Fletcher was surprised to receive a visit from John Conrad. Fletcher knew the planter by sight and reputation, knew about Belle Meade's revolutionary "bean bag" process of allowing slaves to work off their freedom. Fletcher figured the work-out system wasn't much, but it was a step toward freeing the slaves. John was interested in Fletcher's wagon, how the springing worked, what was involved in carrying merchandise over long distances.

Fletcher allowed John to check out the wagon in the warehouse. It was a thorough inspection.

"Mind if I take some measurements?" John asked.

"I got them written down someplace," Fletcher said. "I can bring them out to you, if you'd like."

"Come out anytime. Figure on having a meal with us."

"You planning on going in the peddling business?"

"Making wagons for peddling." John was impressed with the construction of Fletcher's rig. It had been given careful attention during construction. "Never seen anything put together like this one."

"Bought it off a Yankee peddler," Fletcher lied. His father-in-law and his abolitionist friends had seen to the wagon's construction. It was a fine job. "They know how to build things up there."

"Hope I can do half as good as this," John said, bending down and looking at the undercarriage.

"Yankees maybe are a little flinty," Fletcher said, "but they do good work."

John stood up and glanced at a large stack of bottles capped and waiting to be boxed. "Business good?"

"We're thinking about heading out again. But," smiled Fletcher, "I get awful lazy in the summertime."

"Heat gets us all." John extended his hand and thanked Fletcher for his time. "Come and see us. We're planning an open house soon. I'll see you're invited."

"I'd enjoy seeing Belle Meade," Fletcher said.

They walked out of the building. John left. Doc Fletcher's mind was going over the possibilities of stealing slaves off Belle Meade and shipping them north.

III

Jumbo was sunning himself in a chair in front of his shack. He heard the back door of Madame Rose's brothel slam shut, opened his eyes and saw Rose come stomping off the porch. Her face was set tight with anger. She walked up in front of Jumbo, put a fist on each hip.

"The girls tell me you had company today," she hissed.

Jumbo roused himself. "Yeah, Rose. Mr. Conrad from Belle Meade come here to see me."

"What did he want?"

"Wanted to give me a job."

"Dammit! You got a job."

"Well, I reckon a man can listen to a planter make an offer."

"Don't I take care of you?"

"Well, I ain't got any complaints, mam."

"You should have sent that man to see me."

Jumbo nodded his head in agreement. "You was off shopping. I reckon it didn't do any harm listening to the man. He meant well. Seemed like a good sort."

"Hah!" snorted Madame Rose. "I've never seen a cent of his money in my purse."

"Likely you won't. He don't seem the sort."

"I don't like folks coming around to hire away my niggers."

"Miz Rose," Jumbo reminded her, "I am a freed man."

"You were near starving when I put you to work."

"Reckon I won't ever forget that," Jumbo agreed. And if I do forget, he thought, you'll be sure to remind me.

"Another thing," Rose shrilled. "You're getting lazy. The place is starting to look like a trashy crib operation. The windows ain't been washed all summer."

Jumbo smiled. "I don't do windows, Miz Rose. That's woman's work."

"The nigger maid is sick."

"She be feelin' better tomorry," said Jumbo, lapsing into his uneducated routine.

"Don't pull that dumb-nigger crap on me."

"Yes, ma'am." Jumbo stood up. He towered over the woman. "Whatever you say, Miz Rose."

"You don't talk to people behind my back!" She spun around and walked back to the house.

Jumbo settled down in his chair, leaned back against the unpainted wall of his shanty. The sun was warm, but not deadly hot. It was still a couple hours to supper and, in that interval, a man could take a nice long nap.

IV

"You look dressed for courting."

"Just going out to dinner."

"Widow lady?"

"Well, sort of," Big Jesse Hawkins confessed.

Doc Fletcher chided, "You're always crawling in those cold beds with grief-stricken women. You ought

259

to open a service company. Widows welcome! Come get what you've been missing since the mister croaked."

Big Jesse's thick fingers fumbled with the red cravat around his neck. "I never could tie one of these damned things!"

"Let me," said Fletcher, facing the big man and expertly knotting the fabric. "Is this one old, young, middle-aged or just lonely?"

"She's thirty-five."

Fletcher inspected his work. "Not a bad knot. Watch yourself with a thirty-five-year-old widow. You'll wake up at the altar getting hitched."

"I'm just going for dinner because her boy wants me to."

"That kid who's helping in the warehouse?"

"Billy Wells."

"That's worse. You like the kid, I can tell, and that's a sure way of picking up a ready-made family. Jesse, you don't know true happiness until you marry a widow and a passel of kids. Then, my friend, it is too late for happiness. Your nose is to the old grindstone to feed the brood."

"She wouldn't have me, anyway,," said Jesse, stuffing a clean handkerchief in the pocket of his suit.

"A snob, huh?"

"She's real strict with her kids. Reckon she'd be the same with a husband."

"She'll soften up until after the ceremony."

Jesse brushed off his jacket, buttoned it and held himself out for inspection.

"How do I look?" he asked.

Fletcher grinned. "Jesse, I like you better in your wild man outfit."

Jesse picked up his hat. "Speaking of wild men, when are we getting back on the road?"

"Pickings are getting slim around here," Fletcher agreed.

"You mean that monkey business with darkies?"

"That's why I'm here," Fletcher said, seriously. "The tonic is just something to pay our way."

"How is our money?"

"Dipping low."

"We ought to leave soon," said Jesse. "A couple months on the road and I'll feel like a new man."

Fletcher laughed. "You're just spoiling to tumble with all the widows along the way."

"That, too," said Jesse. He opened the door, then paused. "Don't wait up for me, Doc. You never know what a young widow might like to do."

Doc laughed and headed for the kitchen to find something to eat.

Chapter Twenty-Four

Patricia Wells glanced out the front door of her home. Billy was sitting in the rocking chair, his watchful eyes turned to the street. His suntanned, freckled face was absent of emotion. The low summer twilight filtered through the orchard, a shaft of sunlight lighting Billy's hair. He had been sitting there for almost a half hour. His gaze never left the street. He had bathed early, put on his white shirt and black tie without protest, brushed the lint from his black trousers. He polished his shoes to a high gloss, then went out on the porch to watch for Big Jesse Hawkins.

"Billy," Patricia said softly. "I saved the frosting spoon for you."

"Give it to the girls," he said, not moving his eyes from the street.

"Are you waiting for Mr. Hawkins?"

"Yes, ma'am."

"I'm sure he's coming."

"Jesse said he would."

Then Big Jesse Hawkins came into view, turning a corner and strolling through the dusk. Billy leaped from the swing, raced off the porch and out into the yard. He caught himself and, like a man, stood by the gate until Big Jesse came up.

Patricia Wells returned to the dining room to check the table setting for the third time in the past ten minutes. She wondered why her hand trembled; why she felt nervous. After all, Jesse Hawkins was a friend of Billy's. But the notion remained that Billy was playing matchmaker. She decided Big Jesse was looking for nothing more than a good dinner. Besides, she was past all of that foolishness. She removed her apron, folded and placed it in a drawer. Her hands smoothed down her blouse and skirt. She heard the sound of Jesse's footsteps on the porch. She hurried forward, pausing for an instant to check her appearance in a mirror.

"He's here! He's here!" Billy cried.

Patricia opened the door. "Come in, Mr. Hawkins."

"Howdy, ma'am," Jesse said, uneasily. "I brought you some flowers."

Patricia took the bouquet of roses with apprecitiave comments. "Take Mr. Hawkins into the parlor, Billy," she said. "I'll put the flowers in a vase and put them on the table."

Jesse followed the boy into the parlor. The windows were covered with thick-fringed shades and heavy beige drapes. It took a moment for Jesse's eyes to adjust to the dimness. He hadheard of such parlors, but this was his first time in such a luxurious room. The walls were covered with a light brown silk damask. Two handsome oil paintings faced each other from opposite walls. They were romantic scenes of steamboats on the Mississippi River, quite well done, held in large gilded frames. The floor beneath Jesse's feet was covered with a thick Oriental carpet with delicate gold threading. An embroidered Chinese dragon was inlaid into the fabric with many different colors. A dark mahogany stand on one side of the room held a large family Bible, opened to view. The sofa and two matching chairs were upholstered in a beige silk fabric that matched the drapes. The richness of the room was apparent.

"Like the dragon?" Billy asked, pointing to the carpet.

"Amazing," said Jesse, suddenly aware of his boots on the carpet. "You sure we're supposed to walk on it"

"That's what it's for," said Patricia Wells, coming into the room.

Big Jesse looked embarrassed. "I've never been in a room like this," he confessed.

"My husband was a steamboat captain," she explained. "He liked nice things and, knowing New Orleans, purchased things at very reasonable prices."

"This is the best one," said Billy.

Big Jesse followed the boy to a corner, where a lacquered Chinese chest sat. Big Jesse touched the wood, found it was smoothed to a satin finish.

"It even has a secret drawer," Billy said. He demonstrated how a piece of wood could be pressed to open a small drawer near the bottom of the chest.

Big Jesse heard a tiny giggling noise. He turned around and saw three little girls standing in the doorway of the parlor. They wore long white dresses with ruffles and ribbons. Their wide eyes looked expectantly up at their visitor.

"Children, this is Mr. Hawkins," Patricia Wells said. "And this is Deborah, nine; Sally, seven; and this is our baby, Camille. She's five years old."

The girls curtsied in unison.

"Hi, girls," Big Jesse said. "Billy's been showing me the secret drawer."

The girls giggled.

"Time to eat," said Patricia.

She started for the dining room. The girls ran ahead of her, Big Jesse and Billy following.

The dining room was furnished with an oak table with simple lines. An oak sideboard sat at one end of the room and several silver cups and trays were displayed there. The china cabinet, which sat at the other end of the room, contained china tureens, serving platters and a row of crystal goblets. A small crystal chandelier contained candles which were now lit. Their flames sparkled against the crystal, flickered against the silver and china.

"You sit at that end of the table," said Patricia Wells, directing Big Jesse to a captain's chair.

She excused herself, came back from the kitchen pushing a serving cart. Big Jesse had never smelled such delicious soup in his life. Patricia filled the fragile china bowls with a thick potato soup. Big Jesse picked up the largest spoon and took a mouthful.

The girls giggled.

Billy looked surprised.

Patricia saw Big Jesse's embarrassment. "The children are used to saying grace," she explained. "Would you like to lead us, Mr. Hawkins?"

"Ain't much at saying it," Big Jesse said, gruffly.

"Will you do the honors, Billy?" she asked.

The boy closed his eyes. "We thank you for this food, Jesus, and ask your blessing on all those who are not so fortunate." He looked over at Jesse. "It's okay to eat now. Maw won't whack you."

"Billy!" This came from his mother.

They ate the soup in silence. The little girls kept stealing shy looks at Big Jesse. The five year old, Camille, giggled once when her eyes met Jesse's gaze.

When the soup was finished, Big Jesse shoved back his bowl.

"Ma'am, that is the best damned soup—" He sucked in his breath.

The girls were attacked by a spasm of giggles. Billy joined in the merriment. Big Jesse sat with a red face.

"I understand," said Patricia Wells. "You liked the soup."

"I sure do," said Jesse.

Patricia Wells went into the kitchen for the main course. The oldest girl collected the soup bowls and followed her mother into the back of the house. Billy grinned at Big Jesse.

"You messed up," he said, cocking his head in a childish angle. "Mama is liable to whack you."

"My manners ain't the best," Big Jesse admitted.

"You talk dirty," chimed in five-year-old Camille. "Not 'sposed to say that."

"He didn't mean it," Billy said, defensively.

"Why'd he say it if he didn't mean it?" asked Sally. She was seven.

"My tongue slipped," Jesse explained, wishing to change the topic of conversation. He asked, "What did you kids do today?"

"Went fishing," said Billy.

"Catch anything?"

"Couple of catfish," the boy said.

Sally spoke up. "Do you cuss all the time?"

Big Jesse glowered at the girl. "No, darling," he said, sweetly. "Once in a while I hold my breath and quit cussing for a minute or two."

"Mama says people who cuss go to the bad place," she responded. "Don't you ever think about that?"

"That's all I do when I ain't turning the air blue with profanity."

"Spose you'll go there the minute you drop dead."

Jesse suppressed the urge to swat the kid. Instead, he smiled and answered, "Reckon you're right."

Patricia Wells and Deborah came back from the kitchen. The serving cart was loaded with food. Deborah laid out the china plates. Patricia Wells set out huge plates of fried chicken, gravy, corn-on-the-cob, tomatoes, green beans, pickles, corn relish and hot biscuits. Big Jesse was mightily impressed and said so. But cautious as a cat in a dog kennel, he minded his manners. The meal was enjoyable and Jesse ate heartily. Billy was correct about his mother's being a good cook. Dessert was peach cobbler covered with thick cream. When that course was finished, the children cleared the table. Billy agreed to wash dishes, the girls would dry.

Patricia Wells suggested they go sit in the swing. The sun had gone down, but a cooling breeze blew in from the north. Fireflies jeweled the night.

"Lordy, that was a good meal," said Jesse, patting his stomach.

"I love cooking for people who like to eat." A soft, sensuous quality lingered in her voice.

Big Jesse turned and looked toward the woman. A soft light filtered through a window highlighting her face. He was impressed by the serenity of her features. She had to be a strong woman to come out of the backwoods of western Virginia, have four children and still retain her figure. Some women had the grit to get over widowhood, while others turned soft and dependent. It looked as if Patricia Wells had grit enough to pave every street in Memphis.

Jesse wondered where she'd learned her manners. He said, "I was born in the backwoods, Miz Wells. Reckon my manners ain't too good. But I've been over in western Virginia and never met folks much better'n me. Where'd you learn all that?"

"My husband was a remarkable man. He was older than me by about ten years, which was all right, because I needed someone to teach me things." She gave a tiny push with her foot. The swing moved in a gentle motion. "I was born on Big Ugly Creek, which is as far back in the hills as you can go. My father was from Richmond, Virginia, and he settled there to escape some scandelous affair that took place when he was young. My mother died when I was four years old and, what with Daddy being busy, I pretty much rasied myself. Daddy died when I was eleven and I went to Cincinnati to live with a spinster aunt. That's where I met Edgar, my husband. He stayed in my aunt's house when he wasn't out buying and selling land. Edgar, you see, was awful smart with money. He didn't believe in letting it pile up. Invest it and keep it working, that was his philosophy. Edgar demanded that my aunt send me to a female academy. She had the money to do it, but she hung onto every last penny. When she refused, Edgar paid my tuition and even bought some nice clothes for me to wear, so's I'd look as nice as the other girls."

"Sounds like a generous man," Jesse offered.

"He was, Mr. Hawkins," she replied. "Our courtship was something special. We went to the theater, attended lectures and went downtown once to hear the president speak. Edgar had never married. Too busy, I reckon. He claimed nobody had ever interested him until I came into his life. I graduated from the academy when I was sixteen. That's when we started sparking. I was old enough to know what I wanted. Edgar was a kind and decent man. He worked hard. A woman couldn't ask for a better husband and provider. I was very lucky to marry him. When steam power came along, Edgar went crazy over the steamboats. He sold off his land and other investments, invested in a boat of his own. We moved to Memphis and did right well. Edgar bought this place and the furnishings came up from New Orleans. Edgar was always meeting someone sailing to China or places like that. He'd have them buy him a carpet or chests, furniture and stuff."

"I'm sure you miss him."

Patricia Wells sobbed in spite of herself. "Now, don't worry Mr. Hawkins. I'm not going to turn weepy on you. I miss Edgar all the time because he knew so much. If a problem came up, Edgar always had the right answer. He wasn't flighty like some men, didn't womanize or drink. He went to church regularly every Sunday and donated money to help the church keep going."

Big Jesse wondered if Edgar Wells, rest his soul in peace, was a figment of his widow's imagination. Edgar didn't sound like one of the boys, that was for sure, and any man must have a couple bad habits.

"Did he chew or smoke?" he asked.

"Edgar? Heavens, no. Why do you ask?"

"Some men do, you know."

"Edgar said both habits were unmanly."

"Reckon they might be."

She nudged the swing again. "Edgar loved to hear

good preaching. Did you know he always held services on the steamboat every Sunday? Just stopped wherever they were on the river and asked if a preacher was on board. If there wasn't one there, Edgar led the crew and passengers in singing praise to the Lord. He would do the preaching himself, if need be."

"A nice man," said Jesse. Not anyone I'd cotton to right off, he thought. Fact is, the Lord might have had a hand in Edgar Wells' demise. Jesse's mind conjured up a vision of Billy Wells if his father had lived. The kid would grow up to be a pure and simple prig. Yep, Billy seemed to be doing right well for himself without a paw like that.

"He left me well off," Patricia Wells went on. "Edgar believed in life insurance, which most folks don't even know exists. He had two big policies with companies in New York. When everything was settled I was left with enough to school the children and not have to work."

Big Jesse was beginning to hate Edgar's memory. The man was too perfect.

"Billy's my big worry," Patricia Wells went on. "He's been a trial this past year. I've had the preacher over twice to talk with him."

"That's no problem," Jesse told her. "Billy is a boy. They have a natural tendency to do certain things—like wandering around town instead of cleaning out the chicken house."

"Work should come before pleasure, Mr. Hawkins."

"Not all the time," Jesse disagreed.

"Idle hands get into trouble."

"Boys will be boys, Miz Wells. Billy has a lot of

growing up to do. It won't help things having a preacher pray over him."

"You don't know Jesus, apparently."

Jesse cleared his throat. "Well, ma'am, we ain't exactly on speaking terms."

"Religion is the hope of the world."

"Heard it was," Jesse said calmly. "Reckon I'll get around to it someday."

"No man knows when the Redeemer comes."

"I've haerd preachers say that."

Patricia's voice took on a sensuous quality. "If I ever marry again, which looks doubtful, my husband would have to be a man with strong religious convictions. Just like Edgar."

"He must've been a pillar for the Lord."

"Oh, he was, Mr. Hawkins. The preacher said the world could be changed by a hundred men like my husband. Said that many times."

"He must've meant it."

"He did. That's why the women of Memphis have decided to go ahead with Edgar's idea. Sort of a memorial for him."

"Putting up a stone over his grave?" wondered Jesse.

"He's already got that. Edgar was always upset about folks drinking in taverns. Do you go to taverns or drink whiskey, Mr. Hawkins?"

Jesse coughed. "Not often."

"Once is too much. Good men are ruined by whiskey."

"True, I've seen a couple cases like that. 'Course," Jesse said, philosophically, "no one holds their mouths open and pours it down their gullets."

"The men in Memphis need to be protected from

saloon keepers and evil women."

Heaven help me, Jesse thought. "What're you women planning?"

"We're going to close down those evil places."

"Saloon keepers might have a say in that matter," Jesse offered.

"We want to live in a righteous city," Patricia continued, "so we're bringing in a lady from Philadelphia. She's been giving her time and money to closing down saloons in those awful eastern cities. She is a terror against whiskey, I'm told. She comes into a town and organizes a drive against the whiskey peddlers, the taverns and those awful places where fallen women entertain men."

"It ought to be interesting," Jesse agreed.

"Will you come to our first meeting and swear off?"

"Swear off? What's that mean?" Big Jesse was now cautious.

"You sign a paper swearing to never drink another drop of liquor."

"Oh," he said, desolately.

"You could be the first man in town to swear off," said Patricia Wells. "We plan on having the names posted around town. You'll be an example to everyone that grown men don't need whiskey."

"I'll think about it," Jesse said. He stood up and stretched. "Reckon I'd better get home. You probably got to put the kids in bed."

He thanked her for the dinner, went inside and said good-bye to the kids. He shook hands with his hostess and tousled Billy's hair. Then Jesse walked toward home wondering what secret vice had been practiced by Edgar Wells. If he hadn't one, ole Edgar was the world's most perfect man. Jesse didn't think that species existed.

Chapter Twenty-Five

At that moment, Jumbo was engaged in heavy labor. The front porch of the rented house was littered with small pieces of miscellaneous furniture. The yard was covered with straw packing, kitchen utensils, empty bird cages, umbrella stands, and boxes of china. A roll of carpet lay beyond the gate. A great deal of furniture was still in the wagon.

Jumbo was in his shirt sleeves. Sweat poured down his face as he moved the heavy boxes and furniture. Although these moving jobs were sometimes hard, Jumbo picked up extra income helping teamsters move their customers. This particular job involved going down to the steamboat wharf, loading up the household belongings of a Mr. Silas Blackston, who was accompanied by his wife, the former widow, Della Montrose. Mrs. Montrose had been widowed three years previously when her husband, Joseph Montrose, died of a stroke. Her daughter, Regina Flannagan, was moving to Memphis with her mother and step-father.

Jumbo didn't think much of the job. Mrs. Blackston was in charge of putting things away, deciding where furniture went, and the hanging-up department. Mr. Blackston had taken charge of the van, its contents and the work force of teamsters and their Negro helpers. Jumbo was at the beck and call of everyone. One moment he was needed to lift one end of a sofa up on the porch, the next instant he steadied a bureau of drawers being lifted from the wagon. Regina Montrose spent her energy running in and out of the house, looking for this or that piece of furniture. She had an enormous capacity for work, being young and in perfect health.

This was not the first time the young woman had been involved in moving. She had lived in a number of towns since her mother married Silas Blackston. Her first experience came a few months after the unexpected wedding, when her step-father—who was a drummer—moved his small suitcase of clothes into their family home in Charleston.

Shortly after that, Silas Blackston elaborated a plan by which the family would be infinitely better off if a red flag were hoisted out the window and their house sold to the highest bidder. He would then take the money from sale of the house, along with the proceeds of Joseph Montrose's estate, and invest in town lots in a new city being promoted in Georgia. They would have a home of their own, free and clear, and an income from houses built on the other lots. In this new venture, which Silas Blackston assured his wife and step-daughter was foolproof, a total of six homes would be built. They would have a large dwelling in keeping with Della's social aspirations. The income from the rented houses would help his stepdaughter perfect herself in music. He pointed out that Regina possessed a perfect soprano voice, but even the most talented person needed training.

Their home in Charleston was quickly sold, followed by hasty packing and a sudden departure to

Georgia. The lots were bought and construction started immediately on the new homes. None were completed because Mr. Blackston heard of a "Jim Dandy" cotton ginning machine manufactured in New Orleans. He planned on getting rich selling the device. They made the exodus from Georgia to New Orleans, only to find the factory boarded up and the owner leaving town to escape his creditors.

A third exodus took place when Silas Blackston heard of a new steam laundry machine guaranteed to cure the washday problems for every woman. More money was put into what became the United Family Laundry Association, Inc., of Pittsburgh. It was from here that the Blackstons had moved to Memphis, coming downriver on a steamboat. This move had been hasty. The landlord of their rented house in Pittsburgh realized he had traded a year's rent for ten shares of stock in a bankrupt laundry corporation.

These moves had their effect on the family's belongings. Jumbo noticed that the old family sideboard — and every southern family owned one — lacked a brass door handle and was nicked and scratched. Similiar defects were evident on Mrs. Ford's high-poster bed, once the property of her mother, which was missing two of its carved feet.

Regina Montrose was back in the yard again, dragging out a rocker, ordering a crate to be taken to the bedroom, pulling a set of fire tongs from a box. Her stepfather must have gotten in her way. Jumbo was astonished at the authoritative tone in the girl's voice.

"No, Mr. Blackston," she said firmly. "Stop right where you are. Mama doesn't need any more small things until the big ones are arranged. Don't you send them in the house!"

"My dear Regina," Blackston said. "You'll have to take them as they come."

"I'll take things as I want and need them," she said forcefully. "There's plenty of room out here. You've got plenty of men to help. That wardrobe comes next."

"Well, can't you take these here cushions?"

"Send in the cushions. But that's the last."

Blackston's expression indicated his belief that Regina would keenly regret her interference. The girl went back into the house.

Blackston called to Jumbo.

"Here, Jumbo—your name is Jumbo, ain't it?"

Jumbo nodded.

"Well, be good enough to carry this here batch of cushions into the house. And be careful with them, Jumbo."

Jumbo took the cushions and walked into the house. He was making up his mind about the character of these new people. Nothing had escaped his scrutiny. A perceptive student of human nature, Jumbo was usually correct in his appraisals.

Two things interested Jumbo. The first was that Regina Montrose addressed her stepfather as if he were a stranger. The second was Blackston's prefacing his orders with "be good enough." Most people said something like "Grab this!" or "Fetch that!"

Jumbo was also surprised when he got inside the house. "Just put them down anywhere." Regina said in a low, soft voice. This was surprising because Jumbo had heard the sharp edge in her voice when she addressed her stepfather in the yard.

"Thank you, mistress," Jumbo said.

Jumbo went out into the yard. The wagon was

almost empty. The only items left were two pieces of pipe, a burnt-out stove, a big mirror with a gilt frame, a set of wooden shelves, two washtubs and a dainty table. Two black men were lifting the table to the ground.

The noise of glass breaking sounded as Jumbo went toward the wagon.

Silas Blackston went into a rage. He swore in a loud hectoring voice. He ended by calling the whole crew a gang of lunkheads.

"Oh, my poor table," said Regina Montrose, coming up. "I forgot all about it. It isn't anyone's fault. The rest of you do something else. I'll carry it in."

She started to remove the small table from the wagon. The knob on a drawer caught against the stove door.

"Permit me to help you," came a voice from behind her.

Before she could catch her breath, an arm came forth and lifted the small table away from the stove. Without saying anything else, Sean Porter carried the table into the house. He deposited it in the living room, turning around as Regina came through the door.

"That's a lovely piece of furniture," Sean said. "Don't worry about the glass. It can be replaced easily. I must apologize for my intrusion. I came to talk with one of the darkies. But when I saw what a beauty that table was, and heard you say how you loved it, I had to help. There's nothing like lovely furniture and a nice piece like that gets rarer each day."

"It was my grandmother's and I've used it since I was a little girl. Thank you for your help."

Sean Porter introduced himself to the girl. He

asked her name and solemnly took the hand she offered.

"You're a pretty colleen," Sean said. In fact, he had not seen such a striking girl in some time. His gaze took in her healthy color, small ears, and the enchanting mouth above the small dimple in her chin. Her teeth were white and even, unlike many southern belles with crooked teeth. A mass of golden hair fell from beneath her tam-o'-shanter hat. The independence of her speech, and a certain regal quality in her bearing, was a result of earning her own living with music. She sang in private homes for parties and taught music.

"Are you Irish, Mr. Porter?" Regina inquired.

"Aye," he replied. "A son of the auld sod."

She laughed softly. "You don't seem like a typical Irishman."

"I'm average, lass, but I've been luckier than many. I've heard all of the jokes about Irishmen. We're supposed to be dumb, unable to get from one point to another without the assistance of some fine Anglo-Saxon gentleman. My people live a hard life, miss, and those that come to this country still have a hard time. I've seen signs advertising for help that include the line: Irishmen need not apply! But we're human, colleen, and we bleed, cry and have feeling, 'tis true, like every other person in the world."

They talked for several minutes. Sean asked questions about Regina's past, which she answered easily and with good humor. Their conversation was interrupted when Silas Blackston came up and looked at Sean for a long moment.

"Is he bothering you, girlie?" Blackston asked Regina.

Her reply was icy. "I'll be the judge of that."

Saying good-bye to Sean, the girl smiled and went into the house.

Blackston took this moment to chide Sean for his supposed indiscretion.

"I expect you're one of those forward blokes?"

"Nay," replied Sean in a thick Irish brogue.

"Don't bother my stepdaughter."

Sean raised his eyebrows. "Was I bothering the lady?"

"She's not interested in the likes of you. My stepdaughter will marry a gentleman of quality."

Something flickered in Sean's steely gaze, a glint of anger that made Silas Blackston stop hectoring the Irishman. A cold chill prickled his skin with goosebumps. The icy glint in Sean's eyes keyed Blackston's nerves to the quick. The man could be dangerous if aroused, Blackston thought, and then launched into a good-humored attempt to pacify the stranger.

Now, Sean was asking, "I don't measure up to your standards of quality?"

Blackston introduced himself, extending his hand which Sean ignored.

"No offense meant, sir! This here stepdaughter is a pretty girl and all sorts are prowling about, if you know what I mean. My wife is a woman of society and comes from the Montrose family in South Carolina. Fine people, they are, with good breeding. Daughter's the same and I have high hopes of marrying her off to some successful businessman. Speaking of business, I might mention that I am associated with a large industrial corporation that's going to set the world on its ear. Why, I've come to this here town of Memphis seeing these folks ain't got a modern laundry like the United Family Laundry Association, Incorporated, puts out. Someday when you've got some time—do you have a card, sir?—I'd like to show you the plans for the slickest laundry plant in the world, we've put them into all the fancy eastern cities. We buy the best machinery that money can buy, for which we're never sorry, and do the family wash. Women don't have to use a washtub and board anymore, not with our laundry opening up in town. Stock is selling way above par right now. Ain't a man could ever ask for a better investment for his money. Why, you look like a nice person, so I've got a hundred shares of stock that I'll let—"

Sean consulted his watch. "Some other time, I'm afraid."

"You can get rich buying before we open our Memphis laundry. Folk'll be scrambling for this here stock when they see how much we're making every month."

"I'll bid you good day, sir," Sean said, heading out of the yard toward Jumbo, who sat on the back of the now empty wagon.

II

A half hour later, Sean and Jumbo sat at an outdoor table behind a tavern in Pinchgut. They were eating roast beef sandwiches and drinking beer. Sean had been unable to persuade the big Negro to come work on Belle Meade. Jumbo was still playing the role of the dumb darky, unsure that Sean was trustworthy.

"We've got too much work out there," Sean was saying. "We need someone to boss the slaves. Conrad feels you're a fair and honest man."

281

"I don't care much for steady work," Jumbo said, speaking in his regular voice.

Sean did not notice this departure from the man's accented speech.

"We're planning to add a wing to the house and you could oversee that, as well," Sean went on. "We need someone to watch the carpenters to make certain they do good work. Mrs. Conrad is building a library at Belle Meade. That woman must have purchased every book in London. Never saw so many different titles in my entire life."

Jumbo's interest increased with mention of books. He said, "Massa, I nuthin' but a dumb darky. What is hit to be a lie-bury thing?"

"A building to store books."

"Books that folks kin read?"

"Hell, man, that's what books are for."

"How many 'a dem suckers dis lady buy?"

"Including the encyclopedias and everything, at least a thousand."

"How many's that thar?"

"More than I could read in a lifetime," Sean answered. "Bless the lady's heart, but she has an insatiable craving for books. She'll never read them all because while she's reading the ones she's bought, she'll be buying others."

"Dat gwine be a heap 'a books."

"Yes, indeed."

"Darkies 'lowed to read 'em?"

Sean shrugged. "I think there's laws against it. You aren't allowed to educate slaves."

"What about a freed man, b'oss, who knows how to read?"

Sean caught Jumbo's change of speech. "Aye, and

all this while you've been sitting here funning with me. Right, bucko?"

"Didn't mean nuthin' by hit."

"Can you read?"

Jumbo grinned. "Tol'able well."

"And if we let you read all you want on Belle Meade?" Sean looked expectantly at the big black man.

"Wild horses couldn't keep me away."

"You like books that much?"

"I love to read. Most folks won't give books to a black man."

"I've heard that."

"They're afraid we'll learn something," Jumbo explained.

"Suzanne—that's the lady who buys books—won't mind your borrowing them."

"What if she changes her mind?"

"I know the lady. She's nice."

"Maybe we better go find out for sure," said Jumbo.

Sean was delighted to know Jumbo loved books. It was a powerful incentive to lure the black man to Belle Meade. Sean went inside the tavern, came back with a pitcher of beer. They sat at the outdoor table and Sean questioned Jumbo about his background. When the beer was gone the Irishman decided to sweeten the deal.

"Lad, you're living in that shanty behind Madame Rose's?"

"That's home."

Sean told Jumbo about the two plantations that made up Belle Meade. "Conrad got an offer he couldn't refuse," Sean explained, "so he bought the second place from a Mr. Burnside."

"That the planter named Burnside?"

"I suppose so."

"He was one of Miz Rose's best customers."

"Anyway, we own the place. I'm living there with a young man who's an inventor. I'd make it part of your working on Belle Meade to stay at the house with me and Rusty. You'd have a room of your own, wouldn't have to cook any meals, be a part of the family, so to speak."

"Folks might talk about that," said Jumbo.

Sean shrugged. "Let them."

"And the books?"

Sean laughed. "Thunderation! If there's not enough on Belle Meade I'll buy them for you."

"Miz Rose might get mad if I leave. She'll try to start trouble."

"You done anything bad?"

"No."

"Then *be* a free man. Come on out to Belle Meade. Give it a try. If it doesn't work out, you can always come back and work for this madam."

Jumbo thought about that. He didn't have anything to lose. And a library of books like his old master owned would be a pleasure to dig into.

"I might not be as good as you folks think," Jumbo ventured.

"With your education you're not helping yourself being the bouncer in a brothel."

Jumbo extended his hand. They shook.

"Welcome to Belle Meade," Sean said.

Jumbo smiled.

Chapter Twenty-Six

The events of the next few days were etched in Jumbo's memory. The morning after talking with Sean, Jumbo waited until Rose was having her first cup of coffee at noon. He went inside the house to explain he was going away. He did not mention going to work at Belle Meade, figuring that was none of the madam's business.

Rose threw a fit. She whined about ungrateful niggers, untrustworthy employees and colored the kitchen with her expressive profanity. She shrieked about Jumbo's intelligence, his sexual preferences, and his parentage. The big man let her ramble on. He stood there with a small bag containing his belongings and submitted to her screaming.

Next, Rose started crying. That triggered the other girls to gush tears. Rose blubbered that Jumbo was a good man, who would be missed by everyone. She recalled run-ins with customers in the past, the escapades that came with running a brothel. Those memories got everyone laughing and, on that note, Jumbo decided to depart.

Rose would not let him go until a collection was taken up. Half laughing and crying, the madam and her girls pressed eleven dollars on Jumbo in appreciation of his services.

After much hugging and kissing, and more tears, Jumbo said farewell. He slipped out the back door and walked over to the tavern. Sean was waiting there with his rig. Donald was perched on the driver's seat, brightly costumed in his gaudy uniform. Their first stop was a tailoring shop. Sean insisted on purchasing new trousers, shirts and a suit for the black man. Jumbo protested but not enough to dissuade the Irishman. After that, they went to a dry-goods store and purchased socks, boots and a hat. The Irishman seemed to enjoy outfitting his new companion.

They rode directly to Sean's mansion. Jumbo was given a room in the bedroom wing, a few doors down from Sean's room. He met Rusty, who stammered a welcome to the plantation. Dinner was served promptly at six that evening and, for the first time in his life, Jumbo sat with the white folks and ate. He enjoyed the experience because Sean and Rusty talked about the wharf, the problems in construction and design of the structure. They paused to brief Jumbo on their plans. These were men, Jumbo decided, who judged people on their abilities. Skin, coloration, parentage, or a man's past, the richness or thinness of a purse, did not matter. They judged by who you were now, not where you had been or what you'd done.

After dinner they had whiskeys in the library. Jumbo inspected the books and saw a hundred titles he wanted to read immediately. More so, he was impressed with the number of magazines and newspapers lying about. The library was a repository of good literature. Jumbo saw copies of Shakespeare's plays and decided to read them first. He'd heard of the English playwright, but had never read the man's work.

Jumbo read long into the night. He was a bit red-eyed the next morning when they rode over to meet John Conrad. Here, too, Jumbo was accepted as an equal. He was told to pick himself out a horse from the corral, using the animal as his own, or pick and choose until he found a suitable mount.

The first four days went fast. Jumbo rose each morning, left Belle Meade II, and breakfasted with John, Suzanne and the nurse. Over bacon and eggs, John and Jumbo discussed the plantation work to be done that day. Jumbo liked John's philosophy of farming. Next they rode out and inspected the work crews. A close bond developed between the two men. Jumbo was intelligent, articulate and not given to excitement. He gnawed at a problem until a solution came forth. On the fifth day, John stayed at the house to work on the plantation's account books. Jumbo did a creditable job as overseer.

The slaves took a strong liking to the new overseer. Jumbo was one of their own, which they felt was to their advantage. He did not play favorites, nor did he rant and rave when something went wrong. One afternoon, a slave got a wagon mired in a mudhole down by the creek. Jumbo rolled his eyes, said "Dat dere were a stu-pid thing to do!" Everyone laughed, then set forth and pulled the wagon to dry ground. Workers were not threatened. They were given their head, encouraged to think on their own, so long as their solutions were credible.

The slaves were confused by Jumbo's language. He talked to them in the language used by blacks in the South. He sounded more southern than most people.

But when the white folk came around, Jumbo's speech changed to clean and precise pronunciations.

This habit bothered Uncle Eli, the elderly slave. He hunted up Jumbo one afternoon, found the big man getting ready to ride up to the sawmill.

"Ah got's a question," Uncle Eli said, coming up.

"Hope Ah kin hep yuh, grandpaw," said Jumbo.

"It be 'bout the way yuh talk."

"Dere somethin' wrong with hit?"

"Yuh sound awright now. But when massa John come 'round yuh talk funny. Lak white folks."

Jumbo grinned. "Speck yuh might git addled."

"Oh, Ah is."

Jumbo told him about being educated by his master in Louisiana. He summed up, "So's Ah talks lak whoever Ah's with."

Uncle Eli pondered on that for a moment. "'Spect it hep to keep 'way trouble."

"Some white folks don' lak uppity niggers!"

"That be factual."

"Saved lots of messing 'round."

Uncle Eli asked, "Yuh read books?"

"Reckon so."

"Cipher any a'tall?"

"Real good at it."

"Yuh do an old darky a favor?"

"Reckon I might."

"Stop 'n see me sometime. Lak to have yuh count beans in my bag. Bin wonderin' if'in they's enough for m'freedom."

"Massa John watches that."

Uncle Eli nodded sagely. "Knows massa does hit. Lak to have yuh 'splain it t'me."

Jumbo slapped the old man on the shoulder. "Uncle, I'll stop the first chance I get."

"Reckon Ah'd owe yuh for hit."

"Never mind. You want to do it now?"

"Yas suh!"

They walked over to Uncle Eli's cabin. The old man dug deep into the corn husk mattress on his bed, came up with a small black bag. He poured the beans out on a small table. Jumbo went through an elaborate ritual counting the beans. He pulled a bean from the sack, studied it for a moment, then placed it in a row on the table. When the counting was done, Jumbo said, "Uncle, I'll check with Master John to see how many more beans you need."

Tears glistened in the old man's eyes.

"Ah's hopin' to be free 'fore Ah's daid."

"Uncle," Jumbo said, heartily, "you'll outlive all of us."

"Dyin' free means a lot t'me."

"To us all," Jumbo agreed.

He gave Uncle Eli a promise to check his bean bag account in the plantation books.

II

Design after design had gone down on paper, only to be discarded when Rusty Ward came up with a fresh idea. His drawings had been finalized, shown to the carpenters, and a crew was busy building the wharf. Rusty had developed the wharf like a drawbridge. It rested securely on the pilings most of the time, when the Mississippi river was at a normal flow. But if the water level rose a foot or two, and the river did fluctuate, the wharf came up and an iron block was added to each piling. These blocks were secured by iron fastenings. Regardless of the level of water, the wharf would be operable. During floods, men drew up the wharf and let the river run itself out.

In addition to building the wharf, Rusty spent time in Memphis selling the idea to various steamboat captains. Whenever he saw a boat headed upriver, the young man leaped in his carriage and rode into town. He met the captains, explained the project and promised a steady supply of wood. The rivermen were amused at first with Rusty's stammering words. But once the young man got over being tonguetied, he offered something that every steamboat needed. Rusty spent as little time as possible with the capatins, racing back to Belle Meade to check on the progress of the workmen.

One evening Rusty came home early to enjoy a meal with Sean and Jumbo. During the soup course, Rusty asked Jumbo about the cotton crop.

"Should be a record year," Jumbo ventured. "I'm not the greatest authority on cotton, but John says the plants are doing well. We'll have a good harvest."

"Another back-breaking season hauling the bales to Memphis," Sean said. "I wish there was some way to avoid that." Then, a sudden brightness quickened the Irishman's face. "Jesus, Rusty! We can use the wharf this year!"

"Why not?" Rusty shrugged.

"A lot closer than Memphis," Jumbo agreed.

"Miles closer," Rusty added.

"Think of all the planters south and east of Belle Meade," Sean exclaimed. "They'd love to load out of here."

"We could buy cotton at a Memphis price, even pay a little less because they don't have to haul to

Memphis."

Jumbo spoke up. "The big money's in buying here and selling in New Orleans."

"Big money?" Sean's eyebrows shot up.

"The brokers visit Madame Rose's all the time," Jumbo explained. "I eavesdropped on their conversations."

"We'd need boats." Sean was thinking about the possibilities.

"Brokers rent them," Jumbo said.

"Jehosaphat!" cried Rusty. "We're middlemen!"

"Take a lot of money," Jumbo cautioned.

"That's no problem," Sean said, remembering that Israel Goldman had just recently doubled the money on deposit in the London bank.

"Maybe the boats are all took up for this year." This came from Jumbo.

"All we have to do is ask around," Sean said.

They developed a plan during the meal. Sean would run Belle Meade II and take over Rusty's responsibilities overseeing the wharf. Rusty would be free to run into town and check things out. They would have to move fast, because if they went into the venture, a warehouse would need to be constructed before the harvest.

Sean looked over at Jumbo. "What about workers? Will we need more men?"

"Most of the buying and selling takes place after harvest," the big man replied. "That means we're able to use the same workers."

The Irishman jumped up from his chair, did a little jig around the room. "Opportunity! Opportunity!" he cried. "The ways of making money in this country are limitless!"

Regina Montrose ran an advertisement in the Memphis newspaper announcing her services as a music-and-voice teacher. Her first client was a gentleman who clerked in the bank. He willingly agreed to pay twenty-five cents each week for voice training, he had a good baritone. The second client was the mother of a young girl who wanted lessons on the piano. She would also pay twenty-five cents per week and, if the woman's husband agreed, both mother and daughter would be taught for forty cents a week.

The third person to come to the teacher's home was Mrs. Patricia Wells, who had her four children in tow. The three girls would be given piano lessons—an hour each week—for sixty cents for the group. Billy, who was reluctant about any form of music, would be taught alone. One half hour each week for ten cents. When these business matters were concluded, Regina looked over at Billy and asked, "What would be the best time for you, Billy?"

"Never," he grumbled.

"Young man!" Patricia Wells' voice was sharp. "You're going to learn to play the pianoforte."

Billy looked down at the carpet. "The gang's gonna laugh at me."

"Going to," his mother corrected.

"Fatty Johnson ain't taking lessons."

"Billy will be here any time you wish," said Patricia Wells, smiling at the teacher. "He may be reluctant, but you let me know if he doesn't show up."

"Every Monday afternoon at two o'clock," Regina Montrose said. She was scheduling her clients on

Monday, hoping to eventually fill up the entire week.

A discreet cough sounded close by. Everyone turned as Silas Blackston walked into the room with a hearty smile. "I see daughter's doing well in her little venture," he said.

"I'm busy," Regina snapped harshly.

"Always glad to make the acquaintance of folks in Memphis," Blackston extended his hand to Patricia Wells. "Glad to meet you, Mrs. . . ."

Regina Montrose did not make the introduction.

"I'm Mrs. Wells," Patricia said. They shook hands.

"Glad to meet you," said Blackston, stepping back to look at the children. "Daughter's been—"

"Stepdaughter," Regina imposed.

"My stepdaughter's a fine teacher," Blackston continued, unmindful of Regina's icy stare. "I've been too busy to meet many people in Memphis. The duller business gets these days the busier I get. Common sense, ain't it? Early bird gets the worm, as the saying goes. Come to think of it, most of the big deals I've put over have come from gittin' up early—gittin' at 'em—gettin' to the other fellow before he gets you. When you have as many irons in the fire as I have, Mrs. Wells, it doesn't pay to let 'em get cold. Nosiree! Why, ma'am, stepdaughter hasn't offered you a chair. Sit right down and make yourself to home."

"Don't you have an appointment?" said Regina, glaring at her stepfather.

"Never too busy to talk to your friends," Blackston said, smiling broadly at Patricia Wells. "Sit right down in that rocker, Mrs. Wells. Best on the market, it is, and Sid Witherall made that rocker. You know the Whiterall brothers up in Cincinnati, I suppose; slipped right into the furniture business as easy as slidin' off a log. That's one of Sid's patents. Spring-balanced rocker. The spring keeps her rockin'. Sid made a heap of money on that contrivance. Sells 'em like hot cakes. Just the thing for porch or shady nook, country or seaside, an ornament to the house and a joy to young and old. Well, say—when it comes to advertisin', Sid's about as cute as they make 'em, regular persuader in print. Though if I do say so, Mrs. Wells, he'll have to hop along some to beat the latest prospectus of the U.F.L.A. corporation. Cast your eyes on this, Mrs. Wells!" Blackston pulled a circular out of his pocket that was fresh from the printers. He handed it to Patricia Wells with a triumphant air.

"Thank you," she said, sitting in the rocker. She began to read the latest circular of the United Family Laundry Association, Inc. Blackston stood with his thumbs inside his vest.

"Pretty neat, ain't it?" he declared. "Gets the customer first crack out of the box with a good headline. That there line," he pointed to a large inset of type, "is mine. Thought it up myself. Don't sweat over a washtub. U.F.L.A. does the Sweating for you!" Yesiree, no need for women to break their backs washin' clothes with our laundry setting up in Memphis."

Regina Montrose came over and took the handbill from Mrs. Wells' hand. "I'm sure you're quite busy, Mr. Blackston. Mrs. Wells and I were just discussing the hours to teach the children."

"Some folks say I got an inborn talent at catching the public," Blackston went on. "Fact is, it does take a bit of knowin' just how to appeal to folks with a good deal."

"Mr. Blackston," said Regina in a venomous tone, "I'm sure you must be going."

"Yes, I've got things to do. A lot of important people to meet and settin' up the laundry ain't easy."

"Now, Mrs. Wells," Regina said, turning her back on the man. "I'll give your children a few lessons. Then we'll get together and you'll be informed if they have talent. I don't believe in taking money if a student doesn't have the talent for music."

"Reminds me of when I was a lad of sixteen out on the road and selling—"

"Good day, Mr. Blackston," Regina said, firmly.

"Oh, yeah!" He picked the circular out of Regina's hands. "Got things to do. Be seein' you again, I hope, Mrs. Wells. Daughter does a good job of teaching music. Real talented. I tell Regina that she must have inherited her musical talent from me."

"Inherited?" Patricia Wells looked surprised. "I thought she was your stepdaughter."

"Well, of course, she is. Not inherited her talent exactly—I being her stepfather and all, but anyway," he forced a hearty laugh, "music runs in my family. Never took a lesson in my life, but I can sure blow a cornet."

Seeing the angry glint in Regina's eyes, the promoter quickly departed.

"He seems to be a very good businessman," said Patricia.

Regina did not answer her. "Now we have Billy down for Monday afternoon, and the girls can come at three."

Billy watched the two women discuss his fate. He just hoped Fatty Johnson didn't hear about his piano lessons.

Chapter Twenty-Seven

The steamboat from Cincinnati turned sharply in mid-river, churning the muddy water, and wheeled toward the wharf in Memphis. Passengers lined the railings on each of the boat's three decks. They did not look around when the door of a cabin opened and an angular woman in a severely cut black dress walked on deck. She moved toward the railings with an intense, jerking motion, almost like a small child learning to walk. Her black hair was twisted into a tight bun beneath a plain black hat with a tiny veil. The angled thinness of her face made her head appear too small for her body. Her shoulders were small and without strength, seeming to sag into her body.

The most striking feature of this black-clad woman was her restless eyes. Dark and intense, they moved to and fro along the Memphis riverfront. She did not notice the warm sun reflected off the polished surface of the water, but her moving eyes caught sight of wagons and carriages moving through the town. She took in the unpainted shacks set along the river banks, the shantyboats moored below the steamboat wharf. Her mouth tightened grimly at the sight of a gang of small children playing in the mud along the river bank.

"I declare," said the woman to no one in particular, "I've never seen a town as filthy as this in my born days." Her voice was grating, like a fingernail drawn across a blackboard. "Memphis must be the dirtiest city along the river. All of this mud and filth right here on the riverfront where decent folks come off the boat to visit their city."

A drummer was standing next to the woman. He seemed startled by her remarks. "I beg your pardon," he said, tipping his hat. "Were you talking to me?"

"I said this was the dirtiest town I've ever seen," the woman said again.

"Memphis?" The salesman grinned genially. "It isn't all that bad. Just another growing little city. Good business town. Some of my best accounts are here."

The woman looked at the drummer. She asked, "You're a salesman?"

"Yes, ma'am."

"What lines do you handle?"

"Mmmmm, just merchandise of various sorts."

"You're shamed of your goods?"

"It isn't that, ma'am," replied the drummer. "Some folks don't take to my line of goods."

"Which are?"

"Wines and cordials." The drummer withdrew a card from his pocket. "I'm Marvin Smith. I represent Independent Wine and Cordial Company of New York."

"I knew you were a whiskey seller," said the woman in a stern voice. "You might as well mark

298

Memphis off your map, Mr. Smith. Whiskey selling is about to end in this town."

"Never happen," said Smith with a small chuckle.

"Living off the money of drunkards," declared the woman.

The drummer felt uneasy. "I don't believe I caught your name, Ma'am. . . ."

"I didn't give it," the woman said in a pleasant way. "But since you've asked I will give it. Does the name of Henrietta Pugh mean anything to you?"

"She's the old battle—the lady who tore up half the saloons in Cincinnati last month." Marvin Smith looked uncomfortable.

"I'm Henrietta Pugh," the angular woman declared. "I am here to declare war on the whiskey sellers in Memphis."

Marvin Smith made a low noise of rudeness under his breath. "You're really Mrs. Pugh?"

"I said so," she said sternly.

"Oh, Lord!" There was genuine fear in Smith's voice. "Why don't you go down river to Natchez? That Under-the-Hill crowd needs cleaning out."

Henrietta Pugh smiled thinly. "Your territory must end in Memphis, Mr. Smith."

"It does. When do you launch your crusade?"

"Tomorrow night we hold our first meeting."

Marvin Smith's mind was working furiously. If the saloon keepers did not know of Mrs. Pugh's arrival in town, he could still get some sizable orders. Marvin cleared his throat and bowed in Mrs. Pugh's direction. "Madam, I have heard of your exploits up and down the river. I will not sell to the saloonkeepers on this visit."

Mrs. Pugh smiled again. "There will be no future

visits, Mr. Smith. We intend to turn off the whiskey in Memphis. Lemonade and tonic will be the only drinks sold in this town. The Lord has blessed my work. I shall march forth and close the saloons! I shall . . ."

But Henrietta Pugh stopped in midsentence because her audience, Marvin Smith, was disappearing into his cabin. By the time, an hour later, when Henrietta Pugh was in a guest room at Patricia Wells' home, Marvin Smith was working hurriedly to visit his customers. Marvin was grateful that the saloon keepers knew nothing about Mrs. Pugh's visit. He did not mention the woman's arrival. They would know soon enough, and meanwhile Marvin was getting sizable orders for his spirits. He would be gone from town before trouble started, and with Henrietta Pugh in Memphis, it was sure to erupt.

Marvin's last call in Memphis was the Green Parrot Saloon on Main Street. The establishment was in a nice brick building containing stained glass windows that hid the interior from passers-by. The Green Parrot was one of the favorite drinking spots in Memphis. It featured a long mahogany bar, genial bartenders and a free lunch of classical variety. It was also the only spot in Memphis where Italian food was served. In a clean room in back of the bar, a man could purchase a spaghetti dinner, selected from a variety of sauces. The saloon also featured bread in long loaves personally baked by the proprietor each morning in an outdoor oven behind the building.

The owner of the saloon was a stocky Sicilian, Vito Santino. Vito claimed to be thirty-five, but was actually forty-two years old. He lied about his age to quell any talk about his young wife, Athena. She was a sixteen-year-old olive-skinned beauty from his home village in Sicily. Vito Santino had left the island when he was twenty-five years old and about to be drafted into the army. Stealing a small sailboat, he made his way to what is now the Italian peninsula. Once there, he was impressed into a prince's army and sent to fight another nobleman's army in a neighboring state. In those days, Italy was subdivided into numerous small principalities, whose chief business seemed to be waging war against their neighbors. Vito Santino's detachment raided a small town one night. During the fighting, Vito headed for the town's bank and carried away a great many gold coins, then he started walking north toward France. There he booked passage to the United States. Upon arrival in New Orleans, he discovered a sizable settlement of Italians there. He stayed in New Orleans for several years, learning the language and customs of the new country. When he decided to start his own business, he went to his employer, a restaurant owner. Vito was advised to go up the Mississippi and establish a business there.

"Vito," the restaurant owner said, "start a tavern. Americans are crazy for drink!"

And so Vito Santino, from the hills of Sicily, settled in Memphis. He brought with him a parrot with light green feathers. The bird became a fixture in the tavern, a novelty in the community. Vito prospered and saved up enough money to send to his home village for a wife. The elders in Sicily selected Athena to be his bride. Their selection pleased Vito, for Athena was a lovely girl with a pleasing personality. She was also a hard worker who enjoyed keeping house and cooking her husband's favorite dishes. Athena was always mindful of her husband, and that pleased Vito.

Marvin Smith liked Vito Santino, treasured the Sicilian's friendship. Marvin never left the saloon without eating a free spaghetti dinner. Vito purchased most of his liquor from Marvin, took the drummer's advice on what new lines to put in. Marvin did not betray his trust, so a strong bond developed between the two men. It was natural that Marvin would warn Vito about Henrietta Pugh's presence in Memphis.

The last customer left the tavern a few minutes past eleven that night. Vito led his friend into the back room and filled two plates with an enormous mound of spaghetti. He ladled out thick dippers of sauce and buttered slices of homemade bread. As they ate, Marvin Smith explained about Henrietta Pugh's visit to Memphis and the upcoming battle, the wets-versus-drys.

Vito did not understand. He jumped up from his chair, jerked his arm upward in salute.

"*Va! Va!* What kinda shit they got for saloon owners in Cincinnati? They are gutless Germans. Let a *basta* woman close down their businesses? Ridiculous! Someone should shoot this woman! She should be home having babies and pleasing her man!"

"She gets the Christian women behind her," said Marvin.

"A priest would never do that!" stormed Vito. "Protestants! They crazy! No man will allow some woman to tell him if he can have a drink of wine. Right, *paisano*?"

302

"She's trouble, Vito. My advice is to close down the saloon while she's in town." Marvin took a mouthful of spaghetti, washed it down with a sip of rich red wine.

Vito sat back down. "She carries a big stick?"

"She gets the women riled up."

"Women!" Vito twisted spaghetti on his fork. "Who can understand such illogical creatures? Now, my Athena, she is different. A beautiful child who is obedient and understand the husband is boss of the home."

"Henrietta Pugh is not like Athena, I'm sure of that."

"This Henrietta—she is *poco disoro!*—a pig of the devil!" Vito looked grim. "Come to stop honest men from doing business. Didn't I save money to bring Athena over here? Don't I send money back to my home village? Am I not saving to bring my brother here to help me? Plus my sisters and their husbands, aunts and uncles and cousins. I save to—"

Marvin laughed. "You'll have all of Sicily over here."

"Damned right! This is good place. No one tell Vito what to do. Until this *Signora* Pugh"—he pronounced the name as if spitting—"this whore of the devil comes to ruin my business. Who is she to do that? Why didn't those Germans in Cincinnati shoot her? For a few dollars, they could have someone drown her in the river like a kitten that scratches its master."

"We don't do things like that here," said Marvin. "Close your doors for a little while and let the storm blow out. Mrs. Pugh will be leaving town in a few days."

"What if it is weeks?"

Marvin didn't have an answer for that. He shrugged.

"I will starve," declared Vito. "Athena will waste away. There will be no food for our *bambinos*."

"Hell, Vito," Marvin Smith pointed out. "You don't have any babies."

"I'm trying! I'm trying!" grinned the Sicilian. "When they get here I want to have money to buy food for them."

They finished the meal, discussing business and Vito's order and avoiding any further mention of Henrietta Pugh. Vito doubled his usual order.

"If this she-devil's as you say," Vito declared, "a few owners may close their doors. I'll pick up their extra business."

"Pretty good reasoning," admitted Marvin.

Vito tapped his skull with the tip of a finger. "*Signora* Santino did not raise dummies."

"One more thing," Marvin said before they parted. "A couple of taverns were burned during the big shebang up in Cincinnati. I figure a couple lunatics got riled up and set them afire. Anyway, I'd keep someone around here while Mrs. Pugh's campaign is in full swing."

"Maybe she did it," said Vito, looking suspicious.

"She's a Christian woman who hates booze," Marvin said. "She's not an arsonist, for God's sake!"

"I'll watch out," Vito promised. "Take care of yourself."

"I will," the drummer answered. He waved and went out the door and walked through the night to his hotel.

Henrietta Pugh lay between the crisp clean sheets in the guest bedroom of Patricia Wells' home. Although she had retired early, wanting to get away from the woman's four loud children, Henrietta could not sleep. She always spent a restless night before a new campaign. She lay in the warm room and thought of Mr. Pugh, who had drunk himself to death.

They had been married a decent interval after the death of Henrietta's mother, who died from consumption one dark morning in February. Delbert Pugh was a strange, reclusive woodcarver who lived in a small house on the edge of town. His carvings were very creative, especially a cross commissioned for Henrietta's church. The huge wood cross contained intricate scenes from Christ's life.

Mr. Pugh was twenty-three years older than Henrietta and, living alone, she welcomed his attention. A year after her mother died, they bundled up in a sleigh one afternoon and rode to a neighboring town to be married. Unfortunately, Mr. Pugh brought along a bottle of gin. What with toasting their future, each other, and their love on the ride back, her husband was unable to consummate the marriage that night.

Henrietta was horrified to watch the hung-over groom have several gin-and-tonic cocktails for breakfast the following morning. Lunch was the same. From daylight to far into the night, Del Pugh drank. As Henrietta was independently wealthy from the estates of her parents, Mr. Pugh laid aside his chisels and mallet and got down to serious boozing.

So far as Henrietta knew, he never drew a sober breath in the thirty-nine months they lived together. He never touched her as a husband, gave no indication he loved her.

Delbert Pugh was buried in the church cemetery. The town's saloon keepers and whiskey sellers attended his funeral. Henrietta wondered if it was due to friendship, or to their loss of a valuable customer whose like would not soon be seen again. She went home after the funeral, determined that other women would not lose their loved ones to drink.

The night after the funeral she spent sitting before a large fire, thinking about the future. She had money, more than enough to last a lifetime. But her life was pointless, without purpose. So, Henrietta Pugh decided to punish the whiskey sellers. Her first efforts were feeble. She lectured around Connecticut on the evils of drink. Pledge cards were passed out, but she knew her work was not effective. Attendance at the lectures was seldom more than a dozen people: a handful of women, a couple of males who already practiced temperance.

She was horrified by the stories of families ruined because the wagearner was a drinker. Wives told of being beaten by drunken husbands, of houses set afire by enraged men. One woman displayed her left hand with a finger missing. She swore a drink-crazed brother had chopped off the finger to sell her wedding ring for drink. Some of these stories were true, others were the products of imaginative saloon keepers with a bent for practical jokes. The lady with the missing finger had been mangled by machinery in a mill. Her boy friend, a bartender, encouraged her to testify at Mrs. Pugh's meeting.

They regaled their customers with the story that same night.

Hatred for drink grew like a glowing red ball in Mrs. Pugh's mind. The breakthrough came in a small rural community in upstate New York. A particularly vile saloon keeper, so the ladies said, encouraged youngsters of seven and eight years of age to drink. The ladies were enraged, and decided to rid their community of this devil who pushed booze on small children. Leaving the church, they marched down the street and into the saloon.

Once inside, no one knew what to do. Henrietta saw their hesitation, the waning conviction in their expressions. With a shrill cry of anger, long pent up inside, Henrietta raised her parasol and jabbed the belly of the nearest drinker. He let out a loud yelp, then fled out the door as Henrietta rained blows down on his drink-reddened head. By now, the other ladies were also attacking the customers in the bar. These men were soon driven out of the establishment, so the ladies turned on the saloon owner. While a half-dozen women attacked the man with purses and parasols, the others drained his beer barrel, broke bottles of wine and whiskey.

The saloon keeper fled into the night, his bar in a shambles. A formal complaint was made to the sheriff, who refused to get involved.

"Bob, you've been getting away with murder in that saloon," the lawman said. "Been thinkin' about closin' you down myself. Now, why don't you just skedaddle out of the county and be happy those women didn't kill you."

After a few dozen saloons were wrecked in other towns, Henrietta Pugh was arrested for the willful destruction of property and assault and battery. Although the sheriff pleaded for her to make bail, Mrs. Pugh went to jail. She stayed there awaiting trial and, when she walked proudly into the courtroom, had become a national heroine. Newspapers in New York and Boston were looking for a new sensation, and they found it in the widow lady who loved to break up saloons. At her trial she was found not guilty.

When Henrietta returned home, she received letters from women all over the United States. They pleaded with her to visit their hometowns and drive out the whiskey sellers. Going through the mail, Henrietta Pugh knew she had found her true calling.

Now, lying in Mrs. Wells' bedroom, Henrietta began to drift off to sleep. Tomorrow would bring a long and arduous campaign.

Chapter Twenty-Eight

Caroline Spearman sat at the table in the dining room of her home. The girl was plainly bored as her gaze moved lazily about the room. She stared for a moment at the floral pattern of the wallpaper across the room. Then, she shifted her attention to the window. Outside, a summer shower had begun to fall. The big drops of rain came from a sky clouded with a purplish mist. She looked past the windows and saw the raindrops lying on the hollyhock blossoms that ran up the outside wall.

Caroline's mother, Margaret Spearman, was sitting across the table. She talked earnestly with Rev. Adam Matthews, a minister who had come knocking at the door of their home an hour ago. Reverend Matthews wore a plain black suit, thinly layered with dust from his journey to the Spearman plantation on his hoof-weary mule. His white shirt was grimed with dust and his thin black string tie now held a grayish coloration. The minister was a man of average height, normal build, with a thin mouth in his craggy face. He was clean-shaven and, to Caroline, held an expression of utmost serenity.

The minister was forty-two years old. For the last

twenty-two years, since graduating from Allegheny Seminary in Pennsylvania, he had been bringing the Gospel to the backwoods of the South. He had stood above the multitudes in the valleys of Kentucky during the Great Revival, listening to the other preachers and delivering sermons when their voices grew tired. Hundreds had accepted Jesus Christ as their savior during that great gathering.

Reverend Matthews had also traveled through the hills and valleys in remote areas to comfort dying men, baptize children, marry young men and women, and bring the Gospel to the sick and ailing. He had presided at more than four hundred funerals, bringing comfort to the grieving relatives and friends with his eloquent services.

He had ridden through long, dark wintry nights to reach a dying man's bedside, bundled in a great-coat, hopeful that his mule would not stumble in the darkness. He had sweltered in the summer's heat, thirsty for water, hungry for food, to comfort the parents of a child killed by snakebite. And his only companions through the years were his sure-footed mule, now old and tired, and his worn Bible bound in black leather.

The reverend's message was simple and direct: Accept Jesus Christ as your savior. The word had been delivered to rich and poor, young and old, and hundreds had accepted the invitation. Some slid back into sin, but a great number remembered the minister's serene acceptance of life and remained among the faithful.

Caroline rose from the table and went to the window. The rain was letting up. It seemed to her, standing beside the open window, that the morning was a perfect time to make love. The scent of roses, moist and heavy, wafted in and Caroline felt like crying. The thin violet light reminded her of the good times she'd had at school in Boston. Although there were strick rules enforced about men, Caroline had switched her attention to the other female students. She wished for a willing maiden to lie with this morning, or a man who was kind and gentle.

"Enjoying the view, ma'am?" inquired Reverend Matthews.

Caroline turned and smiled at the minister, an insincere gesture.

She didn't understand why her mother put up with such trashy people. Here was this man sitting in their dining room, acting like he was a man of God. Didn't her mother see that the visitor was as black as midnight? How could a nigger go around telling people how to live their lives? It wasn't right. And here was this darky talking to her mother about starting a church. She sat down and sipped at her tea, listening to their conversation.

Reverend Matthews was discussing his desire to settle down. "I've spent twenty-two years as a circuit rider, Mrs. Spearman. Now the Lord has called me to set up a church. Reverend Girard suggested that I visit with you and see if a church is needed here."

"It is definitely needed," Margaret Spearman agreed.

Reverend Matthews nodded solemnly. "Would my color be a problem?"

"I don't know," Margaret admitted. "Has it been until now?"

Matthews laughed. "I've seen a few surprised looks when I first visited someone. But once I started talk-

311

ing and ministering to them, the Holy Spirit erased their prejudice. A few years ago a man up in the mountains refused to have his baby baptized by what he termed 'a nigger.' I've prayed for him every day since then in hopes that he'll change his mind. The messenger is unimportant. The main point is the word. The Gospel. We must bring as many souls as we can to the altar."

Caroline asked, "You mean folks aren't taken back by you?"

"Of course not. They judge my message and my preaching, not the color of my skin or who I am."

"What do you think about slavery?" the girl demanded.

"Young lady—" Margaret blurted out in a shocked voice.

"No! No!" Reverend Matthews held up his jet black hand. "I've been questioned about slavery before, Mrs. Spearman. My feeling"—and he looked directly at Caroline—"is that slavery is wrong. The Bible speaks of slaves and how the slaves live a free life. I know that your father owns slaves. I would hope that someday he will be willing to free them. But I will not actively support any movement for that to come about. I am more concerned with preparing everyone for the moment when they are judged before our Creator."

"How'd you get to be a minister?" Caroline asked in a harsh voice, her tone indicating that such professions should be beyond the mental ability of blacks.

"I studied at a seminary. If you would like, I'll go out to my saddlebag and bring in my certificate of graduation and my ordination papers."

"You must excuse my daughter," Margaret Spearman said to the minister. "She's been raised as a southerner."

"Well," Caroline sniffed. "I never thought the day would come when a nigger would sit at this table."

"Caroline!" Her mother's voice was sharp with anger.

"Lord! What's Daddy going to think if he walks in? He'll throw a fit if he finds this darky sitting here."

"Your father knows Reverend Matthews," Margaret told her daughter, "and he is aware of the good work Reverend Matthews has done."

"Well," said Caroline in a pouting tone, "I don't like it."

Reverend Matthews coughed. "Perhaps I'd better be going, Mrs. Spearman. I don't want to cause trouble. I've—"

"Caroline is going to her room." Margaret threw a venomous glance at her daughter. "Aren't you, dear?"

Caroline sighed. "That's better than sitting here having tea with niggers."

Just then, Albert Spearman came in from the fields. He stopped in the doorway, shaking the rain from his drenched shirt. His eyes took in the scene and his expression brightened.

Caroline jumped up from her chair. She ran across the room to her father.

"Daddy!" Her voice was fearful. "Mama's been making me sit here with a nigger—right here in the dining room."

Albert Spearman appeared not to hear his daughter's complaint. He swept past the girl, thrusting out his hand toward Matthews.

"Adam, you old scoundrel!" cried Albert Spearman. "Dang good to see you. I should have known you'd be here when I saw that flop-eared old mule tied up outside. When're you going to retire that poor animal and let me give you a nice young one?"

"Good to see you, Mr. Spearman." Adam Matthews stood up and shook hands with the plantation owner. "Just don't be downgrading my mule. He's been a faithful servant of the Lord for longer than either of use can remember.

"Adam's thinking about setting up a church here," Margaret said, a pleased smile on her face.

Albert Spearman's expression was solemn. "You mean it, Adam?"

"Just testing the water, sir."

"Daddy! He's a nigger!" Caroline said, pointing out an obvious fact.

Albert Spearman looked at his daughter. He spoke in a stern voice. "If you ever use that word along with Adam's name I'll punish you, young lady," the planter declared. "Adam Matthews saved my life many years ago."

"It wasn't quite that way," said the black man.

"You could have made it to shore a lot easier without me."

"I just did what any person would do."

"Most would have left me to drown," said Spearman, who first met Matthews one night when a steamboat had caught fire north of Natchez. The captain and crew had abandoned the burning vessel and gone ashore in the few lifeboats carried aboard the craft. Albert Spearman had been sleeping in a top-floor cabin when the cries of the other

314

passengers awakened him. He left his room to find the lower decks a blazing inferno. His only hope for escape was to make a running dive into the dark river. His head struck something—he never knew what—during that dive. He did not recall hitting the water, but came to a few minutes later, being pulled to shore. Adam Matthews had been burned on the arm, but he kept Spearman's head above water until they reached a sandbar. Spearman did not know his rescuer was a black man until the first rosy light of dawn. He was forever grateful to him, figuring the black minister had given him every moment of life since that moment when he'd hit his head against something hard diving from the boat.

Albert Spearman did not mention the details of this accident to Caroline. In fact, he ignored the girl, and no one seemed to notice when she left the dining room and went upstairs. Her room was hot and humid from the rain. Caroline removed her garments and, running her hands over her body, struck a nude pose before a full-length mirror. Her fingers touched the tufts of hair at the apex of her legs. She began to softly strum lightly against that secret, sensitive spot.

Lightly.

As soft as the caress of a butterfly's wing.

The lightness of a hummingbird's tongue.

She stood there as a wave of pleasure surged through her body, and her mind flashed with visions of the nights spent with Frieda, her favorite at Miss Markson's school in Boston. Frieda was a plain-faced girl from Maine, but she had the most voluptuous body Caroline had ever touched. She had lured Frieda down a dark hall and up the attic stairs one night. The girl had not drawn back or protested when Caroline kissed her boldly on the mouth. Surprisingly, Caroline felt Frieda respond to her kiss. Her heart quickened with Frieda, a Teutonic wench according to Caroline's views, dropped to her knees and lightly touched her wet tongue to Caroline's throbbing hips.

As she brought herself to a climax, the vision of Frieda's ministrations remained in Caroline's mind. She picked up her dress, petticoat and undergarments and put them away. Then, still nude, she laid down on the bed to nap.

Caroline, look out for yourself, she thought, and find someone to do it with. Doing it by yourself is not as good as having someone there before you. Her father was distant and unwilling to resume their affair. The available men in the neighborhood were stand-offish. She thought of going into Memphis and picking up a man. But talk would get started if she followed that source. Courage, she told herself, courage! She didn't dare get involved with another slave as she did with Sam. Besides, Daddy frowned on having any male servants in the house. And those field hands were so crude, smelling like animals and never taking a bath, wearing one outfit of clothes the whole summer.

Some little idea within Caroline's mind began to grow. While most of the women were as smelly as the men, a couple of pretty young maidens with dusky skin were living in the slave quarters. There was Olivia, that tall and high-hipped bitch who wiggled so seductively when she crossed the yard. And that other one, she didn't know her name, but she was endowed with a magnificent buxom body.

Either of the two would do.

She would ask Daddy to let one of the girls become her personal maid.

A very personal maid.

II

Jumbo was in the study at Belle Meade watching John figure up Uncle Eli's freedom account. Jumbo was sitting in a comfortable chair beside the desk, facing the master of Belle Meade.

John closed the books. "Another thirty months and Uncle Eli will be freed.

"Too long," Jumbo responded.

"Why is that?"

"Uncle Eli's getting old. He's also like most of the darkies here. He doesn't fully understand the arithmatic involved in collecting a bean each month."

"I've explained it several times."

"I'm sure that's true," Jumbo said. "But you're a man who understands numbers. These people don't have any comprehension of mathematics. They can maybe count to five or ten, using their fingers. But that's as far as they can go. After, say, ten they get lost. That's causing a bit of a problem in attitude. They know they've got something, but they can't really understand what it means. Worse, a lot of these people haven't been in this country for more than a year or two. They were kidnapped from their homes and brought here, and they've lost all hope. So what I'm suggesting is that we use Uncle Eli as an example. Hell, he's an old man anyway and about all he does is carry around the keys to the smokehouse and storerooms — and I figure you gave him that job to have something to do."

"True," John agreed. "But also because he's an honest man who wouldn't let anyone raid the supply rooms."

"If you give Uncle Eli his freedom, then the other folks will know they can get there someday."

"Sort of an example?"

"Right," said Jumbo. "I'm even suggesting a little ceremony, with everyone called out to witness you handing Uncle Eli his papers. Makes a big-to-do about it. Maybe even have a little celebration with extra food, a barbecue or something like that. Make it a big deal, so's the rest of them get the idea they can someday stand up there and get that sheet of paper spelling out their freedom."

John was thoughtful for a moment. "Okey," he said agreeably. "I'm busy, so you handle the details."

"I'll get things started right away. Figure we'll give Uncle Eli his freedom papers and also titlement to maybe an acre of land back up in the mountains. I'll have a little cabin built there so Uncle Eli becomes a symbol to the rest. They can look up on the mountain and see the old man sitting there in his rocking chair, taking things easy."

"Do whatever you want," said John, turning back to his books.

On his way out of the house, Jumbo met Suzanne in the dining room. She was feeding one of the babies. Suzanne looked up and smiled at the big man.

"How are you doing with Shakespeare?" she asked.

"Tough reading," he replied.

"What's the problem?"

"I don't understand some of the words he uses."

She nodded. "He was writing in the language of his time. Have you asked Sean for help?"

"He's been too busy."

"Maybe you should back off and try something else."

Jumbo nodded. "Except I don't know where to begin."

"Have you read anything by Sir Walter Scott?"

"No, ma'am."

"The language is still a bit rough," Suzanne said, "but the stories are fantastic. Here, sit down and feed the baby and I'll give you a couple novels to start on."

Jumbo took the tiny sterling silver spoon offered by Suzanne, then sat down and dipped into the soup. The baby was propped up in a small wooden highchair. The infant girgled as Jumbo spooned in the soup.

"Kind of a nice chile," Jumbo said. "Got a nice mama and papa, too. Reckon you got the world on a downhill pull. Be master of Belle Meade, 'cepting maybe you're the girl chile."

He fed the baby until Suzanne returned with two of Scott's novels. She laid the leather-bound volumes on the table, then took the spoon and resumed the feeding.

Jumbo flipped the pages of the books.

"You'll love *Ivanhoe*," Suzanne told him. "That's one of his most exciting books. I've also given you *Kenilworth*, another of his best. If you have any trouble with words, or the language, make a list and I'll help you."

"I'd appreciate it," Jumbo said with sincerity.

"Have you had lunch?"

"I planned on skipping it."

"Join us," she invited. "John and I will be eating as soon as the baby's done here. I've got some newspapers to give you from London."

Jumbo looked pleased. "All the way from England."

"I subscribed to the *News of the World* and the *London Times* while I was there," she told him. "They're both interesting reading."

Jumbo smiled. "Ma'am, I'd work a week for a copy of a newspaper from England. And all I have to do is sit down and eat? I'm going to pinch myself to make sure I haven't died and gone to Heaven."

Chapter Twenty-One

"Ladies! I have told you of how our work has dried up hundreds of saloons in scores of cummunities," said Henrietta Pugh, standing before the crowd in the Baptist church. "We have saved thousands of men from a drunkard's grave. Now, I'd like to pause at this time and listen to your testimony on the problems of drink in Memphis. Perhaps liquor is not a problem here."

"No! No!" the women cried.

"The men are crazed with it," shouted a large woman from the rear of the church.

A dozen hands went up, some waving eagerly, to indicate they would give testimony on drink-drenched Memphis, and Henrietta pointed to a smartly dressed young woman sitting in a pew near the front. "Would you like to talk?"

The young woman reddened slightly as she stood up. "My name is Gladys Titus. My father died last year. He drank himself to death. During the last days, when he couldn't move from his bed, he cried for whiskey day and night. He was seventy-two years old and wept like a baby."

This wasn't quite what Henrietta Pugh had in

mind. Seventy-year-old men were a rarity among the population. Someone might say that the old gentleman had preserved himself in alcohol as a way to live a long and healthy life.

Next, Henrietta indicated that a shabbily dressed woman should rise and speak.

"I ain't an edjicated woman," the middle-aged lady said in a tight, nervous voice. "But I knows what drinkin's done to my mister. He usta be real good at pervidin'. Always pervided for me 'n the chil'lun. But he took to goin' into saloons and gettin' hisself drunk. Weren't no time a-tall till the mister stopped workin' and took up drinkin'. He don't do much perviding noways now. Pervidin's been left to me and the eight kids we got. If it wasn't for the oldest, that's Ted, workin' at the brickyard we wouldn't get no pervidin' a-tall. The mister lays 'round the cabin smokin' 'n drinkin' always."

"Close the saloons!" someone cried.

The middle-aged woman sat down. Others got up to speak and told of homes ruined, marriages shattered and children starving because of drunkenness. After the tenth woman had spoken, Henrietta Pugh raised her hands for silence.

"Are we going to let them do this?" she cried.

"No! No!" roared the crowd.

"What'll we do to stop it?"

"Close the saloons!" came the reply.

"When do we close the saloons?"

"Today," came the roar.

Henrietta's jaw came forward. "Ladies, let us march!"

"Down with demon rum!" a woman yelled, standing up and opening the doors of the church.

Reverend Michael White, an ordained minister of the forty-gallon variety, sat off to the side and watched the women march from the church. He had counted the crowd, judged there were at least 125 women going forth to battle the saloon keepers. Their eyes blazed with the zealous glint of the true believer. When the last woman had left the church building, Reverend White walked outside and gazed at the scene.

The minister moved swiftly to the side of the churchyard. He wanted to remain as inconspicuous as possible. Although his church had been used for the rally, Reverend White did not intend to march with the women. He was thoroughly shaken by the presence of Henrietta Pugh and her followers. God help the whiskey sellers, he thought. There were women in shabby calico dresses, or worn black skirts and patched blouses. Some women wore rough shoes. Others were garbed in fashionable garments, wearing expensive hats and the latest style of shoe. Henrietta was handing out sticks about a yard in length, gnarled wood to be used to destroy the saloons. A number of women had brought their parasols, dangerous weapons tipped with sharp points. Over near the street, a large woman began to pound a large bass drum.

"Sisters! Sisters!" cried Henrietta Pugh. "Line up for the march!"

Across the street, a discreet distance from the churchyard, about thirty men had gathered to watch the procession. Among them was Bull Frazer, sheriff of Shelby County, who viewed the women with an unkind gaze. The sheriff had been bothered all morning by saloon owners who, to a man, demanded protection by the law. Saloon keepers were influential men at election time, often voting their customers in a bloc. This fact was mentioned numerous times during Frazer's conversation that morning. Bull Frazer had assurred the saloon owners that no woman from out of town would be allowed to cause trouble. He reckoned maybe a half-dozen men would show up for Mrs. Pugh's rally. "Just go about your business, boys," the sheriff had told everyone. Now, hearing the drum pounding a call to arms, watching the women line up and shoulder their clubs, Bull decided to act before someone was injured.

He elbowed his deputy, Roger Regenmeyer, in the side.

"Rog, go over there and tell those women to go home," the bull said.

Roger gulped. "Sheriff, look—'

"Just go explain that the law maintains order in Memphis."

"Bull, I appreciate everything you've—"

"Go!" roared the sheriff.

"They'll hit me with them sticks."

Bull glared at the deputy. "You 'fraid of a couple old biddies? You're supposed—"

"Yeah, Bull, I'm afraid of them. I do most things you ask. But I ain't going near that bunch."

A bystander chimed in. "Roger, you got good sense."

"I'm the judge of that," snapped Bull.

The bystander chuckled. "If the women are harmless, sheriff, why don't you go quiet 'em down?"

Bull looked around and saw a number of faces with smirking grins. He sighed. There was nothing for him to do except walk over and read the law to that bunch of hopped-up women. He was worried about what course of action they might take. Nonetheless, he swallowed hard and headed across the street as the men watched him go.

A man told Roger, "Son, you got a good head on you."

"My mother didn't raise no cowards," Roger replied, "but she didn't bring up any fools, either."

"I got a buck says the sheriff gets clobbered."

Roger looked aghast. "They wouldn't dare."

"Want to bet?"

Roger hedged. "Well, maybe not. Never know what a bunch of women will do."

What the women did was gather around when the sheriff came up. Bull found himself surrounded by grim-faced women who looked like they were intent on mayhem.

"What're you doing here?" demanded a woman, brandishing her stick at the sheriff.

"I come to talk to this woman who's trying to start trouble," Bull said gruffly.

"An elderly woman with gray hair shook her stick in Bull's direction. She cried, "You leave Mrs. Pugh alone, sheriff. Else you'll have to contend with us."

"Now, ladies," Bull smiled. "You can't go around chopping up saloons. That's against the law."

The grandmaw type was back. "*You* won't close 'em down!"

"They ain't breakin the law."

"They're ruinin' homes," shouted another woman. She seemed downright hostile from Bull's vantage point. "Whiskey sellin's endin'."

Bull was decidedly uncomfortable. The ladies

behind him were gently hitting his back with their sticks. Not wild swinging blows, just a steady jabbing tattoo that made a man want to leave.

"Where's this out-of-town agitator?" Bull demanded. "She's the one I want to see."

"Mrs. Pugh is busy." This from Grandmaw. "And you better make tracks, sheriff, afore you get hurt."

"Now, granny," bull began. "I got—"

"I ain't your granny," yelled the woman. She jabbed Bull's big belly with her stick.

"Ouch!"

"Want more?" The woman's eyes blazed with a fantastic glimmer.

Another woman jabbed Bull in the side.

He spun. "Quit that! Damnation! You ladies got no respect for law and order."

Henrietta Pugh came through the crowd and smiled at Sheriff Frazer.

"I'm the organizer of this group," she said.

"Whyn't you call off your biddies 'fore they peck me to death with these sticks?" Bull asked.

"Ladies, be calm! Our quarrel isn't with the sheriff."

"I ain't no biddy," declared the grandmotherly type. "He's got a big mouth and a small brain!"

"Yeah!" cried another lady.

"I ain't standing for no busting up of saloons," Bull told Mrs. Pugh.

"Then close them down."

"I can't."

"Why not? They're ruining lives."

"The law says they can sell whatever people want to buy."

Mrs. Pugh smiled brightly. "Then we have no

choice but to destroy the saloons before they destroy our husbands, sons and daughters."

Bull growled, "It ain't like that at all."

Sheriff, we have a march to do," said Henrietta. "I will stand here and guarantee your safety to leave the churchyard. I'll count to three. After that, you're on your own."

Bull glanced around into the sea of hostile feminine faces. He gulped.

"See you around," he said, moving through the crowd.

"Coward!" cried the elderly woman.

"Come back and fight," yelled another zealot.

"Watch the sheriff run!" shrilled a young woman, who waved her club above her long blond hair.

"The bull's met his match," cat-called a middle-aged marcher.

Bull Frazer did not hesitate leaving the churchyard; he walked swiftly back to the group of bystanders.

"Great Godfry," exclaimed one of the male onlookers. "You're lucky to get away with your skin!"

"Dang fantastic!" said the sheriff.

"I was willing to bet against you, sheriff," said another man. "But Roger wouldn't take the bet."

"Lunatics!" roared Bull, glancing across the road to the churchyard. "They ought to be locked up!"

Someone snickered. "Ain't that your job, sheriff."

Bull sighed. "Roger, you hurry downtown and tell everyone to close their saloons. Tell them there's at least a hundred crazy women coming down to tear their places apart. You got that?"

"What if they won't close, Bull?" Roger asked.

"Then I sure ain't responsible when this mob gets

there. Now, skedaddle and spread the word."

Roger and a couple other men took off in a fast trot.

"Damnation!" Bull Frazer watched the women line up for their march, listened unhappily to the boom-boom of their drum. From some place, two women came forth with a banner on two lofty poles that read: DRY UP MEMPHIS! DOWN WITH DEMON RUM!"

A bystander said, an admiring edge in his voice, "Lordy, that Mrs. Pugh must be hell on high heels!"

"See how they chased the bull off their pasture?" giggled another man.

Bull snapped, "Next smart-mouthed remark and I'm arresting the guy."

"C'mon, sheriff, we're just joking," came the reply.

"Better'n that," Bull said, "I'll deputize the bunch of you and send you over there to stop them!"

Everyone went silent.

II

The women paraded into the business district of Memphis. The drummer, a thirty-eight-year-old mother of two children named Cassie Royalton, pounded an ear-shattering tattoo on the big bass drum. Cassie was followed by two women carrying the banner. Behind them came the main procession of women marching five abreast through the dusty street. By the time they came to Main Street, their noise had attracted a hundred or so curious onlookers. They marched to the side of the women, or well behind them. Running in and out of this crowd were a large number of yelping dogs, gangs of whooping children and a white-bearded old man astride a small gray mule. Their first stop was in front of the City Tavern, a drinking spot favored by Davy Crockett during his visits to Memphis. The proprietor had locked and barred the doors, after shooing his customers out into the street. He refused to step forth and do battle with Henrietta Pugh and her ladies.

They marched on to the Mississippi Club, a drinking spot attracting a clientel of businessmen. The bartender had wisely locked the door, but had forgotten to pull the shades. When the women caught sight of the barkeep and a half-dozen customers inside the tavern, they hooted for the men to show themselves. The bartender, an Irishman with a handlebar mustache, was named Tom Clancy. The Irish have never been famous for their patience, and Clancy was no exception. Unwisely, he plodded up to the front window, wiped his hands on his big white apron and delivered a signal recognized throughout the world. He brought up his hand, middle finger held high.

That was Clancy's first mistake of the day.

His second error was to grin widely, waggle his head and deliver a finger to the ladies a second time.

Clancy was considering a third salute to the women outside his saloon when the glass shattered on the front door. All geniality left the bartender's face. He was paralyzed and completely speechless as a half-dozen women came charging through the front door. They held their skirts up, stepping through the door frame, walked over the broken glass and came to Tom Clancy with their sticks held high. Their faces were grim and, still not moving, Clancy recognized the serious nature of the incident. He took off for the back door with utmost speed.

The ladies turned their attention to a couple of men sitting at the bar. They were small merchants who had dropped in for their morning beer. Both men were serious drinkers and fantastic chess players. Dan Adkins was fifty-two years old, a saddlemaker with impaired hearing. His drinking companion and chess opponent each morning in the Mississippi Club was the town's furniture maker, Abner Lambert.

Neither man trusted his opponent because, as most patrons of the club knew, each was willing to cheat to win a game. Once a game started, neither man would remove his gaze from the board, for to do so might mean their opponent would move a crucial piece and win the game. So Dan Adkins and Abner Lambert did not look up when the glass door was shattered. They heard Clancy go pounding toward the back door, reckoning the Irishman was probably having another fit.

But now Cassie Royalton marched into the tavern with her bass drum. She kept up a steady beat, the noise reverberating off the tavern walls.

Abner Lambert kept staring down at the board. He yelled, "Tarnation, woman! Ain't you got someplace else to make noise?"

"Give up the devil's brew!" cried Cassie.

"What'd she say, Abner?" inquired Dan Adkins.

"Give up the Devil's brew."

"The devil who?" Adkins cupped his ear with his hand.

Abner roared, "They want us to quit drinking."

Dan asked, "Are they crazy?"

"Danged if I know, partner."

The grandmotherly type came forward, ready to do battle. "You two buzzards get out of here! Go home to your wives and children."

"What's she screeching about?" asked Dan Adkins.

Abner Lambert yelled his reply: "Says you're to go home to your wife and kids."

"That settles it," said Dan Adkins, raising his gaze from the chess board. "A man can't play chess in a room full of crazy women. Whoinhell are they, Abner?"

"Temperance women."

"We're fixing to clean your plows!" cried the grandmother.

"Whatinhell are them sticks for?" asked Dan Adkins, getting up from his chair.

"To beat some sense into your heads," cried the grandmother.

Dan Adkins glanced around the room. There were a whole lot of women with hostile faces carrying sticks.

"Abner, I think we'd better find the bartender," Dan said, edging toward the back of the room.

While the two men beat a retreat, a couple of zealous women broke the bottles on the bar. They found a mallet and knocked open two barrels of beer. The grandmother took a piece of soap and wrote across the dark mirror: *Drink stinks!* Henrietta Pugh walked through the room, as the voices of the women chattered incessantly about their victory. The feverish excitement of the campaign exhilarated her. She didn't enjoy smashing up private property. After all, some pour soul—misguided as he might be—had paid good money for the liquor and beer draining out onto the floor. But each campaign needed these actions, so that the other whiskey sellers would also close down their businesses.

Up and down Main Street, and in Pinchgut, as well, the news about Tom Clancy's retreat had spread faster than any scandalous tale. The bravest of the tavern owners decided to close their doors and open another day. They would wait until Bull Frazer got law and order back. In one morning, Henrietta Pugh made Memphis go dry.

No one realized she intended the town to remain dry.

Chapter Thirty

No one in Memphis was ever certain how it came to pass that Charlotte Ann Peabody, of the rich and proper Peabody's of New York, came to live in northern Mississippi. Even Charlotte Ann Peabody was unsure about the events leading to her departure from the Peabody mansion. She appeared for work one morning at the offices of her fathers' shipping lines. By noon, Charlotte was aboard a ship bound for Philadelphia, then overland to Pittsburgh and down the river to Memphis. Charlotte had been given a letter of credit from her father's bank and a newspaper containing a want ad for a teacher on a Mississippi plantation.

The one man who could solve the mystery was Harold Musgrave Peabody. He had schemed for several weeks to send his daughter packing. Harold Peabody was not a bad parent. It was simply that Charlotte Ann was driving her father toward a nervous breakdown. The elder Peabody had considered sending Charlotte to China, or some other god-awful place on the other side of the world. But Deborah Peabody, Charlotte's mother, plainly would not stand for her daughter to be exiled to a foreign land. That was going too far, she claimed. Harold Peabody had considered sending Charlotte to England, had even consulted one of his ship's captains about her passage. The mariner acted as if his employer had thrown a snake on the floor.

The captain asked, "May I speak honestly, sir?"

"To be sure," said Mr. Peabody.

"She would drive my crew into mutiny, sir. They might even make her walk the plank.

"You men know about it?" Peabody was surprised.

"It isn't your fault, sir. And I'm sure your missus isn't to be blamed."

"She's our burden in this vale of tears."

"I'm sure she is, sir."

After that conversation, Harold forgot about sending Charlotte to another land. Although, at the oddest moments, his mind sometimes conjured up a vision of Charlotte walking a plank, and he usually felt better one of those visions. Even during her childhood, Charlotte had been different from other girls. Most children wanted to get away from their parents and play with each other; they enjoyed running about outdoors. But Charlotte stayed in the house and read. Books became a magical door to strange and unusual worlds, so she read everything in the family library, devoured the books in the New York subscription library, and demanded an allowance to buy more books.

Deborah Peabody was pleased, but Harold was uncertain about such activities. Women should concern themselves with dolls as children. They should be a gracious host and helpmate for the remainder of their lives. At best, they were flighty creatures with little intelligence or knowledge of how the world really ran, and it took the steady hand of a man to check their unstable nature. Charlotte was always talking about women being as good as men, which to Harold Peabody was pure poppycock. Worse, she always succeeded in bringing up feminism during dinner. The result was that Harold Peabody suffered from indigestion.

Charlotte swept through prep school in a couple of years, and then she was to attend a small religious college in Maryland at her father's insistance. She was fifteen when her parents left her on campus, thanked their guardian angel and headed home. They returned four months later to get her, for she had been dismissed from college.

"Her age may be a factor," said the dean to the troubled parents. "The girl is frightfully young to be enrolled here. But"—he paused and his eyes took on a vacant glaze—"Charlotte is mentally equipped to be a perfect student. However, she's somewhat inattentive in class and often doesn't show up for several days, which complicates matters. Her test grades are excellent—that is, of course, when she remembers to show up for a test. Most times, your daughter is off wandering about the campus on some personal studies of some sort. Or else she is holed up in the library reading everything in sight. The problem is, and I've talked to her several times about the matter, Charlotte refuses to discipline herself to the courses required for a degree from this institution. As you know more than us"—the dean coughed delicately behind his hand—"she has a problem relating to people. I thought at first this was a matter of two minds clashing. That was when her first roommate asked to be transferred. Actually she didn't ask, she demanded it. The second roommate lasted ten days and said she'd leave school before she'd share a room with Charlotte. Since then, she's been living alone and, quite frankly, seems none the worse for it."

Charlotte was taken home. Against her father's strong objections, the girl decided to enter business. It was not proper for a young girl to work in an office. Charlotte insisted, and one morning accompanied her father to the office. By age sixteen, she had grasped the intricate principles of managing the family's far-flung empire. The girl had to have an unusual memory, Harold Peabody decided. Once she read a book, or examined a shipping bill, it seemed to be embedded forever in her mind.

Two years passed. Charlotte was now eighteen years old, not beautiful by any measure, but certainly an attractive girl with neat habits. In the two years she'd worked in the office, the clerks had left in droves. Harold Musgrave Peabody was always advertising for new clerks. Some came to work, but stayed only a short while. Others talked a few minutes with Charlotte and departed without inquiring about working hours or salary.

A typical incident took place one afternoon when Harold Peabody was interviewing young men to fill a vacancy on the clerk's staff. Charlotte happened to wander into her father's office. Her work was done for the day and she planned to test her memory by listing every known species of butterfly—first by their Latin biological names, and then by their popular ones. She listened to her father question the young applicant.

"Can you write a clear and legible hand?" asked

Harold Peabody.

"I think so, sir," the young man said.

"Care to write something for me?"

"Certainly, sir."

Harold looked up at Charlotte. "Honey, get a sheet of paper for this lad to write on."

Instead of heading to the stationery drawer, Charlotte came over and sat down beside the young man.

"Did you know," she said, "that the word *paper* is derived from the Egyptian *papyrus*?"

The clerk looked startled. "Ayuh . . . no, I didn't."

Charlotte went on. "Papyrus is a reed that grows in the swamps around Egypt. A big reed that stands maybe eighteen to twenty feet at maturity. It's really quite a useful plant—or at least the Egyptians turned it into that. The lower part—I suppose you'd call that the bulb—is eaten and considered a delicacy by the Egyptians. The inside of the plant is fibrous. It is used to make sails, footwear, baskets, boats, rope, string and, of course, paper. The plant was so useful to the ancient Egyptian economy that the reed was declared the property of the pharaohs. That's understandable because the word *papyrus* in ancient Egyptian—and maybe even today—means *royal*."

"No, I didn't know all that," declared the young man.

"Now the process for making papyrus into paper was a secret for thousands of years," Charlotte continued. "Imagine! The Egyptians were writing their characters on papyrus as far back as thirty-five hundred B.C. They held the secret that long, selling paper all over the world. At least the world as they knew about it. But over in Asia Minor, around the first or second century B.C., King Ptolemy was mad at the Egyptians. Every time the king got a few pounds of gold in the royal treasury, he had to spend it to buy paper from the Egyptians. So he launched a research program and came up with parchment. Parchment, as you know, comes from animal skins. It lasted longer than papyrus, didn't yellow with time, and was available anywhere you found an animal with a skin to process. Of course, it was expensive. About the same time over in China the first true paper was—"

Harold Peabody interrupted. "Charlotte, our guest is undoubtedly a busy man. We can discuss this later."

"I'll be finished in a moment," Charlotte said. "I'm just getting to the interesting part. The Chinese invented the first true paper around one hundred A.D. Imagine! The inventor was the chief eunuch to the Emperor Ho Ti."

The clerk frowned, asking, "What's a eunuch?"

Charlotte told him, adding, "You know, Mr. No-balls-at-all!"

The young man sucked in his breath.

"I must apologize," said Harold, frowning at Charlotte. "My daughter believes in women's rights. She goes against convention by discussing such matters in public.

"He asked me to define eunuch," Charlotte said. "Now, once again the process was surrounded by high-level secrecy. The Chinese had a monopoly on paper until the eighth century, when the Arabs came storming out of the deserts. They must have gotten as far as China, grabbed a few prisoners and roasted a couple over a bonfire. When they asked the others about the secrets of paper, you can imagine how fast they spilled the beans, so to speak. Under those circumstances, I'd tell everything I knew in a minute. From there, it was another five hundred years before the paper mill was set up in Italy. Don't ask me why they were so slow back in those times. They just didn't move as fast as folks do today."

By now, Harold Peabody's eyes were taking on a glazed look. The young clerk refused to remove his gaze from Charlotte, all the while wondering about Charlotte's sanity.

Charlotte explained, "Of course, the first paper mill would never have been set up without a bunch of really cold winters and the invention of underwear."

Harold Peabody jerked upright. "Underwear? For God's sake, Charlotte, what has underwear to do with paper?"

The young woman held up a hand to signal her listeners to be silent. "Let me explain," she said. "The Bible talks about seven lean years, seven good years. I don't intend to dispute the good book, but the world isn't quite that neat and precise. There appear to be patterns in the weather, which would determine whether you have good or bad crops. A few cold winters and—"

"Underwear, ma'am," prompted the job applicant.

"Oh, I have such a habit of digressing," Charlotte laughed. "Forgive me, won't you? Well, the weather in Europe turned colder for several years and people

339

were naturally uncomfortable. They started wearing an extra layer of clothing to keep warm. But, of course, a couple of dresses and two or three coats made quite a bundle. So someone came up with the idea of underwear and it took hold. When the underwear wore out the rags were sold to peddlers. They went to the mills where underwear was converted into paper. Now, each sheet had to be made by hand and this was a slow process. But it was a great deal faster than turning animal skins into parchment. First, you have to catch the animal, kill it, skin the poor beast and then get on with making parchment."

"Amazing," said the clerk.

"Oh, there's many interesting things in history," Charlotte said. "Those cold winters in Europe changed the very way houses were built. You see, everyone was freezing because most houses didn't have chimneys. Their homes were built around a huge communal dining room. A big hole in the roof allowed smoke to escape. Inefficient. But it was cozy because everyone slept in the big room. Stretched out on the floor in front of the fire. You can imagine the fun that must have been, the master of the manor, his lady, their children, the servants, a few dogs, chickens, and cattle sleeping in the dining room. Think of the snoring, groaning and coughing during the night. But the system had a few advantages. Everyone knew who was sleeping with who."

"Charlotte!" Harold Peabody looked shocked.

"Well," she answered defensively, "they couldn't very well sleep around with everyone watching."

Charlotte knew when her father's patience was wearing down. She said good day to the clerk and swished out the office door to get a cup of tea.

Harold Peabody begged the clerk's forbearance.

"She's a . . ."—the clerk stammered for the right word—"an interesting person!"

"She's driving me crazy," said Peabody in a confidential tone. "She's the cross I must bear. I always wanted a son. I get a daughter that, when you ask for a sheet of paper, delivers a lecture on Chinese eunuchs, Egyptian reeds, underwear and the sleeping habits in Europe."

The clerk was hired. He intended to stay away from Charlotte Peabody, who was the most unusual woman he'd ever met. That night, when he got home from the office, Harold Peabody uncorked a bottle of sherry. He settled back in his comfortable armchair with that day's copy of the *New York Tribune*. The news was the usual fare. Those idiots in Washington City, D.C., were playing politics and acting like lunkheads. A runaway horse and wagon killed a pedestrian in the city. A ship had caught fire just outside New York harbor, ten people dying in the blaze.

Howard was on his second glass of sherry when his attention was drawn to a small advertisement. Someone named John Conrad, of Belle Mead plantation, someplace in Mississippi, wanted to hire a school teacher. Applicants were to write to Conrad's attorney, Roy Manning, in Memphis.

That's what Charlotte should do, Peabody thought. Teaching school. She could talk for hours on any subject. She enjoyed talking. Lord, did she enjoy that.

Harold Peabody was envisioning life, a serene and simple life, without Charlotte in the house. His reveries were interrupted when the call came for dinner. In the dining room, he sat down at one end of the long mahogany table. His wife sat at the other end, and Charlotte was in the middle. The maid brought in a platter of roast beef, and Harold picked up his fork.

Charlotte said, "Did you know that Henry Becket introduced the fork into England?"

Harold Peabody winced. "No, I didn't know that."

"It happened during the reign of Henry the Second."

"Hmmm." Peabody carved the roast.

"They ate with their fingers before that time. But proper folks could only use so many fingers."

Harold Peabody thought about remaining silent. But his curiosity was aroused. He had to ask, "How many fingers?"

"Three. That was the best custom. A mannered person didn't stuff food into their mouth with both hands and, of course, they didn't leave their fingers in the plate too long. That was considered bad manners. They had quite a controversy in England when Becket came up with forks."

"Where'd he get them?" wondered Mrs. Peabody.

"In the early sixteen hundreds an English traveler saw them being used in Italy. He came back to England, told Becket, and the king's chancellor had the king and his bunch of hangers-on start using them. The priests went wild!"

Harold Peabody wanted to eat a peaceful dinner. Nonetheless, he had to know why folks were considered irreligious. He nodded to his daughter and she went on.

"The priests claimed the use of forks meant God's animals were not worth being touched."

Mrs. Peabody glanced at her husband. "Is that true, Harold?"

"How would I know, Deborah?" he answered. "Maybe she makes it up."

Charlotte continued, "Ordinary people laughed at the king for eating with a fork. They thought their use was effeminite and in poor taste. Another hundred years went by before the average family tried eating with forks. Of course, knives have been used since the Stone Age—"

Harold interrupted. "Saw an interesting advert in the paper tonight." He related details of John Conrad's advertisement. "Thought you might like being a teacher, Charlotte."

"Does it pay well?" wondered the girl.

"No matter," Harold said. "I'll send you a remittance each month to cover expenses your salary might not meet."

"Father, you're trying to get rid of me."

"No, I just thought it might be an interesting adventure."

"I'll write a letter tomorrow."

Harold Peabody played his trump card. "You've been working too hard these past few months. Why not go traveling? Visit Memphis and apply for the job in person. This poor chap will have dozens of applications through the mail. You'll be the only one to show up in person."

"The English do that," said Charlotte.

"Use forks?"

"No, they have a system of remittance men. That's what I'll be, you know. The English can be trusted to handle a black sheep in their family in a reasonable manner. When a son became a burden, they sent him to some foreign country and remitted a check to the poor lunkhead each month. Am I to be a remittance woman?"

"That thought never occurred to me," lied Harold. "I'm just thinking of your future. You need to see the country, meet new people."

"True," Charlotte admitted.

"Your mother can help you pack tonight," said Harold.

Mrs. Peabody cried when Charlotte's bags were taken to their carriage the next morning. At the office, Harold Peabody purchased a steamship ticket to Philadelphia and made arrangements for Charlotte to go overland to Pittsburgh, then take a steamboat from there down to Memphis. Each month a sizable check would be sent to the post office in Memphis or to any address Charlotte gave him later on.

By noon, all arrangements were completed. Charlotte Peabody's luggage was placed aboard a ship that was sailing at two P.M. She gave her father a good-bye kiss, then walked up the gangplank. He turned and, with a light heart, headed back to his office.

Chapter Thirty-one

Uncle Eli sat on the small front porch of his cabin and watched the bustling activity in the slave quarters. A half-dozen men were roasting several hogs over an open spit. The aroma of the succulent meat scented the humid air. The day had been hot, but with the coming of night the world had cooled down. No one knew why Master John had declared a special feast for the slaves, least of all Uncle Eli. The old man had tried to wheedle a bit of information from the master, then from Jumbo, and even Mistress Suzanne. They had replied the feast was to celebrate a special occasion.

Uncle Eli wasn't sure what "special occasion" meant, except everyone would have a full belly and a good time. As he watched people move around the slave quarters, Uncle Eli decided it was like his home village back in Africa. Everyone lived together there, huts set close together, in a community of about one hundred people. Take away the cabins, replace them with round wood huts, and things hadn't changed all that much. Except in Africa there had been more free time for everyone. True, life wasn't easy hunting for meat. But his home village sat close by a broad, grassy plain and hunting was not difficult.

Uncle Eli remembered the first hunt, when he was allowed to join the men during the spring. Eli killed a large boar that morning, spearing the tusk-toothed monster as it charged from the bush. The huntsmen liked his courage and, as he grew to manhood, taught their lore to the boy. He enjoyed hunting and was always thrilled by the congratulations when he came back to the village with fresh meat.

Then he remembered the woman he had loved.

Dayhi was her name, a smoke-skinned young woman with graceful manners. She was ignored by the other eligible men in the village. She was a bashful girl who blushed a lot. Dayhi had good sense, was loyal and worked hard. Those were the qualities Eli wanted in a wife. He courted Dayhi under the watchful eyes of her mother. After a year of courting the girl, they obtained permission from the village elders to get married.

The day!

A week before the wedding, Uncle Eli was awakened at dawn by the shouts of terrified people. The Bad Ones had crept into the unguarded settlement. Uncle Eli grabbed his spear. He rushed from his hut. A Bad One was down the street headed into Dayhi's home. Uncle Eli raised his spear and flung the weapon. It drove deep into the man's hip. Eli pulled his knife from its holster, started running to finish off the Bad One.

The man spun around, slashed at Eli with his broad-bladed sword. Eli parried the blow, slipped inside and drove his knife up into the Bad One's groin. He started to withdraw the blade for another thrust. But everything went black.

He awoke a half hour later with a terrible headache. His ankle was gripped by a tight iron ring attached to a long chain. The Bad Ones were standing over his people, throwing water into their faces to revive them. Another group went down the street with firebrands, setting the huts ablaze. Men, women and children were crying. Several dead bodies lay in the street, including the bad one Eli had killed.

An hour later, the men were marched from the village on the long journey to the coast. Eli kept trying to catch sight of Dayhi as they walked through the smoldering village, but he never saw her again. The women were chained together in a separate soffle, and Dayhi was not among them. He never did learn whether she was alive or dead.

The master of the fort on the coast was a lean, angular Dutchman who worked for an English company. He looked upon the fort as a holding pen for animals. The result was relatively good living conditions, plenty of food and good sanitation. Dead men and women could not be sold to the shipping captains who sailed into the bay to buy merchandise. The Dutchman took pride in selling the healthiest, sleeking slaves.

Eli was sick most of the voyage to the United States. He spent those days chained in the hold of the ship, retching with seasickness. Upon arrival in Baltimore in 1801, Uncle Eli was sold to a planter from Virginia. He worked as a field hand for the next eleven years, then was sold to a slave trader who came through the area looking for a fresh supply of hands.

His next owner was a tall, lean, sleekly handsome man who was known as a sportsman. Uncle Eli tended to his owner's horses, becoming quite good at diagnosing the ailments of these animals. He remained on the horse farm in South Carolina until 1829. In February of that year, his owner was killed in a duel over a woman's honor.

Once again, Uncle Eli came into the hands of a slave trader. He was part of a small coffle of seven men and women brought to Memphis to stock the new plantations starting there. He had been living on Belle Meade when John Conrad purchased the plantation from Otto Korrman, the pinch-penny German. Things had improved for the slaves since the new master took over the plantation.

Now Uncle Eli saw his master, mistress and that big black overseer come out of the main house. Uncle Eli watched as the trio came up to his cabin.

"This is a special day, uncle," Jumbo said.

"Indeed it is," Uncle Eli agreed.

"Very special for yuh."

"Me?" Uncle Eli was surprised.

"Just wait and see," Jumbo said with a sly smile. He walked over and pulled the rope on a large bell to summon everyone. Even the men turning the spits left their post and walked over to Uncle Eli's cabin.

"Folks!" Jumbo raised his hands for silence. "Massa John got something to say."

John stood up on the porch of Uncle Eli's cabin. He smiled warmly.

"You've known that each month you get a bean which will give you freedom when you have enough," John announced. "I'm happy to say that one slave on Belle Meade has earned his freedom.

That's why we're celebrating today. One of you has saved up enough beans. Along with his freedom, that person will be given titlement to an acre of land up on the hill. We've laid out the plot and we start building the cabin in the morning."

"How 'bout dat?" Jumbo said, enthusiastically.

"Who gits it?" wondered Cotton Top.

"Here's the title to the acre of ground and cabin," John went on. He held a piece of paper above his head. Then, he pulled another document from his pocket. "And here's the papers indicating that person has been freed."

Martha called, "Who be hit?"

John looked down at the gray-haired old man sitting in his chair.

"It's Uncle Eli," he announced.

"Praise Gawd!" someone cried.

"Yuh be free, ole man," said Hazel, a female slave.

"What's it feel lak?" asked Jumbo, grinning widely.

Tears welled in Uncle Eli's eyes. He stood up, supporting himself with his cane, and started crying.

With tears flowing down his cheeks, with a wide smile on his face, Uncle Eli tried to express his gratitude.

"Massa John . . ." His voice trembled.

Suddenly, Uncle Eli's shoulders trembled. He almost lost his balance and narrowly averted falling from the porch. Then, the old slave's head fell forward on John's shoulder. He bawled with joy.

When Uncle Eli regained control of his emotions, everyone went over and ate from the roast pig. Eli was the focal point of everyone's attention. His freed man papers and the title to his cabin and acre of ground were shown again and again to everyone. Before the night ended, the old man came over to thank John for his generosity.

"You earned it," John said.

"Reckon so?"

"Sure did."

Jumbo spoke up. "You be sure, now, y'hear, to tell every'body they work hard 'n the git their papers, too."

"Ah be sure to tell 'em," Uncle Eli agreed. "One thing's bin abotherin' muh mind. What happens if'n I lose these papers?"

John explained, "Those papers are also on file at the courthouse in Memphis. They'll be there if you should lose these. Folks can go to the courthouse and look them up."

Suzanne came over and Uncle Eli stood up. She put her arms around the old man, gave him a strong hug.

"Bless yuh," Uncle Eli sobbed.

"I love you, uncle," Suzanne whispered.

Tears started gushing again from Uncle Eli's eyes. He rubbed his fingers to erase them, then said: "Ah be cryin' awful lot t'be so happy! Ah best git inside 'n catch mah breath."

Jumbo helped the old man up the steps and into his cabin.

He came back and joined John and Suzanne on their walk back to the house.

"I feel awful," Suzanne said. "That poor old man really appreciated what we did."

" 'Course he did," agreed Jumbo.

"But we did it to convince everyone that they can

get their freedom," she pointed out. "The gift was not from love."

"In a way it was selfish of us," John agreed.

"Yuh white folks sure talk funny," Jumbo said in a genial tone. "Yuh got to realize that darkies don't care 'bout your motives. They's one happy ole man back thar carryin' his freedom papers. That's what counts!"

II

A great drought had struck Memphis. Every saloon in town was closed. Madame Rose heard about Henrietta Pugh's followers and their nasty way of entering the Mississippi Club. With a solid chunk of money earned while the slave traders were in a town, Madame Rose decided to give her girls a holiday. A couple of them went home to visit the old folks on the farm, but most of the girls had lost contact with their relatives a long time ago. They stayed at the brothel, whiling away the days and nights with conversation and rich food.

They settled in the kitchen and dining room each morning, wearing their frilly robes, and launched several conversations at the same time. The topic of conversation was mostly men. That they were still little boys, no topic of conversation was mostly men. That they were still little boys, no matter what their age, they agreed. All men wanted was three meals a day, a place to sleep at night and a willing woman to tumble. Madame Rose pointed out that some men were ambitious, willing to forego pleasures of the flesh to pile up money. The girls agreed this type of *homo sapiens* did exist, but they were a throwback to some Stone Age heritage.

The girls also discussed cosmetics, the latest fashions, and the quickest way to fix a hair-do. They talked at length about what Bull Frazer would do about Henrietta Pugh — "*that woman*," they called her — and her lawless band of followers. The old biddies had clearly broken the law at the Mississippi Club. The girls wanted to see the sheriff throw a few of those law-breaking, butter-won't-melt-in-the-mouths women in jail. That would teach them that everyone was equal under the law. Something had to be done or Memphis would gain a bad reputation and become known as a religious town. That would mean the sporting element would have their good times someplace else.

There were other people in Memphis wondering when the sheriff would move. Dan Adkins and Abner Lambert missed their daily chess games at the tavern. They were becoming short-tempered and openly hostile to everyone except their best customers. Roy Lanning, the attorney for Belle Meade, purchased several bottles of booze from a steamboat captain. The lawyer sold drinks to the courthouse crowd, earning the nickname of Liquir Lanning.

The serious drinkers pleaded with saloon keepers to open their doors.

"Not for all the money in the auld sod," declared Tom Clancy to anyone who asked. "That woman has spies out. They're watching us like chicken hawks eyeing a plump pullet. Nay, lads, I'll not tempt the devil herself by serving liquor while she's in town."

Some tavern owners sneaked into their places during the night, carrying out bottles for their favorite customers. But, as most men reflected, it wasn't like going to your favorite bar. Hoisting a few at home was tame stuff. A man needed companionship and a good bartender before drinking was any fun.

They also talked about Hodge Walker, the town drunk, who hadn't drawn a sober breath in years. Hodge had come into a sizable inheritance as a youngster, spent his life trying to pickle himself. He had done a fair job, but was now under doctor's care. Folks said Hodge was having some godawful withdrawal symptoms, seeing snakes, demons and a raft of other things. The doctor swore Hodge would recover, that a few weeks off the sauce would do his health some good.

By the fourth day, the tavern owners gathered in the sheriff's office and complained mightily. They were angry, sullen and worried about the money being lost. Each of them demanded that Bull Frazer exercise his duties as sheriff. It went on like that that most of the morning, because the tavern owners were without a business needing attention. So they hung around the sheriff's office and demanded action.

Bull let them stay. Boots propped on his desk, smoking and drinking coffee, he suggested any tavern could open whenever they wished.

Tom Clancy objected. "They'll burn us out. We can't open 'til you throw those fillies in the jail."

"I can't do that."

Clancy glowered. "They broke the law by shattering the glass in my door, chasing me and my customers out. They must've poured out a hunnerd dollars of my booze."

"You ever hear of a law about provoking an assault, Clancy?"

The Irishman looked dully at the sheriff. "Can't say I have."

"Provoking an assault's when you rile someone up and they beat the crap out of you."

The Irishman nodded sagely. "Yeah, I can understand that."

"You provoked those women."

"Me?"

"Didn't you give them the finger?"

"I was waving at 'em."

"That mistake cost you a front door and a hundred bucks of liquor."

"Maybe they don't know about that law."

Bull said, "They know."

"Well, you ought to get them on something," whined a bartender known as Dean. "I'm losing money sitting around. My boss says no work, no pay. Next thing, it'll be no work, no pay, and no eat for Deno."

Vita Santino leaped up from his chair. The Sicilian shook his finger at the sheriff. "You are supposed to enforce the law, no?"

"Yes." Bull took a long, deep breath and thought about the money he would get from the store. That would be nice. He could wander around the whole year round, not have to sit in an office and have idiots shaking their fingers at him. "When they break a law, I'll be the first to go and bring those ladies in. 'Course, you boys know that's what they want."

"They do?" Everyone spoke in unison.

"Make a martyr for their cause," he explained. "They'll be shouting from the pulpits, praying outside the jail and holding rallies to whip up the

354

faithful to a feverish pitch."

"We shoot that bitch!" cried Santino.

"Take it easy," Bull said. "She'll be leaving town soon."

"Somebody ought to give her what she needs," Clancy chimed in.

"A kick in the behind," said Santino.

"Naw, a tumble in the hay," said the Irishman. "You fellows know how women are after they've lost their husbands. A colleen starts getting some regular stuff, then the old man conks out. She misses him real bad."

Vito Santino looked doubtful. "Who you get to service this heifer?"

"I admit she's ugly."

"Ugly?" Santino started to spit, then rememberd he was in Bull Frazer's office. "Ugly, you say! She looks like the dogs have played with her for the past year. A man's tool would fall off if he went into her bony body."

"What do you think, Deno?" Clancy turned to the man next to him.

Dean answered. "She's probably sincere about what she's doing."

"You service her," Santino told Clancy.

Bull spoke up. "You fellows know that rape is against the law."

"Rape!" Vito Santino's fist shot into the air. "Tumbling her would be a public service."

"Public service like that's get you hung," Bull advised.

They wrangled on through the noon hour.

"Someone ought to run her out of town."

"Tar 'n feathers and a little lime to burn her tail."

"Losing money every minute."

"Poor Hodge is over there seeing giant spiders."

"Doc says Hodge thinks they're real."

"Are we men or worms?" asked Vito Santino.

No one answered the Sicilian.

"I am a man," Vito said. "I'm opening up this afternoon."

"You mean it?" Tom Clancy looked thunderstruck.

"No woman pushed me around."

"Vito, you ain't seen them women with the sticks coming for you."

"I got a stick," said Vito, rubbing his crotch, "to take care of those biddies."

"Don't do anything to provoke them," Bull suggested. "I'll have a deputy standing by. I think you're making a mistake, but every man does what he thinks is right."

"I'll show her," Vito said, a defiant look on his face.

He left the sheriff's office with the other saloon keepers following behind. They didn't want to miss this show for the world.

Chapter Thirty-two

"I see you wear a rabbit's foot on your watch fob."

"Brings me luck."

"Do you know how that superstition started?"

"No, but I'll wager you're going to tell us."

Charlotte Peabody lifted her position on the seat of the stagecoach. "Back in primitive times each tribe worshipped an animal. They refrained from killing that particular species. One tribe undoubtedly had the rabbit as their totem. Hence, their belief that a part of the rabbit brought divine intervention into their lives. Thus, even today, some people still think a rabbit's foot brings good luck. I suppose you also carry a locket of your sweetheart's hair with you?"

The passenger across from Charlotte was middle-aged, sitting straight and stiff, his face holding a perpetual frown. "Young lady, you should speak only when spoken to. That's the lady-like way."

"No matter," laughed Charlotte. "I never said I was a lady. Actually, carrying a lock of hair goes back to primitive times. Folks used to think the hair was the most vital part of the body. By delivering up a bit of hair, you 'gave in' to the holder. Because it was thought that witches could influence the behavior of any person with a single strand of their hair."

The man looked grim. "You say your father sent you out here?"

"I think he got tired of me at home," Charlotte admitted.

"Understandable. Quite understandable." The man closed his eyes as if to sleep. Charlotte was going on about an ancient civilization believing that man's soul resided in the eyes.

II

They were gathered in the Baptist church, singing hymns, when a breathless woman came running through the doors, she dashing down the aisle, crying that Vito Santino had reopened his saloon. Everyone began to talk at the same time. Vito's defiance meant demon run would once again flow through Memphis.

"He's got to be stopped," cried a woman.

"We have to do something," yelled another.

Henrietta Pugh waited until the woman turned toward the altar of the church. "Ladies, we have plenty of time to take care of Mr. —"She paused. "What was his name?"

"Vito Santino. He's a foreigner," said Cassie Royalton, pleased that Vito had decided to defy the group. It would provide another opportunity to carry the big bass drum. She liked marching at the front of the group.

"We'll visit Mr. Santino in due time," said Mrs.

Pugh. "He cannot defy our ban on liquor in Memphis. The will of the women will be heard in this city and, eventually, throughout the land. We need to gather our sisters who are not here today. Pass the word to everyone that we're holding a rally tonight in front of Santino's place of business at seven. Bring your sticks and as many believers as you can round up."

"Let's have a torchlight parade," cried Cassier Royalton.

The idea appealed to Mrs. Pugh. "Can we find torches on short notice?"

"My mister will fix them," declared Cassie Royalton.

"Okay," said Mrs. Pugh. "We'll gather here at the church at seven and proceed from here to Mr. Santino's tavern."

III

Construction of the wharf was almost completed; Rusty Ward agreed to spend the afternoon overseeing the final details while Sean Porter rode into Memphis to call on Regina Montrose. Silas Blackston answered the Irishman's knock, inviting Sean into the house.

"Daughter's gone shopping," Silas said. "You thinking about taking music lessons?"

Sean grinned. "I'm afraid my talents lie elsewhere."

"Sit down! Sit down!" Blackston said, waving a hand toward a shabby chair across from his position on the sofa. "Been busy with business, of course, but this here afternoon I took off to rest up. Usta work a lot longer'n most folks but time catches up with a man. I used to be pretty light fingered with a cornet when I was a young man. Traveled in them days and when I struck a fresh town I used to lead the church choir. Nothing like a cornet to fill a meetin'-house. That always got me a five dollar bill. Not bad pay for doin' something to help the Lord's cause."

"You traveled, eh?"

"Been traveling since I was a boy. Selling things always come natural to me. I warn't seventeen when I was out for myself on the road makin' sometimes as high as a hundred and fifty dollars a week sellin' 'The Elixir of Youth.' Went clear up to Massachusetts and across over to Vermont during fair time. When them way-backs would crowd up to m'booth and slap down a dollar faster'n a trout grabs a grasshopper."

"Harmless, I trust," said Sean.

"Harmless!" Silas Blackston scratched his head. "Well, sir, I wasn't taking no chances. A tad of Epson salts and brook water, tinctured up with a little port wine never hurt 'em any, I guess. Then, of course, they got a dollar's worth of excitement waitin' to get young. Usta throw in a mirror and a pocket-comb with ever' three bottle sale. That made the rubes buy faster'n ever as I told them the comb was gold. It warn't, of course, but many's the man who went away thinkin' it was. Right purty comb, all yellow and shiny. Don't make things like they usta, which means a person has to keep a sharp eye on what you buy these days."

"A hundred and fifty dolars a week! Imagine!"

"That's what it amounted to, my friend—clean

velvet profit — from Monday til Saturday night. Not bad for a youngster of sixteen, was it?"

"And you picked up an extra five at church on Sundays."

"I was somethin' in them days," said Blackston.

"Now, Silas," said Mrs. Blackston coming into the room. She wore a lavender silk dress and a strong odor of violet perfume accompanied her.

"My wife, Mr. —" Blackston stopped, realizing he did not know Sean's name.

"Sean Porter," said the Irishman, taking Mrs. Blackston's plump hand and rising from his chair.

"Silas has spoken of you often," Mrs. Blackston said.

"Delighted to meet you. I regret not having the double pleasure of seeing your daughter. Your husband tells me she's out shopping."

"Daughter should be back any minute," Mrs. Blackston said. "She was going across town to give singing lessons to the Van Cortland's little girl. Of course, I'm sure you've heard of the Van Cortlands — as if there was anyone in Memphis who didn't. Did you read about the magnificent dinner in the papers the other day? It must have been a grand affair."

"I've been busy," Sean replied.

"Why, Mr. Porter, the papers were full of it! As I always tell Regina, when you do go into society, the best is none too good. It is often shockingly bad!"

"You are correct, madam."

"But, of course, the Van Cortlands. Their wealth and position —"

"Regina says their house is like a palace," Silas Blackston exclaimed.

"Window curtains cost a thousand a pair," his wife added. "Well, when you're wealthy beyond anyone's dreams. Do be seated again, Mr. Porter. My husband says I do rattle on at times."

"Van Cortland. He must be worth more'n any man in town," Silas said.

"I've heard that."

"Wasn't it him that made that big play in land over in eastern Tennessee about ten years ago?" asked Blackston.

"Yes," said Sean. "People say that was Sam Van Cortland."

"Biggest thing ever pulled off, wasn't it?"

"It was a piece of scroundrelism," declared Sean. "Pure piracy if the facts I've heard are true."

"Why, Mr. Porter, you surprise me," said Mrs. Blackston.

"He's a crook, madam."

"Um!" exclaimed Blackston. "You call Van Cortland a pirate and a scoundrel because he's successful—because he's got grit and nerves and brains enough to pull off a great feat of salesmanship."

"I do," snapped Sean. "Especially when the deal means financial ruin for thousands of honest people. Sam Van Cortland ruined them by the wholesale. He ruined them from London to New Orleans and New York. Many of the people who bought his land have never recovered."

Mrs. Blackston raised her eyebrows in astonishment.

"It was crooked from the start," Sean went on. "Van Cortland promised people there would be a town established there. The land was nothing but a bog. You couldn't put up a tent, let alone a good sturdy building. The folks who bought his land were people looking for a new start in life. They gave Van Cortland their money, quit their jobs, sold their homes and came to New Hope—that's what he called that swamp—and found they'd been swindled. He should have been sent to prison because he drove more than one man to suicide. Instead, people fawn over Sam Van Cortland as if he's a great financier. You brought up his name. I've told you about him."

Mrs. Blackston did not utter a word. She sat on the sofa opposite Sean and was none too willing to believe his words. The Van Cortlands were the richest people in Memphis and she envied their social position.

Silas Blackston looked up and cleared his throat. "Ain't you exaggeratin' a little, friend?" he ventured blandly.

"Exaggerating!" Sean's face jerked up. "The man's a crook."

"But all that which you mentioned, Mr. Porter is—well, that's all in the past," remarked Mrs. Blackston sweetly. "I tell Silas that we should always be willing to forgive others their—their little mistakes. Oh, I believe strongly in forgiveness, Mr. Porter. I'm just that way; always have been, and always will be, I guess. My southern blood, I guess."

"What's past is past," said Blackston with a profound expression. "He got his money anyway. If he'd laid down and give up, somebody else would've took them folks—done the trick, and got it for themselves—wouldn't they? Sides, folks should look at things before they buy somethin' as important as land in a new city. Folks're too trusting. Why I don't know how many's the time I've not let people buy stock in my laundry corporation because — while their money might be doubled every six months — they weren't quality people. I guess when you sift the whole thing down, friend, you'll find Sam Van Cortland was up against a pretty big operation. He won out and the rest of them folks got trampled. Life ain't nothin' but win or die."

Mrs. Blackston heard a familiar footstep on the front porch.

"There's Regina now," she said, glad to interupt the conversation. She got up and ran to the door. There was a refreshing cheerfulness to Regina Montrose when she came into the room. Her charm and refinement appealed to Sean, even before she stretched forth her hand. He noticed that her cheeks were rosier than usual this afternoon. There was a warm radiance in her eyes as she tossed her sheet music on the piano. It seemed incredible to Sean that Regina Montrose lived in the Blackston home. The Irishman was appalled by the ill-disguised social aspirations of the girl's mother. Silas Blackston was worse, a montebank with a crude, mercenary view on life.

Sean said, "Your mother tells me you're giving lessons to the Van Courtland girl. I'm sure you'll do well at it."

She flushed under the compliment. "I do the best I can, Mr. Porter." She forced a little laugh.

"She's going to be teaching the Van Cortland girl three times each week," declared the mother, triumphantly.

"Well, say, girlie, that seems like success to me," broke in Silas Blackston.

"Are you interested in lessons?" Regina asked Sean.

"Even your talent couldn't help me," he replied. "I'm too far gone to even whistle a tune. No, I was in Memphis this afternoon and wondered how you were getting established. It occurred to me that you haven't seen any of the country around here. I've got a carriage with me and—" He smiled expectantly in her direction.

"Now see here," interjected Silas Blackston. "I ain't sure—"

Regina smiled at Sean. "I'd love to, Mr. Porter."

"I'll go along as chaperone," chimed in Mrs. Blackston.

"I've seen Mr. Porter's carriage parked outside," Regina said. "There's only room for two people."

"And after the drive," said Sean, "we'll have dinner at my favorite restaurant."

"Now, see here—" Blackston started again.

"I'll freshen up and get my parasol," Regina said, giving no heed to her stepfather's remarks.

They drove north along the river road. Sean was pleased to find that Regina Montrose was a pleasant companion. She had a warm, pleasing personality and appeared to enjoy his company. When they got back to Memphis Sean suggested dinner at the City Hotel though he was somewhat disgruntled to learn about the temperance campaign—a meal was incomplete without wine.

Their appetites sated, they stood for a moment in front of the hotel. The sound of a bass drum came booming down Main Street. Regina explained that Henrietta Pugh and her followers were marching on Mr. Santino's tavern. Sean and the girl watched as the women came walking down the streets carrying lighted pine torches.

"I hope," he said, "they don't plan on burning the poor man out."

Regina laughed. "The torches are strictly for theatrical effect."

"This Mrs. Pugh. Who is she?"

"A lady who believes in a dry town."

Sean took the girl's hand as the last row of women marched past. They walked along in the crowd of onlookers following the parade.

He asked, "The evidence indicates she hates booze," he said. "What I wonder is what started her on this crusade."

"I've met her, but I never thought to ask."

"She a nice lady?"

"A widow."

"Husband probably drank himself to death," Sean ventured.

A hundred or so ladies made up the parade. When they arrived at Vito Santino's tavern, Bull Frazer and his two deputies were stationed outside the door. The women were furious.

"Don't you try and stop us!" cried Cassie Royalton.

"I'm here to see that law 'n order is preserved," Bull said gruffly.

Cassie continued to beat on her drum, which caused a painful look to come over Bull's face.

"You have to pound that noise box?" he demanded.

"No law against it!"

"How about disturbing the peace?" said Bull.

"We got rights!" shrilled Mrs. Pugh, coming up where Bull and Cassie stood.

"You don't have the right to break up Mr. Santino's tavern."

"We want Memphis to be a dry town," Henrietta said.

"Any blamed fool can see what you want," the sheriff told her. "I'm just here to see that there's no property or tissue damage."

"Can we enter Mr. Santino's place of business?"

"Of course, but I'd be careful. He's Sicilian. You know how they are with quick tempers."

Henrietta Pugh called upon twenty women she knew to be the worst singers in the group. Their untrained voices were remarkably bad. Mrs. Pugh led these women, and Cassie and her drum, into Santino's tavern. They found a half dozen men inside. Santino was behind the bar with a frown on his face. He gave the women a hostile look when they came through the door.

"We no serve women," he said.

"We don't want your demon rum," yelled Cassie.

"Then, go away!"

Mrs. Pugh paid no heed to Vito Santino. She directed her girls to stand in the center of the room. Under Mrs. Pugh's leadership they began to sing a hymn. Cassie pounded her drum. The ladies outside the tavern raised their voices to join their sisters inside the *Green Parrot Tavern*.

Sean saw Bull Frazer standing steadfast by the door. He walked over, introduced Regina, and chided the sheriff about the temperance campaign.

"No jokes, Sean," Bull said. "I've heard them all."

"Ever hear singing like that?"

"Like cats howling on a fence," Bull agreed.

"Who's going to win?"

"Mrs. Pugh. Nobody can stand cauterwauling like that. Santino will cave in."

True to Bull's prediction, Vito Santino did something he'd sworn not to do. After thirty minutes of hymns screeched inside his tavern, he sent his patrons home and closed the door.

The victory belonged to Henrietta Pugh.

Chapter Thirty-three

Silas Blackston's rented house sat across the street from the home of Patricia Wells. Silas quickly became interested in the widow lady's financial status. The Wells family appeared to be prosperous, just the sort of folks to buy stock in his laundry firm, so Silas became friendly with the Wells children. Although he ordinarily paid little attention to kids, he handed out candy, and told jokes and entertained them with riddles. Eventually, through artful questioning, Silas learned from Billy Wells that the family had received several insurance payments after his father died.

That was why Silas Blackston knocked on the front door of Patricia Wells' home early one afternoon. He had sat and rocked on his front porch, saw Henrietta Pugh walk toward town. The children were playing down the street in a neighbor's yard. When Blackston knocked, Patricia Wells was mending a girl's skirt. She barely had time to hide the torn garment and seize her knitting before Silas poked his head through the door.

"Got so pesky lonesome acrost the street, I thought I'd just come over here and cheer you up,"

Silas said. "Hope I'm not intruudin', Mrs. Wells, but my wife and girlie have gone downtown to do some shopping. Grand day, ain't it, Mrs. Wells?"

Patricia Wells sprung from her chair and stood helpless before the man, blushing with embarrassment. By now, Blackston had gained the center of the room, an old trick he'd learned during his years of selling.

"So you've been left alone, Mr. Blackston," Patricia Wells said with dignified reservation.

"That's about the size of it," he chuckled, selecting a sofa and crossing his legs. He threw his head back at ease when Patricia Wells resumed her seat across the room. "I'm not much on goin' shoppin'. Seen too much of stores 'n such in my days. What I'd like would be a good show. Used to always be goin' to 'em. There wa'n't a troupe that come to our town that didn't have me taggin' after 'em to catch their performance. Since I've had so many business worries I've kinder gotten out of the habit of goin' to the theater. S'pose you're crazy about 'em, ain't you Mrs. Wells? Most women are."

"My husband used to take me," she answered. "That was mostly concerts because he didn't approve of popular theater."

Silas shot forward with a surprised smile. "Well, say, that beats all!"

"He was a conservative man," she added.

"Well, I reckon you ain't been missin' an awful lot," he conceded. "I've seen some shows where you got your money's worth; then again I've seen 'em that weren't worth twenty-five centers—your husband didn't have nothin' against the circus, did he?"

Patricia Wells looked at him with a hesitant smile.

"I'm afraid our views on life are—well, different, Mr. Blackston. To be frank with you, Mr. Blackston, when you consider their lives, the people who appear on stage—"

"Don't you tell my wife," he intervened, paused and added in a confident manner, "but I knowed an actress once—finest little woman you ever see, Mrs. Wells."

The needles in her hands moved furiously.

"Wish I could remember her name—hold on, I got it.. Nell Little. 'Little Nell' I used to call her. Come up with a show from New Orleans and took sick at the Eagle House hotel in my home town. Had a little dog with her, I remember—one of them shiverin', tinklin' poodle kinds. Nell sure thought an awful lot of that little cuss. Seems he's saved her life once in a stagecoach wreck. She'd got thrown out in the brush and his barkin' led 'em right to her. Well, when she took sick at the Eagle House, and the rest of 'em had to leave her—no, hold on, I'm gettin' ahead of my story."

Mrs. Wells' needles dropped a stitch.

"It was Ed Stimson come to me—that's it. Ed bought the Eagle House from old man Williams' widder, and Ed and me was pretty close partners in them days. 'Silas,' says he, 'Doc Rand claims number nine's got pneumonia. She's been out of her head since daylight. She's been askin' for you. Guess you're elected, Si.' "

Silas rambled on, oblivious that every word he uttered was far from welcome to his listener, who sat before him helpless, dazed and indigent. Yet Patricia Wells was too hospitable, even to an uninvited guest, to stem his tide of worldly anecdotes. He

enlightened her to the fact that he and Little Nell
had supped together only two days before in an
oyster bar owned by a friend of his. He insisted she
had taken a shine to him from the first, that the
only decent thing to do was pay for the doctor and
hotel bill, insisting he was human and wanted to
help any woman in distress. When this tale ended,
Silas Blackston stretched his arms over the back of
the sofa, smiled with satisfaction, and stifled a yawn.

"Seems warm today, don't it?" he declared, breaking the silence in the room.

Mrs. Wells agreed the day was indeed hot. Her
knitting needles had slowed down to their normal
speed.

"It ain't a mite too hot for me," Silas remarked,
displaying a drooping sock above his cracked patent
leather shoes. "Warm weather means plenty of
business in the laundry field. A feller can get along
all right in cold weather, but when she gets to
collar-meltin' time and clean shirts are a necessity,
that's when we do a boomin' business. Ever stop to
think how many fancy duds are ruined by washin'
'em at home with lye soap? Or how many people
don't iron right and scorch a dress or petticoat? If
clothes don't get chewed to death, the iron ruins
'em."

Mrs. Wells laid her knitting in her lap in forced
attention. She was worried about a letter from a
lawyer in Cincinnatti, who informed her that her
aunt was ill and money was needed to pay medical
bills.

"I don't mind tellin' you, Mrs. Wells, a little
secret," Silas continued. "Seein' we're old friends and
neighbors. It's sort of lettin' the cat out of the bag,

but I've been thinkin' it over. Besides, I don't know anybody I'd rather help than you." He fished in his pocket and pulled out a square chunk of dark rubber.

"Purest kind there is," he announced gravely, holding it up for her inspection. "Take a good look at it, Mrs. Wells; you don't often sees it. It ain't worth its weight in gold, but it is close to it when it comes to running a laundry. See, them steel washboards are what does the dirty work to clothes. You don't know how many fine things have been ripped to pieces on washboards. You wouldn't care to wear clothes that come out of most laundries. Right off, we got the rest beat hands down."

Again, his long hands fumbled in his pocket. This time he withdrew a folder paper with a mechanical drawing, depicting a large washboard and a clothes wringer.

"Thare she is," he declared with conviction. "Looks pretty neat, don't it? See, we cover the metal on the washboard with a layer of pure rubber. That does the trick. And our laundry don't do no hand-wringin' 'cause the clothes are sent through these two rollers and every last drop of water is gently squeezed out of 'em. Saves time! One turn of our patented speed-accelerator crank and clothes are dry enough to wear. Can't jam, won't tear up clothes, don't rust and every nut, joint and screw is special treated to last longer'n anything on the market. Gives even pressure on ever' thing from a lady's lace handkerchief to a baby's bib. Got any idea what it costs to deliver such a nice contraption to sufferin' women all over the world? Four dollars. Got any idea what women do when they find out they can buy this little gadget and end their wash-day blues? They beat down doors to get themselves one of these contraptions. Got any idea how much profit you make on somethin' like it?"

"I haven't any idea," confessed Patricia Wells.

"Course you haven't, Mrs. Wells, because you're a woman. Be a little surprised to find that old Mrs. Miggs, one of our stockholders, doubled her income. She's already got a couple thousand dollars laid away for a rainy day. She wouldn't have that extra money 'ceptin' I come along and gave it to her in a friendly way. I don't know that I've ever seen a happier woman. Her mortgage on her house in Pittsburgh is paid up, a nice little house for her and a niece. She's got a tidy sum in the bank—a sum that's growin' ever' day, friend, without gamblin' or speculatin' on the stock market. I'm sellin' somethin' that folks need—honesty made and honesty priced. Folks who have one and used it swear by our contraption. An article that enters the home circle as a helpin' hand; that makes the home happier, and keeps the doctor from the door. No more backaches for mother; a child can turn the handle on this little wonder. Friction is down to a minimum. Any wonder that it sells? The patented speed accelerator tends to that. As my New York sales manager wrote the other day, 'It wrings out the dollars as easy as it does a heavy day's wash.'"

Silas Blackston laughed softly.

"I'm confused," said Mrs. Wells. "Your wife mentioned something about setting up a laundry downtown."

Silas Blackston's face dropped for just an instant.

"That's one of our other divisions," he announced,

suavely. "Yeah, this little wonder has given the regular laundries a real tough blow—even put a few washer women out of work, I'd judge. Doin' a peaked amount of damage to the National Flat Iron Company because Hiram Sidwell, president of that big corporation, was in town just a few days ago tryin' to sniff out some stock to buy. 'Sidwell,' I said to him, 'you ain't got enough money if you was pilin' it to the ceiling to buy a part of my little contraption.' He sorter laughed. He knowed there wa'n't no use. He pleaded like a baby to get in on the ground floor, claimin' our company was goin' to be a gold mine. Which it already is, of course. But I don't sell no stock to somebody who runs a rival company. First thing you know they're be wantin' more and they'd have me out on the cold—"

"Are you offering me a chance to buy stock in your company?" asked Patricia Wells.

"I got a few shares left."

"I'll speak frankly to you, Mr. Blackston. My husband is deceased and I have the children to raise. I barely have enough to get by on until the children are grown. There isn't enough to provide an income, so I have to spend so much of it every year. I tell you this frankly, for I want you to know and understand it. I can't afford an investment that wouldn't make money."

Silas Blackston was alert to her every word and gesture.

"If I was to invest in your company and anything happened to it—"

Silas sprang to his feet. "Can you doubt it," he asked earnestly. "You're starin' at a gold mine. You don't suppose, my dear friend, that I'd lead you into a risky investment, do you?"

Blackston hooked his thumbs inside his vest and began to drum the lapels of his coat with his fingers.

"Suppose I let you have a thousand shares?" he said with a benign smile. "Think what it would mean to you. No more worryin' over little things; you'll have money enough then to have peace of mind."

"I have been worried," she admitted. "There won't be anything left after the children are raised. And I don't know much about business matters."

"Preferred?" he questioned briskly. "That pays considerable more than the common stock."

"Can I afford it?"

"It always pays to get the best," said Silas. "The best always pays in the end. There wa'n't never yit a couple cheap things worth one good one. I'd like to see you git the best—somethin' you'd be proud of ownin' like our gilt-edged premium preferred stock." He leaped to his feet, rammed his hands in his trousers pockets, and for some seconds paced to and fro in the room, seemingly lost in thought. "Let's see . . . let's see," he muttered.

"Tell you what I'll do," he said, stopping his pacing. "Let us say fifteen thousand shares preferred. I'll waive you what they're worth today and you can have 'em at par value, my friend. That'll be an even fifteen thousand dollars. You deserve it, Mrs. Wells, if ever a woman did."

"But fifteen thousand is more than I've got in the whole world, Mr. Blackston!"

"I see," he said gravely.

She started to speak, but he held his hand up for silence.

"We could start with half—say, seventy-five hundred."

"That's almost all I have in the world," she gasped. "We would have just a few hundred to live on."

"Remember, your money doubles almost every three months with this stock."

"That fast?

"Perhaps, then, I'd better decide," she said.

"That's right!" he cried. "That's the right kind of talk. I know such matters are hard to think over and decide. But we've done the thinkin' and we've done the decidin', ain't we? And all them gnawin' little doubts is over."

"Yes," she answered, looking up at him quickly. "I have decided, Mr. Blackston, and I'll take the whole seven thousand five hundred dollars worth of shares. I want to provide generously for my children and myself."

In precisely seven minutes by Silas Blackston's watch, Mrs. Patricia Wells became the possessor of seven hundred and fifty shares of the Household Gem preferred stock and a receipt for her check. The ink was hardly dry on the check before Blackston had tucked it in his vest pocket. It rested next to a five dollar bill that his stepdaughter had loaned him that morning. He had feared the return of Mrs. Pugh, but she was nowhere in sight. His experience with selling stock to women indicated trouble if someone walked in during his sales talk. He had lost a fine sale one time to a widow lady in North Carolina when her sister came to visit. The sister had urged caution. Blackston tried to remember which stock he'd been selling that day. It was something to do with new stuff. People always liked that, what with reading about new machines and everything changing so fast. The stock had been that secret process for making artificial corn that caused hens to lay double the usual number of eggs. Or was it the company with a secret way of making fertilizer causing things to gain a year's growth in a week? Then again, it might have been those fancy new seed oats guaranteed to increase a farmer's yield ten-fold. Silas had even carried a big oat in an envelope to show the farmers. They were always impressed, not knowing he'd sifted through a half ton of oats to find that single piece of giant grain.

"I wouldn't be mentionin' this to other folks," Silas said, just before departing. "Folk'll be boilin' mad if'in they find out you're in on the ground floor."

This said, he walked briskly uptown to the bank. In a few minutes he handed the check to an astonished cashier, who consulted with his boss before transferring the funds from Mrs. Wells' account. With a fifty dollar withdrawal, Silas now had more money in his account than most people in Memphis. Next, he walked to the City Hotel, purchased an expensive cigar and walked around town with the importance of a millionaire.

II

Albert Spearman had also done a good job of selling his neighbors. While some were taken aback by the idea of a black minister, most went along with Albert's vision of a church in their rural area. Rev. Adam Matthews would have his church and a small parish home beside it. During one of his mail trips into Memphis, Noah heard about the project. That night, when the slaves at Belle Meade inquired about news, Noah told them a black man would minister to the spiritual needs of their masters.

No one believed Noah's information. This upset Noah. For once he had spoke the truth; now he was being branded a liar.

"Yuh're lyin'," said Martha, the cook. "White folk're not gonna let no black man do they's preachin'."

"Ah's just tellin' what Ah heard," Noah said.

"Humph!" Martha snorted. "Yuh don't come round here with them stories. Yuh're fibbin'."

"Massa John giv a hunnerd dollas to pay for t'church."

"I don' b'lieve it," Martha was adamant. "White folks're just wantin' blacks to work alla time."

Noah pointed to Uncle Eli, who was sitting on the porch of his cabin in the slave quarters. "Looka that, woman! Ain't uncle gettin' hisself a new cabin goin' up on the hill."

"That be different."

"Mebbe white folk're changin'."

"I ain't holdin' muh breath," snapped Martha.

"Yuh b'lieved me when I tole 'bout that sass-coon and all that other stuff," said Noah.

Martha smiled sweetly. "Noah, yuh think ah b'lieved that? Furst thing I asked Jumbo was 'bout that talk of yours."

"Yuh did?"

"Ah did."

"What'd Jumbo says 'bout it?"

"Ast if yuh tole interestin' stories. I said yuh did."

"That be factual."

"Jumbo say that all really matters."

"I seen them things with muh own eyes," Noah said, defensively.

Martha chuckled. "Mebbe yuh did, mebbe yuh didn't."

"What's that s'posed to mean?"

Martha went over and put her arm around Noah's neck. She gave him a quick hug. "Nuthin, Noah. Yuh just keep tellin' 'bout the wonderments of Memphis. Gives our people somethin' to ease their minds. But Ah'd sure like to peek inside yore head sometime to find out what's in there. Yore mind must be a wonderment itself."

Smiling to herself, Martha left Noah standing in the slave quarters and walked back to the kitchen.

Chapter Thirty-three

Sam Van Cortland stood on the bluffs and looked westward into the falling sun. It was a habit of his to take a walk after dinner. He was pleased when night came because darkness suited Mr. Van Cortland's personality. Although he was past his prime, Sam Van Cortland was a powerful man. Folks looked past his pot belly, triple chin, and the continual glint of shrewdness in his eyes. Sam Van Cortland was the richest man in Memphis, maybe all of the mid-south, and most people understood the power of money.

Van Cortland enjoyed a form of notoriety, as well, because his money had been earned dishonestly. Americans have always been eager to embrace the rogue, the scoundrel, the outlaw as good fellows. Sam had gulled the life's savings from hundreds of families, selling bog land as the Garden of Eden. Once his money was in the bank, and judges bribed to keep him outside prisons, Sam Van Cortland and his wife, Rose became important people. Their mansion, Roseland, was a showcase for their new riches. They lived there in splendor, entertaining with weekly musicales, by invitation only. People as rich as the Van Cortlands received few regrets. Most people vied for an invitation to one of their gala parties.

Two things disturbed Sam Van Cortland's mind during his stroll this evening. The first was his dislike for the new people who had purchased Belle Meade. The plantation was rapidly becoming a showcase for the mid-south. Important visitors to Memphis were always given a tour of Belle Meade. The mansion on Belle Meade was supposed to be magnificent, much larger than Van Cortland's Roseland, and furnished with better taste. At least that is what the Van Cortlands heard. They depended on other people's impressions because neither Sam or Rose Van Cortland had been invited to the plantation.

Such indifference made Van Cortland feel like a provincial hick. There was also Mrs. Conrad. She was rumored to be related in some way to English royalty, her father is a high mucky-muck of some sort. Mrs. Van Cortland, the former Rose Snell from Turkeytown, Kentucky, focused her anger on Suzanne Conrad. She was filled with that spiteful jealousy that a socially ambitious woman directs toward a person of superior charm and grace. More than once Rose had told her husband that Suzanne Conrad was a "snobbish bitch," as well as "stuck up," "putting on airs" and "acting high and mighty like she's the Queen herself." These phrases came after the Conrads politely refused to attend a musicale hosted by the Van Cortlands.

The second thing to disturb Sam Van Cortland's serenity was his financial affairs. Two years past Van Cortland had gone to New York and looked into the stock exchange, the center of buying and selling securities in the nation. Fortunes were being made buying low, selling high, and Sam Van Cortland succumbed to feverish speculation. He had plunged for the past two years and lost disastrously. How much he dared not confess, even to himself. And certainly he dared not tell his wife. Rose was a strong-willed woman who detested any serious discussions on money. Any hint on his part about the lack of it and she would throw a tantrum. She abhorred any mention of economy past all reasoning. Besides, Sam Van Cortland couldn't understand how things had gone so wrong in his investments.

For the past week Sam Van Cortland had been receiving daily letters from his broker. Fifty thousand must be remitted immediately, they said, or else his position in the market would be wiped out. He was done for, and he knew it. Money to send to New York did not exist. His account at the local bank was dangerously low. The newspapers with market quotations came each day, as well, telling of brokerage firms going down in the crash. Noted financiers were bankrupt. The market was in a tailspin.

These thoughts occupied Sam Van Cortland's mind as he strolled through Memphis. Darkness fell and he continued walking past his usual time. His passage was marked by barking dogs, but Van Cortland paid no heed to the noise. In time he arrived at the street running past the home of Patricia Wells. He stood there by the corner, engrossed in his thoughts. Where the man came from Sam Van Cortland would never know. He became aware of his presence when the dark figure crept from the rear of the home, out of the orchard. The moon peeked from behind the clouds as a ladder was placed against the house. Sam watched as the man moved up the ladder toward an open bedroom window. He debated on awakening the inhabitants of the house, deciding he was in no position to be involved in a scandal. For all Sam knew, it might be a neighbor making a regular call on someone else's wife. He turned and walked toward his home.

II

Vito Santino slipped silently through the window of Henrietta Pugh's bedroom. He knew she would be sleeping there. For two nights Vita had watched the house from a vantage point in the orchard. He had learned which room was occupied by Mrs. Pugh. The next step called for slipping into the room, doing the act to regain his manhood. All of Memphis had witnessed Vito's humiliation. He had surrendered and closed his doors after those screeching harpies entered his tavern. He, Vito, would restore harmony to his town, honor himself by taming that shrewdish woman. He, Vito, would see the woman on her knees begging for more of what every woman craved. And in doing this act of kindness, he, Vito, would have the woman under control. She would submit to his will—which meant reopening the taverns.

Vito stood against the far wall of the bedroom. Off to the left he could see the dim outline of Henrietta Pugh's body on the bed. She was snoring lightly. Not making a sound, Vito removed his shoes and clothes. He thought about his wife, fair and lovely, until he was erect. He crossed the room,

clapped his hand over the mouth of the devil's pig.
The woman tried to bolt upright, but Vito held her
down on the mattress. Keeping his hand tight
against her mouth, he slipped his bare leg over the
lower part of her body.

She fought like a devil.

She wiggled and twisted like a dying snake.

Bony elbows, knobby knees slammed against Vito's
vital points. She tried to claw his face. Once, she
twisted her head and his hand slipped away from
her mouth for an instant, but he regained a hold
before she screamed. She tried to bite, sinking her
teeth at one time into the flesh of his palm. Vito
wanted to cry out in pain, but instead renewed the
silent struggle with more vigor.

Vito pushed the filmy nightgown above the knees
of the devil's pig. He moved over her, pressing down
all of his weight. She held her legs tight to prevent
him from making entrance. Slowly, because he had
to keep one hand over her mouth, Vito Santino
spread those thin legs apart. He worked on her in a
slow, steady manner to wear down her strength.
Once her hand slipped away and fingernails raked
his hip. After what seemed like hours, Vito felt he
had her in position. He brought his long thick
member around and drove forward.

What was this? Vito wondered.

Something blocked his entrance.

Mother of God!

She was a virgin!

Vito did not move. The situation called for much
thought, but he could not lay here atop the woman
forever. His mind reeled. One notion was that he
would take her maidenhead. That would be a

suitable revenge. Another thought suggested such an act would be a favor. Vito wanted revenge — not even a hint of benevolence.

The woman whimpered beneath his hand.

It must be done!

Vito plunged toward her with all of his strength. This powerful lunge broke her maidenhead. Vito began to glide in and out of her tight compactness. The woman moaned quietly for a moment, then went limp. Henrietta Pugh was weak with pain. Vito's entrance had hurt, hurt badly, and she took no pleasure from the act. She willed herself to think about something pleasant: a walk in a pastoral countryside.

She heard his breath coming faster. Then, he stopped with his large organ still inside her. A moment past and he resumed his thrusts. His finger lightly touched her clitoris, began a featherly caress. She fought against the responding motion within her body. She cursed her flesh for its weakness.

Henrietta began to silently recite the Lord's prayer.

Her flesh quickened and, with a will of their own, her hips thrust up against the man.

He laughed, a develish chuckle no louder than a whisper.

Now, the monster changed his tactics. He withdrew from her body, but his hand capped the hair at the apex of her legs. He moved up and down, lightly, like a butterfly's wings, until Henrietta wanted to scream in frustration. One part of her mind wanted to surrender, to enjoy whatever pleasure could be found with this stranger. Another part recoiled against the horror of such a brutal and terrible act.

What Henrietta Pugh did not know was Vito Santino's prowess in the bedroom. He had been trained well in the act of love. In Sicily, his family lived next door to a widow whose husband was killed in a war. He was fifteen, awkward and shy, when *Signora* Uccidato initiated Vito into manhood. One afternoon, when his family was working in the fields and Vito was home recovering from a sprained ankle, *Signora* Uccidato, a plump woman in black dress, black shawl and black shoes, came over and invited Vito to her home for a piece of fresh baked bread.

He received much more than bread that afternoon. *Signora* was hungry for the touch of a man. Before Vito was clearly aware of what was happening, the woman was rubbing her large breasts against his face. Her fingers grasped his erect organ and, before Vito knew what occurred, he had climaxed in her hand. But the widow knew the recuperative powers of young men. She waited a few moments and Vito's potency was restored. They lay in the widow's bed all afternoon making love.

In the years that followed until Vito left Sicily, *Signora* Uccidato taught Vito the art of fleshly pleasure. She instructed him in providing her with satisfaction, opening the mysteries of the female body to the boy. The subject was taught by a willing teacher to an eager student. Back in Sicily, *Signora* Uccidata had found another lover. She would have been amazed to know her star pupil was in a town called Memphis using every trick to bring Henrietta Pugh to a climax.

He touched.

She resisted.

He caressed.

387

She froze.

Vito rubbed.

Henrietta mused.

His fingers danced across her body.

She thought about Christmas as a child.

Vito plunged.

Henrietta resisted.

An hour passed and Vito Santino knew the woman was truly a child of the devil. His amorous skills, his strength, had failed to bring the woman to his side. She continued to fight like a she-bear against his advances. He knew she had won.

Next, he wondered about a way of getting away. He was naked in bed, his clothes lying on the floor before the window. The moment his hand left her mouth, Vito knew the woman could screech like the witch she was. Suddenly, he rolled over and his feet hit the floor. He ran to his pile of clothes, started to grab the garments. He found his shirt, trousers and was searching for his shoes when her feet hit the floor. Vito leaped through the window and hurried down the ladder.

Porco discoro! She was a true pig of the devil!

Now, getting through the window and swinging out onto the ladder took time. More time than Henrietta Pugh allowed the intruder because, as Vito started down, her hands grabbed the top of the ladder. She gave a mighty heave and the ladder was shooting out into the air. But Vito Santino was a survivor. He knew what she had in mind, so his hand grabbed a curtain. The ladder was pulled back against the house.

He was in a quandary. If his hand left the curtain, the woman was certain to push the ladder again. If he didn't do something, he'd be there when the sun rose in the morning. So, Vito gambled and tried to get down the ladder before anything dreadful happened. He knew it! She shoved out the ladder, so Vito shifted his way forward and tried to drive it back against the wall.

The ladder fell one way, Vito went another.

He plunged into Patricia Wells' rose bush.

Mother of God!

The thorns ripped his flesh going down.

They tore at his skin coming out.

Even with plenty of time, no way existed to extricate himself easily from the rose bush. He had to grimly put his foot against the wall of the house, push with all his might, feel the thorns doing their worst on his naked back, hips and legs. As he came to a standing position, Vito heard dogs barking. A particularly loud one seemed to be running across the yard toward him. He wheeled and ran toward the orchard behind the Wells home. He looked back once — a fatal mistake! — and ran head-long into Mrs. Wells' best peach tree.

He went down like a pole-axed bull!

Stars danced in his mind.

Groggily, Vito Santino rose to his feet. Suddenly, a tiny red pinpoint grew in his mind until it became an enraged realization that he'd left his clothes in the rosebush. He was stark naked. But the dog was back there by the bush, barking like a wolf. *Mother of God!* The beast sounded big enough to tear off a man's leg. Lights were going on in the Wells' house. Vito Santino walked slowly through the orchard. No head-long plunge into a tree for Mr. Santino, again, because he was still hurting from that blow. He limped. His ankle had been twisted during his escape. When he reached a street, he was thankful for the lack of street lighting. He raced through the dark town, praying that no one was out and about. There were not any pedestrians, so Vito was unobserved during his flight home.

His wife had many questions. Vito refused to discuss the matter. He mumbled something about working late at the tavern, running into a wildcat on the way home. Mrs. Santino could accept that tale. She washed the blood from her husband's body, tended to his cuts and decided Vito hadn't really ran into a wildcat. It must have been a *pack* of wildcats to slash her husband so much.

Henrietta Pugh treated the matter with a discreetness. She pretended to be asleep when Patricia Wells knocked on her bedroom door to inquire about the noise. When Mrs. Wells went back to bed, Henrietta rose and lit a candle. She went over by the window, picked up Vito's heavy shoes and thick socks. She put them in the baack of her closet. By the first light of dawn, she went outside and carried the ladder back into the orchard and placed it against an apple tree. She inspected the damage to the rose bush, discovered Vito's garments there and took them inside to the closet.

Vito Santino had clearly sneaked into her bedroom for revenge. The man was misguided, if not completely insane. Although she'd not gotten a clear view of his profile, Henrietta Pugh could have identified Vito Santino in the darkest of night. The little Sicilian didn't realize his breath held the offensive odor of garlic.

Unable to sleep, she lay and plotted her revenge

against the tavern owner. Someone had mentioned his wife, a beautiful girl who could speak only her native tongue. It would do not good to visit the woman. Clearly, she had to devise a suitable revenge against Mr. Santino . . .

III

Charlotte Peabody arrived in Memphis the morning after Vito Santino had sneaked into Henrietta's bedroom. She came off the steamboat with two trunks of books, another containing her clothes, and a sizable bank draft from her father. She thought the town was a bit shabby in appearance, but that was to be expected of a frontier community. Her first call was to a local bank. The teller inhaled sharply when he read the sums on her bank draft. He swallowed hard, came around and escorted Charlotte into the office of the bank owner. That worthy financier seemed disturbed by the interruption until he read the sum on the draft and the name of the holder. Then, he adjusted his cravet, smoothed back his thin gray hair and came around his desk and offered Charlotte a seat.

He asked, "Are you one of the Boston Peabodys?"

"They're cousins," said Charlotte. "My father runs a shipping company in New York."

The banker's eyebrows shot up. "That Peabody?"

"My grandfather started the company," Charlotte ventured. "I understand my grandmother was something of a nag. So he went into the shipping business as an excuse to be away for long periods of time."

The banker cleared his throat. "Ah, my wife and

I would welcome you into our home if you haven't made arrangements to stay elsewhere." He looked expectantly at Charlotte, the smell of money in his nostrils.

Charlotte brought out the advertisement. "This explains why I'm here."

The banker looked thoughtful as he scanned the ad. "Mr. Conrad must be starting a school out there."

Charlotte chuckled. "Maybe he collects school marms."

"No," said the banker. "Conrad's an up-and-coming person. Incidentally, maybe you'd like to dine with my family tonight. I know how bad the food is at most of our local restaurants. My son is about your age and he'd be—"

"No, I'll be going out to see Mr. Conrad this morning," Charlotte replied.

The banker's expression went sour. "Well, maybe some other time. I'll deposit this in an account for you." He started to scratch out a receipt, then looked up. "Is this Thursday or Friday?"

"Friday," Charlotte replied.

The banker started to write.

"Amazing thing about Friday," Charlotte went on. "Pagans considered it to be the best day in the week. The name comes, you know, from Friya. She was the goddess of love in ancient times. If you study astrology, you'll find that Venus, that goddess of Eros, is the ruler of Friday. Things stayed that way for a long time until the Christians came along. That's when Friday took on a bad image. Christ was crucified on Friday. There used to be considerable debate over whether Eve ate the forbidden fruit on

Friday. Most clergymen held the opinion that she did. You'll notice that I didn't say anything about Eve eating an apple. The Bible doesn't name the fruit she ate, so it was most likely a fig or an apricot. Once death and bad luck became associated with Fridays, the superstitution spread all over the world. For centuries a ship never left port on Friday. That was because sailors were superstitious. They believed sailing that day would only lead them to disaster. Things were really getting to a sorry state. You couldn't sail on the Sabbath and never on Friday. The British, always known for good common sense, decided to prove the superstition was not based on rationality. They built a new ship and laid the keel on Friday. The vessel was launched on Friday. It was named the H.M.S. *Friday*. They went to great trouble to find a captain named Sam Friday. The first mate was named Harold Friday. Both men were competent mariners with a good record of service. Fourteen of the crewmen were named Friday, including two sets of twins. Naturally, the ship left port for the first time on Friday. Now, here comes the best part: The *H.M.S. Friday* sailed away and was never heard from again!"

A curious expression came over the banker's face.

"You're making this up. Right?" he said with a look of wonderment.

"A good researcher can find it in books."

Then, the banker remembered that Charlotte Peabody was one of the eastern Peabodys. He smiled indulgently. "That's fascinating."

"Want to know about the other days of the week?"

The banker cleared his throat. "Some other time, perhaps, Miss Peabody. I'll have to remember to call your facts to my friend's attention."

Having seen attorney Roy Lannings name in the advertisement, the banker accompanied Charlotte to the lawyer's office. Lanning was surprised to have an applicant for the job standing in his office. He stammered as introductions were made, wondering how to handle the situation. He decided that decision should be made by John Conrad. Charlotte waited around the office until Lanning met with a client later that morning. They rode out to Belle Meade and arrived in time for lunch. Charlotte wisely remained quiet and demure during the meal. John asked a few questions about the girl's qualifications. She gave the right answers and was hired.

"But we've got to build the schoolhouse," John said.

"How many pupils?" Charlotte wondered.

John looked down at his plate. "I'm not sure. We'll have to round up a few when you're ready to go."

Charlotte looked puzzled. "What do I do until then?"

"I don't know," he replied.

"I know just the thing," Suzanne said, eager to play matchmaker. "She can help Rusty Ward with his work."

"Sounds great. Rusty's an inventor," John explained.

"I hope he's likeable," said Charlotte.

"He is," Suzanne told the girl.

Chapter Thirty-four

Another day, in late September. Time had come and gone that summer in Memphis and on Belle Meade plantation. It was a Saturday afternoon and Belle Meade was in motion for the annual open house. A platform had been built on the front lawn, a pavilion that held a dozen long tables covered with snowy cloths. They were set with double rows of expensive china plates and crystal glasses, knives, forks, vases of flowers and huge dishes of cold food, carefully covered. At the end of each table a young boy moved a large fan to keep away the flies. Off toward the slave quarters, field hands carried load after load of firewood to feed the flames barbecuing hogs and beeves. Children ran to and fro through the trees, somethings stopping to look up at the lanterns hung there to illuminate the night's activities.

A few guests stood now on the veranda and talked. Among them were Albert and Margaret Spearman, who discussed their daughter's frightening experience in New York. It seemed Caroline had taken a fondness to one of their house maids on the Spearman plantation. The girl had been brought into their home, been given a great deal of personal training by Spearman's daughter.

"Why," said Margaret, "Caroline spent hours in her room with that girl to teach proper manners to the hussy. Why darkies can't realize we have their best interests at heart is beyond me. She certainly fooled us. Caroline and she seemed to be inseparable. Lord knows, I'd never let them go to New York if anything like this, which a person just never knows will happen, was going to take place."

To those who did not know the story first hand, Caroline had gone to New York to shop for a new wardrobe. She had taken her maid on the trip. They had checked into a nice hotel suite at one of the poshest hotels in town. On their first night in the hotel, the girl had tied up Caroline, using strips of bedsheets. The black hussy had next rifled Caroline's purse, even taking her jewels, mind, you and left poor Caroline to suffer. It was three days and two nights before a hotel maid found Caroline laying on the floor.

"The police, who seem to know about such matters, said it was useless to hunt for the girl," said Margaret. "They suspect she robbed Caroline, left the hotel and took a boat to Canada. Of course, she might have gotten help from those abolitionists. They're getting stronger in the north and, unless we do something about such scalawags, they'll have our slaves revolting like that awful Nat Turner's bunch over in Virginia."

Sean Porter came over from Belle Meade II accompanied by Regina Montrose. She wore a lovely white dress and carried a parasol of the same color. She would be singing for the guests following their dinner. Several folks were shocked to see the girl in public, but John Conrad said the man was her stepfather.

"Besides, we shouldn't judge children by their parents," he added.

Everyone knew that after investing in Silas Blackston's stock, Mrs. Patricia Wells had second thoughts about the investment. She had written to the address on the stock certificates, expecting to receive a glowing letter back. Instead, she was shocked to receive a quick return note from a landlord in Pittsburgh declaring Blackston to be a fraud. The letter urged that Mrs. Wells get in touch with the local authorities, that they be asked to hold Blackston for federal authorities. Warrants existed in several states and territories for his arrest on various fraudulent charges.

Mrs. Wells took the letter to attorney Roy Manning, who took legal action to seize Silas Blackston's bank account. The banker had co-operated and the full $7500 was returned to Mrs. Wells. Roy Lanning also gave the woman a stern lecture about investing in projects she knew nothing about. Next, he took the landlord's letter to Sheriff Bull Frazer, who found Silas Blackston eating a thick steak in a popular Memphis restaurant. The man was held in jail and the eastern authorities notified.

When things were sorted out, it was revealed that Blackston had swindled several prominent businessmen. "That included Sam Van Cortland," said Bull. "Sam was already in financial trouble, I heard, with creditors hounding his heels for payment of his bills. He took the last money he had on earth and invested in Blackston's laundry company.

They're both occupying a cell down at my jail. Blackston will never see daylight. Sam might get out. I ain't sure because he owes a lot of people and he stays in a cell 'til they're paid. I don't like the debtor's law, but he shouldn't been playing the stock market with those fast-talking New York monkeys."

Now, the sun began to drop with a beautiful and colorful panorama in the western sky. More guests were arriving, some who had ridden most of the day to attend the open house. The tables were now covered with many covered dishes. The barbecue fires were banked below the ox, sheep and score of wild turkeys. Bull Frazer, wandering through the crowd, judged at least two hundred people were in attendance. He stood with a sense of satisfaction and watched a Negro go around with a long pole and light the lanterns strung in the trees. Lines had been fixed between the trees running alongside the lane coming up to the great house. Lanterns twinkled on these lines like giant fireflies.

Bull saw Vito Santino and his lovely young wife standing on the fringe of the crowd. Vito looked uncomfortable in a suit, cravet and ruffled shirt. "Hello," Bull said, coming up to pay his respects. "Heard you'd been invited."

"The Conrads sent an invitation," Vito explained, "and I wanted Althena to see the place."

"How's business?" Bull asked.

"Back to normal."

"Temperance campaigns lose their strength after a while," Bull agreed. "But I hear Mrs. Pugh plans on staying in Memphis. You hear anything about her moving here?"

Vito cursed in his native language. Althena reddened. He said, "She keeps poking her nose into everyone else's business."

"She nice," Althena said, awkwardly. "She come see me twice a week."

It was Vito's turn to look embarrassed. "We ain't cottoning up to her," he said defensively. "I tried to tell Althena that she's a bad woman. But"—Vito shrugged eloquently—"Mrs. Pugh's teaching my wife how to speak English. She's holding classes for Althena and other wives two nights a week."

Bull shook his head with a look of wonderment. "Never know about folks, Vito."

Vito agreed.

A few minutes after that, the meat was ready to serve. The word went around for everyone to sit down at the tables. A number of Negro waiters came from the main house. They were dressed in freshly starched white uniforms and they each carried huge serving platters. Several men gathered round the ox and began to carve away huge portions of the meat. Within moments, the platters were being passed along the tables.

Roy Lanning did not join the diners immediately. He went round the house where the black guests were being served. Jumbo was sitting there with a huge piece of beef on his plate. The big man sat across from Rev. Adam Matthews, pastor of the new neighborhood church.

Roy came up and clapped both men on the back. "Eating good tonight?"

Jumbo nodded. "Belle Meade takes care of its own."

"Hear you like it out here."

Jumbo cut off a thick slab of beef. "I'm digging

399

through Shakespeare."

"How about you, Reverend?"

"Have you seen my church yet?" asked the black minister. "It's going to be like a picture. We're going to have a steeple and a bell."

"Ain't been there yet," drawled Lanning, "but I'm going to drop out one of these afternoons before winter hits. You got Jumbo baptised yet?"

Rev. Matthews laughed. "I'm working on him. Indeed, I am."

Lanning inquired, "Jumbo, you hear what happened to Miz Rose's place?"

"Sean told me." Jumbo paused to chew his food, swallowed. "Too bad about that old man. He was crazy. I plumb forgot about him when I come out to Belle Meade. Left that ol' fellow out there on the shantyboat. Awful of me, but I never gave him a thought."

"We should always be mindful of those less fortunate than ourselves," said Rev. Matthews.

"It was a sight," Lanning said. He explained that the preacher who'd started the riot at the slave auction had come off his shantyboat one night. He passed a group of fishermen and grabbed a pine torch, went into Pinchgut, delivered a roaring sermon and then put the torch to the "Hoors of Babylon's temple of evil!" When things cleared away, the preacher was in jail prior to being sent to a mental hospital. Madame Rose and her girls were burned out. No one knew whether Madame Rose would reopen her house. Lanning said, "I don't think she will. She'll probably go down river to Natchez-under-the-Hill or New Orleans."

"I could have stopped the old man if I'd been there," said Jumbo.

"Possible," Lanning agreed. "I'd better grab a plate and start eating before the food's gone."

With talking, laughter and joking, the meal went on. Waiters flew about the tables refilling glasses, serving the roast pig and turkeys. A new group of waiters came out to place punch bowls at a strategic point on the tables. People kept saying they couldn't stop eating because the food was too delicious.

At one table, Henrietta Pugh, Patricia Wells and a group of temperance ladies talked about their new campaign. Big Jesse Hawkins and Doc Fletcher sat on the fringe of the group, listening attentively to Mrs. Pugh's expanded campaign in Memphis.

"More than just demon rum is involved," Henrietta was saying. "We have to bring a sense of responsibility to this region of the country. Look at how men fight with each other, gouging eyes, biting off noses! I've seen some of the world's most repulsive people in Memphis. And the children—especially in the outlying areas—are getting married before the girls have scarcely reached puberty. Some of the grooms aren't old enough to shave. Incredible! And those poor foreign-born women. Disgraceful! They can't speak English, stay in their homes all the time and are totally dependent on their husbands. We have to teach people. Education is the sole answer."

Big Jesse asked, "You've given up your temperance work?"

"Not at all," Henrietta said. "I've informed the tavern owners that we won't allow any misconduct. If they step out of line we'll be on them like a crow on a june-bug."

Doc Fletcher laughed. "Maybe even faster than a crow."

"Won't you join our group?" asked Patricia Wells.

"Big Jesse and I are leaving town shortly, possibly next week," Doc replied. "Winter's coming so we're heading south to sell our remedies."

Big Jesse added, "We've lazed around until we're about broke. We need to refill our purse."

Sean Porter went past Henrietta's group to search for Rusty Ward and Charlotte Peabody. He found the young couple off alone, sharing a table under a lantern-lit tree, Rusty barely conscious of what he was eating. His attention was directed toward Charlotte, whose plate had scarcely been touched. When Sean came up, Charlotte was talking about various African tribal superstitutions. Since coming to Belle Meade, she had interviewed numerous slaves about these beliefs.

Sean smiled at the couple. "Rusty, you get the kinds out of that loading unit at the wharf?"

Rusty nodded positively. "Guy didn't know how to work it."

Sean looked at Charlotte's full plate. "Aren't you eating tonight?"

She blushed. "I've been talking again."

"She can't hardly stop," said Rusty. "But I like listening to her. She keeps me company when I'm working on something. I'm a little bashful and Charlotte would talk 'til the devil hisself turned tail and run off."

Charlotte laughed a delightful giggle. "You can always tell me to stop."

"I like listening to her a lot," Rusty said.

"Enjoy yourselves," said Sean, heading toward the barbecue area to pick up a new plate and more roast turkey. He glanced around the panorama as a carver filled his plate. Everyone was dressed in their finest garments. The men looked courageous and respectable. The women were gay and feminine. Belle Meade looked like a fairyland. Off to the side, back by the slave quarters, the blacks were gathered at tables and feasting.

The waiter handed Sean his plate when Jake Stein came up beside him. The waiter took Stein's plate and went off to refill it.

"How's the store coming?" Sean asked the former peddler.

"I think we'll make it," Jake ventured. "Bull is a little hard to take sometimes. I never met a man who wants so much, so soon. But I'm learning how to handle him."

"Like retailing better than peddling?"

Jake Stein chuckled. "Two different worlds, you know. The peddler is usually the only person who calls on the farmers back in the hills. I miss that air of excitement of walking into a yard and showing what's in my pack. Here in Memphis I have to get used to competition, but that comes with time. We're getting a steady following and, next month, I'm laying in a line of hardware. Sort of a medium priced line, not the junk but not the most expensive. People here seem to like buying in the middle range."

"Found any girls to spark?"

Jake Stein blushed. "Not yet. I'm too busy."

"Heard there's a Jewish family moving into town

next month," said Sean. "They're supposed to have a couple daughters of marriageable age."

Jake looked sharply at the Irishman. "How'd you find that out?"

"Talking to one of the steamboat captains."

It was Jake's turn to ask about business. He inquired about the success of the firewood venture, how Sean had done as a cotton broker during the season.

"Not as good as we wanted," answered the Irishman. "But not as bad as it might have been. We made money."

"Planning anything else?"

"Rusty wants to set up a store. He figures we can sell to the passengers while the boats are pulled in for firewood."

"A big store?"

"He thinks it should be."

Jake was thoughtful. "It might work."

"I'm not sure. Rusty's a good man, creative and filled with ideas. But his plan is to build a huge building, maybe a couple or three stories and sell everything made by a factory."

Jake was awed. "You'd have a lot of expensive inventory."

"Aye, bucko, and what if the plan doesn't work? We'd have a big building filled with merchandise setting out there on a riverbank."

"Go slow," Jake advised.

They walked together on their way back to the tables.

Jake asked, "How is Miss Montrose doing now that montebank's in jail?"

"Better than when he was around to chisel money from her," Sean answered.

"Imagine," Jake said with wonderment. "The old fraud even took Sam Van Cortland. Amazing! One crook taking another."

"If I see either of them on the street, I'll challenge them to a duel."

Jake looked shocked. "That's dangerous. The law may grind slowly, but it grinds well."

They parted and went to different tables.

Henrietta Pugh was finishing her dessert of peach cobbler when she saw Vito Santino standing alone. She had not spoken to the man since their encounter in her bedroom. With her jaw set into a determined jut, Henrietta rose and walked over to speak with the Sicilian tavern owner.

"Well," she said with a sigh. "How is Mr. Santino?"

"Fine, thank you," he replied in a formal tone.

Henrietta ventured, "Your wife tells me you had an accident this summer."

"An accident?"

"Got attacked by a pack of wildcats on your way home one night."

"It was nothing," he said.

"I should think a pack of wildcats would be more than something."

"A man can defend himself."

She hooted. "Some men can—if they're really men."

A startled expression leaped onto Vito's face. "I am always able to do what a man must do."

"Always?" Henrietta arched her eyebrows.

"Sometimes men fail when they undertake a task."

"I do what I set out to do."

Henrietta smiled. "Your wife says you've been having nightmares and sweats."

"My wife talks too much."

"She says the bad dreams started right after you fought the wildcat."

"I know of no such dreams."

"Some men," she said, "bite off more than they can chew."

He looked blandly at her. "I am a simple tavern owner who wants to earn an honest living."

"See that you stay that way," she cautioned him. "I would not go sneaking around at night again. I've bought a pistol since your last visit."

Vito's mouth dropped open. "*You know?*"

"Your breath," she said. "It stinks of garlic."

"You never told the sheriff?"

"I've told no one." Henrietta frowned. "Furthermore, I've grown fond of your wife. She's a nice person. I don't intend to hurt her."

"I . . . I'm sorry."

"I'm sure you are," she agreed, walking away.

Althena came back from washing her hands as Henrietta walked away.

"Isn't she nice?" she told her husband.

He did not reply, but stood and stared vacantly off into the night.

II

When the meal was finished, the guests laid down their forks. The waiters cleared the tables. Everyone stood around in talkative groups as the tables were carried away. Next, several field hands came out and lifted up the carpet. Everyone gasped. They had been dining over a finely crafted and polished dance floor.

The orchestra came forward, tuning their instruments. The sound of fiddles and banjos mingled with the keys of a pianoforte. Soon, the band was playing and couples moved out onto the platform to dance.

Sean wandered out in back of the house. A bar had been set up in a discreet spot near the back porch. A Negro bartender took his order for a cocktail. He took a small sip of the drink, found it was excellent.

Sean felt a hand slap his shoulder. He turned to see John Conrad standing by his side.

"A grand party," Sean said. "I thought they'd drop their eye teeth when the boys unveiled the dance floor."

"Suzanne's idea," John said.

"A nice touch."

John ordered a bourbon and branch water. "When are you going to make an honest woman out of Regina?" he asked.

"Can't get the chance to make her dishonest," chuckled the Irishman. "But I do try."

"Thinking of marrying her?"

Sean frowned. "I'm not sure, lad."

"She seems nice."

"Oh, she is," Sean agreed. "The lady I cannot stand is her mother. Not a brain in the woman's head. Strictly fluff for brains."

"Is she here tonight?"

"No, but she'd like to be. The old biddy's a real social climber."

"I'm sure we sent invitations."

"Aye, but she's in seclusion after Blackston's downfall. Wearing of the black and everything."

John picked up his drink. They walked back toward the barn where they could be alone.

"Life is funny," said the Irishman.

"Another philosophical bent tonight?"

Sean smiled. "I was just thinking of all the things that could have gone wrong. We could have missed each other on the streets of London. I would have died back there if you hadn't risked your skin to save me during the hold-up. You might have gotten caught any number of times. Boyo, that goes for me as well. Christ! I still shiver me bones thinking about the close call we had in Scotland. And our luck—yours and Suzanne's—getting here to buy the plantation at the right time." He drained his glass. "Maybe life's all a matter of throwing the dice."

"No maudlin Irish sentiment tonight," John said in a voice of mock serenity. "We're here to celebrate a good harvest, a fine year with our friends."

Sean cocked his head, gave John and impish look.

"You know all of these people?"

"Part of them."

"Then you're a better man than me," Sean laughed. "I see more strangers than acquaintances here."

"Well, the party list just kept growing," John said.

They were interrupted when Suzanne came rushing up.

"There you are!" she cried, taking John's arm. "Sorry, Sean, I haven't danced in years. John belongs to me for the rest of the night."

John sighed with mock resignation. He said, "The boss has spoken."

Sean raised his empty glass in a salute. "A toast to the most beautiful hostess in the world."

Suzanne giggled. "Watch yourself, Irishman. I've been neglected since the harvest started. You'll be getting an invite if you're not careful."

Sean stood quietly, leaning back against the wall of the barn, and watched his friends walk toward the dance platform. He raised his empty glass and sipped the last drops. Belle Meade was a place of peace, tranquil skies and love—an eternal land created by the angels many eons ago.

He glanced up into the sky as a silver ray of moonlight came through the hosts of dark night clouds.

BESTSELLERS FOR TODAY'S WOMAN

THE VOW   (653, $2.50)
by Maria B. Fogelin
On the verge of marriage, a young woman is tragically blinded and mangled in a car accident. Struggling against tremendous odds to survive, she finds the courage to live, but will she ever find the courage to love?

FRIENDS   (645, $2.25)
by Elieba Levine
Edith and Sarah had been friends for thirty years, sharing all their secrets and fantasies. No one ever thought that a bond as close as theirs could be broken . . . but now underneath the friendship and love is jealousy, anger, and hate.

CHARGE NURSE   (663, $2.50)
by Patricia Rae
Kay Strom was Charge Nurse in the Intensive Care Unit and was trained to deal with the incredible pressures of life-and-death situations. But the one thing she couldn't handle was her passionate emotions . . . when she found herself falling in love with two different men!

RHINELANDER PAVILLION   (572, $2.50)
by Barbara Harrison
Rhinelander Pavillion was a big city hospital pulsating with the constant struggles of life and death. Its dedicated staff of overworked professionals were caught up in the unsteady charts of their own passions and desires—yet they all needed medicine to survive.

Available wherever paperbacks are sold, or order direct from the Publisher. Send cover price plus 50¢ per copy for mailing and handling to Zebra Books, 21 East 40th Street, New York, N.Y. 10016. DO NOT SEND CASH!

FICTION FOR TODAY'S WOMAN!

GOODBYE IS JUST THE BEGINNING   (442. $2.50)
by Gail Kimberly
After twenty-two years of marriage Abby's life suddenly falls apart
when she finds her husband with another woman. From seduction
scenes and singles' bars to the problems, successes, and independence of being an "unmarried woman," Abby rediscovers life and
her own identity.

WHAT PRICE LOVE by Alice Lent Covert   (491; $2.25)
Unhappy and unfulfilled, Shane plunges into a passionate, all-
consuming affair. And for the first time in her life she realizes that
there's a dividing line between what a woman owes her husband
and what she owes herself, and is willing to take the consequences
no matter what the cost.

LOVE'S TENDER TEARS by Kate Ostrander   (504, $1.95)
A beautiful woman caught between the bonds of innocence and
womanhood, loyalty and love, passion and fame, is too proud to
fight for the man she loves and risks her lifelong dream of happiness
to save her pride.

WITHOUT SIN AMONG YOU   (506, $2.50)
by Katherine Stapleton
Vivian Wright, the overnight success, the superstar writer who was
turning the country upside down by exposing her most intimate
adventures was on top of the world—until she was forced to make a
devastating choice: her career or her fiance?

ALWAYS, MY LOVE by Dorothy Fletcher   (517, $2.25)
Iris thought there was to be only one love in her lifetime—until she
went to Paris with her widowed aunt and met Paul Chandon who
quickly became their constant companion. But was Paul really
attracted to her, or was he a fortune hunter after her aunt's money?

*Available wherever paperbacks are sold, or direct from the
Publisher. Send cover price plus 40¢ per copy for mailing and
handling to Zebra Books, 21 East 40th Street, New York, N.Y.
10016 DO NOT SEND CASH!*

SENSATIONAL MISSISSIPPI SAGA